TIPPING THE

BALANCE

CalPac Crew, Book Two

C. Koehler

A NineStar Press Publication

www.ninestarpress.com

Tipping the Balance

Printed in the USA

Print ISBN: 978-1-64890-125-6

First Edition, October, 2020
Originally Published in September 2011

Also available in eBook, ISBN: 978-1-64890-124-9

WARNING:
This book contains explicit sexual material which is only suitable for mature readers, homophobia, homophobic slurs, emotional and physical abuse of an adult child by a parent, and mugging/violence.

The boys from ROCKING THE BOAT are back in TIPPING THE BALANCE. Nick Bedford's best friend Drew St. Charles is a man with a dream. He wants to move from selling real estate and flipping houses on the side into renovating houses. Ideally, he'd find the houses and his boyfriend would flip them. Not that he has a boyfriend.

Brad Sundstrom, fresh out of college and working for his father in the family construction business, never believed he could dream of more...until he met Drew. When Drew wins a contract to restore the historic Bayard Mansion, they become the solution to each other's problems. Drew needs someone to oversee the renovation and offers Brad, who wants out from under his father's thumb, the job of project foreman.

Working in close contact makes the sparks between the two men burst into flame, and Brad takes his first hesitant steps out of the closet. Before long, spending the day together at work leads to nights spent together. It looks as if Drew's dream is coming true, but then he is savagely attacked in a hate crime, and Brad panics.

Brad faces a crucial test. Will he overcome his fears and take his place at Drew's side? Or will he retreat to the stifling familiarity of the closet?

To my parents, because while they may not have always understood, they've always believed.

Author's Note

The story starts not long after CalPac College let out for the summer, overlapping slightly with the end of *Rocking the Boat*.

Chapter One

"Are you sure you can't get a general contractor's license?" Drew wiped the sweat out of his eyes.

"Did you just whine?" Nick grunted as he muscled a cherrywood cabinet into place. "Besides, what about the one you already work with?"

"Shut up. Bob's great, but I'm getting tired of hiring an outside contractor so this work passes inspection, and anyway, you'd be cheaper." Drew set a level on the cabinet Nick had just installed and squinted at it as the bubbles moved sluggishly in the yellow fluid. "It's not...quite... plumb."

"How come you don't have a contractor's license?" Nick squatted down to tap a shim into place under the cabinet. Sweat soaked his shirt, as portable fans cooled the kitchen in theory only, but with the HVAC unit out, fans were all they could get in the summer heat.

Drew looked up from the level, struck once again by just how attractive his best friend was. Coaching the men's crew at California Pacific College certainly encouraged Nick to keep himself fit—that, and his smokin' hot boyfriend, Morgan. Some coaches let themselves go, but not Nick. Not for the first time, Drew found himself wishing they could've worked out, but they'd given that a whirl as undergraduates and both agreed they made better friends than lovers.

And what friends they were, pulling each other through hard times and celebrating the good. Drew had helped Nick win and keep Morgan. Nick worked like a dog all summer for Drew's home renovation business. He was one of the few people Drew trusted besides himself to supervise each project from start to finish, the only other person whose eye for detail and quality touches matched his own. Nick treated the jobs done by St. Charles Renovations like it was his own name on the line, not Drew's.

"Because getting my real estate license took all my time and money when I was younger, and now selling houses takes all my time." Drew sighed. "The flipping was just a sideline, and now reno work for other people? It's killing me, I tell you."

"A sideline." Nick snorted. "The best home flip in the area. Isn't that what *Sacramento Magazine* named you this year? Spend the time on this it deserves, and the St. Charles property empire could grow by leaps and bounds."

"It still will. I like a challenge." Drew grinned wolfishly. "Besides, sleep is for sissies."

"You would know from sissies." Nick watched Drew carefully to gauge the reaction, faintly disappointed when Drew barely even rolled his eyes. "Is it level?"

"Yes." Drew straightened.

"Good, now you can use those over-gymmed muscles for something besides filling a polo shirt and help me hang the next cabinet. That'll be the last of the uppers on this side of the kitchen. The guys can help me hang the rest later."

"I can't get too sweaty. I have to show houses this afternoon," Drew said.

"Don't worry, princess, you'll still be the prettiest girl in the room." Nick laughed. "I just need someone to steady it and hold it while I get it bolted to the cleats. The pilot holes have already been drilled."

"Seriously, Nick, how am I going to replace you?" Drew asked. "You'll go back to coaching and your grad work all too soon, and I'll lose my best crew leader."

"I'm your only crew leader," Nick pointed out.

Drew made a face. "Don't remind me."

"You and Renochuck have me for another two months, so make the most of it," Nick said, "because after that I go back to just being your friend."

"Renochuck?"

"That's what Octavio and the guys call it."

"Some of them barely speak English, and they still came up with Renochuck." Drew shook his head. He wiped a speck of dirt off the rich red wood.

Nick eyed Drew askance as he bent over. "Bend from the hips, not your lower back."

"Yes, Coach," Drew sighed.

"Did you enjoy throwing your back out last fall?"

Drew smirked. "Oh hell yes, I had a fabulous time. It was *the* event of the season."

Nick didn't reply. He just glared at Drew, warm brown eyes to merry blue ones. "Did you enjoy the aftermath? No? Then do it my way. I do know something about bodies in motion, thank you very much."

"Yeah, that's what Morgan tells me."

"Hands on." Nick loftily ignored his friend. He squatted down and put one hand under the cabinet and used the other on top to steady it. "In three. One, two, and *up!*"

"Now I know," Drew grunted out, "where that coxswain of yours gets his abrasive tone from."

"No, that's totally Stuart's," Nick said. "Besides, we're crew. We're not real bright, but we can lift heavy objects. Now, put those muscles to some use, Muscle Mary, and hold this steady while I drill it."

"I'm sure you're very good at drilling, seeing how much practice you've been getting." The muscles of Drew's arms and back strained to hold the cabinet in place as Nick hurried to secure it to the wall. Then he noticed something. "Why is the taller of the two of us the one who's not holding this up?"

Nick grinned at him. "Because I'm the drilling expert, remember? There," he said as he put the last bolt in. "That'll hold it while I finish up. You can let go."

Drew lowered his arms. "Seriously, how's it going with you and Morgan?"

He pretended to listen as Nick rattled off a list of his boyfriend's virtues, but Nick's syrupy smile answered the question well enough. "I'm sorry, what'd you just say?"

"I asked if you were going to be around this weekend," Nick said. "I'm meeting his parents for the first time, and I'm scared shitless. I'm hoping you'll be around so I can send panicked text messages from the bathroom."

"Meeting the parents? It must be serious." Drew smiled.

"You know it. He's it, the only one I'll ever want."

"Some of us might like the chance to find that for ourselves, you know." Drew pretended to be very interested in a small pile of loose screws.

"Aww, jeez, not Brad Sundstrom again. I keep telling you he's straight."

"Just his phone—"

Nick put the drill down. "Look, Drew. You know I can't give out his information without his permission. It's a confidentiality issue, among other things. I was his coach, technically a college official. I can't just hand out phone numbers like that."

Drew knew all about Nick's scruples, having listened to him endlessly gnaw his guts out about his interest in Morgan. He supposed he ought to be grateful to Morgan for taking matters into his own hands, if not because Morgan made Nick happy, then because it shut Nick up. "Then will you at least give him my number if he asks for it?"

"Drew—"

"C'mon, Nick. It's a fair question. Don't I at least deserve the chance to get shot down?"

"I just don't want to see you hurt," Nick said quietly.

"I'm a big boy, babydoll. I can take care of myself."

"I know, and yeah, if he asks, I'll pass your number on."

Drew looked at his watch. "Shit, it can't be that late, can it?"

"It can be, yes. Late for the showings?" Nick asked.

"Just about. Everything looks great so far, but keep in touch, and let me know if you hear from the counter fabricators, will you?" Drew said, already heading for his car.

"Of course." Nick picked up his drill.

Drew tried to mop the sweat off his brow as he rushed for his car but only succeeded in pushing it up into his brown locks. He had just enough time to run home and shower before he showed the first of the homes to his clients. Yeah, rummaging around in the dirt and sawdust probably wasn't the best idea, but he couldn't give up fixing up homes, he just couldn't. What he hadn't told Nick was that some days, he felt like he'd made a huge mistake in getting a real estate license instead of going directly into repair and improvement. Working his way through the building trades might've seemed strange after getting his bachelor's degree in business, but it would've been handy when he got a contractor's license. While he'd never wanted to be a designer, there was something almost magical about watching a dump of a home rise from the depths to become a showplace, limited only by budget and imagination. The cabinets with their reeded glass inserts, the soapstone counters that were supposed to have arrived last week, the reclaimed Indonesian teak floors covered with marine varnish to repel water, the lighting, all of the pieces fitted together like a three-dimensional jigsaw puzzle only he could solve—that was why he couldn't keep out of it.

But how—oh how—was he going to replace Nick?

Brad Sundstrom looked at the clock. *My, how time flies. Those five minutes just raced by.*

He sat at his desk in the sales office of a subdivision no one wanted to live in. Shitty little houses on tiny lots out in the middle of nowhere. As far as Brad could tell, Randall Sundstrom didn't own the land between here and civilization, so this place wouldn't serve as an anchor to further development. When he'd asked about this, his dad had just snapped, "You create the demand, son. You should know that. Build the houses and the rest will come."

Come? They weren't even breathing hard.

Brad glanced around the office, anything to relieve the tedium. There weren't even games on the computer. He'd checked. There were two other empty desks for non-existent salespeople and a display of the entire subdivision with little plastic Monopoly houses on the few lots that had sold and the few more that had been built on but languished, unsold and unloved. The people who lived there were sure going to be pissed when this place went belly-up, which Brad figured would be sometime early the middle of next year, at the rate this place wasn't selling. His dad would probably find a way to blame him for it too.

The view out of the picture windows depressed him. Inexpensive landscaping had been slapped down to gussy up the parking area in front of the sales office, but beyond that was nothing but the seared brown fields of the Sacramento Valley in the middle of summer. Heat mirages shimmered in the air over the blacktop, making Brad's battered Lexus waver and flicker in the midday heat, magnifying the scratches and dents the two Sundstrom boys had put in their mother's old car since her death.

He flicked a bit of onion, fallen from the sandwich he'd picked up on the way in, off his desk. He'd learned the second day he'd worked out here in this godforsaken pit not to eat the burritos from the local stop-and-rob attached to the one gas station on the feeder road to the subdivision.

Brad put his long legs up on his desk. He couldn't believe this was what his life had become. He'd graduated from CalPac over a month ago, and the contrast was just killing him. He'd only dimly realized it at the time, but those five years at CalPac College had been the best years of his life. More or less out from under his father's thumb, he'd been one of the big men on campus, literally and figuratively. Sure, there'd been classes to contend with, and Coach Bedford could be a real asshole when he wanted to be, but that had been part of the fun too.

He smiled for the first time in days. Crew really had been fun, maybe even what made the rest of school worth it. Despite the blood, sweat, and occasional tears, he'd never felt more alive. Even his rivalry with Morgan Estrada, which had led him to do the one thing he regretted in life, had been part of the experience. He'd lost. Morgan was stronger, maybe even the better oarsman, but even losing to Morgan had been as important to his experience as anything else. It meant something; he was sure. He just couldn't figure out what. He and Morgan and the others had shared the big win at the Pacific Coast Rowing Championships, so even though his unofficial rivalry had come to nothing, his rowing experience had still meant something.

That race. Brad dwelt on it quite a bit on those long afternoons when it was too hot even for hungry real estate agents to drag wary clients out to this "entry-level" subdivision. Sure, the race itself had been one for the CalPac record books, but it was the aftermath that he returned to again and again. Coach Bedford had stepped down after dropping an atomic bomb on the crew: he'd been dating one of them! Brad hadn't been surprised— after all, there'd been that day in the boathouse—but he acted like it. Morgan had gone off after their coach, and on a whim, Brad followed.

What he saw had stopped him in his tracks, and every time he thought about it, it still had the power to freeze him in place. Morgan Estrada and Nick Bedford locked in an embrace, kissing like they were the only two people in the world. The sight of it had puzzled his brain at the time, but the more Brad thought about it, the more he understood it. That kiss had nothing to do with sex and everything to do with love, a love he'd never experienced. He'd thought he had, but that day after the race, watching those two men, Brad knew he'd only been fooling himself with all those chicks he'd banged in high school and beyond. Nothing with his last girlfriend, the one who'd talk about marriage, had ever felt like that kiss between Morgan and Nick looked, like for that moment, they were all that mattered. Each was the air the other breathed, the sunlight that warmed them, and the ground beneath their feet.

Brad, a little wistfully, wondered what that might've been like. Then, like the caboose on a runaway freight train, came the thoughts of Drew, Coach Bedford's fairy friend. Brad was uncomfortably aware that once upon a time he might've called a man like Drew St. Charles a homo, not that he'd have meant anything by it. It was just a word.

But that was...before. Before the kiss. When he thought about it, and lately it seemed like it was all he thought about, maybe his attitude toward gays had started to change before the kiss. He'd never been homophobic; gays just weren't on his radar. But at some point, Brad noticed Drew. He tended to show up at the local regattas, and Brad figured it had been because he was Coach Bedford's friend. Had he and Coach...?

Brad shook the image out of his head. It was nowhere he wanted to go. Drew. Brad had noticed him everywhere that spring, and now he seemed to be a permanent resident of Brad's imagination. He couldn't figure it out. He only knew he kind of enjoyed the fluttery feeling in his stomach that came with the thoughts.

Brad spun in his chair and flicked his computer back awake. Damn thing was as bored as he was. He opened up the web browser and his mail account, his private e-mail, not the company account. He wasn't that stupid.

He started typing a note to Morgan. He wrote to him more and more lately, sometimes just to say howdy, sometimes to talk about crew, sometimes...sometimes to beat around the bush for a while before asking Morgan to ask his boyfriend for Drew's e-mail. Brad had already looked Drew up on Facebook. Drew seemed to have two accounts, a personal one and a professional one. The personal one was locked down tight, and Brad didn't have the balls to friend him out of the blue. Instead, he chewed his guts out and perused the professional one for glimpses of Drew. They were there, obviously. Drew showing houses. Drew renovating, including one tantalizing pic of Drew in a tight, sweaty shirt.

Morgan had yet to come through, but he was weakening, Brad was sure of it. Brad could be a pretty charming guy when he wanted to be, and right now, he really wanted Drew's e-mail.

Brad wasn't much of a letter-writer, and the e-mail, including beating around the bush, was soon sent, and reality once again intruded. He was still stuck where he didn't want to be, living at home, earning money at a job he hated, and a boss... He wasn't fond of his boss, either. He missed his old life, and if he'd known what the new one held, he might've gone for that sixth year. He went back to staring out of the window.

It felt like hours later, but someone drove up the feeder road. Brad watched with unseeing eyes. Then he jumped as the dust cloud registered. That meant traffic. That meant something to do. That meant human contact.

The dust cloud resolved into a pickup truck. Okay, that didn't necessarily mean one of the construction crews. But then he caught sight of the sunburst logo of Sundstrom Homes, and his dad, Randall Sundstrom himself, got out of the truck.

Brad sat up, pulling his feet off his desk. He rubbed one hand across his cropped hair nervously. He watched his dad approach, practically strutting. His father was shorter than he was, but broader, if that were possible, and built like a fireplug where Brad was just big and heading for beefy. Despite the weathered appearance a career spent outdoors had given him, Randall's hair was still as blond as it had always been. Sometimes Brad wished he'd inherited his dad's genes for hair, rather than the baldness from his mom's father, but mostly he'd made peace with his thinning hair.

Randall walked in the door, a battered leathern portfolio tucked under one arm. "Bradley." He crossed the room and went directly to the file cabinets where Brad had been told to store the files of pending and completed sales, as well as the design records on each inhabited house. "There's nothing new here, Bradley."

"Randall, this place blows," Brad complained without stopping to think first. "You told me when I agreed to come work for you that I'd be in the custom end of things."

Randall looked up from the file he was reading. "First of all, there was no 'agreed to come work for me.' I hired you because with your qualifications, I'd be paying for your upkeep regardless, and this way I'm getting some work in return. Or I would be if you'd actually sell some homes."

"How am I supposed to do that when no one ever comes out here?" Brad grumbled.

"You're here to prove yourself." Randall shrugged as if it weren't really his problem.

"How can I, when this place is dead?" Even Brad could tell the conversation had already curved back around on itself.

"Bring it back. That's one of the reasons you're out here. Since you're so smart, it shouldn't be any problem for you," Randall said.

And there it was. Sooner or later their every argument came down to that. Randall thought Brad was stupid, and never missed a chance to remind his younger son of that fact. Every time they had this conversation, Brad felt like a naughty six-year-old caught with his hand in the cookie jar or breaking a window. Or breaking a window with the cookie jar.

Brad knew he wasn't the smartest guy around, but he also knew he wasn't dumb, either. He'd done all right in school, graduating with a respectable GPA, even if he'd been a physical education major. But Randall had decided that of his two sons, Brad was the dumb one, and no amount of evidence to the contrary would be entertained.

Brad took a deep breath and tried again. "You specifically told me that I would be working in the custom division, not here. This isn't even the active part of the tract-home division. This place is going to fail, and you know it."

"Prove yourself, then talk to me about a transfer."

"How can I do that when this place is dying?"

Another parental shrug. "That's why I've put you here. New blood, fresh ideas."

"Well, gee, Dad, I'll just rewrite the marketing plan since this one's not working so well. Oh wait, I never studied marketing!" Brad tried to sound like Drew, the wittiest person he knew. He slapped his forehead. "That's right, you pay some company for that. You're sure getting your money's worth. You never even asked me. You just plunked me down out here after telling me—guaranteeing me—that I'd start in the custom division. If I'd known I was going to be stuck out here in Outermost Bumfuck, I'd have taken another job."

"What other jobs?" Randall asked pointedly. "Did you even apply for anything else, or did you just assume I'd carry your ass like I always do?"

Brad looked down. "I didn't apply for anything else because you promised me a job."

"You've got no experience," Randall said with exaggerated patience, "and—"

"You mean besides every summer since I started high school? I've done everything on the homes you build but pick out carpet in the design center. I've even led crews," Brad pointed out.

"No experience that counts," Randall snapped, "and you're lucky to have this one. Grow up."

"I am grown up."

"You can't be a teenager forever, but that's what you act like. Man up. It's time." Randall shook his head. He opened the leather folder and pulled out a business card. "Here's the number for that worthless advertising agency. Call our sales rep and see what you can come up with to turn this place around."

"Oh yes, sir," Brad muttered as Randall stomped back to his truck. He glared at the clock. Fifteen whole minutes later than the last time he'd looked. At this time just a few months before, he'd have been carrying oars down the dock to get ready for practice. The realization made the office around him look smaller and tackier than it already was.

He picked the business card off the desk and stared at it for long moments. How the hell was he supposed to come up with a marketing plan, advertising agency or not? He almost wished he'd studied something useful in college, but CalPac didn't offer building management, and the communications major was aimed at broadcast journalism rather than PR. But somehow, he was supposed to convince real estate agents to bring their clients out to this godforsaken wasteland.

Wait a minute. Brad sat up a little straighter in his chair. Drew was a real estate agent. He grinned, the first time since he'd started working there, as an idea sprouted.

Chapter Two

"Good, you're here," Nick said when Drew walked in to check the progress of the Abernathy renovation early one morning. "The flooring finally arrived, and we're behind here, but you also want me to oversee the start of the demolition at the McKinley Park property and then place that order at the hardware store before I deal with the other five things you've got on the list for today. Despite my reputation for awesome studliness, I can only do one thing at a time, and there are only twenty-four hours in a day. Pick one."

"God, you're up early. Don't you ever sleep?" Drew said, squinting at Nick over his bladder-buster-sized coffee.

"It's six and I'm a rower. I've been awake since four thirty. Besides, you're the one who said sleep is for sissies." Nick grinned at Drew's obvious pain.

"And you said I'm a sissy, so it's your fault," Drew muttered.

Nick laughed. "Seriously, I can't be everywhere at once."

"Yeah, I know," Drew said, thinking. "Call the flooring contractor and beg. All that reclaimed teak doesn't do a lick of good if it sits in the garage. I just hope we haven't lost the window of opportunity and have to go with someone else. She's one of the best in town."

"Will do." Nick nodded. "Then?"

"The demolition, then the order, and then the list, which is exactly what you just told me. Why did you even need to bother me with this?" Drew asked.

"Because you're the boss, and I'm not a contractor. Seriously? Wood floors in a kitchen? I don't care how much marine varnish we put on this, water'll get under it."

"I know, but we're not the decorator. This is kind of an unusual case. When Emily Schoenwald called begging, I couldn't tell her no. Her regular contractor flaked and is now her ex-contractor. But that left her without someone to oversee the reno, and this is a chance for me to build my renovations portfolio. We're kind of in the middle between the decorator and Bob Miller, the tame contractor I keep on a string who checks off all my work before it's inspected."

Nick shrugged. "It's not my kitchen, but I've seen what water does to the docks at the boathouse. They'll be yanking this out within five years, tops."

"Speaking of crew and tops," Drew said, drawing a sharp glance from Nick. "Can I please, please, please have Brad's number?"

"I told you—" Nick began.

"Yes, you did," Drew said, "and your integrity is one of the reasons I love you, but damn, man. Help me out."

Nick leaned against the counter, regarding Drew. "What is it about him that gets to you?"

"He's just... I don't know. Something about him grabs hold of me and won't let go." Drew didn't feel like getting into it right then with Nick. It made him feel defensive. He knew Nick didn't mean it that way, but still.

"He's been e-mailing Morgan a disturbing amount this summer. I'll remind Morgan that he can give Brad your info if Brad asks for it, but honestly, that's the best we can do," Nick said.

"I know." Drew sighed, wishing it was more.

Nick looked at his watch. "I've got my marching orders for today, but I've also got a time slot in the human performance lab at school. As much as I use all those erg tests in my research, I need more data points than I can wring out of my crews. I'll call the flooring contractor on my way to school and get on the rest when I'm done."

"Thanks, buddy, I appreciate it. I'll check on the work crew myself. Keep me posted on the flooring situation," Drew said as Nick headed out to his car.

As long as he was there, Drew decided he'd better inspect the rest of the job very thoroughly. Hopefully, the snafu with the flooring wouldn't push the job too far past the due date, but in case it did, he needed to be able to justify it to the designer and the homeowners. He grabbed the file and a pen and started prowling. He needed a contractor of his own, or better yet, he needed to be a contractor, but how was that going to happen? He couldn't just quit real estate to work for his contractor's license, even assuming his home reno experience would give him enough background in the necessary trades. He had bills to pay, and that meant selling houses.

He was stuck in a holding pattern. Real estate was slower than it had been and home reno was booming, but he couldn't afford to jump into reno full-time because he financed his reno business through selling homes. Until he figured out a way out of this puzzle, he couldn't really grow either aspect of his business.

As he went over each room from ceiling to floor, looking for flaws in the install or even just too much dust from the plaster, Drew's mind moved to his usual favorite subject these days.

Brad.

Drew couldn't shake the guy from his mind and when it came down to it, didn't want to. The attraction mystified him, but it was there, and it was real. Brad wasn't gay. He wasn't beautiful in the usual sense. He wasn't scathingly intelligent, although Drew had no data for that beyond Nick's comments.

Like he'd told Nick, there was just something about him, something Drew found compelling beyond his "big lug" looks. Sure, the beefy build and shaved head hit all the right notes for him, but there was more. That shy smile Brad gave him when Drew helped after regattas. After the last one, the big win at the PCRCs, Drew was pretty sure Brad had been looking for him and didn't relax until he spotted him. That shy smile went right to Drew's heart...and groin.

But was Brad gay? Sure, there was that smile. But what else, besides the vague feeling that where there was smoke, there'd be fire? Drew liked to think his gaydar was highly developed, but where Brad was concerned, he wasn't sure. Brad pinged on his screen, but Drew knew very well that wishful thinking overrode gaydar every time, and where Brad was concerned, Drew wished pretty hard.

But then Drew remembered the last time he'd spotted a closeted jock about whom he just hadn't been 100 percent sure. He'd studied the guy and then made his move, luring the guy out of the closet and into his life, and now Morgan Estrada reaped the rewards for Drew's perseverance all those years before.

Nick had been a challenge, but Drew had always thrived on those, even as a child, defiantly and, at times, flamboyantly himself in the face of his family's horror at the bird of paradise amidst the sparrows. Once they'd come around, he'd used their love as a shield behind which he'd stared down high-school bullies and tackled other perils of adolescence and adulthood.

Now Drew had found a new challenge. Sure, Brad was a little rough around the edges, but that was part of his charm and attraction. Drew'd dated plenty of suave and polished men, and none of those relationships had lasted. No, Drew had the desire and the drive to coax Brad out of the closet, and as soon as he had the means to do so, like a phone number and address…

Address. Shit. He looked at his watch. He also had a meeting with his broker and then an appointment to show clients a handful of houses. It was going to be a long day.

Morgan came through! Good ol' Morgan, Brad thought. He was a stand-up guy, and when Brad had checked his private e-mail upon getting to work that morning, a message from Morgan had greeted him. With bated breath—and really, when had Brad ever done anything with bated breath?—he'd opened the e-mail, and pay dirt! There it was, contact information for one Mr. Drew St. Charles. E-mail, cell phone, even the landline. How cool was that?

Suddenly Brad was as nervous as a long-tailed cat in a room full of rocking chairs, as his grandmother used to say. Pits and palms started to sweat, and his chest was tight. What if Drew didn't remember him? What if he'd just been acting nice at those regattas? Just humoring one of his friend's jocks and not interested at all? He'd probably laugh at Brad as soon as he hung up the phone, maybe call some of his gay friends to howl with laughter at the bumbling straight guy.

Why was a straight guy like him calling someone so...so...*out there* as Drew, anyway? Why was he spending so much time thinking about Drew? That couldn't be good. He needed to find something else to do, something to distract him from this unhealthy obsession. What else could it be but an obsession? Why else would he be so hung up on some other dude?

Yeah, something to take my mind off Drew. That's what I need. He bounced up from his chair like he had a spring in his ass and paced restlessly around the sales office. He spotted the folders containing the floor plans and design options. One was turned the wrong way!

He pounced, disassembling the stack entirely before carefully restacking them, one atop the next, Sundstrom Homes' sunburst logo proudly displayed. He'd seen that logo as long as he could remember, but it was still kind of a trip to see his name in print like that, all official and everything.

Just like it had been a trip the first time Drew had tried to carry the oars up after the disaster of a race. What had the guy been thinking, trying to pick up all those oars? Sure, Brad could carry all eight at once if someone stacked them in his arms, but Drew? That had been funny. Drew'd looked at him with such gratitude, such a warm smile that went right to Brad's groin, never mind how tired he'd been. Drew'd smiled at him and Brad had lit right up, even throwing a little wood. For a guy.

That was so wrong.

Damn, he was turning into a girl, Brad thought. Was this what chicks did if they called a guy? Had any of his girlfriends gone through this? If so, he promised to track down and apologize to each and every one of them.

Had he always been like this and never noticed? *Pick up the damn phone*, he told himself. *Call him*. Yeah, sure, call him and sound like a doofus. What if he said the wrong thing? What if he couldn't say anything at all? That'd be just like him.

He picked up one of the yellow pads of paper on his desk. He'd better write down everything he planned to say, from hello on down to goodbye.

"Hi, Drew," Brad mumbled as he wrote the words down. Then what? That was always the problem with "Hi." You had to follow it up with something.

He glanced around the office. Drumming on his desk with the pencil. Exhaling noisily. Hoping for inspiration.

He looked down at the pad. At last he figured out why he was going to call Drew. Drew was a real estate agent, and Brad needed some input from a pro, from one of the people Sundstrom Homes hoped would be bringing their clients in but weren't. That was the easy part.

That done, he still had an entire conversation to script. He needed an outline. He had an entire notepad. Hell, when it came down to it, he had a stack of notepads he wasn't using for anything else.

So. A conversation. He had the meat of the conversation. Now for the skin and bones. Cool. He could do this.

He flipped to another page and jotted down observations about the weather. That was child's play. It was summer in Sacramento, so the weather came in two varieties, hot and hotter.

Another page, terrifying in its blankness. What had he been up to since he graduated? *Nothing, that's what*. Wait. Duh. That's what he'd been up to. He'd graduated and started this job for the family firm. No more rowing.

Brad brightened. Crew was another topic. So was Coach Bedford. Or should that be a separate topic? He agonized over that for a few moments before jotting his former coach's name halfway down the page for crew.

He puzzled over the pages more, trying to elaborate on each one. It felt like writing an essay. He'd thought he was done with that, but no. Actually, he felt proud of himself for his hard work. That communications professor who said he'd never amount to anything should see him now. Brad. Making an outline. To call Drew.

Right, get to the point. He brightened. That was gold, that was what that was. *Let...me...get...right...to...the... point*, he wrote in big block letters on another page.

Hmm, small talk. You don't dive right in, not when you want something. You have to mosey up to it, make it look like you aren't a user. It was good manners. Those gay guys always had good manners, and business always seemed to involve the kind of pointless conversation that froze him to the floor.

So, what did they have in common? Brad thought. And thought. And thought. *Well, we've both got cocks.* Brad started to write that down and then scratched it out, shaking his head. He was so not going there, because what they did with them? No.

With a sinking feeling, Brad figured he was screwed. He was noisy, obnoxious, and wasn't above belching in public. Loudly. His car smelled like a locker room, and most of the time, his clothes, even when they were clean, looked like he'd wadded them up in a gym bag for a few days before wearing them. But Drew? Brad sighed, staring out of the window, a soft look on his face. Drew was always so...so...suave. That was the word. Put together. He seemed like the kind of guy who always knew what to say, what to wear, and how to act. No wonder chicks liked the gays.

No wonder they didn't like him. Brad knew he could hold it together for a date or two, but sooner or later he was bound to burp at the wrong moment, and from what he'd gathered from his dating history, there was never a right moment. Maybe it'd be different, being with a guy.

Who was he kidding? Brad was just a big, dumb oaf like his father said he was. He was screwed.

Then he flinched. "Screwed" was so not the word to use, not when he was...

Brad groaned, leaning back in his chair. He covered his face with his hands. Not when he was thinking about calling another guy, not when he wanted to ask that other guy out but didn't know how, not when he thought about that other guy touching—

"No!" Brad bellowed, standing up. "I'm not thinking about guys touching anything. I'm not!"

He looked at the clock. It was almost noon. He couldn't believe he'd spent three hours on this, but he had. Close enough. He was going to lunch.

He wasn't gay. He couldn't be.

The restless, thudding anxiety robbed him of his appetite, so instead of eating, he just drove around. Driving was good. Driving cleared his mind. Driving gave him a break from thinking about gay men and conversations and other things he didn't want to think about.

But when his lunch hour ended, he was back to calling Drew. He had to. His original idea might've been a ruse, but it also had merit. He needed some ideas from a Realtor about how he could make Suburban Symphony attractive to house hunters, since the marketing firm apparently had none.

Chapter Three

Drew arrived a few minutes early for lunch with Brad. The restaurant was a good one, located on a busy corner of the part of Midtown called Lavender Heights, but just on the far side of trendy, so tables were relatively easy to get and the waiters didn't glare if you lingered too long over lunch.

When Brad had called him yesterday, he'd almost lost the power of speech. When Brad had asked to meet him for lunch, he'd started babbling. Drew hoped it didn't run Brad off. He wasn't sure what to make of Brad's request for advice on that frankly dire housing development, but he'd do what he could if it meant staring at Brad across a table even for an hour.

Drew could've gone inside, but he had work to do, so he sat in his car, resisting the impulse to bang his head onto the steering wheel. His new clients wanted a house that had been on the market for a while, so Drew knew the homeowners should be willing to bargain, *should* being the operant term, but first someone had to explain the facts of life to their agent, and Drew figured he'd drawn the winning ticket.

"Yeah, I get that they're home, but do they get that they're selling their house? It's been on the market for six months. I've got clients who want to see it, but the last time I brought people by, they tried to take over the tour… Yes, I know it's their house, but if they scare people…well, scared people don't buy houses. And one other thing—

Get. The. Taxidermy. Out. Of. There." *Do your job, asswipe, so I can do mine*, he screamed silently. "Haven't they ever heard of staging? Haven't you? They're going to move anyway, so they need to get a jump on the packing."

Drew half listened to the listing agent for a few more moments. The agent swore up and down his clients wouldn't spoil this, but Drew paid more attention to cars pulling into the restaurant's parking lot. Excuses were like assholes: everyone had one. "Look, we'll be by at six p.m." A battered Lexus had parked while Drew was laying down the law. It wasn't until a man got out of it that Drew paid attention. It was Brad. "Look, make sure those freaks are out of there and they take the dead petting zoo with them."

Then Drew killed the call. For a moment, he just looked. Brad still caused a hitch in his breath. Unlike a lot of former college jocks, Brad hadn't started packing on the pounds, even though without the intense demands of crew, his caloric demand had surely dropped. Drew very much appreciated Brad's efforts to keep fit, even if he looked out of place in khakis, a dress shirt, and a tie. Some people just looked better in shorts or jeans and a T-shirt pulling tight across those muscled pecs.

Drew could see Brad had the tiniest hint of bearish endomorphic belly, just the way he liked it. He hadn't seen Brad since the Pacific Coast Rowing Championships in May, but he still felt the old tingle deep in his belly as he responded to the sight of a man he thought was sex on legs. That Brad looked sweetly nervous was too adorable.

"Brad, hi!" Drew said, getting out of his car.

Brad turned to face him and smiled shyly. "Hi, Drew," he said, hands in his pockets. "Thanks for meeting me."

"Any time." Drew extended his hand, and Brad shook it awkwardly, as if he weren't quite sure what to do or how to act. "Let's get a table and then you can tell me all about this development of yours. I had no idea you were going into real estate after you graduated."

"Yeah, it just sort of happened."

"I hear that. I'm not sure many children dream of growing up to sell or flip houses, but it's still kind of fun," Drew replied.

Drew watched Brad surreptitiously as they entered the restaurant. He saw Brad wipe his palms on his pants several times and glance around repeatedly, far more than necessary to look where he was going. Oh yeah, this guy was nervous. He wondered what might be driving Brad, because he sure hadn't struck Drew as the type to be nervous in his own skin.

"So...do you come here often?" Brad asked after they'd sat down, glancing around warily, as if he expected to be attacked before ordering or perhaps ambushed by the woman filling their water glasses.

Drew looked up from the menu. He smiled, trying to put Brad at ease. "From time to time. The food's good, and they're usually not so busy that they resent you if you linger over lunch."

"Oh. That's good."

Drew'd had a date like this once. It hadn't ended well.

With one last glance around, Brad picked up his menu. Drew hoped he didn't get hung up on the prices. They were pretty reasonable for a Midtown restaurant, and besides, Drew was paying. He would've, even if it weren't deductible, just for the privilege of having an excuse to stare at Brad Sundstrom. He wanted to pinch himself.

"So, I have to admit," Drew said after they placed their orders, "I've been dying of curiosity since you called me yesterday. You said you had some questions for me?"

"Yeah. I really appreciate you meeting me like this. I know you must be busy and all." Brad picked up his knife and tapped the hilt on the tabletop.

"It's my pleasure," Drew said, and it really was.

But Brad didn't reply, and Drew sat there, waiting. Expectantly. Waiting.

When the seconds threatened to lengthen into a minute, Drew kicked himself mentally. The guy was nervous. It was time to fill empty space. "After all, you were one of Nick's favorites. He talked about you all the time."

"Really? I didn't know that." Brad smiled his anxious smile again. Drew felt it in the pit of his stomach.

Yep, because I wouldn't quit pestering him about you. "So, your questions were about real estate, I'm guessing? Since we both know I can't help you with rowing."

"Oh." Brad colored. "Sorry. I guess I'm kind of nervous."

"Really? I hadn't noticed," Drew said blandly.

Brad looked at him for a minute like he was trying to figure out if he was being made fun of, but Drew simply sat there expectantly. "Yeah, I got put in charge of Suburban Symphony when I started working for my dad after graduation."

"Oh. I mean, wow, that's great. Right out of school and already in charge of an entire development."

"It sucks ass," Brad said bluntly.

The combination of Brad and sucking ass took Drew to a place he really didn't want to go. Rather, he did, a lot, just not in public. He'd never been more grateful for a tablecloth in his life because he'd gone from zero to painfully hard in seconds.

"Drew?" Brad said.

"Oh, sorry. I guess I'm not seeing the problem."

"Yeah, well, people aren't seeing the houses, either, and the old man's riding my ass to turn it around," Brad grumbled.

Drew closed his eyes momentarily. His cock had zoomed from painfully hard to crammed up against the fly of his pants in a second.

"Hey, man, are you okay? You kind of whimpered or something," Brad said.

Drew shook his head to clear the visual. "Bit my tongue. I'm sorry, you were saying something about Suburban Symphony?"

"Yeah. It's dying, and it's trying to take my career, such as it is, with it. It's not like I've got any cred with my dad as it is, but if this goes under, I'm sunk."

"I see."

They were silent as lunch was placed before them. When the waiter was out of earshot, Brad said, "So, what do real estate agents look for in a subdivision? What makes you bring people who want to buy a house to one place instead of another? What makes you drive right on by a development?"

"Well," Drew drawled, stalling like an American car with air in the fuel injectors, "that all depends on the needs of the client, of course."

Shit, he wants my help to save that subdivision!

Brad bounced his foot up and down, the tapping muffled by the carpet. "No, I get that, but houses are pretty basic when you think about it—bedrooms, bathrooms, kitchen, living room, maybe a dining room. But this place is...I mean, almost no one comes to see it. No one wants to live there, but I'm supposed to turn it around." He sounded bitter. "Somehow I'm supposed to come up with something to save the place when the marketing people can't come up with anything. You gotta help me, man."

Drew shrugged. "There are intangibles too, like the vibe people get off it, or what they think of the way the rooms are arranged." But that place—ugh, he didn't want to tell Brad the truth. Those shy smiles Brad had flashed him at the regattas that spring...he didn't want to be the one to kill them. "And of course, there's always the famous 'location, location, location'—"

"Stop playing me, dammit. I asked for your help because I need it, not because I want smoke blown up my ass," Brad hissed.

Drew took a bite of his sandwich, chewing slowly and taking his time choosing his words. His appetite was gone. He took a deep breath. He had to do it. Even if he never saw Brad again, at least he'd be able to say he'd been honest with him. "They say there's a house for every buyer, but there's going to have to be a whole lot of desperate, clueless people to fill that place up and real estate agents who don't care about their clients to bring them there."

Brad slumped in his chair. "That's what I was afraid of."

"There are virtually no neighborhood amenities, because whatever county agency's responsible for planning out in that former cornfield apparently thinks driveways and streets count as 'open space,'" Drew said, plowing on. "The floor plans could only have been designed to generate maximum misery for the people dumb enough to buy there. And the location? Please, Brad. It's out in the middle of nowhere, the backside of beyond. Did you know I went out there a few months back?"

"No." Brad appeared surprised.

"Oh yeah." Drew rolled his eyes. He took a swig of his water. "Every time a development opens, they invite any and every real estate agent from miles around to come see it, and so when I saw that Sundstrom Homes—and I had no idea you were *that* Sundstrom, by the way—had something out there, I went to look. I only found it because I got lost. When I got back to my office, I got online to locate the nearest grocery store to see just how bad it was. It'd take someone almost half an hour just to get there."

"Shit," Brad breathed. "I knew there was nothing around there for lunch, but I didn't know it was that bad."

"Look, Brad, these kinds of developments are meant as commuter communities, so I guess people could buy food on the way home from work, but what the fuck? Twenty-seven minutes to get from the Suburban Symphony to the parking lot of a back-country Safeway? Why did you guys saddle yourself with that place?"

"I don't think it was ever our idea. My dad acquired it along with the company that originally developed it," Brad said glumly. "Now you know why the original developer got into trouble and made himself vulnerable."

"Only now it'll take Sundstrom Homes down?" Drew suggested.

"I doubt it, but it's not helping my career any." Brad picked at his pasta.

"I wish I had better news for you, but I'm not really sure how to help you with that place." Drew smiled at Brad, who seemed calmer now that he'd gotten what he wanted out of Drew. "You've only been out of school for a few months. Still learning the ropes, are you?"

"Not really. I've worked for the family business every summer since I started high school."

When he didn't elaborate further, Drew didn't push it. "So, tell me what else you're up to."

"Now why would you be interested in that?" Brad smiled a real smile for the first time since they sat down. He started eating.

"I might have my reasons," Drew said with an arched eyebrow.

Brad laughed, and it warmed Drew right down to his toes. It was a loud laugh, almost a guffaw from a man Drew was learning didn't do things quietly. A few people turned their heads to glare, but he didn't care. Drew was glad Brad had shaken off the glum demeanor that horrendous subdivision inspired.

Afterward, conversation flowed like water, sometimes like a gentle stream, sometimes charging ahead like the varsity eight at the PCRCs. Drew still thought of that magnificent sight, the CalPac V-8 surging ahead of the other crews like eight thoroughbred stallions (and one tiny jockey) moving in perfect synch, backs bending, chests heaving, oar blades knifing into the water.

Drew had never witnessed the human body pushed to the brink like that before. That he'd been there for Nick, his best friend, was special. That he'd gotten to see Brad in his native element—that'd been something else.

For all that Brad set off his gaydar, Drew didn't know for sure if Brad was...questioning, and straight men could get pretty freaked out by the obvious signs of gay interest.

"Brad, look... I'll bring clients by Suburban Symphony. At the very least, it'll leave records of increased traffic," Drew said impulsively. He couldn't help himself. Something about Brad made him want to keep him smiling. "It'll at least show your father you're earning your keep."

But Brad shook his head. "No way, you were right. It's a dump, a tacky little subdivision that's too far from anything. Suburban Graveyard is doomed. How I'm supposed to bring it back is anyone's guess."

"It can't be that bad. If someone wants something in that price point, I'll keep it in mind," Drew said. Brad quirked a smile, and Drew felt all goofy.

The waiter left the check, and they both grabbed for it. "My treat." Drew pulled it close to him. Brad had long arms. He wasn't taking any chances.

Outside the restaurant, Brad shook Drew's hand. "Here," he said, handing Drew a card. "My contact info."

"I've already got it," Drew said with a smile.

Chapter Four

Brad spent the drive home flying on an adrenaline high. Drew rocked. That man was awesome, no two ways about it.

He laughed out loud. He hadn't made too big a fool of himself, not since he'd picked up the phone and called Drew in the first place. At first, he'd been so nervous he could barely speak. But he'd planned ahead, and he'd stuck to his script, pages arrayed before him on the desk. The conversation was probably a little stilted, but it helped put his mind at ease.

And then Drew had asked him a question he hadn't planned on, and Brad panicked. He'd never been one of those people who thought fast on his feet, and as nervous as he'd been, Brad froze.

Then he'd frantically rifled through his papers, trying to find something he could modify on the fly.

"Are you reading from a script?" Drew had chuckled.

"No," Brad had said, letting his pages of scribbled conversation scatter as he dropped them on his desk. "No, what gives you that idea? Just busy...with paperwork."

At the time, he'd been petrified, but there in the car, Brad thought it was pretty damned funny. Making a script to call someone and then getting caught at it and playing it off. He still wasn't sure if he'd gotten away with it, only that Drew had let it go.

Drew was a class act, Brad could tell. A man more sophisticated and suave, if that was the word, than he'd ever be. He was a big lug, and he knew it. You could put him in a fancy suit and teach him to tie a Windsor knot and curl his pinky while drinking tea, and he'd still be a big lug yanking on his collar because it felt like it was strangling him.

Just the thought of himself all dressed up like that made him snicker. Brad, with his neck like a tree trunk and thighs to match. In a suit. Drinking tea.

But Drew... Brad stopped laughing. He hadn't been able to take his eyes off Drew the entire lunch. Every time he felt uncomfortable or even scared and started glancing around, the sight of Drew pulled him back.

"Fuck, he's handsome," Brad whispered. Drew was average height, but Brad liked that better. He'd been around tall and rangy rowers for five years, and not one of them had ever caught his eye.

Drew's brown hair sparkled in the sunlight when they stood in the parking lot to say goodbye. That was the word, sparkled. Maybe it was some gay super hair product or good genes or something. Brad had brown hair, at least what was left of it from where it was noticeably thinning on top. He clipped it super short every other week and left it at that. But even when he'd had enough hair to style, it had never looked like Drew's.

Blue eyes that danced when he smiled. That was weird. Blue eyes usually bugged him. There was something off about them, the way they were different colors from ice blue to flat-out gray, but all still blue. His dad had blue eyes, and they'd never held a hint of warmth. But Drew's...they looked so friendly, so inviting.

Muscles that showed, even through his business-casual clothes. Brad wasn't cultured or sophisticated, which he imagined meant things like knowing about art or fancy food or...something. He didn't know. That was him. But he knew muscles. He knew what time in the gym felt like, and what it looked like later, after you'd recovered and built the muscle. Drew had muscles.

Drew had earned his muscles the hard way too. Brad had never juiced. He knew people who had, people who'd done Deca and then Clomid to keep their balls from shrinking. He could always tell. The thought made him curl his lip in contempt. Juicing was cheating. That was for pussies, pussies and...

Fags?

Brad had forgotten Drew was a homo, that it was another man whose appearances he was so hung up on. But damn, those pecs alone, hidden behind Drew's dress shirt, they'd taken a lot of time to sculpt. A lot of guys just did the bench press for their pecs and left it at that, but it took a lot more to achieve perfection. It took time with the incline press, the dumbbell flies, pull-ups... No, those muscles made Drew look like a man, not just someone who was male. Maybe that was it. There was something manly about Drew.

Was it gay to appreciate another man's masculinity? Brad shook his head. It couldn't be. It was simply acknowledging all Drew's hard work in the gym, that was all.

But even if that was the case, that he just appreciated Drew's efforts in the one area he happened to know something about, Brad was forced to admit there was more to it.

Brad shifted uncomfortably as he drove. He'd boned right up as soon as Drew got out of his car. He was glad Drew had gone into the restaurant ahead of him so he couldn't see the wood Brad had been pushing. But he'd been hard for the entire lunch, balls so tight they ached.

That was totally gay, and Brad knew it. That pissed him off. It scared him. That wasn't who he was.

Was it?

That wasn't who he wanted to be.

But what if he secretly did?

"Damn it!" Brad yelled, bellowed, as he pounded the steering wheel in frustration. "I'm not gay!"

Then he noticed the dashboard clock.

"Shit!" he screamed, well and truly pissed.

It was 4:00 p.m. Lunch had lasted hours, and he'd never noticed. He'd been gone from the office all afternoon. If his dad had dropped by...

Brad gunned the engine. He had to get back to work.

Brad pulled up outside his house—his dad's house, really, even though both Sundstrom boys still lived at home—with a feeling of dread curdling in his guts. It wasn't that Randall Sundstrom was physically abusive, but he sure yelled a lot. Brad was sick of the yelling.

His shoulders slumped, and he got out of the car. He swung the disreputable backpack he still carried over one shoulder and looked at his house, wishing he were anywhere but there. He might as well face the music, but coming hard on the heels of his afternoon, he was so not in the mood for this.

Brad had barely shut the door behind him when he looked up to see Randall standing there waiting for him. "Hi, Randall."

Randall acknowledged the greeting. "Where were you this afternoon?"

"I'm sorry, I just lost track of time. It won't happen—"

"I'm tired of your excuses, Bradley," Randall said calmly.

"Look, I said I was sorry—"

"Sorry doesn't cut it in the grown-up world, Bradley. You've always been feckless. You treat life like a joke. When're you going to grow up?"

Maybe when you treat me like a grown-up?

"What—"

"The sales office was closed all afternoon. That's simply inexcusable," Randall said. "Where were you?"

"Meeting with a real estate agent to find out what I could do to make Suburban Graveyard more appealing to his clients," Brad snapped, voice dripping sarcasm. That was it. He'd had enough. Pushed by his fears and insecurities, he'd hit the limit of what he was willing to swallow. "That not what you were expecting to hear, *Dad*? Figured I took the afternoon off to go joyriding or something? Sorry to disappoint you, Dad, but I'm trying to do the job you dumped on me. Besides which, there weren't any cards stuck in the door when I got back, and no messages on the voice mail."

Randall stared at him for a moment. "We don't want Realtors bringing people in, Bradley. You have to share the commission." He emphasized the *you.*

But Brad was having none of it. "Right now, there's *no one* coming in. So, all of nothing is...nothing. You told me I had to do this. If you're not going to tell me how, then back off."

"No cards just means no real estate agents, Bradley," Randall said with exaggerated patience, "it doesn't mean that no one came by. The people we want don't leave their business cards in the door. They're just ordinary people who want to buy a house."

"Yeah, they're beating a path to our door, that's for sure." Brad laughed. "Whole busloads of 'em, all panting to buy one of those horrible houses. Whoever designed those must have a lot of hostility to work out."

Brad didn't wait for an answer. He stomped off to his room, ignoring his dad's demands that he come back. He threw his backpack into a corner of his room and slammed the door behind him. If Randall was true to form, he'd leave Brad alone in his room.

Brad relaxed fractionally now that the door was shut and locked. Whatever else he could say about living at home as a college graduate, at least he had a spacious room to call his own, including an attached bath. If it had had a kitchen beyond the small dorm-style fridge he stored beer in, it'd have been like living on his own. His dad was an asshole, but he was still a home builder and developer, and the Sundstrom house showed it through details, finishes, and touches large and small.

Part of him wondered if it was his dad's way of keeping his sons dependent, but mostly he just liked hiding in his room, kicking back in a battered recliner, and cracking open a beer or four. But if this job Randall had dumped on him ever started paying, he was off like a prom dress, out of there, and into his own place.

He didn't figure the shit job was his dad's way of keeping him down, as his brother Philip made bank with his job at Sundstrom Homes. Why Philsie didn't leave was anyone's guess, but he was the oldest and clear favorite. Brad had a shit job because he was Brad.

He sighed and opened a beer.

Brad was pissed but unsure why beyond the catch-22 his dad had put him in, although that was enough. It angered him that he was playing by a set of rules he didn't know and, for all he did know, changed on him at his dad's whim. Brad felt like he'd had a good idea and taken positive steps to do his job, a job he didn't want, and then got crapped on.

No, he brooded as the booze worked its liquid magic, there was something else going on. He and his emotions and motivations weren't really on a first-name basis. He'd always been content to go with the flow, riding the wave of whatever he felt without bothering with the whys and the how-comes. Life was simpler that way, and Brad liked simple.

But lately, his emotions were turning on him. Starting this summer, he'd been buffeted by an unaccustomed melancholy. He'd looked the word up once, and it seemed to describe his mood. He missed his old life, plain and simple. The parties. The gym.

Crew.

He missed that most of all. He'd proven himself there. Even if Morgan had finally beaten him on the ergs, proving once and for all that he was faster, Brad had enjoyed the process.

But the thought of crew led him directly to Drew. Crew and Drew. On his third beer, the rhyme made him snicker. But the direction his mind—liberated by alcohol and an empty stomach—headed when he thought of Drew, that scared him.

He thought about how hard he'd been during lunch. That scared him too. He'd sported a monster boner for another man.

Brad leveraged himself out of the chair and headed for the bathroom to tap a kidney. He finished up and glanced at his underwear as he was putting his cock back in. The gray of the boxer-briefs was damp with darker spots of pre-cum.

Standing before the toilet, junk still out, Brad could only stare at the physical evidence of his attraction for another man.

That is it, that is just it. I'm not gay, I'm not attracted to Drew. He helped me out with a work problem, but that is it. Over and done with.

This...*thing* of his where Drew was concerned was a thing of the past. It was over and done with.

Drew left the restaurant thoroughly charmed by Brad. He didn't know what Nick's problem with the guy was, because lunch only confirmed Drew's hunch that Brad was worth getting to know. A few hours of face time across a table from him, and Drew knew he couldn't get enough of that double handful of big lug. He was just so appealingly gauche, but once he warmed up and started smiling...that was even better. Drew wanted some more of that.

Drew wanted all kinds of things from Brad, starting with a little help for his hard-on. But he also knew the chances of that were slim. As he puttered back to his office to prepare for taking his clients to that freak show of a house in a few hours, he realized he also wanted to be Brad's friend.

Based on what he'd seen of the crew and Brad's place in it in previous years, and what Brad had let slip, he had the sense Brad might not have had too many friends—real friends, not just people he made trouble with.

It was probably wishful thinking, Drew cautioned himself as he pulled into his parking space at the realty office, but it had really seemed like Brad had opened up over the course of lunch, from the closed, even hostile person who'd greeted him in the parking lot, to the laughing and joking guy he said goodbye to.

Drew knew he had to play it cagey, since he had only a few fleeting smiles, a vague sense of the fey, and wishful thinking to go on where Brad's sexual orientation was concerned. The last thing he wanted was to come on strong and scare him off. If he was the older gay perv hitting on the hot young guy, he wouldn't even have Brad's friendship to show for his efforts.

"Hi, Drew," the admin said as he walked into the office. "You've got a small pile of messages on your desk, but otherwise, it's been pretty quiet for you."

"Thanks, Serena," Drew said, blowing her air kisses as he walked by.

She laughed. "You always promise but never follow through."

Drew sat at his desk and sorted through the promised stack of messages. Most weren't urgent, but he was surprised a few weren't smoldering. He set them aside. He'd have to return to them before he drove to meet his clients for that 6:00 p.m. meeting.

He woke his computer up and set it to downloading e-mails, but his mind was still at lunch with Brad. As much as he'd enjoyed himself, and as happy as he'd been to help (once Brad had seen through his attempts at dodging being honest about that development), it hadn't required a face-to-face meeting, let alone a lunch that lasted several enchanting hours. A real estate agent's perspective on Suburban Graveyard could've been solicited via e-mail or even telephone, and it wasn't like he hadn't given Nick permission to pass his contact information along to Brad via Morgan.

The more Drew thought about it, the more lunch felt like an excuse. That Brad might've been looking for an excuse to see him thrilled him. He grew warm all over as a goofy smile stole over his lips.

Brad was going to be the death of him, however, if he didn't change his vocabulary. All that talk of Brad and ass had Drew hard and wanting.

Drew snickered at the name Brad had come up with for Suburban Symphony as he reluctantly got back to work.

Chapter Five

As the days headed for a full week with no contact from Brad, Drew faced the fact that he'd misjudged Brad and his interest. He tried to shrug it off. He tried to be philosophical about it. After all, as he well knew, wishful thinking trumped gaydar every time. But no calls, no e-mails, no nothing from Brad cast a dark patina over Drew's mood. He'd been so sure...

But Drew had other things to worry about that summer afternoon. The economic climate might not have been the best, but for some reason, Drew had never had more business, and that was the problem. What he didn't have was people to do the work.

He sat in traffic on the freeway, wondering if he could possibly have found a worse time of day to check out another potential reno. Even though it was where he wanted to head in terms of his business, he was practical enough to realize he wasn't there yet. He just didn't know how he could handle another renovation right then.

But then Emily had called. Actually, she'd done more than call. She'd driven to his office and begged.

"Even if I take out a hit on my old contractor, which, believe me, is growing more likely by the minute, it won't save this project," Emily had said.

"I'm not a contractor, you know," Drew'd protested.

"No, but you've got one you can work with, and these days, that's a miracle. You also do good work, which is a nice bonus. Please, just tell me you'll come look at it." When he'd looked like he was about to turn her down, she'd added, "Mary and Fred Abernathy love your work so far. You're on budget and slightly ahead of schedule. As far as they're concerned, after hearing horror stories about home renovations, you're a miracle worker. I need another miracle."

So, there he was, wondering how the hell he was going to pull off another miracle and rotting on the elevated Capital City Freeway while down below, Sacramento went about its business beneath a leafy green canopy. At least it wasn't a complete house renovation, just the master bedroom and bath. That was the only reason he was even considering it.

But it wasn't just another possible reno for Emily. It was the job already under way and the one lined up, waiting for his crew to become available. Every day those properties went unrenovated and unsold cost him money.

The flips he could handle. That was what he did. He knew how they worked. But the flips, along with the not-nearly-as-complete-as-Emily-claimed   Abernathy renovation and a new reno on top of his stillborn love life...

The thought of it all made Drew a little queasy.

He didn't know how helping his friend out and keeping everything else going was going to be humanly possible. Sure, he could find the labor. This was California, after all, and so long as you didn't look too closely at immigration status, labor was there for the asking. It sucked, and it was exploitative, but there it was.

Drew made sure his crew checked out, and he knew he could trust Octavio to find more help, if it came down to it. But Octavio wasn't interested in the headaches that went along with being a project leader. He'd made that much clear the first time Nick had had to go back to coaching and grad school in the fall a few years before.

Crawling down the highway at thirty miles per hour, Drew realized he needed a business partner, not just more labor, and where he was going to find someone he could work with, he had no idea.

Finally, traffic opened up, and he drove to meet Emily to see this latest nail in his coffin.

"You know, we actually used to socialize outside of home improvement," Nick said the day after Drew had gone to check out the next proposed reno. He placed a level against a cabinet door in one bathroom of the Abernathy renovation to make sure it was hung correctly.

"We used to socialize more before you got a boyfriend," Drew said from under the bathroom sinks where he was adjusting a leaking cold-water feed. "It's just the way things go."

"Yeah, I guess. The truth is I miss talking to you without hardware in my hands or worrying about deadlines."

"I know what you mean, but summer's almost over, and we'll get back to normal in a month or so. And speaking of which..."

Nick put the level down. "I know that tone. Spare me the buildup and cut to the chase."

"I've got another reno I want to take on, and that means you." Drew leveraged himself out from under the sink. "For starters, it's a small one, just a master bedroom and bathroom. I think we can bang it out before you go back to school."

"Maybe, maybe not. But you said 'for starters.' What else is going on?" Nick leaned against the counter, arms crossed over his chest.

"This is what I want to do. Flipping's all well and good, but I'm limited to what I can do alone during the school year and what we can accomplish together during the summer, and you—"

"Graduate next spring, yes."

"I don't even want to think of that yet," Drew admitted.

Nick shrugged. "I know, but you're going to have to one of these days."

Drew looked up. "You and Morgan will graduate, probably move away, and then where will I be? Here without my best friend."

"Maybe, maybe not. A lot depends on where Morgan goes for his teaching credential. Don't borrow trouble. So. A bed/bath in a month before school starts?"

"Yes. This place is all but done. We've got one reno in progress and another ready to go, but if I charge Emily enough, this job will more than make up for putting that one on the slow track."

Nick thought about it. "The only way this can work is if I put my research on hold for that month and if you scale way back on selling houses so we can both put all our efforts into this."

"I can do that, I think, if you can."

"And I have to talk to Morgan about it," Nick cautioned.

"You have to ask your boyfriend? Dude, you are so married." Drew laughed. Secretly, he was a little envious. That kind of accountability to another sounded pretty attractive to him, but it wasn't looking like a possibility any time soon.

Nick shrugged. "It affects him too. Not only will I not be around as much the rest of the summer, it means I won't be around as much this next school year, since the research won't happen by itself. Between that, teaching, and the last of my own coursework, to say nothing of coaching... There are only so many hours in the day. Of course, it'll be his senior year, so he'll be pretty busy too."

"Fair enough," Drew said. "Let's get back to work. Whatever happens, I want this place done. It'll only help Renochuck in the future. Jeez, I can't believe I just called my own company Renochuck."

The next day, both men were back at the Abernathy place for their last inspection before the homeowners had their final walkthrough.

"So, I can do it," Nick said, "but Morgan wants you to pay me more."

"He what! That little—"

"Man I love," Nick said flatly. He sounded gruff, but Drew could tell he was kidding. Mostly.

"Yeah, I'll pay you more. It's only fair." Before Nick could change his mind, Drew pulled out his cell phone and called Emily. "Okay, I know this is voice mail, but I'm suddenly very busy. I'll do the bed/bath job for you, but this is the last job for a while, do you hear me? The very last! Love you, babe. Bye."

"That'll learn her," Nick snorted. "You also just caved like a spelunker."

Drew shrugged. "Yeah, I know. But what can you do? She's a good friend, and we help our friends out. Thanks for helping me out with this, friend."

"Any time."

They worked their way through the Abernathy house one room at a time, going over the work with the proverbial fine-toothed comb. The silence was companionable, but Drew could tell Nick was working his way around to something.

"Drew..."

"Yes?"

"I'm almost afraid to ask, and I think I can guess, because quite frankly, you've been a bit of a downer for the last week or so, but what's up with Brad?"

"Nothing, that's what," Drew said. "A big fat nothing."

"I'm sorry. I tried to warn you. I just don't think he's into you, not like that."

"I know, and I don't actually hate you for that 'I told you so,' but I thought there was something there... The looks, the shy smiles."

"I don't know what to tell you that I haven't already said before, but you know I'm here for you, and so is Morgan," Nick said quietly.

"I know, and I appreciate it," Drew replied.

Nick regarded him for a moment and then hugged him.

"I thought I was happy with my single life," Drew said, face muffled by Nick's chest. "I've got a great job, keep myself busy, but then this spring...when I saw Brad. When I thought I saw something in Brad and thought maybe he saw something in me... I realized I want what you've got with Morgan. I want... I want to share my life with someone."

"I'm sorry," Nick murmured. He kissed Drew's head softly.

"It's okay." Drew sniffled. "Maybe he'll still be my friend. Jeez, that sounds pathetic."

"A little, yeah."

Drew let go of Nick and wiped his eyes with the back of his hand. "I don't know when I turned into such an emotional bag of slop."

"Feeling doesn't make you a bag of slop, and you'd pinned your hopes on Brad. It's natural to be disappointed, to be upset."

"Thanks, Oprah. Good to know."

"Aaaand he's back!" Nick laughed. "I'll be right back. There's something I need to get out of my backpack."

When he returned to the bathroom they were inspecting, Nick handed Drew a piece of paper. "I can't believe I'm doing this, and in light of previous discussions, I run the risk of hypocrisy, but this may take your mind off Brad."

Giving Nick a skeptical look, Drew took the paper and read it silently for a few moments. "Holy shit," he breathed.

"About that, yes," Nick said. "That interest you?"

"Are you kidding me? The city's calling for bids from up-and-coming designers and architects for the renovation of the Bayard House." Drew's gaze was glued to the circular. "This is what I want to do, but...it's too soon!" He met Nick's eyes. "I mean, I can't pull this off, not yet. We're freaking out getting this project done and then a bed/bath. The mayor's residence is an historic house that goes back to the Gold Rush, when Sacramento was built on stilts because the American and Sacramento Rivers flooded like clockwork every winter. I don't know much about historical preservation, let alone how to update and adapt such an old and important structure. I..."

Nick let Drew sputter on for a few more moments but then cut him off. "Look, the city obviously knows this is a huge undertaking, but they're calling for up-and-comers anyway. You've got some experience and you've got a contractor you can work with. Give Emily a call. She's got the design chops. Between the two of you, you should be able to come up with something."

"You think so?" Drew said.

"Drew, I know so," Nick said gently. "This is your big chance."

"The only way I can do this is if you help me." When Nick started to protest, Drew cut him off. "No, seriously. We work well together. You've been helping me with flips since you moved up here. You're the only crew leader I've ever had. You probably know more than I do at this point, frankly."

Nick shook his head. "There's no way on earth. I'd have to take a semester off school, and that's just not happening."

"Please, Nick, I'm begging. I went along with your insane scheme to get Morgan off your scent before you two decided to give it a go. Now it's time to return the favor."

"This is totally different, and you know it." Nick had an edge to his voice. "That turned out to be one night out. You're asking me to take half a year off school. It's not just me anymore. As it is right now, Morgan and I will finish up at the same time. There's no way I'll screw that up.

You're my best friend, but he's the man I'm going to marry."

"Fine. I can't believe you're going to be that way, though, not after all we've been through together."

"Don't make this a choice between you and Morgan," Nick warned. "We've been friends a long time. Don't fuck it up."

"But the Bayard House!" Drew wailed. "This could make me."

"I know it could, Drew, and that's why I brought it to your attention, but reno isn't what I want to go into. It's your dream, not mine. I do this to make money on the side and as a favor to you, but you can't ask me to derail my life for it, to say nothing of Morgan's, you just can't."

"I know," Drew said softly, deflated.

"Talk to Emily," Nick urged him. Then he smiled. "Save your manipulation for her. After all, she owes you a few favors, now, doesn't she?"

"You're a baaaaad man, Nick Bedford." Drew smirked. "That's why I like you."

Nick winked. "Now let's get back to work. If you're going to go after the Bayard House bid, you need this and that bed/bath to be perfect."

"So, you've heard about the Bayard House, have you?"

Drew sat across from Emily Schoenwald at a small table at a trendy coffee shop. Both had notebooks and calendars open in front of them. Drew stared at the blank page open before him, toying with a pencil. "My crew leader showed me the circular. What do you think?"

"I think it's a tremendous opportunity," the small blonde spitfire said. "I'm just not convinced it's an opportunity for us."

"It'd be a stretch, that's for sure, but then, that may be the point of aiming it at younger designers and builders. It's supposed to be a stretch, and it'll turn into a boost up."

"I'm just not convinced that either of us operates at the scale this job will require. You do fantastic work, but you handle only one or two jobs at a time. I usually have a few more jobs going at once, but we're neither of us used to handling things like this."

Drew shifted in his chair. "Of course, we don't operate on that scale. The point is to make the jump up to that scale."

"Possibly," Emily replied. She took a sip of her latte. "It's also a gamble. You'd have to back way off on selling houses, and I'd have to devote most of my resources to the project too. That means either we need to have money in the bank to carry us or we have to secure loans until the city pays us, and in this economy, I'm just not optimistic we could get the financing."

"We work pay as you go, you know that. I don't see how these public projects would be that different," Drew said.

"You know these government contracts don't tend to have large profit margins." Emily looked at him.

"Maybe we should stop thinking about why we can't do it and start thinking of how we could do it." Drew was beginning to lose patience.

Emily smiled. "I was wondering how negative I was going to have to get before you pushed back."

"You bitch." Drew laughed as he sat back in his chair. "All that caffeine in your blood is making you mean."

"I could tell you wanted to do it just by the way you brought it up, but you needed to get the reasons for not doing it out of your system." As Emily spoke, she brought a laptop out of her briefcase. "Let's look at this and start brainstorming. This is the chance we've both been waiting for."

Drew pulled his own laptop out, and together he and Emily called up the webpage devoted to the contest. There they found the information they'd need to start their bid, including detailed schematics of the existing Bayard House and a list of requirements for the renovated structure, along with so much more.

Two hours later, Drew and Emily felt a lot more optimistic about the possibility of making a go of it.

"So, what do we need to update this thing?" Emily said, thinking aloud. "HVAC, for sure."

Drew nodded. "Probably two separate systems, one upstairs and one down." When she looked at him quizzically, he said, "Because the building is so old, the walls may not take well to having ductwork run through them. Separate systems for the upstairs and then the downstairs and basement gets around that."

"But what about new wiring? Won't that need to go through the walls?"

"Yes, but if we have to run conduit in the walls first, it'll be much less intrusive than effective HVAC ducts. Even if it turns out that the walls just can't take that much, conduit is unobtrusive, and can be run along baseboards. You see it in a lot of old homes. But one thing may change all this, and it's going to involve some research. Seismic upgrades."

"I hadn't thought of that," Emily admitted, "but you're right." She thought for a few moments. "Okay, one real problem I've got as a designer is that this is an historical building, and the city very explicitly wants it preserved as much as possible, even as we adapt it to modern needs like the HVAC or wiring for computer networks."

"Would we even need it to be networked? It's the mayor's official residence, not the working offices," Drew pointed out. "We might be able to solve that problem with Wi-Fi repeaters. They're small and can be hidden almost anywhere. Something else to check into."

Emily scribbled a note. "I'm on it. Let's do this."

"Not so fast. Another issue is that we're not contractors. This is a problem I face in my flips, and since Bob Miller's retired, he may not want to commit to something this large. He'll need to be paid, too, and that means more money in our bid beyond what we might need for salaries. It reduces our competitiveness."

Emily shrugged. "That's just something we have to face. Others might not have it. We will."

"Let's both look into how little we really need to live on while this is going on," Drew suggested.

"Short our salaries?" Emily wrinkled her nose.

"Says the doctor's wife. Besides, you said this was a gamble. Talk to Missy and see what she says. If we don't pay ourselves as much so we can pay for someone to sign off, that might make us more competitive."

"I guess," Emily sounded glum.

"Hey, no guts no glory."

"I wish you were a contractor."

"And I wish I were taller and hung like a horse. I guess we'll both have to smile through the tears."

Emily laughed as she shook her head. "Now who's the bitch?"

"You love it."

"And you," she said. "I think we can do this."

"I do too," Drew said as they gathered their things and left.

It was the same old problem, and it reared its head every time he turned around. He wasn't a contractor. He needed a contractor, and not just one who signed off on things.

He felt like he was spinning his wheels on this one. It was time to let it go for a while, since he couldn't put his own affairs on hold long enough to get a license himself. It was time to think of something else.

He tried running through the list of current homes he had listed, along with clients who wanted homes. Neither was as long as he'd have liked, but with the economy so uncertain, home sales were off. One more reason to head into renovation. Since people couldn't afford to move, they were renovating.

And so, he was back to the contractor issue.

"Enough!" he yelled as he came to a stop at a light, bouncing back against his seat. He leaned his head against the headrest.

Inspiration struck as the light turned green.

Brad.

Brad didn't come right out and say it, but he sure hadn't sounded happy talking about work at lunch. He did say, however, that he'd worked for his dad every summer starting in high school. He clearly had some experience in the building trades.

Drew wondered how Brad would feel about entering into a partnership and working toward a contractor license. Drew and Emily would have someone they could trust overseeing the renovation of the Bayard House, and they could still work at their own businesses to an extent, even if they were working to pay Brad. Then Bob could work as needed. Anything to keep the bid costs down.

But Drew was honest enough with himself to admit it was more than that. Despite the radio silence from Brad, he just wasn't ready to abandon the idea that there might be some chemistry between them. Working with Brad—strictly platonically, of course—would give him a chance to suss him out. And who knew, maybe a business partnership between St. Charles Renovations and the younger Sundstrom boy might lead to a partnership of another kind.

Chapter Six

Hot as balls.

Hot as fuck.

Hot as...

Damn. That was all he had.

Brad sat at his desk, sweat streaming down his face, his untucked shirt darkened with the runoff. It was the end of July, and Sacramento sizzled. The cooling evening breezes from the delta where the Sacramento River entered the San Francisco Bay hadn't risen for the past week. Every day was hotter than the last, and this day, the air conditioner, pushed beyond endurance, sputtered and coughed and died before 10:00 a.m.

Coming up hard on lunch, he didn't know how he was going to make it the rest of the day, not when Sundstrom Homes' own HVAC crews were busy elsewhere and outside repairmen couldn't make it until the next afternoon. Apparently his wasn't the only AC to have given up the ghost in the heat wave, and many people were a lot worse off. This was just where he worked. His home would be fine. Better he should sweat at work than some old lady die in the heat. He knew it could happen.

But that didn't make work any easier to take, especially given that he'd already finished all the cold water in the little fridge.

So, he tried to take his mind off the heat by coming up with all the things it was as hot as without saying *hot as hell*. It didn't take him long to give up. It was just too hot, and word games had never been his thing. That was why it took him a few moments to realize the phone was ringing.

"Suburban Symphony, this is Brad, how can I help you find a home today?" Brad answered. He didn't even make a face anymore at the stupid way he had to answer the phone.

"Hi, Brad, I've already got a home, thanks, and honestly? It's a lot nicer than those, but thanks for asking."

"Hey, Drew!" Brad said, grinning like an idiot. Before he knew it, his heart was soaring.

Then he remembered he'd sworn off Drew and forced himself to stop smiling, because that...that *thing* he felt for Drew was done for, even though the tickling in his stomach shouted *liar!* He mopped his forehead with a paper towel, angry with himself for getting so excited. "Yeah, what'd you want?" he snapped.

"Well hello to you, too, sweetness," Drew said. "Who pissed in your Wheaties?"

Brad couldn't help it. He laughed. The comment was just vintage Drew. He hadn't known Drew that long, but he already knew he had a ready snap. "Sorry, man, it's just too hot. The AC died in the office this morning, and it's going to take me with it."

"Well, then I have a proposal for you," Drew proclaimed grandly.

Brad's mind inserted the word "indecent," and his balls tightened right up.

"...at the water park?"

Brad's mouth went dry. Drew? In a swimsuit? "I'm sorry, what'd you say?"

"I said, it's just too hot to do anything today. Do you want to meet me at the water park? You know, Raging Waters. It's at the state fairgrounds."

Brad agonized for a moment. He knew he'd sworn off Drew, but that sounded like fun, and he was surprised how much he missed the sound of Drew's voice.

Mistaking Brad's silence for hesitation, Drew said, "C'mon, you know you want to. You said yourself the AC was dead. What else are you going to do? You can only pretend your office is a sauna at a fancy gym for so long before you give it up."

Fuck it, gay guys and straight guys can be friends. Hell, a gay wingman could be just the thing. *Women are drawn to gay men, and then I'll be there to reap the benefits. Yeah, that's the score*, Brad told himself, even if his dick was sitting up and begging at the thought of Drew rather than the disappointed women crying in his wake.

And it was far too hot to get all choosy. "That...that sounds like a lot of fun."

"Yeah? Great! How fast can you get there?" Drew asked.

"Gimme forty-five minutes," Brad said. "I'll meet you out front. Shit, make that an hour and a half. I have to go home for a swimsuit."

"I've got one that'll fit you."

"Dude, I'm about six inches taller and fifty pounds heavier," Brad scoffed. "How do you have a suit that'll fit me?"

"I didn't say it was mine. People leave things here all the time. Trust me."

"Forty-five minutes it is, then." Brad ended the call and then called his dad. Predictably, he got voice mail. "Hi, Randall, it's me, Brad. Listen, the AC is dead in the office, and it's almost a hundred inside. The foreman here's already sent his crews home, and I can't get anyone out here until tomorrow to deal with it, either one of our own HVAC crews or the outside service we use. I'm closing down. I'll leave an outgoing voice mail to that effect, along with a sign on the door instructing people to call my cell phone. Bye."

With unaccustomed diligence, Brad printed out a variant of the proverbial "Gone Fishing" sign and taped it inside the glass front door of the sales office and was in his car—his beautiful air-conditioned car—in minutes.

His subconscious wanted to know why strange men left clothing behind at Drew's house "all the time," but he steadfastly refused to take the bait. He tried to shove the thought out of his mind, but it kept coming back.

"Look at you, playing hooky," Brad said as they met in front of Raging Waters.

There was an awkward moment where Drew couldn't figure out if they should shake hands or hug or what. If he'd been with gay friends, they'd have hugged, but he didn't want to make Brad uncomfortable. So, he settled for keeping his hands in the pockets of his shorts.

"Who's playing hooky? I just finished the final walkthrough on a renovation this morning, and I don't start the next project until tomorrow. Besides, in this heat, it's not safe for people to work in the house I'm renovating, so I sent the guys home. Excepting the unlikely event of a real estate emergency, I'm free for the afternoon."

"I'm just using this heat and a dead air conditioner as an excuse." Brad sounded a little glum.

"Well, I'm glad you are, because doing this by myself? Pathetic."

"Couldn't find anyone else, huh? What about Nick or someone?"

Drew wasn't sure what to say. Brad was his first choice, but that apparently hadn't occurred to him. He figured someone had done a real number on Brad's self-confidence.

"Nick had to get some research done. He's doing me a major favor by overseeing this next renovation for me before school starts. I didn't want to distract him, and more to the point, I didn't want to get Morgan pissed at either one of us."

Brad smiled. "I can see that. We had an unfriendly rivalry thing going for a while, did you know that?"

"No, I didn't," Drew said.

"Yeah, he didn't get mad or say anything, he just did his thing real quietly and totally cut my throat at it. It really made me mad at the time, but now I just think it's kind of funny. He's an okay guy. But...him and Coach Nick? I didn't see that coming."

"I did."

"No shit?"

"You forget, Nick was never my coach, so he never hid who he was from me. I wasn't even that surprised he was hot for one of his rowers. No, I had to listen to him whine about the ethics of it all."

"Well, it's all water under the bridge. Let's get inside. It's hot, and I want to cool off. You've got a swimsuit for me?"

Drew patted the duffel bag slung over one shoulder. "Right here."

They paid their admission and headed inside. Drew wasn't sure what to think. There'd been that long silence from Brad, and then a bit of awkwardness when Drew had finally called him at work. But that seemed gone now, and Drew was glad. He'd had time to accept that Brad wasn't gay. He'd thought there was something there, and there wasn't. Fine. Moving on. He still liked Brad as a friend, and friends could do things together.

Besides, Drew thought as he followed Brad through the turnstile into the locker room, if he were to convince Brad to come work for and with him, there had to be some kind of relationship there, even if it wasn't the kind he wanted.

"So, wait," Brad threw back over his shoulder, "you said Nick worked for you? On houses?"

"Yeah, I needed some help a few summers ago, and he needed money. It's not like coaching pays that much, and it's basically seasonal," Drew said, pleased at the chance to bait a trap. "So, he helped me out, and apparently he's quite handy. It didn't take long before we realized if I put him in charge, we got more done. Every summer since, he's my crew leader. I don't know what I'm going to do when he graduates and moves on."

They found a bank of lockers with open doors. Drew handed Brad the swimsuit and towel he'd brought for him.

"That's so cool!" Brad said. He held the suit up. It was volleyball-length and made of an iridescent purple fabric.

"Yeah, it really has been. I've gotten to work with my best friend, and we've stayed friends."

"No, I mean the suit, but do I want to know why you've got clothing in a size that will never fit you?"

"I don't know, do you?" Drew said coyly.

Brad looked pained. "I asked, didn't I?"

Drew laughed, trying not to read too much into it. "I've got a hot tub and a wide circle of acquaintances. People crash at my place after going to the clubs or after parties, things get left behind. See? Perfectly tame."

"Glad to hear it." Brad unbuttoned his shirt.

Drew looked away quickly. There was no way he could risk looking. He'd brought a square-cut Speedo, and he'd be unable to hide the tumescence that would inevitably result from watching Brad strip. But he was freakishly aware that the subject of his fantasies was taking off his clothes a few feet away. He turned slightly away from Brad, just in case, the same old story of the gay man in a straight man's locker room.

"I didn't know you were in construction," Brad continued as he changed.

"I just kind of stumbled into it, really. I started flipping houses on the side not long after I got into real estate. It seemed like a natural progression," Drew explained, "and it turned out that I really liked it. Maybe even more than real estate, if you want to know the truth."

"That's cool."

"It's nerve-racking. I've got a major opportunity coming up, one that might allow me to move more into renovation, but without Nick there, I'm really not sure how it's going to work." Drew's mind was full of everything he wasn't telling Brad. But springing, "Hey, wanna come work for me?" on Brad seemed a little sudden. He knew he had to work his way around to it, build a case and pique Brad's interest, and then spring it on him.

"Hey, Drew?"

Drew looked up. "Yeah? Ouch!"

"Surprise!"

"You just whipped me with a towel."

"Uh-huh," Brad laughed. He had a huge shit-eating grin.

"So that's how it's going to be," Drew said, nodding slowly. He finally got an eyeful of Brad, whose tree trunk-like thighs were barely contained by the borrowed bathing suit. And that fur on his belly! Drew's throat went dry.

Brad's eyes were bright. "C'mon, let's go play in the water."

The first bracing plunge into the water felt balls-shrinkingly cold compared to the oven-like heat of the air, but after the initial shock, the water was refreshing, and Brad and Drew had a great time racing down the flumes. The faster runs, in particular, were largely rug rat free, and in any event, the lifeguards did a good job of keeping the fully grown from plowing into smaller, lighter people by making them wait a few extra moments before barreling down the flumes on their rubber mats.

"Oh, man, that was just what I needed today," Drew said as he flopped down onto his beach towel on the grass under an enormous shade structure.

"That was a blast," Brad said. "Thanks for calling."

Brad stood, looking down at Drew, who fortunately had his eyes closed. He paused with the towel over his head, the water running down his shaved head unheeded. Water ran onto his chest, tracing rivulets around his pecs, pulling his chest hair together. It trickled its way down over the merest hint of a belly and disappeared into the borrowed swimming trunks, but Brad didn't notice.

He'd been right with his speculations about Drew's body at lunch almost two weeks before. Drew obviously knew his way around the gym. He was toned and built but lacked that fake shredded look of the dedicated gym rat who lifted lots of weights but did nothing with them. Whatever Drew did for exercise and fun was clearly working for him because Brad couldn't take his eyes off him. He looked like what Brad thought a man should look like, not a 'roid droid.

Brad swallowed the lump in his throat. Then his eyes traveled further down Drew's body, and he forgot how to breathe.

He'd been around guys in spandex before, seen plenty of packages barely contained by the stretchy fabric of high school wrestling or collegiate crew unisuits. He'd even seen guys popping boners in uniforms that left nothing to the imagination. They did nothing for him. Nada. Zilch.

But Drew in that little Speedo?

He was mesmerized. He was entranced. All he could do was stare at...it.

Brad wanted it. He didn't have a name for it, but he wanted it.

Actually, he did have a name for it.

He started drying his head vigorously, even roughly, hard enough to leave the skin of his scalp red and angry.

"You're quiet," Drew said, propping himself up on his elbows.

"Just thinking," Brad said.

"About?"

"About that big opportunity you were telling me about. Sounds cool. What's up with it?" Brad tossed the towel on the ground, awkwardly smoothed it out, and lay down next to Drew.

"I'm trying not to think about it," Drew groaned.

"If you don't want to talk about it..."

"No, it's cool. You've heard of the Bayard House, right?"

Brad nodded. "It's supposed to be the mayor's mansion, but it's totally uninhabitable or something."

"Basically, yeah." Drew sat all the way up, facing Brad. "What updating's been done hasn't been all that compatible with the rest of the building. The city government decided it's time to get serious about preserving the mansion, because there's so little of the old city left. So, there's a call for bids specifically aimed at younger firms to preserve and adapt the old mansion to the needs of the twenty-first century."

"Wow," Brad breathed. "That sounds...awesome."

"It sounds terrifying," Drew said.

"Terrifying? It sounds like a blast."

"I mostly do flips, but lately I've worked with a designer on actual renovations. She thinks we should do it. We're both young, new in this business and all that, but..."

"But you're not a contractor?" Brad prompted.

Drew plucked at a grass stem. "No, and that's the big stumbling block, or one of them. I've got a contractor I usually work with. He's retired, but he's willing to inspect my work and sign off if I pay him as a consultant. But by no stretch of the imagination is he new to this business, one of the requirements of the job. That's even assuming he'd be willing to work on this. It'd be pretty big, and that's another thing. It'd take all my time." He groaned and lay back on his towel, covering his eyes with one arm.

Brad watched him, considering. He was kind of jealous. When it came down to it, he liked the housing trades. He liked being physical and working with his hands. He liked being outside, at least when it wasn't quite so sweltering. That was why crew had been such a good fit for him, and the same things that had drawn him to rowing were what he liked about home building—working with his body in the outdoors, working as part of a team for a greater whole.

Despite his dad and that damn double-cross about where he'd be working, he liked the idea of his job. It was at least familiar territory while he figured out if this was what he wanted to do with the rest of his life. But for someone with some experience in the home trades, someone adrift and looking around after college, this sounded like a dream job. That said, he knew he could never do anything like that.

"So, are you going to do it?" Brad said, trying not to sound too excited.

Drew looked up at him. "Probably," he said. "Yes. I don't know."

"So long as you're sure and all that."

"I'm sorry, I'm sure this sounds pretty pathetic." Drew sat up again. "Sorry to dump all this on you."

"No, it's totally okay." Brad smiled. "I like hearing about it."

"Oh." Drew smiled shyly in return.

Brad looked back at him for a few moments. Then the tingly fluttery feeling got to be too much. "Hey, let's slide some more. I'm getting hot again."

Drew didn't say anything for a minute, but Brad could tell he was up to something. He could see the muscles in Drew's legs bunching.

Sure enough, Drew sprung up. "Last one in buys dinner!"

And he was off, pelting across the pool deck, Brad in hot pursuit, the booming voice of the lifeguards chasing after them, demanding they walk.

Laughing like maniacs, the pair of them, they slowed down fractionally, each trying to beat the other to the stairs leading up to the top of the water slides.

A few hours later on the way home, Brad felt let down, as if going back to the ordinary world were a return to the world he'd seen on old TV shows, a world of monochrome where the afternoon had been in laughing, breathing color.

He realized he'd been happier that afternoon than he had all summer, happier with Drew. He frowned, thinking. Drew was his old coach's best friend. In some ways, maybe Drew was his last connection to crew, his last connection to the best part of college. That had to be it.

But that didn't change the fact he'd spent the afternoon romping and playing with a half-naked gay man and had a fine time doing it too. Drew was Drew. There was something about him that Brad liked being around, and if Drew liked dick, then Brad had spent the afternoon with a man who liked dick. That was all. It didn't have to Mean Anything. He could almost see the capital letters floating in the air.

Brad wasn't one to analyze things, but there wasn't really anything wrong with a straight guy like him having a close gay friend, was there? If that was what this was. He squirmed. He so didn't want to think about this.

Chapter Seven

Thursday afternoon, Emily met Drew at his house. Thursday was usually Drew's day for getting things done. Saturday and Sunday were his busiest home-showing days, and Friday was spent preparing. Thursdays were for errands.

It was time to pool research and brainstorming about the Bayard bid. Drew had spent the morning with Nick getting the bed/bath reno off the ground, and now was prepared to spend the rest of the afternoon working on the bid for a project that looked like it could not only take on a life of its own, but take over both his and Emily's lives too.

"The site tour's set up for Monday. You'll be there?" Drew said.

Emily nodded. "I wouldn't miss it for anything. I'm coming back early from a romantic long weekend at the coast to beat this heat. My wife's not happy, but it's not like her job's never interrupted things."

"Poor little surgeon. She finally takes some time off, and then her wife ups and gets busy." Drew pretended to pout.

"I'm always busy, I'm just not adjusting to her schedule this time." Emily snickered. She shoved some books across the table to him. "Here. I've marked a few things for you to look at. These are illustrations and pictures of period furniture. It's what would've been found in east coast homes of the wealthy when the Bayard House was built."

As Drew looked at the illustrations and photographs of Civil War-era furniture and fixtures, Emily looked around. "What I could do with this room. Such good bones, but it's a blank slate."

"You say blank, I say clean and uncomplicated," Drew sat back in his chair and tried to see his dining room through Emily's eyes. It was plain, even austere. He was fine with that.

"You've been here how long? What're you waiting for?" Emily said. Then she peered at him. "That's it, you're waiting for something...or someone."

"I'm just not in a hurry." He cringed. He sounded defensive even to himself.

"Mm-hmm. So, what about this guy you were telling me about? The one who might be able to help us out."

"I'm still sounding him out." Drew crossed his arms over his chest.

"Hurry up about it. We don't have all that much time, you know."

"I know, but I don't want to rush things and scare him."

"You still think he's the missing piece of our puzzle?"

Drew nodded slowly. "He just might be. He's not a contractor, but he knows what goes into it, and I think he might be open to getting his license. He's certainly not happy in his present job. Most important, he's really interested in this. He can't hear enough about it."

Emily gazed at him shrewdly. "Sounds like a good possibility. Anything else? Something else you want to tell me about him?"

Drew looked at her, his face expressionless. "No, not that I can think of."

Emily knew him well, almost as well as Nick, but there were places he just wasn't ready to go with her yet. He knew he had a crush on Brad but wasn't ready to say it aloud yet. Interested, absolutely, if Brad were gay. But crushing on a straight guy was just pathetic, and he didn't want to hear about it from her. None of that changed the fact that Brad could be a real asset to what he and Emily had planned. If he had to, he could keep his feelings under control.

"So, you'll call him, right?" Emily said.

"Yeah, I'll call him," Drew said, laughing a little. It was all he wanted to do, but he was trying not to be a stalker.

The next evening, a Friday, found all three Sundstrom men at home, much to Brad's irritation. His relationship with Philip was complicated, and he plain didn't like Randall. It was so time to move out. All it took was money.

Work was work. The air conditioning had been fixed early enough that morning that the day hadn't been a total waste from a deodorant standpoint, and he'd shown some of those dismal houses too. Still, given his tendency to sweat like a racehorse, he came home from work, showered, and then scrounged for dinner while he decided how to avoid his family for the rest of the evening.

Friday evening. At home. How pathetic was that? A few short months before, Friday meant parties. Now it meant boxers, beer, and television. It was yet another sign college was over and being an adult sucked.

"Can you not put some clothing on, Bradley?" Randall said, making a face as he entered the kitchen where Brad stood at the counter, pouring cereal into a bowl.

"Boxers are clothing," Brad said sullenly.

"Street-legal clothing, Bradley. That's not asking too much, is it?" Randall replied.

Brad shrugged. "It might be."

"Hmmm, chest hair in Cap'n Crunch. How appetizing," Philip said. "Keep eating that and you'll get fat right quick. In fact, is that a tummy you're building? College athletics are over, you know. You're going to have grow up sooner or later."

"Fuck you," Brad said, milk dripping from the corner of his mouth.

"Nice manners. Were you raised in a barnyard?" Philip asked.

"Yep," Brad said. "And college athletics isn't over. I got an e-mail from the crew's alumni oversight committee. They want me to join, since I just rowed and since we won that big regatta."

"They just want Dad's money. He should never have given them that boat when you graduated." Philip shook his head.

"So?" Brad shrugged. "He asked what I wanted for graduation. That was what I wanted. What'd you care?"

Randall watched the exchange with amusement. "Actually, I was impressed with his request, Philip. I half expected him to ask for some booze-filled trip to Cancun. Instead it was something that will only benefit other people. Are you going to accept?"

"I dunno. I might," Brad said.

"I think you should, Bradley," Randall said, "because then you can do something about that fag coach." Brad clenched his teeth at that, but Randall didn't see. "Philip, I've got two tickets to the ball game tomorrow night that I can't use. Do you want them? They're great seats. A client gave them to me."

Philip shook his head. "Nope, I've got a date, and Angie hates baseball or any other kind of sport."

"Hmmm, shame, that. I'd hate for them to go to waste," Randall said, considering the matter.

If this sort of thing weren't standard operating procedure, Brad would've been floored. He was right in front of his dad, after all. "I'll take them, Dad."

"What'll you do with them?" Randall demanded.

"Uh...find someone to go to the game with?"

"I suppose it can't do any harm," Randall said. He handed Brad an envelope.

Brad tucked it into the waistband of his boxers with a cheeky grin. "Thanks, Randall. I'll try not to wear my Sundstrom Homes T-shirt and scratch my butt in public or anything."

"You're an ass, Bradley," Randall said. "Thank God your mother can't see how you've turned out."

Maybe if Mom was still here, I wouldn't have turned out like this. Baiting his dad might be petty, but most days, it was all he had.

"I'm going to shower. Try to be dressed by the time I get out," Randall demanded as he headed to the stairs and his own suite on the house's second floor.

"Thanks for the tickets!" Brad called. He belched thunderously. "I'll try not to embarrass you any more than I already do!"

Philip shook his head. "That was childish."

"So? That's how he treats me, that's how I act," Brad said. He hunched his shoulders as if that would ward off his brother's accusation.

"Maybe he treats you that way *because* that's how you act," Philip pointed out.

"Whatever. Shouldn't you be upstairs spit-shining his shoes or something?"

"Dude, you've got a social life? Since when?" Philip ignored Brad's jibe.

"Since Dad didn't want the tickets. Duh. You were standing right there. You didn't want them, and it'd be a shame to let box seats go to waste."

Philip shook his head. "No, it's been longer than that. You've been taking afternoons off. You've been enjoying yourself." He said it like it was an accusation. "So, who're you going out with? It's *someone*, not just a random friend. You're going out with someone."

"I'm just going to the ballgame with a friend of mine from crew, okay? Don't make a big deal about this." Brad rolled his eyes. He flushed. He felt like the time when he and Philip were kids and his brother destroyed a lamp their mother had loved. Philip had blamed him, and nothing Brad had said exonerated him. Helpless. Sick to his stomach. Suddenly, he couldn't breathe.

He had to get out of there. He dropped his cereal bowl in the sink and charged out of the kitchen, elbowing Philip aside on his way by.

"Jeez, Brad, I didn't mean anything—"

"Get over yourself already, Philip. Didn't you hear Randall? I have to put clothes on."

Brad slammed his bedroom door behind him, and he leaned against it, gasping for air. "Get a hold of yourself," he whispered.

He dropped into his armchair. Was he "going out" with someone? With Drew? He thought it was just two dudes going to a ballgame. Or would be when he called Drew.

And he would call Drew, he knew that much. Somehow, and in a very short time, Drew had become his go-to guy for fun. There was something about him... Drew got under his skin. He liked being around him. It made him think of those times when Drew grabbed the oars after regattas, or at least tried. Sure, the sight of him trying to carry all eight oars with them sticking out in all directions had just been hilarious. But it had also been damned nice of Drew to try, and he'd been so grateful when Brad had come to his rescue. After the balls-out effort at the PCRCs, when all Brad wanted to do was vomit and die, he'd looked up, and there'd been Drew, waiting for the oars. Waiting for him. No one had ever waited for him before.

And there was that fluttery, tingly feeling in his gut when he saw Drew in that Speedo.

Steadfastly ignoring reality, he rooted through his wallet for Drew's card, even though his number was already in Brad's phone, because it let him put off the inevitable that much longer.

"Drew? Hey, it's Brad..."

Saturday evening found Brad and Drew at the ballgame. They still drove separately, which Drew supposed allowed them both to maintain the fig leaf that this wasn't a date. Drew didn't really know what to think on that score. Brad didn't seem to be gay, but he sure seemed to be in Drew's life all of a sudden, and that was no bad thing.

Fortunately, the delta breezes had returned, and the night was cooling off nicely, so sitting in the open-air box was a treat. "So, this is how the other half lives," Drew said, kicking back and putting his feet up on the chair in front of him after they sat down. "That was great of your dad to give you the tickets."

"Yeah, I guess," Brad said, shrugging.

"Free tickets for box seats at the baseball game isn't generous? I know it's minor-league baseball and all..."

"No, it's not," Brad said, explaining how he came by them.

Drew looked around the mostly empty box. "Embarrass who?"

"That's just my dad. That's always been my dad. Randall's always liked my brother better; Mom liked me. Too bad Mom died when I was in middle school."

"I'm sorry." Without thinking about it, Drew placed his hand on Brad's arm.

Brad looked down at Drew's hand, clearly puzzled but not unhappy. He shrugged again, a casual gesture of dismissal that Drew could tell hid a pain Brad might not even acknowledge. "It's just the way it is, you know?"

Drew didn't. His family had his back, and he knew it. But Brad really needed to get out of his dad's house. It was just one more datum for Drew's plan to lure him to working with him and Emily on the Bayard House project. Time to lighten things up. "So other than that, how was the play, Mrs. Lincoln?"

Brad looked at him for a moment and then laughed. "That's horrible! And to answer your question, things're okay. Did I tell you the latest?"

Drew shook his head. "Latest about what?"

"I was invited to join the crew's alumni oversight committee." Brad snorted at the thought.

"Seriously? I've heard Nick mention them before."

"Yeah?"

"Yes, as a vague and shadowy cabal of people looking over his shoulder micromanaging his program in return for every penny they spend."

"That's about what I figured. Philip—my brother—thinks they want me because my dad donated a boat for my graduation. They scented the money and thought they'd lure me in."

"Your dad bought them one of those shells?" Drew arched an eyebrow. "Aren't they kind of expensive?"

"Twenty to thirty grand, depending. I'm not sure how much Dad finally spent, probably right in the middle."

Drew whistled. "That's quite a graduation present."

"I didn't really need anything that I couldn't get some other way, and this way I can leave something behind for the crew," Brad said softly.

"Are you going to do it?"

"I don't know." Brad was silent for a while.

"You miss it, don't you?" Drew said, barely audible over the noise of the crowd in the stadium below them. When Brad didn't answer, Drew continued, "Nick's talked about this before too. I guess it's pretty common. Crew's a huge part of your life. It required nearly total dedication and a lot of your time, and now it's gone."

Brad nodded absently, unfocused eyes staring out over the game.

"You could always buy an erg," Drew said, thinking of the specialized rowing machines the crew trained on.

"Oh, hell no!" Brad exclaimed, jerked back to the here and now by the thought.

"That sure got your attention." Drew snickered.

Brad elbowed him. "Mean!"

"Ow! Brute!" Drew yelped.

Brad eyed him askance for a moment. "Someone's ticklish!"

"Am not! No fair!" Drew gasped out, doubled over, trying to reduce the vulnerable areas.

Then Drew met Brad's eyes and Brad froze.

"Sorry, man," Brad coughed. He returned his attention to the game, resolutely looking straight ahead.

Drew got up and wandered off to the concession stand and brought them both beer and popcorn. Brad muttered his thanks but still wouldn't look anywhere but at the game.

Drew kicked back in his seat again and pretended to care about the game. He was really just there to spend time with Brad, but he was willing to play along.

He looked at the posters of who he presumed were famous athletes, ball players by the looks of their uniforms, but he wouldn't have bet money on it.

That took all of three minutes. For lack of anything better to do, he started tossing popcorn up and trying to catch it in his mouth. His aim was lousy, but he persevered.

Once Drew mastered the basic toss and gobble, he increased the difficulty by increasing how far up he tossed the popcorn before catching it. Points off for choking.

During one particularly challenging toss, Drew bumped smack into Brad while trying to get his mouth under the kernel during its descent.

Brad glanced at Drew. "What're you doing?"

"Pretending I'm a seal and catching fish tossed at me?" Drew said, eyes merry.

"You don't actually care about this game, do you?"

"Nope." Drew grinned. "But I'm still having a good time."

"Then why'd you come?"

"Because you asked me to," Drew said cheerfully. "You said you wanted company, and here I am. What're your other two wishes?"

Brad laughed. "You're impossible."

"No, just highly improbable." Drew smirked.

"Huh?" Brad shook his head. "So...how're the plans for that renovation of the Bayard House coming along? I tell you, that's just too cool. Getting to do that, I mean."

"I haven't gotten the bid yet," Drew said dryly. But there it was, an invitation to make his pitch to Brad if ever there was one.

Brad grabbed a handful of popcorn and leaned forward. "So, how're the plans going?" he asked eagerly.

"It's nerve-racking, and to tell you the truth, I'm not sure this is something Emily and I should be contemplating at this stage in our careers. Another two or three years, sure, but now?"

"Yeah, good thinking. You wouldn't want to reach for the brass ring. You might throw your back out." Brad shook his head. When Drew stared at him, Brad said, "What? I heard that somewhere. Look, it's a good thing Stuart didn't talk that way before the PCRCs this spring. That kind of talk gets you nowhere fast."

Drew looked at Brad long enough to make him squirm. "How'd you get to be so smart?"

Brad shrugged uncomfortably. "Even a blind man hits the target once in a while. Seriously, tell me everything about this."

As scared as he was by this greatest challenge of his life to date, he found Brad's enthusiasm intoxicating. So, Drew told him where they were in the design process, from issues about preservation versus adaptation to just how close to period style they were taking the furniture. "I've actually got some sketches in the car—"

"Then why we're sitting here watching the home team get slaughtered?" Brad demanded, jumping to his feet. Drew made a show of hesitating, one final check to make sure the hook was baited.

Brad grabbed his arm. "C'mon. I want to see your plans."

Smiling faintly, Drew led Brad out to his car. Drew pulled his design books out of a leather messenger bag, and they sat in the back seat of Drew's BMW, where there was more room. Brad pored over each one, holding them up the better to see them under the car's dome light and asking probing questions. At one point, Drew just sat back and watched him, wondering how anyone had ever thought Brad was nothing more than a dumb college jock.

"What kind of conduit are you using?" Brad said at one point.

"Well, given that we haven't had the tour of the site yet, I'm tentatively planning on—"

"What're you doing in there?" a voice demanded from outside the car as something tapped on the window.

Brad put the window down. Outside, the parking lot was empty and the summer sky almost dark.

"Now, you boys need to go find a hotel room, and not...what're you doing, anyway?"

"Sorry, sir," Brad said sheepishly to the private security service patrolman. "We're going over some renovation plans and lost track of time."

The patrolman leaned closer to the open window and shone his flashlight onto the plan. "Humph. That's a new one, and with twenty years in private security, I don't get to say that very often. This isn't the best neighborhood, boys, and it's getting late. I'd be a lot happier if you took this to a coffee shop."

Brad looked at Drew. "Sure. Unless we're done?"

"No, actually, there's quite a bit more to see, and I had some questions for you," Drew said.

"Have a good evening, boys," the patrolman said as he walked to his golf-cart.

"I know where a twenty-four-hour restaurant is not far from here. I don't know if the food's up to your standards..." Brad glanced at Drew.

"I'll be brave," Drew said.

"Cool! Then follow me." Brad shoved the papers aside.

"Why don't I drive you to your car?" Drew suggested. "As the rent-a-cop said, it's getting late, and this really isn't a good part of town."

Chapter Eight

Twenty minutes later and they were in a booth at Denny's, coffee, drawings, and plans spread out before them. Drew watched with amusement as Brad set each drawing out in sequential order based on the photocopied layout of the original mansion.

"So, walk me through it," Brad said.

"Well, as you can see, I've only got rough conceptual sketches, and at that, only for about half the rooms," Drew said.

"So, when's this bid due?"

"A couple of weeks." Drew bounced his leg up and down. He oscillated between trying not to think about it and thinking about it too much. He liked his challenges, but that didn't mean they were easy on his nervous system.

"Like living on the edge much?" Brad said with a small smile that made Drew's heart beat a little faster.

"It does add a certain zest to my life, yes."

Brad looked at the plans again, a little enviously to Drew's eyes, but that could've been wishful thinking, and where Brad was concerned, Drew's wishful thinking seemed to be in overdrive.

"This sounds really great," Brad said wistfully.

"There's one problem. Neither my partner nor I know enough about the building trades. I know real estate, and that's not the same thing. I flip houses and am new to renovation, but that may not be enough. Emily's a designer. She'll make the Bayard House look like it did the day after the servants cleaned up after uncrating all the furniture. She'll find just the right chiffonier to hide the receptionist's workstation in for the front hall, but making sure the wiring works? Not so much."

"You'd need a contractor, ideally." Brad leaned back against the booth's vinyl back. "But the only ones I know work for my father. No offense, but I don't think you could afford to poach them, even if they'd be interested in something like this."

"I don't want your dad's contractors, I want you." *In more ways than that one too.*

"I...don't understand." Brad looked puzzled.

"What if you joined us?" Drew said softly.

Brad shook his head. "Dude. I'm not a contractor."

"Yet."

"Are you telling me I should go to contractor's school or something?" Brad scoffed.

Drew shrugged. "You can't tell me you don't like and know home building, and it'd be one solution to my problems. Yours, too, potentially."

"I don't know, this is big, real big. Are you sure about me and are you sure this is even something you want to bite off?"

"Hmmm, what was that you were saying?" Drew arched one eyebrow. "Something about brass rings and pulled muscles?"

"Oh, yeah," Brad mumbled, flushing. "It's just... I'm not sure this is all a good idea, you know? That place is a wreck. It's been a firetrap for decades."

"The renovation's a bad idea? Is that why you've hung on every word I've said about it? Why we've spent hours going over my rough sketches? You want to do this, and you know it."

"I know," Brad said softly.

They were silent for a while. Their waitress came and refilled their coffee, and still they said nothing.

"I'm going to have to think about this," Brad said.

"I know," Drew said, echoing him.

Brad stood up to leave. Then he sat back down. "Shit. Tell me how you see this working."

"Well, I need a contractor to work with me on supervising the renovation, as well as making sure it passes legal muster. Then...I guess I should back up a step or three. I never got a contractor's license because at first, I just didn't think about it, since I was working on my real estate license. Then I was busy getting that business going, then busy flipping houses. That's when the need for a contractor became all too clear. Having to pay a general contractor on top of the subs really cuts into profits. In a perfect world, I'd form a partnership of some kind with a general contractor. I'd find houses to buy, and the contractor would oversee the renovation with my help as time permitted. Then I'd sell the houses, presumably at a profit, and we'd do it again."

"But if I did this, you'd be paying me a salary," Brad pointed out. "You were going to be paying me, weren't you?"

"Duh. Of course, we would." Drew rolled his eyes. "But I always try to think a few steps ahead. You doing this would solve a problem in the short term, on the renovation of the Bayard House, but could also point the way to the future."

"You've given this a lot of thought."

Drew smiled. He had indeed, and not just a partnership in the business sense. He'd just about abandoned hope that Brad was gay or bi, but he really liked spending time with the guy, a big lug in the best sense of the term.

"I really am going to have to think about this and how it might work. I mean, I don't think I could just quit my job with Sundstrom Homes. Don't take this the wrong way or anything, but I'm hearing a lot of 'ifs' and 'maybes' here. I'd need something to fall back on, at least at first, especially since I'd be an employee and not a partner," Brad said.

"That makes sense." Drew didn't want to admit it, but Brad was right. It was a huge gamble, and it wasn't like he could judge. He still had his real estate business, after all. "And you'll need to meet Emily."

"I'll call you soon to give you my decision." Brad got up again. He set a twenty on the table.

"I can't wait to hear from you." Drew smiled, meaning it. "If you want, and if you can get the time off, you can come with us on the site tour on Monday."

"I'll keep it in mind. And Drew?"

"Yeah?"

"Thanks for thinking of me with this. It means a lot."

Drew watched Brad leave the restaurant. The die was cast. All he could do was wait and keep in touch with Brad to stop him from talking himself out of this. And Drew knew Brad would try. Someone had done a real number on that man's confidence in himself and his abilities, and Drew had an idea who it might be.

Even as he drove home, Brad knew he was going to do it. The whole thing was just too cool, from the renovation of the Bayard House to Drew's proposal that they work together. Never mind his attempts to shoot it all down. Where'd that buzz killer come from, anyway? He liked Drew, who dangled a tremendous opportunity in front of him, and it was the first thing he'd gotten excited about doing with his life since he'd found crew. He hadn't said anything to Drew, but he even had a small trust fund that would be his as soon as he "made something of himself," whatever that meant. The trust wasn't enough to live the life of the idle rich, but it'd certainly be enough to pave the way forward, if he could talk the lawyer who controlled the trust into it.

The fact that he was excited about his future was reason enough to do it, Brad figured as he bounded up the steps to his house.

Then he paused, key in the lock. He had to find a way to tell his father he'd be working only part-time at Suburban Symphony.

Shit. He was sunk. He leaned his head against the door, hating his life, hating Randall. Hating himself for not being able to stand up to him.

Feeling a little sick, Brad let himself into the house and went directly to bed. He didn't bother undressing, and he didn't sleep. The rump end of the night was short, but it felt like forever as he tossed and turned, never quite comfortable enough to drop off to sleep, never quite comfortable enough in his own skin to tell his old man where to go.

Red-eyed and baleful, he glared at the alarm clock. Five thirty a.m. He hadn't gotten up this early since the last morning practice for Coach Bedford. "Damn it," he growled, throwing the covers back.

He squinted and stumbled his way to the kitchen, where his nose told him there was coffee.

"You're up early, Bradley," his father commented, not looking up from the morning paper.

"Yeah," Brad grunted.

"Usually when you're this hungover, you don't get up until at least noon."

"I'm not hungover, I just couldn't sleep." Brad tried and failed to keep his irritation to himself. He poured himself a big mug of coffee.

"I don't care for that tone," Randall said.

"I didn't get drunk last night, and I didn't embarrass you. I was just up late and then tossed and turned all night, okay?" Brad snapped, holding the mug under his nose and letting that magic coffee smell clear his mind.

"Of course."

Randall's tone told Brad he didn't believe a word of it. The story of his life, Brad reflected. If he told his dad the sky was blue and the sun came up in the east, his dad would tell him how stupid he was. Most of the time, Brad just ignored it.

That morning, it rubbed him the wrong way, and he couldn't stomach it. "Suffering Christ, would you give me a break? I had one beer last night. I didn't sleep well. That's all."

"Poor child," Randall said. "Maybe you can catch up on your rest at work today."

Stripped of his usual defenses by sleep deprivation, he blurted, "I need to go to part-time. At Suburban Symphony, I mean. I can only work there part-time."

"Don't be absurd, Bradley. I need you out there." Randall finally looked up from the paper.

Emboldened by fatigue, Brad felt something inside him give. "Let me rephrase it, I'm going part-time."

"And let me be clear, no you are not." Randall slammed his coffee down. "You can't just go skipping off when the mood strikes you."

"I can't believe this! You don't even know the reason why, and you're already assuming it's a bad one!" Brad yelled. He'd always been the go-along-to-get-along younger brother, the one who swallowed the insults because it was easier than arguing, but it had to end sometime.

Randall leaned back in his chair, arms crossed. "Fine. Tell me about this grand reason of yours."

"Just do it more quietly," Philip said as he made his way to the kitchen, blinking in the light.

Brad took a deep breath, steadying himself. "Sorry, Philip. Listen, I've got a tremendous opportunity, and I don't want to lose it."

"So, what's this scheme of yours, then?" Randall said.

"A friend of mine flips houses, and he and his partner are submitting a bid for the renovation of the Bayard House," Brad said. "They've asked me to come work for them."

"What on earth do you know about renovation, to say nothing of preserving historical buildings? And a house-flipper? Good luck with that." Randall laughed harshly.

"Interesting," Philip said, "but you're not a contractor. What do you bring to the table?"

"First, I'd start working toward my contractor's license, but you can't say I don't know the building trades," Brad said.

Philip nodded slowly. "Yes, I can see that, and the Bayard House is certainly the biggest thing going around here these days."

"You and your friends don't have a shot," Randall scoffed.

"We won't know if we don't try," Brad said. He hated it when Randall got like this. He hunched over, as if he could protect himself and his plan at the same time. "It's a chance to get in on the ground floor of something, a chance to grow into the job as the job grows."

Randall rolled his eyes. "And you'll do this and work at Suburban Symphony, how?"

"Like I said, I'd have to work at the sales office half time," Brad admitted, still defensive, "but be honest. Suburban Symphony is doomed. It's not as if my working there half time will cut into sales. You could put some intern in there the rest of the time, or even go 'appointment only' and have me on call."

"Yes, that'll work very well," Randall said, making a face to show his sons just what he thought of what he saw as Brad's latest harebrained idea.

"It might, actually," Philip said. When Randall glared at him, he continued, "Dad, that place has more problems than Brad—or anyone—can solve easily, and you know it. You wanted to put Brad in there, and I went along with it, but cut him some slack, for once. It's an interesting opportunity he's been presented with."

"That place is a wreck, and the plans to preserve it are doomed from the start. They should just admit that they've screwed around too long and lost it, just like they did with the old town. The city should tear it down and either preserve the façade in a new building or build something new and modern from the foundation up," Randall said. "But this? This is idiocy."

Randall glared at his oldest son, but Philip stood his ground. "He needs to make his own way. You've got the heir, so let the spare go."

Randall nodded his head slowly. "I see. Fine. You go right ahead, Bradley. This project is doomed to failure, just like everything else you've ever touched. You'll come crawling back, you'll see."

Brad and Philip were silent as their dad set his coffee cup in the sink and stalked out of the kitchen.

"Thanks, Philip. It's been a long time since you stood up for me."

Philip shrugged. "Maybe too long. At least one of us has a chance to get away from him. Don't screw this up, Brad, or he'll never let either of us forget it."

Chapter Nine

With a brimming commuter mug in one hand, Brad drove down to Suburban Graveyard to spend his Saturday watching tumbleweeds blow by in the hot summer wind. Lately, he did his best thinking in the car. It was relatively free of distractions, and thanks to the ban in California on driving and cell phone use, he had an excuse for turning his phone off.

At least one of us has a chance to get away from him.

Philip's words were fresh in Brad's mind. He and Philip had been close as kids but had grown apart as they grew up. Once their mom died, Philip had clung pretty tightly to their dad. No, he corrected himself, that was when Randall began grooming Philip to take over the business. By any objective sense, Philip had done well at Sundstrom Homes, working his way up to a vice president.

It had never occurred to Brad that Philip's place in their father's regard came at a price, although, he thought dryly, the fact that Philip still lived at home, too, should've been an indicator the two were in the same boat.

But Philip had gone to bat for him. He still couldn't get over it. It made him all the more resolved to strike out on his own.

He got the office open, the signs out, the jaunty helium balloons filled from the small tank in the back room and out by the road, bobbing in the breeze. "Pig, meet lipstick."

The morning startup routine observed, Brad sat down at his desk and fired up the computer. While he waited for it to boot, he pulled out his phone to call Drew.

Then he stopped. No. He'd spend the weekend doing some research on contractor's education and licensing and on the preservation of historical buildings. Then he'd call Drew Sunday afternoon.

Brad pulled out one of the ubiquitous pads of paper intended to work out deals with nonexistent homebuyers and started feeding terms into a search engine. Even though the hits came back almost instantly, he sat back in his chair to think.

He'd been told most of his life he wasn't the sharpest tool in the shed, just as he knew he had the rep for being even dimmer than that. But some of that was an act, and sometimes he thought before he acted, or thought while he acted, or thought by acting. Try something, see what happens, assess. Repeat as necessary. It had worked up until now.

But maybe it was time to try a little harder, to think things through before he made big changes. He was finally striking out on his own, at least a little, if you didn't count that he was still working for his dad's company and living at home.

It was a process he'd started when he joined crew, something he'd picked out on his own and done pretty well at. His dad had chosen his college for him because of its proximity to home and its lax admissions standards, but crew? That'd been his and his alone. He'd thought maybe success there would earn him Randall's notice or even his respect. The fact it hadn't didn't change how Brad felt about rowing.

This offer to come work for Drew on a job that might lead to bigger and better things was his chance to build on that, and Brad knew it. The questions were, how and what were the implications? The how seemed to be working itself out. He would work part-time for his dad and the rest of the time for and with Drew.

Brad figured the "with Drew" part might be interesting. On the one hand, he'd be working with someone who made him laugh and smile. Someone he had fun with, like that time at the water slides. The thought that coming to work might be fun and not like walking into a cellblock energized him. Moreover, he'd be working with someone he liked at something that might be really satisfying, that might matter more than suckering fools into buying a home in this disaster of a subdivision.

Brad exhaled noisily, spinning himself around in his desk chair. But there were the implications to think about. They made him nervous. Drew made him nervous. Drew raised feelings in him that he wasn't prepared to admit existed. He'd always thought of himself as straight, but on some level, Drew made him question that. Instead of running the other way, which was what he should've done, he was running right for Drew.

It didn't make sense to Brad. When there was something dangerous in front of you, you turned and ran the other way. Duh. Instead, he was charging ahead at full speed to work with someone who made him feel things he didn't know how to feel.

Brad rested his head on the desk. He'd gotten a boner thinking about Drew in that Speedo, for fuck's sake. Hell, he was getting one right there at his desk. He simply wasn't ready to deal with feeling like that about another guy or what it said about him.

So why do this? Why push through the fear to take this opportunity that put him in the gay lion's den? Because that was what he was doing when he stopped to think about it, and why he didn't stop to think about things very often. He was afraid of what he felt and what that meant, but he was going to do it anyway.

When Brad thought about it, however, he knew it wasn't a lion out to devour him, it was Drew. They had similar professional interests and got along well. Drew had offered him a job and a chance to get away from his dad. He'd be a fool to turn those down because of that other thing. He could control those feelings. He knew he could.

He lifted his head off his desk and shifted around, trying to make his cock behave. Damn, he was hard. That Speedo...

Brad shook his head. Research. He needed the details of what getting a contractor's license involved. Then he could call Drew like he knew what he was talking about, like he had something to bring to the table too.

Brad's week started out decently enough. He called Drew on Sunday evening after finding out everything he could, from the options available for getting his contractor's license to going to the public library to read up on historical preservation.

Then he met Emily and Drew for an early breakfast on Monday, and they'd gotten on well enough, he and Emily. She seemed nice, and he figured once he got to know her, that impression would hold. For her part, Emily had no problems with him. He could be charming when he wanted to be, even if it was a hassle to keep it going for too long.

The only odd thing was Emily was the kind of woman he'd usually have noticed for her looks, since she was a sizzling blonde and all. But strangely enough, her looks weren't the hot issue that Monday morning. He barely noticed them, and he only realized he hadn't noticed when she got a wolf whistle from some construction workers as they approached the Bayard House behind its chain-link hazard-zone fence.

"Nice manners," Brad said.

Emily rolled her eyes. "It happens."

"Yeah, but it's gross." Brad looked around for the jerks responsible.

"What're you going to do?" Drew said to Brad.

Brad smiled. "I'm going to ask them not to do it."

And off he went. He knew how to play the game, and he might've worn chinos, a blue shirt, and his second-best of two neckties, but he still looked like a bull moose on the rampage.

"Hey, asshole! Leave her alone! She's a lady. She doesn't need your kind of crude," Brad said.

"You wanna make something of it?" the worker said.

Brad bared his teeth and puffed his chest out. And out. And out. The buttons strained across his pecs, and his neck bulged over the collar of his shirt. "If I have to," he bellowed.

That was when the construction worker—and the one person nearby—realized that Brad was a lot bigger and certainly a lot louder, and in this case, ceding ground was the better part of valor. "Tell her I said sorry."

"Damn straight," Brad said, nodding.

He turned around and saw that Drew had shielded his eyes in embarrassment. But Emily was grinning broadly. "Oh, you'll do fine," she laughed, hooking her arm on his, "just fine."

"Yeah, great, can we please hurry up and get in there before we miss the site tour?" Drew said.

"I've been around construction workers all my life. You can't let them get away with shit like that," Brad said, sparing a wink for Drew. Then he looked at the woman on his arm. That was when he realized he hadn't noticed just how hot she was. But he also noticed Drew glaring at him, and he was suddenly afraid. What if Drew was mad at him? What if Drew was reconsidering him working on the project with him?

Brad spent the tour on his best behavior and the rest of the day seriously worried he'd pissed off Drew. For some reason deep down in his guts, that was something he really didn't want to do.

Worrying about whether he'd offended Drew turned into a weeklong project, punctuated by bursts of reluctant activity at Suburban Graveyard.

Thursday morning, he was in the midst of compiling reports requested by the sales division of Sundstrom Homes when his cell phone rang. His personal phone, not the corporate one no one ever called.

"Brad Sundstrom," he said.

"Hi, Brad, it's Pete Rancilman."

Brad racked his brain to figure out why that name sounded familiar. Oh, yes. "Hi, Mr. Rancilman. I'm sorry I haven't gotten back to you about the alumni oversight committee. I—"

"Not a problem. I just wanted to call and personally extend the invitation," Pete said. "We're very keen to have you, and I hope you'll consider joining the committee."

I just bet you are. Philip's comment about their dad's money sprang to Brad's memory. "I've certainly been giving it some thought, but I'm not sure what I have to offer, since I just graduated."

"That's precisely what you have to offer, Brad," Pete said. "Most of us are long out of college. You'll bring a fresh perspective and ideas as we deal with the coaching situation."

"Coaching situation?" That was the last thing Brad expected to hear.

"Indeed. As you know, there were reports of an inappropriate relationship between the men's varsity coach and one of his rowers, one of your teammates, in fact."

Brad's mind kicked into overdrive. "I thought the school dropped the matter."

"CalPac may have dropped its investigation into the matter, but the NCAA has not," Pete said firmly. "The oversight committee takes this kind of thing very seriously, and we want to make sure this deviant behavior isn't part of a larger pattern."

They were after Coach Bedford, Brad realized. He'd been looking forward to lunch, but no longer. "Deviant behavior, huh? I'm in. Tell me when and where."

This was so not good. This was the opposite of good, he thought miserably, resting his head on the desk. They were after Coach Bedford, the man responsible for some of the best years of his life. He just couldn't let this happen, but he had no idea what he could do. This was like...grown-up stuff, committees and planning and strategy. He was good at the physical stuff, the in-your-face threat of grievous bodily injury, not this.

Like Monday, when he'd gotten in that construction worker's face. Brad groaned. He could really use Drew's input, but Drew hadn't called all week, hadn't even e-mailed him. Drew would know what to do but probably wanted nothing more to do with him after that minirampage. But this was new territory for Brad. He could e-mail Coach Nick directly and warn him, but what if this was nothing, or at least nothing as bad as he was making it out to be?

He spent the rest of the day staring at his computer but not accomplishing much. The thought of the oversight committee upset him and working on what he needed for the Bayard bid made him think of Drew being mad at him.

Friday was more of the same. But after a sucktastic day at work and a fight with Randall when he got home, he needed to hear a friendly voice.

He sat his armchair in his room, staring at his phone, wondering who he'd become. He'd never been one to hesitate before. He was Brad Sundstrom, force of nature and bull in a china shop. But where Drew was concerned, it seemed like he was becoming someone else.

"Man up, you puss," he muttered to himself, picking up the phone and stabbing the button for Drew's number in the autodial. "Hi, Drew, it's me."

Chapter Ten

Drew dropped his messenger bag on the floor inside the garage door, his keys following in a noisy clatter. He leaned against the door, eyes closed, savoring his weariness. It was the end of a marathon week, and tomorrow would be a busy one of showing homes and making time to work on the bid for the Bayard House.

The bleating of his cell phone roused him from his daze. "Drew St. Charles here."

"Hi, Drew, it's me," Brad said.

"Brad! How're you! You've been quiet this week." Drew pushed himself up and shuffled off to his room, stopping long enough to toe off his shoes.

"Look who's talking."

"Ugh, what a week. I've been crazy busy showing and selling houses. Suddenly people are crawling out of the woodwork buying and selling." Cradling the phone between his chin and shoulder, Drew started shedding clothing along the way. He was too tired to care about the mess right then. "It's amazing how much time a closing can take, let alone three."

"So, dinner's on you?" Brad said. The remark sounded brittle to Drew.

"It'll help carry us through the project, if that's what you're getting at."

"If we get it." Brad sighed.

There was a pause on Brad's end. Drew heard him draw breath and then release it as the silence stretched painfully. "Brad?"

"Am I still on the project?" Brad blurted.

Drew shook his head. He couldn't have heard that right. "What're you talking about? Of course, you're on the project. After all the trouble I went to lure you in? Seriously, dude, talk to me."

"Well, I...the thing is," Brad huffed. "Oh jeez, do we have to go into this?"

"I'd say so, yes, since I have no idea what you're talking about, but you're starting to scare me. Just spit it out." Drew said. When nothing was forthcoming, Brad's temper started to slip. "Brad..."

"All right, I just feel stupid. I've been worried about Monday all week. When I went at that construction worker who whistled at Emily. That kind of thing is just so rude. I've seen it all my life, and there's no call for it. None. So, when I heard that whistle, I didn't even stop to think. I just went all alpha male on the guy. But then I looked back at you and you looked so embarrassed. I don't want to be that guy who embarrasses you," Brad said softly. "I...you...you're a nice guy."

Drew knew right then that it was a good thing they were separated by miles and miles, because if they'd been in the same room, he'd have tried to kiss Brad. That was just so sweet. "Oh no, Brad! I didn't mean it like that... Okay, yeah, I was a tiny bit embarrassed, but mostly I was afraid you were going to get yourself creamed."

"By him? God, no," Brad laughed. "I've taken down bigger guys than that."

Drew rolled his eyes. "Do you do this often?"

"Not all the time, no, but when someone I'm around needs protecting? Then yeah, I'm there."

"I can imagine." Drew smiled, wishing he were the one on the end of that protective display.

"Yep, that's me, big dumb lug and bodyguard. Did I ever tell you about the time I scared off some assclown who was hassling Coach Bedford and Morgan Estrada?"

"No, I don't think you did," Drew said. By this time clad only in his boxer-briefs, he lay down on his bed to listen.

"Yeah, it was right after the Pacific Coast Rowing Championship this spring. Coach Bedford had just dropped this bomb that he was going to step down as coach." Brad laughed at the absurdity of the idea.

"I'd heard about that. I'd also heard Morgan wasn't real happy that he didn't discuss it with him."

"I didn't hear that part," Brad cackled. "But when Morgan went off to find Coach, I followed for some reason. Then I saw them kissing. It didn't creep me out the way I thought two guys kissing would've. It was... I don't know. You're gay, so you know. Anyway, someone said something unpleasant to them, and I got right in his face and bellowed. It was like one of those cartoons when someone screams really loud and all the leaves are blasted off the trees or something."

Drew pictured it in his imagination. "You're something else, Brad."

"So...when do we need to get together to talk about the project some more? Because I've been doing my homework."

"Have you now?"

"You bet. I'll carry my weight."

"Of that I have no doubts. I'm booked up this entire weekend, but you can come over for dinner on Sunday, if you want. I should have time to breathe by then."

"Sounds great. This time, I'll have notes for you to look at." Drew could hear the pride in Brad's voice. "Do you mind talking a little longer? There's something I need to run by you."

"Yeah, sure," Drew said. He listened with growing horror as Brad described his conversation with the head of the alumni oversight committee for the crew teams at CalPac.

"So, what do I do?" Brad said. "This is so not my area of expertise."

Drew thought of Brad's description of himself as a bull in a china shop. "E-mail Nick Bedford. I'll mention it to him, too, but I'll tell him he needs to call you for the info."

"Yeah, okay, that makes sense. I'll be his mole on the committee or something."

"That's really nice of you to do that. You're a good friend."

"So are you, for listening to me ramble on tonight," Brad said quietly.

"That's what I'm here for," Drew said. Then he said goodnight, and they hung up.

Drew lay there for a long moment, holding the phone against his chest, and realized the truth of his situation. It was the oldest story in the book, but it was his. He was in love with a straight man.

He had a whole new appreciation for what Nick had gone through this spring when he was crushing so hard on Morgan but couldn't have him. Only then, Morgan made it very clear that he had a say in it, too, and he most definitely was warm for his coach's form.

Drew had no such hope of delivery from this sweet misery. Brad was straight. *It didn't creep me out the way*

I thought two guys kissing would've. Drew cringed. Hardly a ringing endorsement of guy-on-guy action. No, not a chance in hell of getting his man. Brad was a nice guy, but straight.

The one thing Drew disliked about real estate was that his work consumed his weekends. He rolled out of bed early Saturday morning knowing he wouldn't be home until dinnertime, and by that point he'd be too fried to do much. But last night's conversation weighed on his mind, and he needed to talk to Nick.

He glanced at the clock. Seven thirty a.m. Not too early to call grown-ups, and ordinarily, he'd call without a second thought, since he knew Nick kept early hours. But Nick and Morgan had moved in together recently, and Morgan was a college student on a summer schedule.

He risked calling anyway but only reached their voice mail. "Hi, guys, it's Drew. Nick, can you call me on my cell? I've got open houses all day, but I should be able to talk, at least for a while. I'll try texting you too. Bye."

He pulled out his mobile phone, grateful he owned one with a complete if tiny keyboard, and sent Nick a message.

Need to talk and soon.

Drew set his phone on the counter, grabbed his messenger bag from his home office, and checked it for the glossy fliers he'd made for the properties he was showing. It was all about advertising and creating a favorable impression in a potential buyer's mind. He made a note to run by the supermarket to pick up some flowers, just in case.

Then his phone buzzed with a text from Nick.

I'm at the boathouse. What's up?
I'll be there in 20. Don't leave.

He grabbed his keys, his bag, and his mug full of coffee and was out the door.

Blessing the light Saturday-morning traffic, Drew made it to the CalPac boathouse in less than twenty minutes. As he walked into the main bay, Morgan turned and waved before heading down to the dock.

Drew spotted Nick over by his office, talking to that short dynamo of a coxswain, Stuart Cochrane. "We'll talk more, but I'm hoping you can round up some of the guys to coordinate the new guy's welcome to CalPac and the team. You know, show him around campus and town, make sure he knows his way to the boathouse, that kind of thing."

"Sure thing, Coach. I can probably do it myself," Stuart said as Drew approached. "What's his name, anyway?"

"Jonathan Poisonwood. He should be up here sometime next week. I'll forward his last e-mail to you, and you can contact him directly. Thanks, Stuart. I appreciate it. I know how busy this year's going to be for you," Nick said.

Stuart shrugged. "Things haven't gotten crazy yet. Hey, Drew."

"Hello, Stuart," Drew said. He'd always liked Stuart, even if he only ever saw him at regattas, where, in his role as coxswain, he tended toward the bossy.

"Why don't you CC me the first time you e-mail Jonathan? That way I'll be in the loop. Sort of," Nick said, smiling slightly. "All right, Drew. What's dragged you down to the boathouse, of all places?"

"Catch you later," Stuart said, recognizing a dismissal when he heard one.

Nick raised a hand in acknowledgment, but his focus was on Drew.

"What's all this?" Drew said.

"Just a light row for the guys who're back before school starts or who never left for the summer, varsity and JV," Nick said.

"Let's talk in your office."

Nick led him to the coaches' office and shut the door behind them, although they remained standing. "I repeat: what's brought you down here? I know what your weekends can be like."

Drew exhaled noisily. "Two things, and both of them are Brad Sundstrom."

"Oh, jeez, not this again," Nick groaned.

"It's not what you think," Drew said. "We've actually become pretty good friends. I think."

"You think?" Nick cocked one eyebrow.

"I know. He called me last night, just to talk. He's struggling to find his way."

"It's not uncommon. Even a school like CalPac provides a fair amount of structure. Rowing gives them even more. Then, just like that, it's gone. Some land on their feet, some seem to wander for a while. I'm surprised Brad's turning out to be a wanderer. It looked like his life was set for him after graduation, with that job at his dad's company waiting for him."

Drew shook his head. "Looks were deceiving, I guess, and from what Brad's told me, his dad's an asshole of the first magnitude who treats him like he's not only five but simple-minded."

"Brad's not stupid, but he can be a challenge."

"Maybe if his dad tried treating him with a little respect and kindness for once, Brad'd respond in kind."

"Maybe if Brad thought further into the future than his next beer or sexual conquest, he might find he's treated like the adult he's supposed to be."

"He's an adult. He's got a good head on his shoulders." Drew started pacing.

Nick gave him a funny look. "Are we talking about the same Brad? Because the Brad Sundstrom I know is an overgrown child most of the time."

"Not the one I know," Drew snapped.

Nick held up his hands. "Easy there, but I think I know Brad pretty well."

"In some ways, perhaps, but not in others. Did I tell you he may come work for me?" Drew explained the bid for the renovations of the Bayard House and Brad's potential role in it.

Nick looked nonplussed. "I had no idea."

"Sorry. It's been a busy summer, I guess."

"No kidding," Nick agreed. "When I'm done here, Morgan and I are having breakfast, and then I'm diving into that bed/bath reno."

"I'll come by to check it out between open houses today. Anyway, I wish I could help Brad. He's a nice guy. He just seems really unhappy."

"Did he tell you this?" Nick asked.

Drew shook his head. "No, but I can read between the lines."

"Be careful, Drew."

"I just want to help him, you know? Not get in his pants," Drew said quietly. Then he smiled. "Okay, not just get in his pants."

"At least you admit it," Nick laughed.

Drew shrugged. "In the immortal words of Popeye, I am what I am. But this is a hell of a challenge. How do I help someone I'm...?"

"Crushing on without it being self-interested manipulation?" Nick suggested.

"You make it sound so ugly." Drew frowned.

"It sounds like Brad's vulnerable right now. You could easily pressure him into giving you what you want, at least to an extent and at least for a while."

"God damn, Nick, you know I'd never—"

Nick put his hands on Drew's shoulders and looked him straight in the eye. "I know you wouldn't because you're too good a person. But it could easily happen, especially if you're thinking with your dick and you don't realize it. Be careful, that's all I'm saying. I don't want to see either of you get hurt."

"Thanks, Nick. I know you don't." Drew put a hand on Nick's. "I guess all I can do is listen at this point."

"A few strategic suggestions might not hurt either. Sometime when we have time, I want to hear more about your adventures with Brad. It sounds like I've seriously misjudged him."

"You looked at him and his behavior, and you expected something, so that's what he gave you," Drew said, considering. "But I expect something different, so that's what I get."

"What do you expect?" Nick asked.

"I'm not sure how to put it into words, but I know he's more than a beer-soaked poon-hound, and so far, that's what I'm seeing."

"You sound like you're planning a future with him, and he's not gay," Nick pointed out.

Drew thought for a moment. "You may be right. It's just...damn it, I only want what you and Morgan have."

"But can Brad give you that?" Nick said softly.

Drew refused to meet Nick's eyes. "I'll take what he'll give me, even if it's only friendship."

"Oh, Drew, you've got it bad," Nick breathed.

"Speaking of friendship, you need to sit down," Drew said, "because Brad's told me something that proves he's a good friend to you too."

"Oh?" Nick sank into one of the chairs in front of his desk.

Drew sat in the other one. "Yeah. He's been invited to join that alumni oversight committee thingy you've mentioned once in a while."

"He has? Isn't that interesting," Nick mused.

"No, what's interesting is one of the agenda items for the first meeting he'll attend."

"Oh?" Nick freighted the word with a wealth of meaning.

"There's no gentle way to say this, but it's you, babydoll. According to Brad, they're not happy about your romantic life."

Nick blanched. "But the school..."

"From what Brad told me, it sounds like the committee doesn't care that the college dropped its investigation or that the NCAA and USRowing aren't getting too wound up yet,"

Nick closed his eyes, resting his head against the back of the chair.

"It gets worse," Drew said quietly.

Nick looked at him. "Do I want to know?"

"I think you need to. According to Brad, the head of the committee referred to your relationship as 'deviant behavior' and wanted to make sure this wasn't part of a larger pattern of you preying on your athletes."

"'Preying'? Apparently, he's never met my boyfriend, who's not shy about what he wants. I practically had to pepper spray him to get him to back off once he decided to go after me, and I'm not sure even that would've gotten him to back off," Nick snorted. "This is great, just great. How the hell am I going to shut this down?"

Drew was silent for a moment. "Give Brad a chance. He'll come through for you."

"You think so?"

"Nick, the only reason he joined the oversight committee was to spike this."

"I'll have to talk to him, then."

Drew considered that for a moment. "Actually, I think for Brad's sake that'd be a bad idea. If word gets out that you and he are in cahoots, it undercuts his credibility. Let me funnel information."

"I guess that'd be best." Nick nodded slowly.

"I'm not telling you to cool it with Morgan, but be careful, Nick. It sounds like this isn't done."

"That's just the distraction I need going into a new season with new people in the boat, and more people on the team," Nick said. "Did I tell you we're growing because of that big win last year? I've got some hotshot new junior-college transfer student from Orange Coast College coming here specifically because he wants to join a winning crew. School starts in a week or so. Couldn't they have done this earlier?"

"Or never?" Drew said.

"Never works for me," Nick sighed. He was still pale. Drew stood up. "I've got houses to sell."

"And I've got one to renovate. Jeez, I hate the thought of telling Morgan about this, but that's not how we work. Thank Brad for me, will you?"

Chapter Eleven

Brad slammed his locker shut and secured it with a battered old combination lock, the same one he'd had since junior high. Men filled the locker room of the trendy Midtown gym that evening, but Brad didn't mind. On a good day at work, he saw a handful of people. Crowded was good.

He put the earbuds in and started his favorite playlist, and with the high-pitched death metal pumping through his iPod and water bottle in hand, Brad headed out into the gym, first to do a little cardio for a warm-up, then stretching, weights, and finally more cardio. It was past time to hit the gym. His last regular workout regimen had ended with graduation, and he was getting doughy, he thought, poking himself in the side. Beer for dinner came with a price.

Joining a gym on Sundstrom Homes' corporate account had another benefit, as well, really more of a twofer. Brad not only consumed something besides beer and cold cereal for dinner after his workout, he escaped Randall and his barbed comments for an hour or two.

The vast main floor of the gym was divided in two, with elliptical trainers and treadmills and a few unloved and rarely used ergometers occupying one half and weight machines and free weights occupying the remainder. In between lay a no-man's-land of mats and medicine balls for stretching and toning. A flight of stairs led up to rooms for aerobics and spin classes and a gallery where people on the exercycles watched those on the floor below when the canned offerings on television monitors failed to hold their attention.

Brad walked right by the treadmills for his warm-up, aiming for the elliptical trainers. He hated their awkward gait, but he was a big guy and had never been much of a runner, and the ergs? He knew what a great warm-up the ergs gave, but no. It was just too soon.

Back and forth, up and down, Brad quit the elliptical as soon as he completed his ten-minute warm-up, promising himself he'd do more after he lifted.

From there, he hit the mats for a good stretch, just like Coach Bedford had taught him. He started with his arms and upper back and worked his way down, sticking one leg out at a time for a revolved single-leg stretch, hand to opposite ankle, trying to feel it in a line from one end of his body to the other. Then he switched, closing his eyes, enjoying the release, even if his side grew cold when his shirt pulled up.

He sat up and opened his eyes...and met the eyes of the man on the gallery above who'd been staring at him, who didn't look away quite fast enough.

Brad frowned slightly and returned to the exercise mat and the movements he'd been taught as a rower, movements he was pretty sure were based in yoga—not that he'd ever been to a yoga class. Those were for chicks and...guiltily, he thought of Drew.

He got up to stretch his hamstrings by leaning into a pillar, one leg out behind him. The he realized he'd pointed his ass directly at the guy he'd caught staring at him. He hesitated, and then kicked himself mentally. The last thing he needed was to pull a hamstring from deadlifts with cold hammies. Flushing slightly, he stretched anyway, counting to thirty and then switching legs.

Then Brad did something that, later, he still couldn't believe. He looked over his shoulder and winked at the guy.

Then panicked. He just winked at a man who'd been checking out his ass.

He hightailed it to the weight room and the free weights, pulse drowning out his iPod, his face red.

His hands shook on his first sets on the free weights. He watched himself in the mirror, face still burning. *Who are you?* he wondered. *What's really bothering you? That guy who looked at you, or the fact you kind of liked it?*

Brad settled down as he concentrated on his form. The weight room was no place for daydreaming, but in between sets, he looked around. Sometimes, he saw guys looking at him. Most of the time, they glanced away, but sometimes, they kept looking, their eyes lingering on his like they were sending him a message he could almost but not quite make out.

Relatively light weights and lots of reps gave him an excuse not to make eye contact again as he returned to his sets and focused on doing them right. Dead lifts for his legs and core; push presses to work arms, shoulders, and upper back; and then, because that alone wouldn't make him sore enough, thrusters, taking the barbell from a squat up and over his head, arms thrust up and out.

Sweat dampened his shirt, causing it to cling and bind. He pulled it away from his skin a few times, fanning himself with it, even though the gym's air conditioning cooled him quickly.

As Brad sipped water, he glanced around the gym floor. It seemed like all kinds of guys were looking at each other. He'd thought the student gym at California Pacific was a meat market, which was why he'd always used the equipment at the boathouse. But this gym? Wow. Brad shook his head and wondered how long this had been going on. He felt like the air held hidden music he couldn't quite hear, or that they spoke a language he could almost but not quite understand, and if he only listened hard enough, it would come to him.

Just before he got to the elliptical trainers, he glanced at the ergs. Some guy using one was just massacring it. He grimaced. *They're such nice machines. What'd they ever do to you?*

He swerved and sat down at a free erg. Suddenly Brad felt like erging.

He started with the old drills from crew. First his arms, twenty strokes. Then he added the forward motion of his trunk, and twenty more strokes. Finally, he added the legs, first taking the catch at half slide and then lengthening out to the full rowing stroke.

Feeling his neighbor's eyes on him, Brad set the monitor for a reasonable distance and went to work. The distance was enough to give him a good cardio workout without punishing him unduly. It wasn't like he had to qualify for a seat in the boat anymore.

As Brad warmed to his workout, he glanced over to the neighboring monitor and noticed that the guy next to him was trying to match him.

Good and loose and warm, Brad kicked it up a notch, pulling harder on the handle to drive faster, taking a bit less time on his recovery.

Then the man next to him sped up. Brad could tell by the increased noise coming from his erg's air-fed flywheel.

So that's how it is. Brad rowed a little faster.

The man next to him matched him, but badly. His form, not good to begin with, grew increasingly erratic the harder and faster he rowed.

Brad smirked and picked up the speed.

His shadow followed.

Brad rowed faster and harder. He was working hard now, his breath coming in gulps on the recovery, but he knew he could sustain this pace for a while.

"Shit!"

The man next to him let go of the erg handles. He slowly toppled off the erg and lay gasping on the ground.

Brad just looked straight ahead and finished his workout at the fast pace.

Later, after his shower, he stood before his open locker, a towel straining to stay wrapped around his waist.

"Hey, I saw you out there on the rowers. You were working pretty hard there."

Brad glanced over at the man next him, a tall blond who slowly toweled himself off while facing Brad. The man was a little shorter than Brad and a lot less hairy, but chiseled and, he had to admit, pretty good-looking.

Brad shrugged. "I've done worse on those things and for a lot longer."

"Yeah?" the guy said, smiling at him.

Another shrug. Why was this guy talking to him? "I rowed in college."

"And I'm guessing that wasn't that long ago?" The blond stopped toweling, holding the towel over his crotch, but Brad was pretty sure there was something going on down there, even as the man idly scratched one pec.

"I graduated in June. That guy didn't stand a chance," Brad said, shifting uncomfortably. He stared straight into his locker, refusing to look at the guy anymore, even though he felt the blond's eyes on him. There was something going on, something in the guy's stare, that made him nervous. He felt it stirring, a tingling at the base of his spine, a tightening of his sac.

He felt like a doofus, but he quickly shimmied his underwear on under the towel and then dropped it and pulled his pants up fast. He knew the guy was watching him. Shirt and sandals made Brad good to go. The rest could wait until he got home.

Brad didn't exactly run out of the locker room. He was nervous. He had a feeling the guy was hitting on him, like it was more of that language he couldn't quite understand, although if he stuck around, Brad was pretty sure the blond would be willing to translate.

Brad had never really thought of guys as attractive before, but that wasn't quite it. They just drew his eye in a different way than women did, but now that his eyes were opening, he realized there were a lot of hot guys around.

He came to the gym for a vacation back into the territory he'd learned so well when he was in college, but the workout puzzled him. The gym was a familiar place, almost like home, and the notion that it held secrets he'd never imagined threw him off. *Have gyms always been like this, guys looking at other guys like that? Looking at me like that?*

But Brad wasn't upset—far from it—and hadn't dropped the towel to dress because locker rooms made him nervous. He'd dressed under the towel to keep from embarrassing himself.

"Thanks for coming over on a Friday evening, guys. I know it's a lousy time, but I'll be busy showing homes all weekend," Drew said, ushering Emily and Brad into his dining room.

"Not a problem," Brad said, yanking at his tie until the knot came loose. He pulled it off and dropped it on the floor near the door.

Emily shrugged. "Melissa's working tonight, anyway, and we need to get the applications in."

"Applications, as in more than one?" Brad said.

"Yeah, there are all kinds of grants and small business loans from sources public and private," Emily answered. "The more we ask for, the greater our chances."

"Wait...isn't the city paying us?" Brad said.

"Yes, but it typically takes time to get money out of the government, and if the city's getting the money from the state, and the state's budget is held up—again—we'll need money to cover us," Emily explained. "We'd be stupid to turn any source of funding down."

"Especially the grants," Drew said.

"Uh...what're grants?" Brad asked, feeling stupid for not knowing.

"Free money," Emily said. "They might make the difference between doing this project right and eating dinner too."

"Speaking of," Drew said, "is Thai okay?" Without waiting for consent, he placed an order online. "Brad, if you get your laptop out, I'll give you the password for my Wi-Fi network." He smiled. "Something tells me you'll be around to use it for a while."

Brad found himself blushing. "I hope so."

"So, can we just take over the dining room? Because I've got file cases in the car too," Emily said, setting her own computer down across from where Drew sat.

"We might as well set up on the table. It's not like there'll be time to entertain before this is done, and there's not room for all of us in my home office," Drew said.

"If we get this job, we should look into renting an office or something," Brad said as he set down one of Emily's big file boxes. He sat next to Drew. "That way we could come or go whenever we needed to without Drew sacrificing his house, because this looks like it'll take over, and quick, if he lets it."

Drew and Emily looked at each other. "It's an idea," Drew said.

"An expensive one, though. Commercial rent is pretty high, and that's one more line item to add to the budget projections," Emily said.

"Put a line in the budget for a trailer on the job site, one with power, phone, and Internet hook-ups," Brad said. "You run the job from the job site. It's how it's done, and the city will be expecting something like that. If you leave it out, we'll look like amateurs."

When Drew and Emily stared at him, Brad flushed. "Never mind, it was a dumb idea," he mumbled, looking at the ground.

Emily shook her head. "No, it wasn't, Brad. That's why we want you on this project. You know construction on this scale, or better than we do, anyway."

Brad looked up to find Drew's eyes on him, which only made him blush.

Drew just smiled. "Dinner will be here soon. Let's get to work before dinner gets here, though. It's going to be a long night."

His face still aflame, Brad opened the file folder in which he'd haphazardly stored his contribution to the paperwork and the applications, even as Emily and Drew did the same.

Brad had previously given what he thought he'd need in terms of salary, as well as help with tuition for classes toward his contractor's license. Fortunately, he'd still be working part-time, even if it was at that hated job at Suburban Graveyard, and trade school wouldn't cost that much. It was mostly to prep for the contractor's exam. Also fortunately, all those summers working for his dad on job sites counted a long way toward the experience part of licensure, and working on the project would get him even more experience.

But Brad was the junior partner in this endeavor, more employee than principal, and he knew it. Drew and Emily could make a bid for the job without him, but with him, their attempt was so much stronger. That was cool with him; he was in this to learn, after all.

An excuse for spending large amounts of time with Drew, looking at Drew, thinking about Drew, was just a fringe benefit, and with Drew and Emily poring over the electronic applications, he was free to watch Drew.

And get caught looking.

Drew, obviously sensing eyes on him, looked up, and Brad didn't look away quite fast enough. Drew smiled at him and went back to work.

Brad was rescued from embarrassment by the arrival of dinner. "I'll get it!" he said when the doorbell rang.

Before Drew could stop him, Brad bounced out of his chair and made it to the door before Drew or Emily had saved their work, let alone gotten money out.

Brad set the takeout containers on the table. "Stay seated, you guys. Just tell me where the plates and flatware are."

"You mean besides the kitchen?" Emily said.

"Ha ha," Brad said. "Drew?"

Drew stood up anyway. "I'll show you. I need to get drinks, anyway."

Drew led the way into the cozy kitchen. "Plates are there above the sink and to the right," he said, pointing, "flatware in the drawer next to the dishwasher."

Drew reached up to get glasses from the cupboard next to the plates. Brad brushed by him as he reached for the dishes, their bodies almost touching. "Thanks," Brad breathed, almost in his ear.

Drew pulled two bottles of mineral water from the fridge. The kitchen wasn't that small. He wondered if something was up with Brad. It sure seemed like it, the way he'd caught him looking several times. It felt like Brad was trying to send him a message, but he couldn't figure out what. Since Brad was straight—his sexuality wasn't even on the agenda—Drew couldn't imagine what it might be.

Then he stopped cold. What if Brad was pulling out? Granted, they could do the job without him, but not as easily. But if Brad had to back out, why was he even there, and why bother giving them his numbers?

Drew shook his head. This was driving him nuts. He really liked Brad and enjoyed every minute they spent together, but maybe Nick had a point. Maybe Brad Sundstrom just wasn't friend material, at least not for Drew. The thought made Drew sad.

Drew set glasses down in front of Emily and Brad and the water in the middle of the table. "I see you found the pad thai."

Emily beamed. "Thank you so much!" At Brad's quizzical look, she said, "My wife's allergic to peanuts. The only time I get things like this is when she's not around."

"Whoa, that's got to be rough," Brad said.

"You have no idea," Emily said, speaking with a mouth full of noodles.

"Peanuts are in everything," Drew said, slowly licking the sauce off his lips, "but hmmm, oh so good."

Drew felt Brad's eyes on him, burning in their intensity. He felt the air between them crackle with charge. Brad leaned toward him, head cocked...

Then he jumped up, knocking over his chair and spilling his water. "Shit! I...I'm sorry, I can't...I gotta go!"

With a final terrified glance over his shoulder, Brad bolted from the house.

"What the hell was that?" Emily said.

Drew shook his head slowly. "I have no idea. I know he's been under some stress lately, but that..."

Emily tossed her fork down in frustration. "We need his signature."

"I'll get it from him tomorrow," Drew said, wondering how he was going to track Brad down when it was obvious the guy didn't want to be followed. "Besides, he left his computer."

Emily looked at Drew long enough to make him squirm. "What?"

"What's going on between you two?" she said finally.

"Nothing," Drew said, not entirely sure he was right.

"Please, Drew. Even I could feel something in the air between the two of you."

Drew thought about telling her, but as good a friend as Emily was, he didn't want to analyze this right now. They had too much to do. "I really don't know. If you'd asked me this even earlier this evening, I'd have said nothing, but that little performance?"

"Yeah, exactly. You know what it reminds me of?" Emily said thoughtfully. "It reminds me of when Melissa and I were first going out. I coaxed her out of the closet, you know."

"No shit? I didn't know that."

"Yeah, she had a fiancé and everything, but my womanly charms were too much for her to deny."

"They are pretty formidable, or so I'd imagine."

Emily rolled her eyes. "The point is, Melissa had a nearly identical freak-out, only we weren't pushing a deadline for a career-making opportunity."

"Right, back to work," Drew said. "I'll hunt him down tomorrow in between showings and that nervous breakdown I keep putting off."

Chapter Twelve

Ohmygod, ohmygod, ohmygod...

Brad locked the bathroom door behind him and slowly slid to the floor, his mind a maelstrom. He didn't remember the drive home, but he figured it was the blank in between running out of Drew's place and running into his room. He was glad Randall and Philip weren't home.

Ohmygod, ohmygod, ohmygod...

He couldn't believe himself, but he just had to get out of there before he did something catastrophically stupid, and given his lax definitions, that would've been saying something.

Ohmygod, ohmygod, ohmygod...

"Get a grip, asswipe," he muttered as he hauled himself up.

He turned on the faucet and splashed himself with cold water. He slapped himself in the face. Hard. Anything to cut off the loop running through his mind.

He looked at himself in the mirror, water running down his cheeks. His gaze fell to his lips. He raised a hand and touched them.

He'd really wanted to know what Drew's tasted like. He'd been buzzing on Drew all evening, just grooving on being around him, but seeing him lick his lips short-circuited his brain. *Snap, crackle, pop!* He was surprised smoke didn't pour out of his ears.

When he caught himself leaning in to taste those lips, he panicked. He'd almost kissed another man.

Ohmygod, ohmygod, ohmygod...

Suddenly Brad understood that mysterious language he'd heard at the gym. There, at dinner, he finally made out the strange music in the air. It was the language of desire, a song of love, as each man, aware of himself and those around him, sought to draw others to him. When he'd noticed the guy checking out his ass during his warm-up stretch, it had confused him. In the locker room, it had aroused him.

But now he understood exactly what it meant, and it terrified him.

Ohmygod, ohmygod, ohmygod...

Was he gay? Bi? He didn't know. Both terms conjured images that he didn't recognize; that he prayed didn't apply to him. The lisping faggot, the limp-wristed theater crowd, the cocksucker. Even at relatively liberal California Pacific, there'd been the divisions between the jocks, the real men, on the one hand, and the...not-manly-enough guys on the other.

Brad didn't have a word for them besides "fag," even though the word felt dirty. Never mind that there were gay athletes. He'd known some and had his ass kicked in crew by one. His coach had been a gay athlete too. Neither of them was a fag. Was Drew a fag? Brad shied away from the thought.

But somehow, to like guys sexually was to be less than a man. He couldn't shake that idea from his mind. He'd heard it all his life. His dad certainly thought that, at least based on what Brad had heard Randall say and what he'd heard at construction sites. Hell, they were where he'd learned to be macho, to puff up his chest and posture and stare guys down.

But...he'd wanted to kiss another man. Did that make him a fag? The thought made his heart race.

"You're a homo," he whispered, but that didn't feel quite right. "You thought you were straight, but you're not. You're bi-curious," he proclaimed, hamming it up a bit, but he knew that wasn't true either. He felt a hell of a lot more than curious where Drew was concerned.

He'd heard jocks say, "I'm gay for you, bro," around the gym or around friends' frat houses. They hadn't meant it, not like that. Maybe that was what he was. Maybe he was gay for Drew.

He wondered what that would mean. He didn't even know how it would work if they were both guys. Which one of them would be the man and which the woman? He was bigger, so maybe he'd be the man, but what if Drew demanded it? Drew had way more experience like that. Would Drew want to...to...to him? He couldn't even complete the thought.

Ohmygod, ohmygod, ohmygod...

No. Just...no.

He pulled out his mobile phone. There were a couple of messages, probably from Drew. He couldn't listen to them.

He flipped through the address book until he found what he was looking for. He selected the number and hit the call button.

"Hey there, Rico!" he said, voice full of false cheer. "Yeah, not bad... So, listen. I need to get shitfaced and get laid, bro. Where's the party tomorrow?"

Drew woke Saturday morning only reluctantly and only after his alarm clock screamed at him for the third time.

After that, his sense of responsibility took over and he hauled himself upright, but what a night.

He and Emily had finished all the applications last night after Brad's freak-out, but they still needed Brad's signature on those applications that had to be submitted physically, including the one to the city for the renovation itself. He'd left Brad three messages last night and one more this morning, each firmer than the last. He also texted the locations of his two Saturday open houses. If Drew had to, he'd corner Brad at home on Sunday. They had a few days of wiggle room on the submissions that couldn't be turned in online, and fortunately the big one could be delivered in person.

But still.

And the dead elephant in the drawing room needed naming. Last night had just been weird, Drew reflected as he shaved, even before Brad ran screaming out of his house.

Because Emily had been right. There had been a current in the air. Drew had noticed it the first time he caught Brad looking at him, and it continued right up until he thought Brad was about to kiss him...right before bolting.

And what an ego boost that hadn't been.

Drew wiped his face clean, looking at himself in the mirror. He'd really thought Brad was about to kiss him, and apparently Brad thought so too.

He needed another perspective. He glanced at his watch. If he hurried, he might still catch Nick at the boathouse. School started next week, so the returning rowers would already have a steady practice schedule.

Still at the boathouse? Drew sent to Nick's cell phone.

For another 40 minutes or so. Why?

Guess.

Drew flinched as he hit "send." He could just guess how Nick would respond.

Nick didn't disappoint.

Again? This is getting to be a pattern.

Three times is a pattern. Twice is just taking advantage of your sage counsel.

No, three times is a cry for help. Hurry up. Morgan and I are spending the weekend in San Francisco before classes resume.

And once again, Drew was off to the CalPac boathouse before hitting the open-house circuit on a Saturday morning, but Nick was right. It really was getting to be a pattern.

Drew walked into the boathouse with lattes in hand. "Here you go."

Nick took his. "Hmmm, coffee. All may be forgiven."

"I figured I'd better not push my luck, and I drive right by a Starbucks," Drew said, smiling over his own latte. "So...next time, what'll it be, stock certificates? Gold?"

"Next time?"

Drew shrugged. "We both know there'll be one, so what'll it cost me?"

Nick smiled. "Just your eternal regard."

"You've already got that."

"Then everything will be fine. So, what can I do for you?" Nick shepherded Drew out to the deserted dock, where a beautiful summer morning was just getting started. "Since you've got to get to work and I've got a warm and willing Morgan waiting for me to take him to the city for a weekend of debauchery—"

"Yeah, right," Drew scoffed.

"—a weekend of museums and walks along Lands End," Nick continued with a glare, "I'll shorthand this for you. Brad?"

"Brad," Drew sighed.

"I warned you."

"I guess that's better than 'I told you so.' Keeping it brief, we were finalizing the bid for the Bayard House last night. During dinner, I thought he was going to kiss me. You just know sometimes, right? I mean, he leaned toward me and everything, but then he freaked the fuck out and ran from my house like a frightened schoolboy."

"That's an unexpected development."

Drew stared at him. "That's it? That's all you have to say?"

Nick shrugged. "What do you want me to say? You were right, I was wrong. It sounds like Brad may be switching teams. So, what's the problem?"

"So, what's the—the problem is that he ran screaming out of my house after aborting a kiss. Nick, I really like this guy. Help out with some magic coaching words that'll help me unlock his heart."

"I don't have any magic words." Nick put an arm around his friend. "This is why we don't go after men who are 'bi-curious' or 'questioning their sexuality.' It's not because we don't like their answers, it's because we get hurt."

Drew rested his head on Nick's shoulder. "I thought we were friends, he and I, but he's totally ignoring me."

"What do you expect? You've shown him a part of himself he didn't know existed. You're radioactive, now. You're kryptonite."

"But I still need his signature on the bid for the Bayard House. On top of everything else, his personal issues are making this damned complicated, and I certainly don't need any more anxiety about it," Drew said.

"I'd say something about mixing business with pleasure, but I'm dating one of my rowers and have apparently incurred the wrath of the oversight committee, so I'm probably not the best authority to cite."

"Yeah, that does kind of let the wind out of your sails on that score, doesn't it?" Drew agreed. "But dating? You two are so married."

"Not yet. Maybe when Morgan graduates." Nick blushed.

"So, what am I going to do?" Drew said.

"What do you want to do?" Nick countered.

"I want to sit him down and kiss the stuffing out of him after I bitch him out for running off like that. So instead I'll leave him alone until tomorrow and then try to get his signature for the bid. I won't bring up kisses that might've been."

Nick nodded. "Sounds like the right approach."

"And I'll let him take the next step about anything personal," Drew added.

"I'd been hoping for 'I'll give up this notion of luring him out of the closet,' but I guess if you haven't by now, you're not going to, not with him almost kissing you."

Drew's eyes watered suddenly. "It just hurts, you know?"

"That's why they call them crushes. If they didn't hurt, they'd call them something else," Nick said softly.

"Isn't that from *Sixteen Candles*?" Drew said suspiciously.

"Probably, but that doesn't make it less true. There's nothing original anymore anyway." He looked at his watch. "So, are you good? Or at least good enough for now?"

"Yeah, go take your hot boyfriend to the big bad city for a weekend of your tepid debauchery. I'm going to go sell houses so I can afford to reduce my hours if we get the Bayard bid."

"*When* you get the Bayard project bid. Visualizing's half the battle."

"Thanks, Coach." Drew kissed Nick's cheek before heading to his car.

Brad parked his car outside Rico's apartment with plans to crash there after the party. He had no intention of being in any condition to drive home.

"You seem tense," Rico said as they walked the handful of blocks to the frat house hosting the party.

"Yeah, being a grown-up and working and all kind of sucks. Put it off as long as possible," Brad said.

"I'm on it. I just keep changing my major. It's my fourth year, and I'm only a sophomore," Rico laughed. "My folks'll catch on sooner or later, but in the meantime, the beer's cheap and the girls are free."

"Beats the other way around," Brad pointed out.

"It so does not, dude. Are you mental?"

"Yeah, what am I thinking? Free beer and cheap girls for the win!" Brad made himself inject the comment with false cheer.

"Dude, are you okay? You're quiet and kind of moody. It's just not right."

"Yeah, I'm fine." Brad thought about how he'd feel tomorrow, but it was nothing compared how he already felt. Everything he'd thought was Brad Sundstrom had just been yanked out from under him by the realizations of the last few days. He didn't know who he was anymore.

"Whatever, dude, just stay pressed. I don't want to be the one who brought Debbie Downer to the party," Rico grunted.

Stay pressed. Brad had no idea what that meant. Out of college for a few months, and already they'd passed him by. Now he felt worse than he already had. Oh well, there was a cure for that, and they were heading right for it.

But he knew he had to pick up his game, or he'd have to explain why he had his head up his ass. He couldn't stomach the thought of a long conversation about feelings with Rico. He was an emo train wreck as it was, no need to add to the carnage.

Their destination was a frat house around the next corner, and they heard and felt the party before they saw it, a heavy thudding sound cranked up so loud that the words were indistinguishable and the music nothing but ear-massacring audio sludge.

The doors and windows were open to the mild summer night, and in Brad went, right behind his friend. The frat house was in an old mansion a few blocks from campus. It was nestled among other such houses, clustered into a sort of ghetto that made the presence of the small private school easier for the neighbors to stomach, since the damage was confined to a relatively small area.

Large rooms, formerly the formal living and dining rooms, opened off the foyer, and a double staircase snaked up to the second floor and the private living spaces of the frat brothers—or at least as private as a space could be with the front door thrown wide.

Rico veered right, toward the smell of marijuana, pulling a small pipe out of his cargo shorts as he walked. "Coming?"

"No, man, I'm good. I'm gonna go find the beer," Brad said. Smoking anything had never been his thing. Randall had a nose like a drug-sniffing dog, and besides, he'd been into sports. He knew a lot of high school and college athletes who'd used, but he hadn't. Crew demanded too much lung capacity to piss it away with pot smoke.

Chants of "Go-go-go!" told him where to find the beer, so Brad followed his ears, and sure enough, there was a veritable buffet of booze in the living room and a small pyramid of kegs in the kitchen.

Beer, sweet beer. He was golden, and with any luck, soon to be buzzing all those uncomfortable thoughts right out of his head.

Too bad it didn't work out that way.

Brad helped himself to one of the ubiquitous red plastic cups and filled it with beer from a keg. Thus fortified, he looked around for people he knew.

After ten minutes, he changed his plans and started looking for people he liked. He'd seen plenty of people he knew but only one or two he really wanted to spend more than a few moments grunting at noncommittally.

Drifting from room to room, he finally located some guys he knew, brothers of the fraternity, so technically his hosts. They and a whole lot of other people were taking their turn under a beer bong, chugging cheap beer to catch a buzz as quickly as possible.

"Brad!"

"Dude, where ya been?"

"They finally get sick of your ugly face and kick you out?"

"I graduated," Brad said, shrugging. "No help for it. Your turn'll come...or it would if you'd stop flunking classes."

Laughter rolled around the room, and someone got up and pulled Brad to the bong. Brad knew these people, and he knew their capacity. He could best them.

"You're done when you have to breathe!"

Smirking, Brad knelt while someone held the long tube with the funnel on it over his mouth, and the beer started flowing.

While he hadn't trained hard in months, crew had bequeathed to Brad a very useful gift, an ability made for a situation like this. He could hold his breath for a long time—a *very* long time.

One beer followed another into the funnel, one, two, and three before he held up his hand and stood up, wiping his mouth on the back of his hand.

"Damn, man! We shoulda got a deposit from you."

"Bitches," Brad said with a snort.

Brad took his turn holding and pouring, even as the cheap beer worked its magic. He was a big guy, but three beers was a lot in a short period of time, and it wasn't long before he was a bit unsteady on his feet.

Unsteady, perhaps, and buzzing, but with it enough to take stock of the evening. The beer hadn't been the best, he'd known that going into it, but that Blue Ribbon crap? He'd allowed himself to grow spoiled since graduation, developing a taste for locally crafted microbrews that made the stuff coming down the funnel taste like horse piss. He'd had enough of that for this lifetime.

Brad thought beer goggles were supposed to make things look better, but as he roared out a belch, he realized what a dump the frat house was and decided it might possibly qualify as a shithole. Yeah, the brothers were hard on their houses, but would a little paint have killed them? Something just off white, maybe in an eggshell finish for easier cleanup? Was that too much to ask?

He stumbled and decided he'd like to sit down, but one look at the filthy armchair, its dated patterns dulled to a shitty brown, had him reconsidering the idea in a hurry. Did armchairs get bedbugs?

He could only imagine what Drew would make of a place like this and found himself agreeing with what he imagined Drew would say as Brad flopped down into the chair anyway.

No, Drew would take one look at this place and spin on his heel and march back to his car, and Brad wouldn't blame him.

He brooded in the armchair for a while. Then a realization fought its way through the beer's haze, and he sat bolt upright. He had come here to escape Drew, but there he sat, imagining what Drew would think of a seedy frat house. Even in his absence, Drew was right there with him.

He felt like Drew'd worked some kind of gay mojo or something so all the women looked cheap and all the guys hot. The girls at these parties used to be hot, but now they just seemed...sleazy. He knew not all women were like this. Emily sure wasn't like these girls, but she only liked other women. These girls—sorority chicks with too much makeup, too keen to find a husband, and who wouldn't do anything but a hand job; future barflies and biker chicks who put out like photocopiers but who already showed signs of partying too hard; even the occasional Goth girl, and if he'd been into blood sacrifice or looking for spells, he'd be on one like stink on a monkey, even if they frightened him a little.

But these women...these were the ones around, and given a choice—and it seemed that somehow, he suddenly had other options—he'd take the guys he'd seen, the handsome and muscular guys he'd noticed noticing him at the gym or even there at the party, the closeted frat boys he'd made fun of when he was a student.

Given the choice, Brad realized he'd take...Drew. That was who he wanted. He had no idea what it meant or how to go about it or how to tell Drew or even if Drew had any interest in him that way, but he wanted Drew.

Faced with that undeniable realization, Brad did the only thing he could think of: he decided to get drunk, plowing toward the table with the hard alcohol like a cruise ship to an iceberg.

He knew the adage "Beer before liquor, never sicker," but he didn't care. He was still thinking. It had to stop, and a game of tequila pong looked like the magic ticket. It was just like beer pong but looked like it'd work far quicker.

Brad eyed the guy currently winning. Tall, but not crew tall, built. Probably lacrosse or maybe baseball. Or just a gym rat. He didn't know; he didn't care. The guy's hands looked reasonably steady, which suited Brad fine. He figured his own coordination wasn't what it could be, and that suited him too. It meant evicting Drew from his head that much faster.

"I'm done!" giggled the party favor currently playing. She staggered up and fell onto Brad. "You're a big one, aren't you? I could just lean on you all night."

"That might be kinda awkward when the beer starts recycling," Brad said, giving her a gentle push to return her to the full upright and locked position.

"You play football?" the current champion of tequila pong asked.

"Crew," Brad replied. "You?"

"Baseball," he replied, peering at Brad from under his eyebrows in a way Brad was learning to recognize.

Brad couldn't hide his own appreciation, but he'd be damned before he'd respond. "Let's play."

Someone handed Brad the slightly sticky ping-pong ball, and he bounced it off the table and into a shot glass, his aim and reflexes still reasonably keen despite the beer.

"Lucky shot," his opponent said.

Brad shrugged and waited for him to take his turn.

Back and forth they played, shots taken and missed, tequila pounded, and it was just what Brad had sought. He hardly thought of Drew because he had to focus all his effort on the task at hand.

At some point his opponent staggered away from the game with a final glower of regret for Brad, which he ignored in favor of his new challenger.

"I'm Brenda," she said, her voice husky from smoke and alcohol. "I'm not very good at this."

"S'okay, I'm schnockered," Brad said, slurring his words. Talking was hard with a numb tongue. "My name'sh Brad."

But she was right. Despite his impairment, Brad took the first three rounds, but the alcohol paradoxically sharpened Brenda's skills.

After that, Brad knew it was time to quit, since he couldn't quite focus his eyes. "I'm done."

He met Brenda's eyes. "Me too," she said.

Even through his booze goggles, he could tell she was a bottle of peroxide and a pack of cigarettes away from skank, but he didn't care. She was throwing the right signals. She was the right sex.

She'd do.

As others took their places at the tequila pong table, they stumbled away, looking for a dark corner. They pulled each other upstairs and into one of the bedrooms but couldn't quite make it to a bed without falling. Giggling, they rested against each other, and then lips sought lips.

Brad felt no special zing when he kissed Brenda, no strange attraction like the one that had pulled him to Drew's lips last night, but then, he'd had enough to drink that his lips were tingling anyway.

It didn't take long before the kisses turned sloppy and hands started to roam.

"Yeah, baby," she slurred as his hand found its way under her T-shirt.

She pawed at his pants, and he groaned his encouragement.

Then his hand made it further north, up to the bra line and above. Brenda's chest was soft and pliable, supple give and smooth skin.

He froze, and his body told him he wanted hard planes. He'd never wanted hard planes before, and the realization killed the mood for him. He pushed himself up, overcome by the realization he was about to be very, very ill.

Brad stumbled and tripped his way to the bathroom, which was blessedly empty, and just in time. He kicked the door shut behind him, fell to his knees, and made the traditional obeisance to the porcelain idol of those poisoned by alcohol.

Heave after heave brought it all up: all the beer, all the tequila, all the feelings he'd tried to bury. When he was done, he slumped back, tears trickling down his cheeks.

"Are you in there, sugar?"

Brad crawled to the door. He blocked it with his body and fumbled to lock it. "I'm fine. Go away."

"Don't be that way, baby, lemme help you," she cooed, thumping weakly on the door with her fist.

"Go away," Brad muttered.

She continued to thump at the door, but Brad ignored her. He heaved himself up and staggered to the sink. He was still drunk, but he could feel his head clearing thanks to blowing chunks.

He turned the sink on cold, splashed his face and then cupped his hands and sucked down several noisy handfuls.

He looked at himself in the mirror, eyes red from alcohol and the tears he still shed. This wasn't what he wanted. "You're gay," he whispered.

Chapter Thirteen

The phone's bleating from its charging cradle on his nightstand pulled Drew from a semi-futile attempt at sleeping. Those parts of Saturday not spent selling houses Drew spent fine-tuning the various applications for the renovation of the Bayard House. Little remained to be done other than corral Brad long enough for him to sign everything, but that hardly prevented Drew from picking at them. He wasn't sure whether it helped his nerves or only further riled him up. So, while the phone interrupted his sleep, it did nothing to deny him rest.

He glared at it gimlet-eyed, squinting to make out the caller ID without his glasses. If it was one of his clients calling this late at night—he looked at the clock—this early in the morning, his real estate disasters could jolly well wait until daylight hours.

Then he recognized Brad's number and he grabbed the phone. "Brad?"

"Hey," Brad said gruffly.

"What's wrong? Where are you? You sound like crap." Drew frowned in the darkness of his bedroom, torn between relief that Brad had contacted him and anger that it had taken him this long. "What's that noise? Are you at a party?"

"Yeah, I was... I am. I'm in a bathroom. Drew, how did you know you were gay?"

"I...wow. You called me from a party to ask me this? Have you been drinking?"

"Yeah, but I've thrown most of it up. I'm pretty sober now," Brad said. The moments lengthened. "So...how did you? Know, I mean. That you're gay."

Drew exhaled noisily. "You don't pick the easy ones, do you?" He thought about it for a moment. "I've just always known, I guess. There was no great *a-ha!* moment."

Brad was silent for a minute while Drew waited expectantly. "Can I come over?" he said softly, or as softly as he could over the noise penetrating the bathroom door.

It only took a moment for Drew to realize this would be the worst possible time. "I'm not sure that'd be a good idea right now. You've been drinking, so I'm not sure you should drive." *And I want to hold you so bad right now I'd never be able to keep my hands off you if I picked you up.*

"I guess you're right," Brad sniffled. "I just...how do I get you out of my head?"

That flummoxed Drew. "I don't know how to answer that, Brad."

"Yeah, forget I said it," Brad begged.

The hell I will. "Why don't you call me when you get up tomorrow...or later today as the case may be. You can come over. I'll make you something to eat if you're up to it. We can talk."

"That'd be nice." Brad said sniffled again. "Okay, I've got to get out of here. I'll call you later. Bye, Drew...and thanks."

Drew hung up the phone, but sleep eluded him. Brad was gay, or at least bi. His hopes, once grounded, soared again. Brad seemed like he might be interested too. This was what he'd wanted—that double handful of big lug was looking to jump the fence and land in his arms—but right then, he felt nothing but pity for Brad.

Brad rubbed his face as he walked from his car to Drew's front door. Given how much he'd had to drink the night before, he should've felt a lot worse. Water and Tylenol before bed, eight hours of sleep that ended only with Randall banging around the house like a one-man marching band, followed by more Tylenol and a shower. He'd had a slight headache, but the Tylenol banished it.

"You know I don't have a hangover, right?" he said to Randall when he emerged from his room to make coffee. He didn't feel the need to mention it was because he'd puked up most of the hard alcohol. He poured himself a big mug full of coffee and called Drew from his car.

Twenty minutes later, Brad stood before Drew's front door. He knew he should've been more nervous, but he wasn't. Maybe he just didn't have the energy for it that...afternoon. It was after 1:00 p.m., coming up on twelve hours since he'd called Drew. Twelve hours since he'd more or less come out to someone.

Shit.

Suddenly he felt exhausted by it all.

The door opened. "Hey." Drew looked concerned. "How long've you been standing there?"

"I just got here," Brad replied quietly.

"Come in," Drew said, getting out of the way.

Brad entered, and Drew closed the door behind him. "Rough night?"

"Rough night? More like a rough morning," Brad said. "Rough last few weeks, even."

"You want a late lunch, or would you rather talk about it?"

"I'm not really very hungry right now. Maybe we could just talk?"

"Yeah, sure, c'mon back to the family room. It's cozier than the front living room." Drew led the way.

Brad knew leather furniture was actually very comfortable, but it looked cold in the living room, reflecting the light of the summer afternoon in a way that reminded him of ice. But the suede finish on the sofa and chairs in the family room looked more inviting, brown and comfy, and he launched himself onto the sofa without thinking. "Ooops," he said, blushing when the sofa jumped back a good six inches. He stood up in a hurry. "I'm sorry! That was really rude. That's why my dad keeps telling me to think before I act. That was—"

"Perfectly all right," Drew laughed. "At least I know you like it."

"Oh, yeah," Brad sighed, almost a moan, sinking back down. "It's so soft and comfy. I never want to get up again."

Drew looked at Brad in a way he couldn't interpret. "Then stay there. Water? Soda? More coffee?"

"Nah, I'm good." Brad added to himself, *Now that I'm here.*

"Yeah, you are." Drew smiled again. He sat down on the far end of the sofa on the small area not covered by a very large Brad. "So...about last night," he began.

"Aw, jeez, I was drunk," Brad groaned, throwing one arm over his eyes to hide behind it. "Just forget it, okay?"

Drew didn't say anything for the longest time, long enough that Brad hoped he'd win this round, that he'd be allowed to hide just a little bit longer. But Brad still felt Drew watching him, and he held his breath.

"You asked how I knew I was gay," Drew said at last. "Like I said last night, I've always known, I guess. Even as a little kid, I knew I was different in 'that way,' even if I didn't have a name for it. Some friends of mine, neighbor kids, a boy and a girl—he had *Playboy*, she had *Playgirl*. I liked *Playgirl*. There was no question which did it for me, even when I was that young. Later, someone defined 'gay' for me. I thought, *Oh, that's what I am*."

"Really? That young?" Brad pushed himself upright.

Drew nodded. "That young. I didn't know I was supposed to like girls. I knew gay was a bad thing to be. I received that message loud and clear." His voice grew hard. "I kept it hidden in high school until it became impossible to hide any longer."

"What happened?"

"I came out." Drew shrugged, looking uncomfortable. "I won't say I rubbed my family's faces in it, but I was pretty obvious about it, a peacock surrounded by pigeons. They didn't know what to make of me. Sometimes I think my older brother still doesn't know, but they came around. I know one thing, though."

"What's that?" Brad said, wary in the crosshairs of Drew's sharp look.

"My life is infinitely better for having done so. I have a relationship with my family, for one thing, and I wouldn't have if I hadn't come out. The more you hide, the more you have to hide." Drew searched Brad's face as he spoke.

"Oh," Brad said without meeting Drew's eyes. There was an opening if ever there was one, but he just couldn't. He felt like there'd been a moment last night where he might've told Drew what had weighed on his mind over the last several weeks, but he also knew that without the liquid courage, his mouth would stay clamped shut.

But his conflict wasn't so easily squashed. *This is what you wanted, and the man you want.*

But that's just it, he argued back. *The time's not right, it's not when you want him...it. Drew implied the time had to be right. It sure sounded like something was off when he came out, maybe something even forced him out, and he's still uptight about it even now.*

But then, as clearly as if Randall had been standing in the room with them, Brad heard his dad say, "You're a fuck-up, Bradley. The man's handing you the perfect moment, and you're screwing it up, just like crew. You let that kid take your moment from you, and you're throwing this one away. When are you going to be a man?"

"This is hard for me, okay?" Brad said softly.

"I know," Drew replied.

"So, you told them, your family I mean, and they just accepted it?" Brad was still unable to name it. "They accepted you?"

"Eventually, yes. There was some confusion and hurt feelings, but it was just because I'd been hiding it." At Brad's puzzled look, Drew explained, "I'd spent enough time hiding my true self that what I told them didn't make sense with what they'd seen and what they thought, despite the rather obvious signs. Once I explained things, once everything made sense again, yeah, my parents and brother were in my corner. The cross-country team took longer, but I was fast, and that helped."

"I never had that," Brad said softly.

"Had what? I didn't think you were out to your family... I mean, I assume you're gay or questioning."

Brad shrugged uncomfortably, still unwilling to say the words to Drew. "About anything, really. Sure, Mom was pretty understanding, but she's been gone for a while now."

"I'm sorry you never had that kind of acceptance," Drew said quietly.

"It's okay. Like I said, it's been a few years. It's only painful when the day of the accident rolls around."

Drew shook his head slowly. "That's not what I meant. Everyone needs understanding."

"I sure don't have that. I don't know what my dad's problem is, but nothing I do is ever good enough for him. It's like he got the son he wanted the first time, and once I came along, I was just in the way. He took one look at me and decided I annoyed him, and that was that.

"But it wasn't that bad, you know?" Brad continued. "I mean, I had Mom, Philip had Randall. I thought brothers were supposed to be close, but at some point, I guess we took sides too. But Mom's gone, and now... I'm not sure whether being Randall's favorite is such a great thing for him, you know? Our dad's kind of an asshole."

Drew didn't say anything.

"I might've mentioned this, but Morgan and I had a real rivalry going for a while," Brad continued.

Drew shook his head. "If Nick ever mentioned it, I've forgotten. How come?"

"Because I was the fastest guy on the crew until he showed up. I bumped one of the varsity men for a seat, and it seemed like I had nowhere to go but up." Brad shrugged. "But then Morgan did the same thing, and to a guy I'm not sure I could've beaten. Suddenly I had to fight to prove myself in the one place I'd found I wasn't compared to my brother. You know what Randall said when Morgan finally beat me at an indoor-rowing competition?"

"No, but I'm almost afraid to hear the answer."

"No kidding," Brad snorted. "'Well, that certainly didn't take long, Bradley.' Nice, huh? I don't know why I tried...try. I mean, it's like I'm slamming my head into a wall. It hurts like a motherfucker, but I just keep doing it, hoping the next time won't hurt. But it always does. It always hurts."

"I'm sorry," Drew whispered. He reached out a hand to Brad but stopped, clearly unsure if the touch would be welcomed.

"Something like this..." Brad shook his head. "I don't know. I just don't know."

"Then don't go there with your father yet, wherever you're going. Start small. Start with one person, just one person you know is in your corner, who won't judge or reject you," Drew said, eyes bright with unshed tears.

Brad frowned at Drew, weighing his words. He felt a sudden rush of gratitude that Drew was in his life. It was another benefit of crew. It occurred to him that even though he'd only known Drew as a vague presence at the fringe of the CalPac crew for a handful of months, he'd already become his closest friend. Sometimes you just knew about people.

He took a chance. "Can I... Will you just hold me?"

Drew nodded.

Brad scooted the rest of the way down the sofa and laid his head on Drew's lap, facing outwards, his back to Drew's front. He needed the comfort of contact but not the pressure of meeting Drew's eyes.

He closed his eyes and relaxed into Drew, just sagged, the tension slowly washing away as Drew first hesitated to hold him and then gently put one arm across Brad's chest. He hadn't been held in years, not since before his mother's death. He'd forgotten how it felt. But somehow being in

Drew's arms felt nothing like being held by his mother. This felt...like a safe port. Like calm water. Like something he could get used to, fast.

That scared him, but the need for contact outweighed the fear. He tried not to think about why he was cuddled up to a gay man, tried not to think about why being so close to Drew felt so good, tried not to think at all.

"Is this all right?" Drew said softly.

"Yeah," Brad breathed, sighing into Drew a little more. Drew felt so warm, so strong. Somehow, it felt like he would keep all his troubles away just by holding him. It was Brad's tamest contact with another person since he'd hit puberty, and at that moment, he couldn't imagine anything better. There, in Drew's arms, he relaxed for the first time in as long as he could remember.

Brad was scared. There was no two ways about it. His whole life, he'd seen himself as one thing—straight. Since puberty, he'd been all about getting into women's pants. And he'd enjoyed it. But there'd been no connection, no feeling beyond getting off. He'd just chalked talk of such things up to girl talk or soap operas or romance novels or wherever women got those ideas. But now he knew. In those few moments, he had already experienced a deeper connection to Drew than to any of the women he'd been with.

So, Brad made a decision. This? What he felt at that moment, he'd never felt this in a woman's arms. That had been about sex, but this was about so much more. About comfort, about security, about understanding, about trust... The flood of feelings made his head swim.

If this was what it was with Drew, then Brad wanted it. He wanted Drew. Whether that made him gay or bi or whatever, he just wasn't going to worry about it then. He couldn't, not in the face of these feelings.

The feeling of protected comfort turned to something else then. Something that shivered down his spine to settle in his belly, in his groin. Something hotter. He knew that feeling of slithery, anxious need. He had never expected to feel it with another guy.

Brad rolled over to look up at Drew, a serious expression creasing his brow, as if he were trying to determine whether or not this was right. But Brad didn't stop to think. He couldn't.

He sat up, pulling himself onto his knees next to Drew on the sofa. Still deadly serious, he leaned toward Drew, who was frozen in place. Head tilted, he did what he'd wanted to do on Friday. He gave in to the force pulling him toward Drew.

He kissed Drew, lips grazing lips. He gasped, his senses suddenly on high alert. It had never felt like that, lips against lips. He kissed Drew once more before pulling back again.

"Is...is this okay?" Brad whispered. He touched his tingling lips.

Drew nodded. "More than anything," he breathed.

Brad smiled faintly before leaning in again. Their lips touched and the electric feeling of that first kiss rushed back, stronger than before, zinging from his lips to his cock and making his whole body feel alive.

After a moment, he felt Drew move closer, kissing him back, but always letting him take the lead in exploring. Under Brad's guidance, the kisses deepened from short busses on the lips to longer, deeper contact that made his head spin with the newness of the old familiar action.

That Drew kissed him back with equal intensity, and the fact Drew was just as into it as he made it hotter. He knew how Drew's kisses affected him, and the thought that his did the same to Drew... He'd never felt such a rush.

Their bodies hummed together, increasingly in synch, sigh with sigh, moan with moan. Drew's every utterance and sound added fuel to Brad's fire. Without even knowing it had happened, Brad was rock hard.

Their kisses grew sloppier, more heated, and Brad let his hands start to explore, one hesitant hand on Drew's arm, another on his chest. The bicep beneath his hand was firm, bunching and flexing as Drew stroked him back. Drew's chest made his own tighten with the thrill of the hard muscles under his fingers. He thought of that woman from Friday night. In contrast to that encounter, this felt right. His mind flashed to other places where Drew would differ from whatshername, harder places. There was so much he wanted to explore and so much he was afraid to touch.

Drew raised his hand to cup Brad behind his head. Drew's touch made Brad shiver with all the wants he felt but couldn't name. He relaxed back into Drew's caress, his scalp ultrasensitive under Drew's hand.

Then—

Brad froze.

Up until now, Drew had let Brad take the lead, but when he felt Drew's tongue dart against his lips for a moment...

Drew pulled back. "I'm sorry—"

"That was—"

"I know, I shouldn't have—"

"Shut up, will ya?" Brad said. He attacked Drew's mouth with renewed vigor, tongue dueling tongue, sliding back and forth across sensitive, kiss-swollen lips, each stroke sending them higher. When Drew opened for him in surrender, taking his tongue in, Brad all but lost it, almost creaming his shorts right there.

He pushed Drew back on the sofa, the two of them sliding down until Brad had Drew pinned. He looked down at Drew, a big grin on his face. "Now this I like."

"Yeah, I'm helpless under you, you brute. What're you going to do with me?" Drew breathed, running his hands up and down Brad's broad, muscular back.

"This, I think," Brad said, angling in for more kissing.

Then Drew's hips started thrusting, and Brad felt another man's hard member pressing into him. Even with layers of fabric between them, that was all it could've been. A man's cock, a gay man's cock—

Brad froze for a moment, skeeved out and hornier than he'd ever been in his life.

He thrust back against Drew, groaning with the need of it. Hell yes, this was what he wanted, what he had to have. Drew was hard for him. He was hot for Drew. It was a perfect world.

I could make him come, Brad thought fleetingly. The knowledge rocked him as hard as he rocked against Drew's hips, thinking of hands and cocks and mouths and... His balls pulled tight against his body. The power was heady and awesome and pushed him closer and closer...

Brad pulled back, gasping for air.

"What's wrong?" Drew said, frowning at the withdrawal of contact.

"I don't know. This? I mean, I'm totally into you, into this, but it's just..."

"I know." Drew gazed into Brad's eyes. He smiled as his breathing slowly calmed. "Baby steps."

"Yeah, baby steps," Brad whispered, suddenly embarrassed. He rested his forehead on Drew's.

"Regrets?" Drew said, his heart in his eyes.

"No," Brad croaked, his voice cracking. "It's just that...this morning I was straight and right now I almost got off on a man. With a man, I mean."

"That doesn't have to mean you're gay, you know. A lot of guys experiment. That doesn't make you gay."

"No, listen. You don't understand. This isn't an experiment. I came over here because of you, for you." Brad's voice rose.

"It's okay, I get it," Drew said, still pinned beneath Brad.

"No, you don't." Brad was almost yelling now. He forced himself to calm down. "You don't, Drew. If you did, you'd know what you do to me, what you've been doing to me, ever since you first smiled at me at that regatta this spring. You'd know why I can't get you out of my head, and," he said softly, raising his head to look in Drew's eyes, "I don't want to."

"Then help me understand," Drew whispered, stroking Brad's back.

"I can't. I don't understand it myself. I just know..." Brad paused. "I know this isn't an experiment. You opened my eyes or changed me or something. Can't put the genie back in the bottle."

"Are you gay?"

"I...yes. No? I don't know," he groaned. "Do I have to have an answer?"

"No." Drew shook his head. "So where do we go from here?" He wiped a tear from Brad's cheek with his thumb.

"I don't know," Brad whispered, "but I want to find out."

Chapter Fourteen

Drew and Brad spent the rest of that Sunday exploring their new...whatever it was. Drew didn't delude himself into thinking it was a relationship. But they were more than friends, that much was clear. He knew there'd be a backlash, too, that the rubber band would snap back as the no-longer-straight Brad suffered the inevitable freak-out after spending an afternoon rolling around on the sofa with him. It was so much easier, Drew reflected, coming out early in life. The longer you waited, the harder it was.

Drew wasn't sure what to make of Brad's wanting to spend lots of time together in the evenings. New relationship? Escaping paternal influence? While it was Wednesday afternoon and he hadn't yet heard from Brad that day, they were already two for three this week. He told himself just to enjoy the ride, even if he had no idea where they were headed. But he knew where he wanted them to go.

Drew glanced at the clock on his desk. Four thirty-two. He should go home. He was done at the office, and he was the last one there. If he left, then the admin, Serena, could switch everything over to the answering service and pick her son up from daycare early.

Then his phone vibrated. *Free 2nite?* the text read. Drew smiled. Like he'd be anything else for Brad. *Heading home now. See U there?*

As soon as I'm done at Graveyard, I've got the oversight committee. After that?

I'll have food waiting for you, Drew wrote back, thinking about the way to a man's heart.

You're the best. L8r.

"Hey, Serena! Let's get out of here!" Drew called as he shoved files in his messenger bag. He just couldn't take the office any longer.

Drew fixed himself a snack when he got home before showering and then cooking a real meal. He wasn't sure how much Brad would want to eat that late, but he could always live off the leftovers for a day or two if Brad didn't eat anything.

Then he occupied himself with work. He'd landed three new sets of clients that morning, two selling and one buying, and market research awaited him. He doubted he'd get much done, but he had to do something and had too much work to do to justify watching television.

Brad's unmistakable pounding on the door jarred him out of his search for what houses comparable to his two new would-be sellers had sold for recently. That the county tax assessor's records were now online was a boon to him even if they held nothing but bad news for anyone trying to sell a home.

Drew glanced at his watch as he bounded to the door, now reinvigorated after a long day. It was almost 9:00 p.m., and he'd been in front of his computer for close to two very productive hours.

Drew opened the door. "Hey, I'm glad you made it."

Brad pushed in and shut the door behind him. "Of course, I made it. Why wouldn't I?" He looked at Drew for a moment with a shy smile.

"Hug?" Drew said, opening his arms.

Brad returned the hug awkwardly, relaxing into it after a moment's hesitation. It was obvious to Drew that Brad still struggled with his attraction for him. Drew allowed himself to savor the feeling of Brad's arms around him for a moment before releasing him.

"So how was your day?" Drew asked, pulling Brad along to the kitchen. "Are you hungry?"

"I should be, but no," Brad said, making a face. "I'm sorry. I know you made something, but between eating because I'm bored out there at Suburban Graveyard and a snack at the oversight committee, I don't have much appetite."

"Then I'll just get us something to drink, and you can tell me about your day," Drew suggested. He was struck by the incongruity of their situation. He wasn't even sure they were dating, but already they were falling into some kind of *Leave It to Beaver*-like pattern. So long as neither of them took it too seriously, it seemed harmless.

When he joined Brad in the family room on what had in three short days become their customary sofa, he saw that Brad had arrived at a similar conclusion. Brad reached for his glass of fizzy water with a smile. "Ah, the little woman. Where's my pipe?"

Drew's glare had stopped rogue drag queens cold, and it would've taken a stronger man than Brad not to flinch. "Uh...sorry."

"I hope you got that out of your system," Drew said in a low voice.

"It was just a joke." Brad hunched his shoulders defensively.

Drew sat next to Brad and turned to face him, one leg curled up under him. "Really? Where I come from, those're usually funny." Then he smiled to take the sting out of it.

"Thanks." Brad took the water. He met Drew's eyes but couldn't hold his gaze long.

"So," Drew said, "the committee meeting?"

"It's actually kind of interesting," Brad confessed. "When Pete Rancilman contacted me, he made it sound like the whole committee was at his back with torches and pitchforks or something and all of them out to get Nick."

"Yeah, I remember."

Brad scratched his head absently. "The funny thing is, I think it might just be Pete."

"No kidding?"

"Don't get me wrong, people are concerned about the 'Nick Situation'"—Brad set the words off with air quotes—"but Pete's the one who seems like he's out for Nick's balls."

"I'm sure Morgan will have something to say about that," Drew snorted.

"You don't know the half of it. I mean, the guy's going on about Coach Bedford preying on innocent undergrads... Clearly he's never met Morgan." Brad set down his empty glass.

"So how many hours did you have to spend listening to the details of this guy's witch hunt?"

"Not that long, thankfully. Everyone else was buzzing about how many people have already indicated an interest in crew," Brad said, inching close to Drew. "Even assuming half of those people ever show up in the first place, and half of them can hack it, it's still a huge increase."

Drew pretended not to notice. "Is this because of your big win this spring?"

"That'd be my guess. What this means for the oversight committee is coming up with the money for an assistant coach or two. Wonder who they'll find for that chore?"

"It's not much fun?"

Brad shook his head. "Think about it—you get to wake up dark and early, ride around in a launch when it's freezing cold in the morning or boiling hot in the afternoon, depending on the season, but you're the assistant, not the coach, so—"

"All the work, none of the glory?"

"And there's no payoff. The training plan and strategy are the primary coach's. If you're lucky, he'll consult you and let you in on his plans. If you're not, you're just a babysitter in a motorboat."

Drew looked at him shrewdly. "You miss it, don't you?"

"I think I do," Brad admitted. "I didn't know it until just now, but yes, I miss it."

"Maybe Nick'll ask you."

"Why would he do that? I don't know the first thing about coaching."

"Maybe not, but you know the sport and have a little time on your hands."

"Until that bid comes in." Brad elbowed Drew. "Listen to you, Mr. Optimistic."

Drew curled over protectively. "God, don't start tickling me."

But Brad wasn't listening. With a devilish grin, he moved in for the kill, going right for the sensitive spots.

"Just because you—" Drew gasped, swatting at Brad's hands. "Stop that. Just because you tickle me to distract me doesn't change the fact that you'd be a good assistant coach."

"Maybe," Brad muttered, "but it's not going to happen, so forget about it. The oversight committee has to approve hires, and besides, the money hasn't even been set aside yet."

"Okay, but consider this—the very fact you'd be willing to do it might make this oversight committee of yours more likely to agree to it in the first place, and could even reassure the committee that one of its own would be in a position to keep an eye on things for them," Drew suggested.

"I'd never spy on Coach Bedford for them!" Brad said, almost shouting.

Drew put his hands up. "I'm not saying you would, but they don't need to know that, now do they?"

"No, I guess not." Brad crossed his arms. "I just don't like the thought of spying or all this sneaking around."

"I know you don't." Even though Drew's heart was suddenly full of affection for Brad, the irony wasn't lost on him. "That's not who you are. It's one of the things I like about you."

Brad smiled at Drew and then looked away. He quickly looked back at Drew, blushing. "I like that you see that about me."

They looked at each other for a few more moments, and then Drew pulled Brad toward him. Brad sighed, resting his head on Drew's lap and closing his eyes, the tension leaving his body.

Drew closed his eyes, too, for just a moment, enjoying the feeling of Brad's head and shoulders on his lap. He was such a solid, reassuring presence, like his weight on Drew's legs meant he'd be in Drew's life for a while. Drew felt incredible tenderness at that moment, and he never wanted it to end. He tried not to think. He only wanted to experience that moment and that man.

Then Drew opened his eyes to see Brad looking up at him, a gentle expression on his face.

"Hi," Brad said softly. "What're you looking at?"

Drew blushed. "You."

"Good. I'd hate to think anything else could hold you."

"You have nothing to worry about." Drew smiled a goofy smile. He hated that, but Brad somehow just drew it out of him.

"Get down here. You look like you need to be kissed, and I know just the man for the job."

"Oh? And who would that be?"

Drew figured maybe he'd already been a bad influence on Brad when Brad rolled his eyes and pulled his head down, but then their lips met and drove the thought from his brain.

A few moments later, Drew straightened. "This is killing my neck."

"You're getting old," Brad taunted.

Drew stuck his tongue out.

"Nice," Brad said. He sat up and leaned in for another kiss.

Drew grabbed onto Brad and then pushed him over.

"Oooh, pushy," Brad breathed.

"Making out's easier if you're not crushing the air out of me, you big doofus," Drew said.

"Oh, you'll pay for that."

"Yeah, I'm terrified. Are you going to kiss me or what?"

And then Drew lost track of time, spellbound in near-total focus on the man underneath him. They kissed, and there was heat and wandering hands but none of the rolling around or threatened sex.

Drew kept going to play with Brad's hair...which had been almost completely shaved off. He made a frustrated noise.

Brad figured it out quickly. "I'll grow it out for you," he said softly. "If you want. There's probably enough left to make you happy."

"I'm good," Drew said.

"Yeah." Brad smiled. "You are."

Drew thought about what he was about to say for a moment. He didn't want to spoil the moment, but he couldn't avoid responsibility forever. He sat up and pulled Brad with him. Or tried, only tugging on one of Brad's arms.

"All right, all right, I'll sit up. I had no idea you were so pushy," Brad muttered.

"Technically, that was pulling," Drew said.

"I bet you're an expert puller...of something."

"Don't get all cocky on me."

"That was bad." Brad shook his head.

Drew shrugged. "So."

"So?" Brad echoed.

"So, are you ready to get to work on the renovation? I've got another one starting, and Nick's going back to school and coaching. He's agreed to stick around for the first few days of this one to help you learn the ropes, but he's pretty much over and out until next summer."

"Shit, are you kidding me?"

Drew shook his head. "Nope, this is a perfect time. If—when—we get the bid, you'll have some hands-on experience being in charge of these things. Even if we don't, it'll count as hands-on experience toward your contractor's license."

"I didn't think it'd be this soon," Brad said. "I don't know the first thing—"

"Isn't that the point of this? And don't give me that, that's your dad talking. I submitted our applications, remember? You know what you're doing, you just need that piece of paper to prove it to everyone else."

Brad started to retort and then clamped his mouth shut, thinking for a few moments. "I still think you picked the wrong guy."

"No." Drew shook his head. "I picked absolutely the right one."

Chapter Fifteen

Drew didn't waste any time, Brad thought, walking up to a house in a decent part of town. He knew it was the right place because it was a hive of activity in the afternoon heat, even though it was the first day of a new renovation job, even though it was a Thursday.

Brad had bailed on the sales office as soon as his replacement had arrived, and he'd allowed himself time to pick up a sandwich before heading over. He'd wolfed it down, but looking at his watch, he saw that he still had ten minutes before he was supposed to meet Nick. But Nick's car was already parked down the block, and Brad figured he'd better go in, since his former coach was back in school and back to coaching.

Brad got out of the car and stripped off his work shirt. He hadn't thought to bring jeans or carpenter's pants, so his chinos were going to take a beating. He pulled on a T-shirt as he headed up to the house.

"Hello?" he called, opening the door. He knew no one was home. He knew the only people there were Nick and, presumably, the crew he'd shortly be supervising, but it felt weird just walking in. He guessed he'd get used to it.

"Brad? That you?" called a voice he recognized as belonging to Nick Bedford.

"Yep, in the flesh!" Brad called back, pretending he wasn't nervous. That was stupid. Why should he be nervous around his old coach? Maybe because of what he'd been doing with his old coach's best friend.

Brad didn't think Nick could've changed in the few months since he'd last seen him, but somehow, he had. He wasn't taller or more buff or anything. Maybe a bit of a tan from time on the water. But there was something different about him. He was hotter, somehow.

And then Brad figured it out. Nick Bedford hadn't changed. Brad had. How had he never noticed his coach before?

"Coach!" he said, injecting a note of hail-fellow-well-met he suddenly didn't feel. He stuck out a hand. "How ya been?"

"Just fine," Nick said, shaking Brad's hand. He turned Brad's hand over. "Getting soft, aren't you?"

"I still erg," Brad said defensively. "Sometimes. Besides, I'll be roughing my hands up plenty here, it looks like."

"Yeah, there're certainly a lot of chances to cut your hands up in this line of work."

"No kidding. I've been working on my dad's job sites since I was in high school."

Nick shook his head. "I can't believe we went all those years of rowing without me figuring out you were from *that* Sundstrom family."

"Well, we can't help our relatives," Brad muttered, wishing he could do just that. "Did you hear they put me on the oversight committee because of that boat Dad donated?"

"Drew told me."

And there it was.

Brad didn't know how much Nick knew, but Brad had certainly pestered Morgan enough, and he just assumed boyfriends told each other things. Drew had also told Brad how much he'd gotten after Nick for Brad's digits, so there was all kinds of room for gossip and misinformation.

"Right, so you're going to show me around, introduce me to how Drew likes things done," Brad said. Wait...was that a sex joke? As soon as the words left his mouth, he regretted them.

"Right." Nick coughed, and Brad figured he was just as uncomfortable. He held up a somewhat battered three-ring binder. "This here is 'The Binder,' and it's basically Drew's brains for any given job."

"Same binder for all jobs?" Brad asked, grateful Nick had said nothing more about his slip-up.

"Nope, one binder per job, name on the spine." He held it up to show Brad the homeowners' name on it. "But Drew's only just now growing, so it hasn't really come up before," Nick said. Then he froze.

Nick met Brad's eyes.

Then they burst out laughing, the tension broken.

"Thank God you did it," Brad said.

"Couldn't play it straight any longer?" Nick had a wicked gleam in his eye.

"Oh, you're bad." Brad shook his head ruefully. "You should be ashamed of yourself."

"I really should, but I guess Morgan's rubbed off on me."

Brad stared at Nick, trying to figure out if that was another joke, but Nick was all wide-eyed innocence. "I think," he said carefully, "that it's just as well I didn't know this side of you before."

"Touché," Nick said.

"Is that French?" Brad asked.

Nick nodded. "Yeah, for 'Drew wants to touch your monkey.' Or you his. It could go either way."

"Oh, you're so going to get it now." Brad cast his hesitancy around his former coach aside and advanced on Nick.

"No, only when Morgan gets home from school." Nick smirked.

Brad feinted and Nick dodged, but Brad was better at this, and grabbed Nick in a headlock. Nick was laughing too hard to mount a serious resistance, so Brad was able to noogie him with ease.

"Okay, I give up! Stop!" Nick laughed.

Grinning, Brad let him go. "There's more where that came from, and don't you forget it."

"Yes, sir!" Nick said, saluting him with the binder in his hand.

Brad felt a lot better suddenly. Then, as Nick watched him closely, he realized what his former coach had done. "Wow, you're really good, you know that?"

"That's what Morgan said the first time too."

"I so did not just hear that. Seriously, thank you."

"Think you can bring yourself to call me Nick?"

Brad nodded. "Yeah, I think I can manage that."

"So," Nick said, brandishing the binder, "don't let me forget to give this to you before I leave. It's got everything you need to know, from which subs Drew's working with to the master schedule to worker's comp insurance to the contact info for your workers, all indexed by tabs. And there's a section with drawings about what the finished rooms should look like, in this case Drew's, but sometimes he works with designers."

"I've met Emily Schoenwald. Actually, we'll be working with her on the Bayard project, if we get it," Brad said.

"That's great. She's the one he works with almost exclusively. There'll be a workflow chart in the garage as well, just in case."

"The garage? This must be a pretty thorough job."

Nick nodded. "They're not quite gutting it, but a lot of rooms are going down to the studs. That's another thing that's in there—abatements of various kinds and how to be nicer to the neighbors. That's one thing Drew tries hard to do. He even gives the houses on either side and the back his card in case there are problems."

"That's really decent of him," Brad said, thinking of some of the jobs he'd seen. Randall didn't care whose driveway he blocked or whose lawn he killed or who he pissed off with early hours and lots of dust.

"That's Drew St. Charles," Nick said.

It warmed Brad that he knew exactly what Nick meant by that. "I'll do my best to make sure that doesn't change. So...the work crew."

"Right, they're back here." Nick gestured for Brad to follow. "They're starting in on the kitchen and then the bathrooms so—"

"That we can be ready for the subs. I know how this works."

Nick shook his head ruefully. "Sundstrom Homes. Right. There's a reason Drew hired you."

"I guess so." Brad suddenly got what Drew had been telling him all along. He had something to contribute to the operation if they were successful in their bid on the mayor's mansion.

"So, come meet Octavio Perez-Nolan and the guys," Nick said.

A middle-aged man looked up as they entered. He was on the short side, with silver frosting at the temples of his otherwise dark hair. He glared at them with coal-black eyes under bushy beetle brows.

"Don't worry about him," Nick whispered. "He hates everyone."

Then Octavio's face lit up. "You must be Brad Sundstrom! I'm so happy to meet you!" Octavio said, pumping Brad's arm. "Come meet the guys. They don't speak much English, but if they don't understand you, they'll come get me."

Brad cast a startled glace over his shoulder at the nonplussed Nick, but Octavio paid them no mind as he introduced Brad to the handful of guys who worked for Drew's renovation firm.

"If Mr. St. Charles gets that big project he's bidding on, you're going to need to hire some guys. Will you do me a favor and let me meet them before you hire them? I want to make sure they're not dicks."

"Yeah, sure, okay," Brad said, bewildered. He looked at Nick, who just shrugged. "But if you don't mind me asking, how come... I mean, you're not upset that I've got this job?"

"Oh hell no, son," Octavio said. "I spent fifteen years in retail management. I got into this line of work so I could get away from that and make something useful, something enduring, not herd people around so they could. It's bad enough that Mr. St. Charles made me the work crew leader. I guess I'll be your deputy once you hire more people, but any more than that and I'll quit, and Mr. St. Charles knows that."

"Okay, then, good to know," Brad said, still somewhat confused by it all.

Octavio clapped him on the shoulders. "You'll be fine, son. This is Felipe Sandoval, and..."

Five minutes later, after meeting the men who were now working for him, Brad rejoined Nick. "I thought you said he hated people," Brad said.

"Yeah, that was different," Nick said. "But he was right about one thing. If Drew gets this bid, you'll need a lot more people. He can help, even if, as he made clear, you'll be in charge of that."

"I guess I'd better stop by Home Depot," Brad quipped.

Nick stopped and put a hand on Brad's arm. "I know you were kidding about picking up undocumented day laborers, but don't forget that the mayor's mansion will be in the public spotlight. Just assume someone's peering over your shoulder to see if you're spending one dime too much or cutting any corners. Do everything the right way and by the book, no matter how long it takes. So, check Social Security numbers or even immigration status if you have to. Don't do anything to embarrass yourself—or Drew. He's counting on you."

"I know," Brad said softly, aware in a way Nick might not know just how true that was. He was young and didn't have a contractor's license. Working for Drew on simple flips and renovations was a big enough step, let alone that potential job saving the Bayard House from termites and dry rot.

Brad followed Nick through the remodel while Nick showed him how Drew liked things done. Most of it was pretty standard, Brad thought, different from what he'd learned at his dad's feet only insofar as Drew tried to keep his clients and those around them from suffering too much during a remodel.

But there he was, standing in a bedroom, once again coached by Nick Bedford, and never mind the earlier reassurance. "Déjà vu all over again," Brad said. At Nick's quizzical look, he explained, "It's just like crew... You're showing me how to do things."

Nick smiled. "Perhaps, but this time, you know a lot about it, maybe more than I do." He thought for a moment. "But then, by the time you finished your last race...let's just say you know more than you think you do about rowing too."

"Says the man with a what? A USRowing level two certificate?"

"Said the man working toward a contractor's license," Nick parried. "Seriously, man, have a little faith in yourself."

Brad hunched his shoulders uncomfortably. "That's not always easy to do."

"Don't I know it," Nick sighed. "Let's head out to the garage. I'll show you the work plan out there, and then that'll be that. You'll be in charge."

"Scary thought," Brad said.

"Hey now, none of that," Drew called from the doorway.

"What're you doing here?" Nick said.

"Uh...I'm the boss, remember?" Drew said.

Nick rolled his eyes. "I thought you were showing houses this afternoon."

"I was," Drew said, shrugging, "but something came up for some of my clients, and I've got a few hours free. I thought I'd come take pictures for my portfolio. Emily's too. Also, *Sunset* loves 'before and after' spreads, so maybe I'll get lucky and get a spread."

With that, the loaded joking with Nick rushed back like the tide. Brad looked at Drew and suddenly felt very hot in a way that had nothing to do with the summer afternoon. At that moment, he wanted nothing more than to push Drew up against the nearest wall and maul him. He didn't think about why or what it meant, he just wanted.

He caught Drew's eye, and Drew gasped softly. Drew knew.

Nick looked back and forth between them and smirked.

"You told him?" Brad said.

Drew shook his head, frowning. "No, he seems to have figured it out for himself. You didn't actually think he was stupid, did you?"

"No, but I'd hoped maybe Morgan kept him tired enough he wouldn't have noticed right away. Damn. That's kind of spooky," Brad said.

"Do you want me to leave so you can talk about me?" Nick said.

"I don't have anything to say to Brad that I wouldn't say in front of you," Drew said.

"I was hoping maybe you'd learned some discretion," Nick said.

Brad got a sly look on his face. If Nick was so shockable, he'd give him something to be shocked by. As he had several times on Drew's couch, Brad moved in on Drew and started tickling him.

Drew flashed momentary ire and batted Brad's hand away, but his temper was there and gone so fast Brad wasn't sure what he'd seen.

Brad grabbed Drew by the waist and pulled him in for a sloppy kiss. "Sorry, babe, I didn't mean anything by it."

"Okay, I didn't need to see that," Nick said. He handed Brad the binder and then checked his watch. "Just look at the time. Gotta run. And boys? I know there's a bed left in one of the rooms, but it's really bad form to use a client's home for something like that."

Nick left, but Brad ignored him. He knew that look on Drew's face, a look that said he was in trouble because Drew was unhappy. "I'm really sorry—"

"Can you *please* stop tickling me?" Drew said quietly. "It bothers me more than I realized."

"I don't mean anything by it," Brad said.

"You do." Drew sounded pained. "Every time you kiss me, you tickle me first. I'm done with it."

"Aw, babe, don't be sad—" Brad started to say. Where he'd been hot moments ago, he now felt cold all over. He hated it when people were mad at him, and now that Drew was mad *and* hurt...

Drew cut him off. "Don't 'aw, babe' me. I get that this is new for you, that you're grappling with feelings you never thought you'd have, but you need to face the fact that you're in a...whatever this is with another man. Stop hiding behind the tickling because I'm tired of it."

"I'm not hiding behind the tickling," Brad scoffed. "What're you talking about?"

"Oh really? You start out tickling me, and only then do you kiss me, like you're surprised you're doing it. 'Hey, look at that! I was tickling you, and it just happened! Again!' Uh-uh. You want to kiss me—and for the record, I like it when you kiss me—just kiss me. No hiding, no pretending, none of this tickling bullshit."

"I had no idea you didn't like that. I thought it was just fun," Brad said softly.

"It may have been." Drew looked Brad in the eyes for the first time since the tickling started. "For you. For me? Not so much. For the record, there are times when I like being held down by a much bigger man, but not like that."

Brad looked at him, momentarily confused. Then he got it. "Oh. Oh! I...well. I'm sorry. I won't do it again." He hesitated. "Can I kiss you now?"

Drew couldn't shove his camera in his pocket fast enough. "Please."

Brad smiled and held out his arms and Drew rushed into them. The sight of Drew made his heart beat faster, but the feeling of Drew in his arms? Holding him against his chest while they kissed? That was going to make his head explode, he was sure of it.

Drew's lips, soft and slick with lip balm, slid against Brad's in a way that made him tingle like he'd been shocked. Kissing a woman had never felt like this, and kissing a man was so new he could do nothing but explore the sensation for a few moments. When they were apart, whenever he freaked about what they were doing, remembering this feeling brought him back.

Brad leaned back against the wall, pulling Drew with him and supporting his weight. This just felt right, Drew against him, one leg between his legs, lips pressed to his, his tongue oh-so-politely asking entrance. Brad stroked his tongue back against Drew's, and Drew opened for him.

Brad still took his cues from Drew. His experience was with women, and he wasn't sure what transferred. So, when Drew nipped at his lips in between kisses, he moaned. It was familiar, but new and different.

So, Brad nipped back. He needed to be shown what a guy liked, and when a guy—his guy—showed him the way, he took it.

"Yeah," Drew breathed.

"You like that?"

"Uh-huh."

Brad liked to do what his guy liked. The kisses grew heated, plundering, and Brad knew he was hard even without Drew rocking against him, hip to hip, cock to cock. The desire, the rough wanting, the need to grind into Drew made him dizzy.

It made him think of what else they could be doing with those cocks, where else they could be besides trapped behind pants and underwear. He thought about Drew's lips wrapped around his dick as Drew sucked him. As he fucked into that hot and willing hole.

Then Brad felt Drew's stubble, already growing in from his morning shave, press into his lips as he expanded operations, kissing and nibbling around Drew's lips and down his chin. Drew had a nice chin, a prominent chin, a bitable chin, one made for rough kisses.

Like the other times they'd made out, the stubble surprised Brad at first, another reminder he was kissing a man, but just then, it hit. Hard. Stubble. His guy. His *guy*. He was making out with a man. That meant he was....

Brad stopped, resting his forehead on Drew's, really on Drew's head as he was so much taller.

When Drew moved for his lips, Brad said, "I'm sorry."

Drew pulled back a little. "For what? What's wrong?"

"I'm sorry," Brad repeated, whispering. "It's just...weird, sometimes."

"Weird?" Brad could tell Drew was hurt.

"Not bad weird...just weird. Different, I guess. I never thought—" Brad caught himself before he could say he never thought he'd feel this way about another person, but he wasn't ready to go there yet. He took a breath and tried again. "You weren't wrong earlier. This is hard for me. Dude, you're a *dude*. I'm a dude. We're kissing."

"Or we were," Drew said, pulling back a little to look in Brad's eyes.

"I mean, if I'd knocked up the last woman I did, she probably wouldn't even be showing, okay?"

Drew winced. "So not a visual I needed."

"Sorry," Brad chuckled weakly, "but it's the truth."

"What did it this time?" Drew asked.

"Stubble," Brad confessed.

"I can shave more often."

Brad shook his head. "No. I don't want you to. It's different from anyone I've ever been with. It's one of the things I like."

"But you stopped kissing me," Drew pointed out.

"It was a little weird right then," Brad said defensively. "I didn't say I hated it. It reminds me you're you, that you're a guy. Just because it's new doesn't mean I'm not into it." Brad kissed him again. "Or you. Sometimes, for a while anyway, it's gonna be hard for me."

Drew reached down, the first time he'd grabbed Brad's cock so boldly. "Speaking of hard."

Brad groaned. He slumped against the wall, his eyes closed. "You just...you do something to me."

Drew captured his lips, and he surrendered them willingly. "Not nearly what I want to do," he breathed.

"Yeah? What'd you want to do?" Brad said, panting as Drew sucked on his neck.

"Promise you won't freak out?" Drew palmed Brad through his pants. "My cock, your mouth; your cock, my ass."

Brad's mouth went dry. Fuck. That was what Drew wanted. He wanted to fuck. On the one hand, Brad really liked what Drew was doing to him through his pants and would bet good money the man had even better ideas when they were naked.

But that meant sex. With another man. Not making out with a guy, fucking him. That was the final nail in the hetero coffin, wasn't it? He couldn't pretend to be straight anymore, because if he were honest with himself, he'd have to admit that since Drew, he hadn't looked at a woman with anything resembling desire.

"It's okay, Brad," Drew said, reading his silence. He kissed Brad gently on the cheek. "That's just what I dream of. I'm fine with the way things are. I get that there's a difference between making out and a cock in your mouth."

Brad coughed. "Yeah."

"I can wait."

Brad didn't know what to say, so he kissed him again.

But when Drew said, "My cock, your mouth"? His throat might've gone dry, but his mouth started to water. He wanted it. He wanted Drew's cock. He didn't know quite what to do with it, but that was changing.

Chapter Sixteen

Drew liked to work out, and he liked to stay fit. Sure, he knew he looked good, even hot in his better moments, but the habit of physical fitness he'd picked up as an undergraduate when he ran cross-country team persisted. Since he'd graduated, he'd become a bit of a gym rat. His full-service gym allowed him to work out around his other commitments but still keep fitness a priority. But every once in a while, he just had to get outside. Sometimes he biked, sometimes he swam, and sometimes, when the weather wasn't too terribly hot, like that September afternoon, he ran.

Running allowed him to think without needing to focus too hard on what he was doing. It was one foot in front of the other over and over again, and it freed his mind. He needed to think that afternoon.

He and Brad had settled into a steady routine after that afternoon at their latest reno. At times, he marveled that it was "their" latest anything. But sure enough, he and Brad had thus far made a go of it. He knew not to get too far ahead of himself.

And not just professionally. What he hadn't told Nick when he'd badgered him so relentlessly for Brad's contact information was that in his fantasy world, his business partner would be his life partner too. Drew would sell houses and his partner would renovate them. They'd work in the same industry, but not right on top of each other.

They'd save that for after hours. It struck Drew as the best of both worlds.

And that was what brought Drew to the trails along the American River rather than the treadmills at the gym. He liked Brad. A lot. Available evidence suggested Brad liked him too. After all, Brad was coming out of the closet. They'd made out hot and heavy a number of times, and if it had been someone else, Drew knew they'd have fucked by now.

That they hadn't was a testimony to Drew's patience. He knew he could've had Brad naked and begging that first afternoon on his couch, but seduction under such circumstances would've bordered on abusive. That wasn't who he wanted to be, and if he'd given in, he'd have lost the man who gave him those shy, sweet smiles after his races. He'd have lost the fun he'd already had with Brad, the pleasure in just being around him. No quick fuck was worth that.

Drew thought as he pounded the pavement that he and Brad could be more, and that was why he was so patient. He'd had plenty of sex. He'd never had the "more" with anyone. He wanted the more with Brad. He wanted to fuck him and love him both.

He'd started this venture with the plan of luring Brad out of the closet, but it had already turned into more than he'd originally planned. He knew if he took his time and, more importantly, allowed Brad to take his own time, that he stood a good chance of realizing his whole dream of a business partner who could also be his husband. If he was patient for a while, he'd get what he wanted—Brad's car in his garage and his cock up his ass. If he pushed, he'd scare Brad off.

Drew stumbled as he realized that in some ways, he already had the more. Not all of it, not even most of it, but more than he'd ever had before. He really cared for Brad, cared for him in a way that he'd only ever felt about one other person, and he and Nick just hadn't been right for each other. They might've made it work after a fashion, but in hindsight and from watching Nick with Morgan, Drew understood that if they'd forced it, Nick would've missed out on the much better thing he had with Morgan, and he...well, his happily ever after was still up in the air.

But Drew didn't mind. He could be patient or at least try. He knew that was what people did when they loved someone. He'd do his best to wait. Brad was worth it.

It was Saturday night, just eight days after Brad had started working for Drew. While he knew the job, being in charge of it was unfamiliar territory, and he was still nervous every afternoon when he headed over to the job site after putting in a morning at that stupid subdivision.

But he'd deal. The cash flow was less than he was used to, but then he didn't have many expenses to begin with, since he drove an old beater, even if it was a Lexus, and he still lived at home.

More and more, Brad worked for the weekends, because that was when he saw Drew. Sure, Drew dropped by the flip whenever he could, but despite Drew's weekend work schedule, they still had Saturday and Sunday nights. They hadn't been going out very long, but already they had a pattern. Brad liked patterns. They made life simpler. They'd grab some dinner and then head back to Drew's place for some sofa time. Brad liked sofa time.

Actually, Brad realized, feeling more than a little guilty about it, they didn't go *out* much at all.

Like that night. Brad met Drew at his place. Drew drove them to a restaurant, and now they were heading back to Drew's house. Other than the act of eating, they hadn't really gone out. No movies. No more games, not since that first one Randall had grudgingly given him the tickets for, no nothing.

Brad was kind of ashamed to admit it, but he was nervous being seen in public with a gay man. But smart enough to realize it was about him, not Drew. Drew was who he was, and that was one of the things he liked about Drew. Drew didn't pretend. He was out there, living his life.

Brad was still trying to figure out what his own life was, but he was increasingly aware that he was more like Drew than he was like the friends he'd had at CalPac. But it still made him uncomfortable. He just couldn't wrap his mind around the g-word, not yet, not applied to himself. Drew was gay. Dogs and cats knew Drew was gay.

Brad knew he was gay, or least inclined in that direction. His cock told him so every time he saw Drew. Every time he kissed Drew, it stood at attention as if to salute and say, "Ready for action, sir!"

That was where they were heading. Sex. With a man. With Drew. But Brad just couldn't, not yet. Not for what it meant.

Brad could already tell that where Drew was concerned, there would be no experimenting. Sex with Drew would change him. He wasn't ready for that change. Every time he thought about it, he recoiled. He didn't like all this thinking.

But Drew'd been so patient, never once pushing him. He—

"You're awfully quiet over there," Drew said from the driver's seat. "Everything okay?"

Brad looked over at him and grinned. This man, this suave, handsome, sophisticated man, thought he was worth the time of day. "Yeah, I'm fine. Just thinking."

"About what?" Drew asked.

"Kissing you," Brad said, because there was no way he could say any of this to Drew when he could barely articulate it to himself.

They stopped at a light, and Brad leaned over. He gave Drew a quick peck on the cheek. "Mission accomplished!"

Drew shook his head. "You aren't even remotely done kissing me tonight."

That made Brad warm all over. "Good," he said softly.

And before much longer, they'd turned onto Drew's street and pulled into the garage.

Brad followed Drew closely into the house. After that first afternoon at the reno, after Nick had fled and they'd almost gone too far, he had an idea of what his guy might like. To make up for not being brave enough to do more in public than eat out, he planned to give it to him, at least a little.

As soon as the door into the house shut behind him, Brad grabbed Drew before he could get out of reach.

"Wha—"

Brad shut that off by pressing his mouth over Drew's. Then he pushed Drew up against the door. He might be new to guys, but he knew how to be dominant. Some things just came naturally.

Drew's hands came to his back, rubbing him slowly through his shirt. Brad liked that, but he liked the sounds Drew made as he kissed him roughly better. Not quite whimpers, they were needy, wanting sounds.

Brad smiled into the kiss. He'd found one of Drew's buttons, and the sound of pushing it went right to his own cock. He kissed Drew in a way he'd never let himself before: demanding, greedy, hungry.

He held Drew pinned against the door, kissing along Drew's jaw, and the stubble that had broken the moment a week ago just made him hotter, each bristle a goad.

When he reached his neck, Brad yanked the collar of Drew's shirt open. He kissed until he found the pulse point and then sucked. Hard. "Brad," Drew whispered.

"Too much? Do you want me to stop?"

"God, no," Drew gasped.

Drew's knees started to buckle, but Brad had other ideas. He stood back, turned Drew around, and pushed him up against the door. Drew gasped and then moaned, low and needy, thrusting his ass back against Brad's crotch.

"You like that, huh?" Brad breathed in his ear.

"Uh-huh," Drew squeaked.

Brad grabbed Drew's hands and held them over his head with one big paw, leaving his other hand free to maraud around to Drew's front. He grasped Drew around his belly, fingers pulling his shirt out of his pants.

When Brad got his free hand up under Drew's shirt, feeling the skin hot and smooth over his muscled abs, he moaned himself. "Damn, Drew. You feel...damn."

Then Brad pressed his weight against Drew's back, harder than granite himself, feeling the slip and slide of his denim-enclosed erection over the back of Drew's denim-covered butt. He had to bend his legs a little, but he found his cock fit quite nicely between Drew's ass cheeks. He shifted back and forth, rubbing across Drew's backside. The sensation was intense. His head swam from the speed of the lust rising in his blood.

Part of Brad's mind thought this felt awfully like sex, but he shoved that part out of the way and kept rocking into Drew.

Drew pushed back into him, every bit as into it as Brad. "Please," he breathed.

"Please what?" Brad rasped. He blinked several times and shook his head to clear it. "Tell me what you need."

Drew didn't say anything, and then Brad smirked. He'd robbed his guy of the power of speech. He raised his free hand to hold Drew pinned.

On impulse, Brad bit his way down Drew's neck from behind as Drew leaned his head away for better access, his breath coming in shallow gasps. Where the neck met the shoulder, Brad stopped to suck. To mark. He pulled Drew's skin into his mouth, rolling it between his teeth, sucking hard.

"Do it," Drew breathed. "Mark me."

"Want me to claim you? Show you're mine?" Brad grunted out.

His efforts would leave a hickey. He wanted there to be a sign on Drew's neck that he'd been there, even if only he and Drew knew it. But Drew'd see it every time he got dressed for a while. *You're mine*, he thought, not sure he could say it aloud, not sure if Drew felt the same. *You're mine and no one else's.*

As a blissed-out Drew approached dead weight, Brad's arms reached their limits. He put one arm around Drew's chest to support him as he backed away. "I've got you, don't worry."

Drew looked at him, his eyes dilated with desire. "Yes, you do," he said thickly.

"Couch?" Brad said.

Drew stood up. "Oh, yeah."

Drew pulled Brad to the long comfy sofa in the family room, the one that seemed to be the scene for all their making out. "Where were we?" he said, pushing Brad onto the sofa and then climbing on top of him.

"I think I was making you forget how to talk. Someone likes being shoved up against a wall."

"Maybe we can do that again sometime." Drew moved in for a kiss.

Brad met his kiss, and soon Drew's tongue probed at his mouth, and he opened eagerly. It'd only been a few short minutes, but he longed to taste Drew again. The feeling, the closeness, of him started a tingle in his lips that raced south and made him long for more intimate contact.

He needed to feel Drew, not just hold him. He ran his hands under Drew's shirt, thrilling to the touch of another man's muscled back. He'd seen the strong lats that tapered to a trim waist; now he traced those contours with his hands, digging the feel of skin over muscle. The women he'd been with had always lacked this hardness, and the rightness of it blew him away.

Then Brad grew braver. When he ran his hands down Drew's back, he didn't stop at the waist. He worked his hands into Drew's pants to cup that fine, fine ass in his hands. The jock in him knew what it took to get that kind of muscle in the glutes. But the horndog was the one in the driver's seat just then, and he loved the way it felt to hold an ass cheek in each hand, kneading and grasping. Drew seemed to like it, too, based on the noises he made.

That made it so right, so natural to pull Drew down and into him, to guide his hard cock into his own, their clothes in the way. Each grind stoked him higher and hotter.

Then Drew pulled back, eyes dark with lust.

"What's wrong?" Brad said.

"You're not ready for sex with a man, and I'm close. You make me lose control, and I like that, but you're not ready for it."

"I'm sorry," Brad whispered.

"Don't be."

"It just seems like such a huge step," Brad said, cooling and ashamed. He looked into Drew's eyes, but then his glance darted nervously away. "I'm sorry. I...I don't know if I can. Right now, I mean."

"It's okay. Really."

But Brad still felt terrible. "I feel like I'm letting you down, or I'm telling you you're not good enough or something when I don't mean that at all. I don't feel like I'm ready for sex with a man, but I really like the things we do, and I like the way you make me feel." He looked up at Drew. "Does that make sense?"

Drew nodded. "It's a big step. You've got feelings you never thought you'd have for another man, and you're doing things you'd never thought you'd do with another man. You're not giving yourself credit for how far you've come and how quickly. We just started going out, what? A month ago?"

"Yeah, but I started noticing how cute and sweet you are this spring when you were coming to all the regattas with Nick," Brad confessed. "The way you helped with the oars, even though you had no idea how to carry them, and then seeing you waiting for me on the beach at Lake

Natoma? That meant a lot to me. So, it's been more than a month, at least for me."

"Okay, but still. You're twenty-two, right? In less than a year, you've gone from being a heterosexual big lug to rolling around on the sofa with me. I'd say that's pretty significant."

"I am not," Brad said, "a big lug."

Drew grinned at him. "I happen to like big lug. I think it's hot. I think you're hot."

"You think I'm hot?"

"You have no idea," Drew breathed.

Brad looked sly. "Maybe you could...uh, tell me more about that?"

Drew, still laying on top of Brad, sat up so he was effectively sitting on his crotch, a fact not lost on either of them. "You first caught my eye at that disastrous race early in the spring, what were they called? It was the one that was so stormy and the crew's nerve broke or something."

"The WIRAs," Brad groaned. "The Western Intercollegiate Rowing Association's spring regatta. I can't believe you remember that. Not our finest moment as a crew, and not mine as a rower."

"You puked as soon as the race was over." Drew grinned.

"I can't believe you remember that," Brad groaned.

"Something about you that morning caught my attention," Drew mused. "You were—are—so handsome, so masculine, I wanted to climb you like a tree. Still do." He held up a hand to head off Brad's self-recrimination. "When you're ready. But when you smiled at me? Oh, man."

"That's funny. That was when I first really noticed you too. I didn't know what it meant, but by the last race of the season, somehow, I needed you there. And afterwards? After we eked out that win? I didn't relax until I saw you standing next to Nick as we came back in. You have no idea," he said, pulling Drew down to kiss him quickly, "how much that meant to me. In my whole life, no one had ever been there for me."

"I was."

"I know, and I think it was that moment—" Brad started to say, but then he stopped. He was about to say, *It was in that moment when I knew my heart was yours. I didn't know it at the time, but it was.* But he couldn't say that right now. It was too much, too soon. "I...uh, it was that day I knew I needed to know you better, to find out if this... I'm," he swallowed, "gay."

Drew kissed him. "And what'd you think?"

"I think I need to kiss you some more," Brad said, dodging the question.

"Oh, good."

The kisses, which weren't all that chaste to begin with, quickly regained their fire and urgency. Brad loved the feeling of Drew on top of him. He could just let go and feel without worrying about whether he was too heavy for Drew to handle, like he would if their positions were reversed.

He craned his head and kissed the man he was coming to feel so strongly for, strongly enough it scared him. Drew took the invitation and gnawed his way down Brad's jawline to fasten on his neck, and Brad knew he'd have a mark to match the one he'd given Drew earlier. The thought of Drew staking a claim like that went right to his already hard cock, and he thrust up into Drew.

Drew groaned and rocked his hips back against him, and damn, didn't that just make it hotter? The rush blew Brad away. Its intensity blotted out all his thinking, carrying his worries and fears away on a rising tide of emotion and lust. He knew he'd never get enough of the man who made him feel that way.

Then Brad looked up, thunderstruck. "Oh shit!" he gasped as his eyes rolled up and shudders racked his body. The burn of pleasure on his cock lanced out to engulf his entire body. Out of nowhere, his climax smashed into him like planets colliding, like suns exploding behind his eyes.

"Brad! What's wrong!"

Brad pulled away. "Oh my God," he muttered, disgusted with himself but still riding the wave front of pleasure as the most intense orgasm he could remember slowly faded away. "I can't believe I did that."

Drew, a little dazed from his own pleasure, simply rested on Brad's muscled chest, working his arms around the man under him. Brad tried to push him off, but Drew held on tightly. "No, just tell me," he said.

Brad turned his head to bury his face in the sofa cushions. "This is just...oh, jeez, this is so embarrassing. I just came in my pants, okay?"

"Yeah, it's okay. It happens."

"To horny teenagers in the back seats of cars," Brad groaned, his voice muffled by the cushions he used to hide his embarrassment.

"You were really turned on. Your body knows what it likes," Drew said gently. He sat up and then, with a certain amount of effort, pulled Brad up to sit next to him.

"Yeah, it does." Brad looked at Drew, his eyes dark, unreadable. "I feel pretty stupid right about now."

"I can tell, but I can't figure out why." Drew turned to face Brad and pulled his legs up under him so that he knelt before the mortified man.

"I keep going on about not being ready for sex with a man, and then I blow a load in my underwear while making out with a man. With you."

"When you're ready, you'll be ready. There's no rush."

"Dude, I've got a load of jizz cooling in my pants because I can't get enough of you. I just keep overthinking this." Then Brad snorted. "Me. Overthinking things. Who'd believe a big oaf like me would think too much?"

"I would. Anyone who really knows you would."

Brad looked at him with a soft and tender look. "Then that'd only be you," he whispered. "Somehow, and just this summer, you've really worked your way in."

"You too," Drew said, his voice barely audible.

"So where do we go from here?"

"You'll know when it's time, and something tells me you'll let me know." Drew smiled at him.

Brad hesitated. "Maybe...maybe I could spend the night sometime?"

"That'd be nice."

"Next weekend?" Brad asked.

Drew smiled. "I'd like that a lot." He caressed Brad's cheek. "But no sex. I want there to be no pressure. We're just cuddling."

"I..." Brad exhaled. "I want to have sex with you. Officially, I mean. I want us to be together. As boyfriends."

"I like that even more, but even if we just spend the night cuddling in our underwear, it'll be fine because it'll be you."

"If we spend the night cuddling in our underwear, I'll have blue balls for sure," Brad growled. "You don't know what you do to me."

Drew reached down to Brad's pants, running his hand over the dark spot on the front of his jeans. "Oh, I think I do."

Brad groaned and felt stupid all over again. He tried to hide once more, but Drew caught his chin. "Hey, none of that. Not here. Not with me. There's nothing to be embarrassed about. There's no shame in it."

"I just feel—"

"I know," Drew said, quieting Brad with a finger over his lips, "but you don't have to."

"You've had the patience of a saint. You—"

"I'm definitely ready, but it has to be right. For both of us."

"It will be." Brad had no idea how he'd gotten so lucky. "But why're you being so patient? There have to be a hundred other guys out there you could have just like that." He snapped his fingers.

Drew smiled. "Maybe not that many, and I don't want them."

"But why me?" Brad said.

"I'll tell you later," Drew promised. "For now, just hold me."

Brad smiled softly. "I can do that."

Brad didn't squirm as Drew settled back against him, pushing the wet spot on his clothes up against his skin. He owed him that much. He put his arms around Drew and simply held him. It felt right.

He wanted more. He wanted to do more, even if they only jacked off together, even if the thought of holding another man's cock, let alone sucking it, had him shaking inside. Nerves or desire or both, Brad didn't know. But it looked like they'd both find out.

Later that evening, after Brad had gone home, Drew lay in bed, thinking. Brad had been so embarrassed, and Drew knew he would've been, too, if it had been him. But it was also kind of gratifying knowing how easily he'd made Brad lose control. It gave him hope for the future of getting into Brad's pants, but Drew knew it wasn't just that, not anymore. If that was even how he'd started. His feelings where Brad was concerned were complex.

Drew had initially gone after Brad because he thought he was hot and because coaxing a straight jock out of the closet certainly posed a challenge, but he realized that evening it—he—they could become so much more. He sighed, leaning back against his pillows while he waited for sleep to come. So much more.

Chapter Seventeen

Brad sat on the front steps of the reno after work, sipping an ice-cold sports drink. It was after 6:00 p.m., and Octavio and the rest of the workers had gone home hours before. Brad stayed later, working in the summer heat with nothing but the cooling fans, since the air conditioner was offline. But early September was proving to be just as hot as August, and the fans only moved the hot air around. Brad sweated easily, and in the confines of the house, he sweated profusely. He had electrolytes to restore. Funny how the lessons of crew ended up teaching him things about life after college.

He didn't care about the heat or working late by himself. The changes he'd made to his life felt right, like he was supposed to be working on homes, not trying to unload new construction in a useless subdivision. All the changes involved Drew too.

He was musing on that when a car pulled up in front of the house. At first, he thought it was the owners coming to check things out, but then he recognized Nick's beat-up old Honda.

Brad watched Nick come up the walk and stood to greet him. He stuck out his hand. "Hey, Nick. Good to see you, man. But...shouldn't you be running practice?"

Nick shook Brad's hand. "Just got out. I'm on my way home."

"Where's Morgan?" Brad asked, looking over Nick's shoulder, but there was no one else in the car.

"He's got a night class this semester," Nick said, "so he drove himself in."

"That sucks," Brad replied.

Nick shrugged. "I've got one myself tonight, so it works out."

"That makes sense. You're both gone on the same night and get home at the same time."

"Yeah, living together's new enough we like being home at the same time," Nick said with a dopey grin.

Brad rolled his eyes. "You're so gone."

"Oh yeah," Nick said, "and you, my friend, are impossible to get ahold of these days. Do you ever check your e-mail? This summer, Morgan couldn't log on without finding a bunch of e-mails from you, but now? If I weren't standing in front of you, I'd think you'd disappeared. It doesn't matter, because you don't reply, but I never know where to e-mail you, your personal or work account."

"I'm pretty busy at work in the mornings since I've started taking classes for my contractor's license. That sales office is even more dead and just as quiet as a library, and I'm too busy here to think about e-mail," Brad said. Then he smirked. "Just e-mail my personal account, and I'll remember to check it at Drew's house. That's where I am most nights."

Even in the heat, Brad could see Nick's blush. "Damn, I walked right into that one, didn't I?"

"You kind of did. What happened to that hard-ass coach I used to know?" Brad asked.

"Morgan's the one who's tough as nails, not me."

"Don't I know it. What he sets his sights on, he gets."

Nick nodded. "He decided he was going to be the fastest and went about doing it, but he might have some competition this year."

Brad rolled his eyes. "I was thinking more along the lines of your ass, but yeah, that too."

"What is this newfound fascination you have with tormenting your old coach?" Nick demanded. "But speaking of coaching...that's what I wanted to talk to you about."

"This about the assistant coach position?" Brad said, taking a swig of sports drink.

"It really needs to be coaches, plural, but yes, it is. I'm getting slammed out there."

"Do you need me to take it up with the oversight committee?"

"That'd be great if you could pry more money loose, but no, that's not why I'm here." He looked Brad right in the eyes. "I want you to be my assistant coach."

Brad stared at him. Then he sat down on the steps. Hard. He knew Nick needed one. He'd just never imagined that Nick planned to ask him.

Nick swooped in and removed the bottle of sports drink from his hand. "Easy there, big guy." Then he laughed. "I can't believe I've managed to render Brad Sundstrom speechless."

Brad shook his head. "I must be hallucinating from the heat. For a minute there, I thought you asked me to be your assistant coach."

"I did," Nick said. He sat down next to Brad. "Why's that so hard to believe?"

"Dude, I'm not even remotely qualified, for starters," Brad said, the "duh" hanging unspoken between them.

Nick shrugged. "Beyond rowing for four years, neither was I when I started, and you've got that much under your belt."

"I don't know, Nick..."

"I think you'd be really good at it, and an asset to the crew," Nick said softly.

Brad didn't say anything. Wow. Assistant coach. His mind raced with reasons to refuse. He was busy enough as it was between working part-time for his father and more than that for Drew, plus working on his contractor's license. Adding coaching to the mix would mean a lot of early mornings on top of everything else.

And Drew. Their relationship took time now that they were boyfriends. He'd better talk to Drew. It wouldn't be fair to him to take on another time commitment without checking with him.

He rested his chin on his knees, arms wrapped around his legs. He felt Nick watching him but ignored him. Crew. He'd missed it. He hadn't known how much until Nick dangled the chance to get back into it in front of him. It had been such a big part of his life for so long. To have it back... Longing overwhelmed him.

"Just promise me this, that'll you'll at least do a ride-along with me in the launch before you make a final decision," Nick said, mistaking his silence for refusal.

Brad looked up, blinking away his dithering. "Yeah, I can do that. Maybe Friday morning?"

"That'd be great, Brad, and thank you," Nick said. He stood up. "I have to run if I'm going to eat and make class on time. See you Friday morning."

Brad watched Nick jog to his car and drive off. *Huh, go figure. Assistant coach.*

"Knock, knock!"

Drew looked up and smiled when Brad opened the door. That Brad felt comfortable knocking and entering delighted him, and he'd taken to leaving the door unlocked when he expected him. "Hey, you!"

Brad walked in carrying a duffel bag in one hand and a brown paper shopping bag in the other. He stopped in the living room just off the foyer where Drew was at work on a laptop. He leaned in to kiss Drew. "Hey, yourself."

"Long day?" Drew said.

"You know it," Brad replied, dropping the duffel.

"Go shower, and I'll go throw something together for dinner."

Brad held up the paper sack. "No need. I hit the deli at Good Foods."

"Then I'll set the table. Go get cleaned up," Drew said, giving Brad a playful push.

"I smell that bad?"

"No, you stink. I smell...*you.*"

"I'm going, I'm going!" Brad said. He picked up his duffel bag and headed to the back of the house and Drew's guest bathroom.

Drew saved the search on his computer. More clients, more comps, followed by home inspections, pest inspections, and arguments about staging. His job, he reflected, would be so much simpler if his clients simply stopped living in their houses.

"Ah, it's nice to relax after a long day," Brad said ten minutes later when he sat down next to Drew on the sofa in the family room. "Cool, that show's on."

Drew rarely ate in front of the television, but somehow kicking back with Brad felt right, even if he

knew many of his other friends would never believe that
Drew St. Charles *ever* ate in front of the television. "It's
very nice to relax with you. But—and don't take this the
wrong way, because I'll take every moment with you I can
get—doesn't your family object to you being gone all the
time? Do they even notice?"

"Yeah, right," Brad said. "Actually, my brother Philip
asked me where I was. I just told him at a friend's house."

"What'd he say?" Drew asked. He'd wondered himself
if Brad's family cared at all. Brad was at his place nearly
every night. They pretended it was to go over the day's
work on the reno and upcoming small jobs that Drew
could now contemplate taking on while they waited to
hear back on the bid for the Bayard project, but he was
pretty sure they both had the same ulterior motive.

Brad shrugged. "He didn't say anything. It's not like
he's there much either. He hides at his girlfriend's house
when he can."

"Why don't you guys move out?" Drew asked.

"I can't afford to yet, or believe me, I'd be out of there
so fast I'd get whiplash," Brad laughed without humor.
"Philip? I don't know. He certainly earns enough. But he's
always been Randall's favorite, and that means he's on a
real short leash. I used to resent it, but lately...."

Drew waited to see if Brad had more to say, but as
usual, the subject of his family shut him down. "You're
realizing you're a grown-up, perhaps in a way that Philip
isn't, maybe in a way your dad doesn't want you to be. I
don't understand it, but whatever."

"Whatever is right. As soon as I've saved enough for
first and last month's rent, I'm gone. I've got a small trust
fund from my mom, but it's supposed to be used 'to help
me get ahead in life and not for daily expenses,'" Brad

said. "That's a quote from her will, by the way. How's that for a kick in the pants? I've actually got money; I just can't touch it."

"At least she cared enough to set you up and cared enough to make sure you did something with yourself," Drew said.

"Yeah, she did. You'd have liked her."

"If you're what she turned out, I'm sure I would've."

Brad smiled at him. *Time to lighten the mood, or at least get off the serious stuff,* Drew thought. "So, how's the reno? How was your day?"

"Funny you should mention that. Guess who came by after work today?"

"The building inspector?"

"I'd have sent you a text message. No, Nick Bedford."

"Good ol' Nick. Now that he's back in school and back to coaching, I don't hear from him as much. This sounds bad, and don't take this the wrong way because I'm nothing but happy for those two, but it was kind of nice when he and Morgan were trying to get their act together. It meant I heard from Nick a lot."

Drew felt Brad look at him. "You've known him a long time, haven't you?"

"Since we were freshman. That's eleven years now," Drew replied.

Brad put his hand behind Drew's neck and rubbed it. "I can't wait until I've known you that long."

Drew leaned over and rewarded Brad with a kiss. "Me too. So, what'd Nick have to say?"

"I think I told you how the oversight committee authorized money for an assistant coach for the varsity?" When Drew nodded, Brad continued, "Nick wants me to be his assistant coach, if you can believe that."

"Assistant coach," Drew said.

"Yep," Brad replied before taking another bite of food.

"So now darling Nicky's poaching."

Brad stopped chewing and swallowed. The gulp was audible even to Drew. "You think he's after me?"

Drew stared. "Oh, God, I'm sorry! No, not that way! Jeez. This spring, back when Nick was first going out with Morgan, I—" He stopped, the color rising up his neck when he remembered where this story ended. "Are you sure you want to hear this?"

"Since you're as red as a tomato? Oh, yeah. You're adorable when you blush, by the way."

That just made it worse. Drew felt like his face was burning. "I was pretty into you by this point—"

"Really? That early? You hid it well." Brad grinned at Drew's discomfiture.

"You were just clueless," Drew said, his face afire. "Do you want to hear this or not?" Brad mimed zipping his mouth closed. "Anyway, you'd definitely caught my eye, and I joked that since Nick got to have a hot rower boyfriend, why couldn't I? There. Are you happy?"

"Oh, yeah," Brad said cheerfully, snuggling down into the cushions. "So, what do you think? About me assistant coaching, I mean."

"Honestly? I can't say it thrills me," Drew said. When Brad opened his mouth to protest, he held up one hand. "Let me finish. It doesn't thrill me because I'm already worried about how busy you are. You work part-time out at that awful subdivision six days a week, then you work more than half days a week on the reno. We're talking about taking on more jobs since you're here to lead, and even though those'll be small jobs, it's still a demand on your time and mine, and they bring with them more responsibilities. And then there's your contractor's license."

"Yeah," Brad said, "I know, but still..."

And that was it, that *still*. Drew looked at Brad, who was now staring glumly at the television. He knew Brad had felt rudderless since graduation. Working on renos seemed to help, but he also knew Brad missed rowing. Maybe this would help. "All of that said, I can't really point fingers, because I'm just as busy trying to sell lots of houses now, in case that needs to carry us, assuming we get the bid on the Bayard project. If this is something you want to do, we'll find the time."

Brad looked back at him. "I guess it couldn't hurt to go talk to him. I mean, it's crew. And Nick." Then he smirked. "And Morgan. I'd be coaching Morgan."

Drew laughed. "Just don't start any fights with Nick, I beg you."

"All right, I promise," Brad said. "So, you don't mind if I take this on?"

Drew nodded. "I said I don't."

"I just want to check to be sure it's okay with my boyfriend." Brad smiled shyly.

Drew replied with a smile of his own. "Boyfriend. I sure like the sound of that, you big lug."

"Just so long as I'm *your* big lug."

"Oh yeah, you are," Drew said, happier than he remembered being in a long time. "You are."

Friday morning found Brad up dark and early and down at the CalPac boathouse. His dress clothes for the sales office were in the back of the car, along with the carpenter's pants and old T-shirt he wore when he worked on the reno. Despite the fact the September day would warm up nicely, it was still cold down on the water, and he had his parka on and a lightweight fleece cap.

Brad paused in the open doorway of the boathouse. Nothing had changed, but somehow things appeared different. All the familiar sights were there, the boats, the ergs, the locker rooms... He flushed when he thought of the time he'd seen Nick and Morgan rushing into them. Now he had a better idea what might've gone on. Now he wanted that himself with Drew.

He shook his head to clear it. He really didn't need the distracting mental image. No, the boathouse was familiar, yet somehow not. He recognized people, varsity rowers from last year, junior varsity rowers who hoped to make the jump to varsity this year. Across the boathouse, Morgan raised a hand in greeting as he sat on the ergs to warm up. Brad smiled and waved back.

It was still the CalPac crew, and people still took oars down to the dock or stretched or, like Morgan, warmed up on the rowing machines. Brad knew what they were doing because he'd done it so many times himself, even if he didn't know most of the faces anymore, even if there were now so many more bodies than when he'd rowed just a few months before. He wondered if any other members of the oversight committee had set foot in the boathouse recently. The numbers, at least for the two men's teams, had skyrocketed, and Brad was proud to be part of the reason why, proud to have achieved so much under Nick Bedford's coaching.

Brad nodded in satisfaction. None of that mattered. Even though the boathouse was now filled to bursting with bodies and even a new eight in slings in the middle of the bay, it was still the boathouse. It still felt like home. What had changed, Brad realized, was him. He'd changed. He no longer studied, if that had ever been the word for his five years in college, at California Pacific. He was an alum, and he was back in the boathouse to coach. *It feels right*, he thought, nodding slowly.

Then Nick himself came out of his office.

And grinned. "Brad! You made it!" Nick pulled him into the coaches' office.

"Yeah, here I am, Coach, just like old times," Brad said.

Nick looked at him closely. "But it's not, is it?"

"No, I guess not," Brad agreed, "but it's still good to be back."

"I'm really glad you are, and I hope you seriously consider coaching with me. As you can see—" Nick gestured at all the people outside the office door "—we've got a lot of bodies out there. Even just from a safety standpoint, we need more launches on the water."

Nick was right. Brad knew that. "The oversight committee's just going to have to come up with more money. Even if I bounce back and forth between varsity and junior varsity—"

"You won't really be able to help with either one," Nick said. "But Brad? I hope you know that's not even remotely why I asked you to help."

"Couldn't get anyone else?" Brad joked.

Nick rolled his eyes. "Granted, people in the area with the time and knowledge to coach are few and far between, but no."

"Seriously, Coach, I don't know why else you'd ask," Brad admitted.

"Someone's really done a number on you," Nick muttered. "I asked because you know a lot about rowing. You bring something that I can't, and that's recent experience in a boat. The rest of it, like the periodization of training and what drills work for what issues, I can teach you. But you just went through them as an oarsman a few months ago. Don't sell that—or yourself—short."

Hearing those words from Nick warmed him, and Brad smiled. "Got it, Coach."

"And stop calling me 'Coach,'" Nick groused. "You knew my name this summer. Besides, you're a coach, too, now. So, for this morning, just follow me around. Tomorrow, I'll give you a practice plan and throw you in a launch."

"Got it."

A knock on the door halted further discussion. "Coach? You in here?"

Brad looked over his shoulder and grinned. "Hey, Cockring, how's it hanging?"

He laughed as Stuart Cochrane gritted his teeth so hard Brad could practically hear his fillings crack. "Don't ever call me that again," Stuart snapped, smacking the back of Brad's head.

"Hey!" Brad yelped.

"Who or what is that?" someone behind Stuart said like Brad wasn't even there.

Brad looked around the still-seething coxswain and saw a much taller man with light-brown skin and a bushy thatch of hair a shade darker that made his moss-green eyes appear more vivid. Brad thought he detected a slight British accent. Whoever he was, he hovered protectively over Stuart.

"That's Brad Sundstrom, an asshole from last year's varsity crew who's apparently back to plague and vex me," Stuart said.

Brad stood up, smirking. He stuck his hand out. "*Coach* Sundstrom. Nice to meet you."

The stranger shook his hand warily. "Jonathan Poisonwood. Pleased to meet you, as well. I've heard about you."

"No doubt," Brad said, still smirking.

"No," Stuart breathed. "Just...no."

"Coach Sundstrom's doing me the favor of checking you all out to see if you're worth his time," Nick said.

"I knew him leaving for good was too much to hope for," Stuart sighed. "Anyway, the crews are out running to warm up, and then they'll do their dynamic movement drills to stretch. The coxswains are ready to go over today's practice plan."

Nick nodded. "We'll be right out."

As Stuart and Jonathan left, Brad looked at Nick. "Who or what was that?" he asked, mimicking the new rower.

"You know Stuart," Nick said with a laugh, "and that was his shadow, Jonathan Poisonwood, my star acquisition. I recruited him from Orange Coast College down in the OC."

"What's going on between those two?"

Nick shrugged. "Who knows at this point, but you saw it, too, huh?"

"Blind people can see it," Brad snorted.

"Everyone but them, according to Morgan." Nick laughed again. "Come on, let's go herd some cats. Just stand behind me and look confident while I tell the coxswains what's what today."

"Any of 'em besides Stuart any good?" Brad asked.

"I nabbed one of the JV coxswains who wanted to follow her boys up to the varsity, Evangeline Chin."

"You stole Evie from the JV? Way to go. Anyone else?"

Nick shrugged. "We'll see. Let's go meet them."

Brad listened closely while Nick went over the plan for the day. It was early in the season, still in the "getting the rust out" phase after summer vacation when some of the guys hadn't touched an oar or erg, so for that morning's practice, Nick planned some basic drills to get the oars in the water at the same time, followed by rowing—first by a rotation of six of the eight rowers and then all eight. Pretty standard stuff when Brad thought about it.

"Let's get out of the way," Nick said, steering Brad toward the launch once he'd gone over the day's practice with the coxswains. "Normally I'd have the leftover rowers in here, but I put them on the ergs this morning. Today I just want it to be us so we can talk freely. Once you're up and running as a coach, we can put the leftovers in smaller boats, the singles and pairs I bought this summer."

Brad pulled on his cap while they puttered out into the river, careful not to kick up a wake that might push the expensive and somewhat fragile rowing shells into the dock. "Today I want you to observe. The perspective's different out here," Nick continued over the farty sputter of the motor. "I think you'll find that you'll learn things about rowing just from watching. I know I did. I'll point things out to you, and if anything jumps out at you, speak up."

"Will do," Brad said. He pulled his gloves on. "Is it always this cold in the morning?"

Nick nodded. "You might want to put long johns on under your jeans. That helps."

So, Brad kept quiet and watched as practice got underway. It didn't take him long to realize that Nick was right. He saw everything from the launch, every late catch, every squirm of the rowers' bodies out of place, all the little things that could upset a boat, and the more he watched, the clearer those mistakes became. Nick looked over and nodded, like he'd heard Brad's thoughts.

"How come we didn't do this launch lizard bit?" Brad asked, almost accusingly.

"Numbers. We had eight rowers and one coxswain. We could've borrowed a four from the women, I guess, but you'd have spent more time fighting the set in a smaller boat than rowing, so it didn't seem worth the hassle to me. We made do with what we had, and we did all right," Nick said.

Then Brad connected some dots. "That's why you filmed us."

"Yep, and I'll do it for these guys, too, even though we now have enough for some real competition for seats in the A boat. One of the things having an assistant does is free me up to concentrate on one group or another and still have someone to run a safe practice for the rest."

They stopped talking then. Nick had a practice to run, and Brad knew he could either focus on the crews or talk to his old coach. He chose to watch the crews. He still thought it was a trip there were enough rowers for a B boat, plus some spares. The guys were going to have to hustle, and Brad wondered if he'd have made the cut. Then he realized it didn't matter. That was then, and now he was out of the competition. No, he was helping run the competition. He smiled. This could be fun.

After practice, Brad tagged along behind Nick as he debriefed with the coxswains. His attention wandered as they discussed specific people whose names he hadn't yet learned. There, in the middle of the bay, was a gleaming vision in white, the latest in carbon-fiber hull technology from one of the boat makers. Brad couldn't tell which one, and right then he didn't care. He just wanted to admire the boat.

"That's yours, you know," Nick said, coming up behind him.

"What're you talking about?" Brad said, frowning.

"It took me a while to figure it out, but you asked your dad to donate a boat when you graduated, didn't you?"

Brad blushed. "Yeah. I...uh...I also figured it might give the athletic department some incentive to get off your case about Morgan."

Nick stared, stunned. "You did that? For me?"

Brad shrugged, and his blush turned to one of shame. He couldn't tell Nick he was the one who'd turned in the anonymous note that lit the match to the whole powder keg. He didn't regret much in life, but his actions that spring filled him with shame. He squirmed. "Can we not talk about this? Ever? My dad's got more money than he knows what to do with. I thought about a car, but I like mine okay, and this way I could help someone else out, help out the crew, you know?"

Nick gripped Brad's shoulder. "You're a good man. C'mere, there's something I want to show you." He led Brad around to the boat's bow. "There. See the name?"

Brad froze and time stood still. *Helena Sundstrom.* His mother. They'd named the boat for his late mother. "I..." he started, but his mouth was dry. He coughed. "I don't know what to say."

"I thought you might like that," Nick said softly.

Brad's thoughts raced. His dad named the boat for his mother. The news shocked him. He really didn't think the old bastard was capable of caring that much. Hell, at all. Where Brad was concerned, his dad usually parachuted in, spent what he had to spend to maintain appearances, and then bailed out just as quickly. That Randall first bought a boat for Brad's old crew and then named it after his mother...

"Didn't think he had it in him," Brad whispered.

Nick scratched his head uncertainly. "That's the thing. Once your dad donated the money, we never heard back. You're on the oversight committee, so you should know."

"This went down before I joined. I think that's why they wanted me, so they could juice some more out of my old man."

"Usually the person who donates the money names the boat, but your dad won't return my phone calls. It's pretty frustrating."

"Then...how'd you pick the name? How'd you know?" Brad's heart sank.

Nick looked Brad in the eye. "Drew thought you might like that."

Drew. Brad's vision blurred. He blinked the moisture away. *I don't care about Randall's neglect*, he insisted silently. *I don't.* But Drew... All that time Drew had listened to Brad miss his mother, he'd really listened. Brad knew he'd harbored feelings for Drew for a while, but this? This filled him with something he couldn't name. His feelings for Drew just kept growing stronger.

Drew's kindness and thoughtfulness humbled him, but rather than feeling ashamed of his own shortcomings,

Brad longed to prove his worth to Drew in return. Right there in the boathouse, with Nick hovering expectantly, he knew he had to have Drew in his life for the rest of his life. He shoved questions of gay or straight or bi aside right then. He was for Drew, whatever that meant. That a man he'd known—really known—less than a year had thought of the one gesture that would mean the most to him while his dad ignored phone calls summed up his life pretty well.

"I don't know what to say," Brad sniffled. Then he thought of something. "I'm kind of hurt I wasn't invited to the dedication."

"There hasn't been one. Like I said, your dad won't call me back." Nick hesitated. "If this is what your dad was like growing up, then some of the things I...uh, found abrasive when I coached you make more sense."

Brad shrugged. "You could've called me."

"I did. That's why you're here now. We'll either dedicate her here on our home water before our first race, or we'll do it at the first race and her first victory."

"If there is one." That was not a tear in Brad's eye. It wasn't, damn it. "Can...can Drew be here? He was there for the win that's made all the rest of this possible."

Nick looked at him like he knew there was more to say, but Brad didn't feel like breaking down in the boathouse, and he knew he was close.

"I think that's only fair. We can do it next weekend, maybe Saturday after practice, if you can stick around for a few. If we both call Drew, I bet he'll make sure not to schedule any viewings or open houses. After all," Nick said with a tight smile, "he pestered me about you the whole season."

"Shut up, he did not." Brad blushed. Even though Drew told him he had. Hearing it from Drew in the moment was one thing, but hearing it from Nick? That was just disturbing.

Nick just rolled his eyes. "So, what'd you think? This something you can help me out with?"

Brad nodded slowly. Just sitting in the launch with Nick watching the crews row...it felt right. He knew he needed this. "Yeah," he said, smiling. "I think so. I checked with Drew and—"

"You checked with Drew? You got permission?" Nick smirked.

Brad turned as red as a Coke can. "We...uh, we might've had the 'boyfriend talk.'"

"Brad, that's fantastic," Nick's words were for his ears alone. "While I have questions, I hope you know you'll never get any grief from me about this development in your life."

"As long as I treat him right?" Brad knew how close Nick and Drew were.

"Oh, if you fuck him over, there's no hole deep enough to hide you," Nick said cheerfully. "From me or Morgan."

"Well that's not gonna happen." Brad got a dopy grin. "He's..."

Nick nodded. "Yes, he is. But spare me? Brad Sundstrom, nice guy and assistant coach, I'm all for, but Brad Sundstrom, goofy romantic? I don't know if I can handle that."

"You and me both," Brad muttered as he headed to the locker room to change for his shift at Suburban Graveyard.

Chapter Eighteen

A week and a day after his Friday ride-along, Brad was still finding his way as assistant coach. His confidence on the water grew with every practice, but the organized chaos of the boathouse after practice on Saturday mornings still threw him. All those new faces. Almost new, he corrected himself. After a week of staring intently at rowers from his launch, he knew faces. But names? That was going to take time.

But right then, it didn't matter. In a few minutes, once the dedication started, he wouldn't be there as a coach but as Helena—Ellie—Sundstrom's son, and the only representative of the family who cared enough to come to the dedication. He'd left messages for Philip and Randall but hadn't heard back from either one. He hadn't expected to.

"You okay?" Nick said, coming up to him.

Brad shrugged. "I will be."

"I'll handle most of this." Nick looked at him sympathetically. "And a lot of what I say will be for the benefit of new members of the team and anyone else who isn't part of our traditions here."

"Which would mean just Drew, since none of my lame family could bother to come," Brad muttered. He looked around but hadn't seen him yet. He knew Drew wouldn't let him down, but he worried just the same.

"We'll give him a few more minutes to get here." Nick glanced at his watch. "We ended practice a little early."

Brad scanned the parking lot and finally relaxed when he saw the familiar BMW pull up. He smiled and waved; then he caught himself and looked around, feeling guilty. How much was safe to show at the boathouse? He didn't know how much he was comfortable with his athletes knowing, because he wasn't yet comfortable with himself.

He turned around and caught Nick nodding to Morgan, who smiled knowingly. He realized just then that he'd seen no overt demonstrations of affection between the two, but he didn't have time to dwell on it, because Drew came up behind him. Anyone watching would only see one man tap another on the back as if to say "excuse me," but Brad felt Drew's hand linger and heard his greeting, pitched for his ears only.

"I'm sorry I'm late," Drew said. "Wait...am I late?"

Brad shook his head, smiling at Drew despite his nerves. "No, we just ended practice early."

"Thanks for waiting, then."

"You had to be here." Brad hadn't said anything about the new boat's name to Drew all week. It was hard for him then, but he pushed on. "You knew," he said thickly. "You knew what this would mean to me. You had to be here. We'd have waited."

They might not have been boyfriends for very long, but Brad could tell Drew was itching to hug him. He could also see how Drew fought the urge. He appreciated that. He wasn't ready to be...whatever he was to the crew yet.

Drew smiled shyly. "You're not mad?"

"How could I ever be mad at you for that?"

"Those things were said in confidence. I was hoping

you wouldn't think it was a betrayal, but when Nick told me he was getting frustrated with tracking your dad down..."

Brad brushed a tear out of his eye with the back of his hand. "Let me show you the boat, maybe you can take a look around. I'll see when Nick wants to get started."

"I've been down here before, but not with so many people around," Drew said. "Operations have sure expanded." He looked around again. "In fact, I'm not even sure this is the same boathouse. Did they build a bigger—"

"Heads up!" a woman's voice called.

"—boathouse?" Drew asked, looking all around.

With a quick look of apology at the tiny woman standing with her hand on the bow of a boat, Brad took Drew firmly by the arm and pulled him out of harm's way. "I know you've been around Nick a lot, so I'm sure this is just a reminder, but 'heads up' really means duck, and for the record, she'd have run you over."

"Rude," Drew hissed.

Brad shrugged. "Boats have the right of way." He knew he had to distract Drew before things got out of hand. "Look outside the boathouse." He pointed out of the bay doors to where Stuart directed some of the varsity men as they put the *Ellie* into slings. "Nick might be ready for us."

With his hand on Drew's lower back to guide him, Brad pushed the still-simmering Drew out into the yard.

Nick looked up and smiled. "Drew! Glad you could make it."

"Thanks for asking me," Drew said, hanging back a little.

Nick frowned and pulled him into a hug. "What, you're shy now?"

"I didn't know how out you were at the boathouse, after..." Drew's voice was muffled by Nick's chest.

"It's a hug between old friends, not sex on the dock," Nick said. He shook his head and released Drew. "Anyway, now that you're here, we'll get started. It's pretty straightforward. Brad's seen dedications before, but this is the first one he's participated in, yes?"

Brad nodded.

"So, you'll stand near me while I say a few words about the CalPac crew and its traditions, and then you'll talk briefly about your mother. That's really all there is to it," Nick explained. "Then you'll pour champagne over the bow and the *Helena Sundstrom* will be ready to row. Some of the varsity men will take her out for a spin, and then that's that. Any questions?"

"Where do I stand?" Drew said.

"Over there near Morgan," Nick said. "I promise he won't bite."

"That's not how I remember it," Drew said.

"You should live so long." Morgan rolled his eyes.

Drew smiled. "How're you?"

"Hush, Nick's about to start," Morgan said.

Nick held up an air horn and let out a deafening blast to get everyone's attention, and in short order, both men's squads, the junior varsity and the varsity, had gathered around. "Thanks for sticking around, guys. This won't take too much of your time, but today's an important part of our life here at the CalPac boathouse. Today, we dedicate a new shell, a men's heavyweight eight, and she's a beauty. You'll have to earn your places in this one.

"As a coach, dedicating a boat is both a joyous and a melancholy privilege. It's a privilege, because another boat, whether it's a used single or a flagship eight, is a cause for celebration. The crew is growing. One of our alumni, one of the great PCRC Eight from last year, thought so much of this sport and this crew that when his dad asked what he wanted for graduation, he said a boat for the men of the CalPac rowing team.

"But it's also melancholy, because it's our tradition at California Pacific to name boats for the dearly departed. Every name on the bow of one of these proud shells represents a life ended. Some died young, taken from their lives and crews, immortalized in carbon fiber by their grieving parents and rowed with pride by former teammates. Some shells are named by children, themselves well into middle age, to celebrate their parents' lives, and we cherish these boats no less for all that their namesakes' exploits in the sport took place long before any of us was born."

Nick paused to look around at his crews. "Young or old, the people whose names you see every day, who you may not even think about, these people live forever, honored every time we launch and every time a novice rower reads the legends in the crew handbook.

"And their names and legends live on even beyond this boathouse, because once CalPac no longer needs these shells and sells them to clubs or smaller schools that lack our resources, no crew will ever change the name of a boat. They know what naming a boat means.

"So today we gather to dedicate a new boat," Nick concluded, "donated by the generosity of our new assistant coach's family. Brad, would you say a few words?"

Brad stepped forward. He swallowed and wiped his hands nervously on his jeans. He hated speaking in public. "Uh...Mom died before I discovered crew, but she always supported my decisions and encouraged me to chase my dreams. She never got upset with me when I failed, but if I didn't give something my all, well...then she got mad." He swallowed, his throat dry. "I think she'd be proud to know that her name lives on to help a new generation of men row beyond the limits they knew through crew." Brad turned to the varsity squad, sparing a quick smile for Morgan and Stuart and the others he remembered. "The *Ellie* will carry you as far as you can go. Because this is a sport about limits, she'll take you beyond what you ever thought possible. Row her well, men. Make her proud."

Morgan started clapping, slowly, loudly, followed quickly by Stuart, as the rest of the crew joined in. To the sound of applause, Nick handed Brad an open bottle of champagne. "Just dribble it across the bow deck. If you break it against the bow, you'll scratch the carbon with the broken glass."

Brad nodded, his chest tight, his eyes stinging. "Here's to you, Mom," he whispered as he trickled the champagne across the white hull and watched with unseeing eyes as the pale liquid flowed across the cursive script of the new boat's name in the bold blue of the CalPac Titans.

"All right, men!" Stuart cried. "Hands on the *Ellie*! Act like you know what you're doing."

Brad stood back as eight of the varsity rowers stepped forward to flip the boat up and out of the slings and onto their shoulders for the *Ellie*'s maiden row.

As Brad watched the new varsity A boat head down the dock on the shoulders of eight of CalPac's best, Drew slipped under his arm. "You okay?"

"Yeah, I guess," Brad said. The PDA made him squirm a bit, but he also liked how Drew felt under his arm. A lot.

"I've got to take off, but I'm glad I could be here," Drew said.

"Me too," Brad replied, staring out at the water as the rowers lowered the *Ellie* into the river. He squeezed Drew and, with a furtive look around, kissed the top of his head quickly before releasing him.

Drew looked up at him and smiled. "I'll see you tonight, okay?"

"Definitely. Have a good afternoon, and thanks again for coming."

"That's what boyfriends do, right?"

"Right." Brad glanced around and then took a deep breath. "Drew?"

"Yeah?"

Brad dove in and kissed him. It was a quick peck on the cheek, but it still made his heart slam. "See you later."

Drew smiled. "Bye, Brad."

Brad turned and headed for the coaches' office and his duffel bag. He'd thought maybe he'd reclaim his old locker, but as it was, Nick had given up his own locker and was giving serious thought to restricting lockers to the varsity squad only. He made a note to himself to warn the oversight committee again that they needed to expand the boathouse.

Then he saw what he was sure was his brother's retreating back—Philip's *and* his girlfriend's. Shit. How much had they seen?

Brad sat at the desk—he refused to think of it as "his" any longer—and drummed his fingers on the laminate top. *The original builder sure spared no expense,* he thought acidly. *Nothing but the finest quality plastic to lure people into mistakes with thirty-year mortgages.* From what Brad had seen when he went snooping around the home sites, the concern for quality materials and fine craftsmanship extended to the homes themselves. Not even the pricey upgrade options changed that equation much; not even the better designers Sundstrom Homes had lured in with grand promises and fat commissions could slather on enough lipstick to disguise the ugly porkers for sale at Suburban Graveyard. It was a lesson he took into his work with Drew. They'd never talked about it directly, but he was pretty sure Drew shared his commitment to quality work with the best materials the budget afforded.

When it came down to it, he knew he was pretty sure about Drew too. As sure as he could be about anything in a post-graduation life filled with doubt. Speaking of...just how much had ol' Philsie seen? Brad's hand on Drew's back as he led him out of the boathouse before the dedication? Drew under his arm for that hug afterward? The kiss?

The kiss. He must've been crazy, kissing Drew in public, right there in the yard at the boathouse. But then he remembered Drew's smile. Ever there in that crappy sales office, the memory of that smiled warmed him. That couldn't be wrong.

But Brad's guts still churned thinking about getting caught. How could he face his family when he didn't have answers to the obvious question? He didn't know if he was gay or bi. He just didn't. Yeah, women still kinda caught his eye, but so did guys now. That didn't mean he wanted to lick any of them from head to toe like he did Drew. Did that make him gay? He was pretty sure it did. It at least made him not straight.

The g-word and the pictures it brought to mind scared Brad. He thought of the crazy images he'd seen from Mardi Gras or the leather street fair in San Francisco, or the magazine one of his friends had shown him once when they were drunk after a frat party their freshman year.

Those images still made him shiver. Was that guy trying to tell him something? Maybe find out if he were gay? The memory itself was too fuzzy, even if he recalled those pictures of hardcore bondage with perfect clarity. He knew that wasn't him. Tying someone up a little just for play sounded fun, but not that hard stuff. Different strokes and all that, but not him.

All Brad knew was that he was Drewsexual. Why couldn't that be enough for now? Somehow, he didn't see Randall accepting that explanation, but what the hell business of his father's was it? Just as soon as he could swing his own place, he was out of Randall's house and his life for good.

Speaking of Drewsexual...Brad wanted to be right then. A lot. His body did, anyway. The thought still scared him because there'd be no turning back. You can't unring a bell, after all, but Drew sure seemed to ring his bell. Firing off in his pants like that proved as much.

No, the thought of sex, full-deal, all-the-way sex still petrified him when he thought about it, but where Drew was concerned, his body knew what it craved. He'd spent his life following his body's lead, and maybe it was time to let it lead again. Because all this worrying about it? It only confused him.

He leaned back in his chair and let his body do the thinking. What did his body want? He thought of Drew. He thought about tapping that fine bubble butt, and he was halfway to hard before he knew it. There was his answer. It was time to do and not overthink. He'd leave that to Nick and Morgan.

Damn. Enough of this. Time to get back to doing. He was going to take his boyfriend lunch. He knew Drew didn't have a lot of time on these Saturdays packed with open houses and showing homes. Bringing him lunch would be the perfect boyfriendy thing to do. Fortunately, open houses were just that, and he could walk right in.

Brad glanced at the clock. Close enough to lunch. It wasn't like frenzied would-be homebuyers were beating down the door. His replacement would be there in a little over an hour, and he felt no need to hang around. If no one arrived to open the office, it wouldn't be his ass in a sling. It wasn't so much that his loyalties lay with Drew and Renochuck, although he could see that happening, it was that they didn't lie with Randall Sundstrom and Sundstrom Homes.

Chapter Nineteen

Drew closed the door to the garage behind him. Long day. He was ready for some rest and recuperation with his boyfriend. He loved being able to say Brad was his boyfriend. Speaking of whom, where was he? His somewhat disreputable-looking car was in front of the house. Maybe he was napping.

Then Drew heard the sliding glass door to the backyard open. "I'm home!"

Brad came in, wearing cargo shorts that hung on his hips like sin and a T-shirt that didn't make it all the way down. Only an apron covered up the fine, furry belly and prevented Drew from embarrassing himself right then and there. "Hi, honey! How was your day?"

Drew grinned. "Better now that I'm home. What's with the apron?"

"I'm cooking you dinner. Grilling, actually," Brad said, grinning. He jutted his jaw out like a Neanderthal. "Me caveman. Me cook food with fire."

Drew smiled. He loved seeing this side of Brad.

"Lunch, then dinner? That's so sweet of you."

"Yeah, well, you keep feeding me. I figured it's my turn." Brad blushed. "But lunch doesn't count. That was just because."

"Well, I appreciate it anyway." Drew tipped his head up to kiss Brad's nose. "How long until dinner's ready?"

"Maybe another five on the steaks. Salad and bread are from the deli at the store." Brad shrugged apologetically. "It's nothing fancy."

"It's food I'm not cooking. It's my favorite meal *ever*."

"You're easy," Brad said, snorting.

Drew arched an eyebrow as he turned and headed for his bedroom and a change into comfortable clothes. "You have no idea."

"That's dessert," Brad smirked.

"Oooh," Drew exclaimed. *Looks like the night just got interesting.*

Five minutes later, the scent of dinner pulled him out of the bedroom and into the kitchen, where he was pleased to see that Brad had ditched the apron.

Drew came up behind Brad, who was standing at the counter gussying up the bagged salad with some croutons from a box. He wrapped his arms around Brad's waist and pressed himself against his broad, muscled back. "Thanks for this. That's really sweet of you."

Brad put his hands over Drew's and leaned back into the hug. "You're welcome. I want to do nice things for you." He shrugged. "I'm glad you were there this morning...it meant a lot to me."

"I'm glad I was there too," Drew murmured, enjoying just being close to Brad.

When Brad took his hands away to resume doctoring the salad, Drew ran his hands up under Brad's shirt, drawn by the gap between the shirt and the shorts. He couldn't help himself. He just had to feel Brad's furry belly.

"Someone's frisky tonight," Brad said.

"If you had any idea what the sight of your hairy abs peeking out from under your shirt was doing to me, you'd cover it up," Drew said.

"Oh, I think I've got some idea what it does to you," Brad laughed softly. "I—ohhhh."

While Brad had been talking, Drew allowed his hands to roam further, up to Brad's pecs. He flicked at Brad's nipples while biting his back. The feel of muscles and skin and just the right amount of hair...yeah, Brad had it all going on. He ground himself into Brad's ass and even tried to gnaw on his back as need rose like the tide. He knew he said he'd wait, but damn.

"I said that was dessert." Brad sounded breathless.

Drew stopped his assault on Brad's back. He looked up and laughed. "Sorry about the wet spot on the back of your shirt."

"And the one in my underwear. Damn, Drew. You sure know how to short-circuit my brain. But dinner's ready. You seem to like this big body I've got, and while I've got no complaints about that, it takes a lot of food to keep running."

Drew dropped his hands, albeit reluctantly. "What can I do to help get dinner on the table?"

"Dishes and beer."

"Coming right up!" Drew said, and in short order they sat down to a simple but tasty meal. "This is really nice."

"Thanks," Brad said softly. "So how was your day after the dedication?"

"Really good. The first open house didn't have much traffic, but the second one? Wow."

"Good?"

"Bidding war."

"What's that?" Brad asked in between bites.

"Just about the best thing ever in real estate," Drew said with a shit-eating grin. He loved this part of his job, and for purely mercenary reasons. "It means more than one person wants the property, so I can drive the price up, sometimes well above the asking price. It's rare to begin with, and in this market even rarer."

"Whoa, dude, that sounds harsh." Brad laughed.

"Maybe, but it's just business. When there's demand for something, the price goes up. In this case, it's a great house and a fair price."

"Not for long, it sounds like."

"No, probably not, and it's not uncommon for people to drop out of a bidding war if the price goes too high."

Brad looked puzzled. "So how do they know if they've won?"

"The way this one works is that the two couples who definitely want the house, along with a third who might, have a fifteen-minute window tomorrow morning starting at 9:00 a.m. I'll check in with my clients, but I'll also let the low bidders know what the highest one was and give them a chance to revise their offer."

"Upward, of course."

"Of course," Drew smirked.

"Still sounds kind of harsh," Brad replied.

Drew shrugged. He took a sip of beer. "It is what it is—product and demand, and no one's going into this blind. I represent my clients, the sellers of the house. The people who want to buy it also have people representing them. The only advantage anyone has is financial... Someone's going to have or be able to borrow more money than the others, and that person will win. It's my job to get my clients an offer for as much as possible. They don't have to take it. They could decide they like one bidder over another. I'll advise them, but the choice is theirs." He paused, thinking. "Think of it this way. Real estate may carry us for a while if we get the bid on the Bayard House and the city takes its sweet time paying us, so the more houses I sell for more money means freedom later."

"If we get the bid," Brad pointed out.

"Then it means more leeway on flipping and renovation once you get your contractor's license." Tomorrow would probably be a long, complicated day dealing with the bids, and he didn't want to spend any more time on it then he had to. "So how was your day? You seemed kind of...somber this morning. Even this afternoon when you brought me lunch."

"I was, but that was this morning." Brad hesitated. "On my way out, I thought I saw my brother Philip and his girlfriend leaving."

"Oh?" Drew stilled. "What'd he say?"

Brad shrugged. "He didn't. I didn't call out to him or anything."

"Your family." Drew shook his head. "So, what're you going to do? Are you going to talk to him?"

"Why would I do that?" Brad asked.

The thing that made Drew want to scream was that Brad was serious. "I don't know... See if he has questions? See if he's going to tell your dad? See if he's got your back? I mean, he showed up, after all, right?"

"He hasn't had my back so far." Brad took a long pull on his beer.

"It's a wonder you turned out sane." Drew shook his head.

"Who says I did?" Brad stuck his tongue out. "Besides, it's not like it changes anything."

"No, I guess not."

After that, they switched to safer topics like coaching or renovation for the rest of dinner.

"So, what's for dessert?" Drew said once they were done and the dishes cleared. He knew what he wanted, but it had to be Brad's choice. He was the one who had the most to lose, even if only how he thought of himself.

"You want to know what's for dessert?" Brad said, suddenly up close and in Drew's personal space. He moved forward, crowding Drew.

Drew stepped back a little, tilting his head up, and still Brad loomed. "Uh-huh."

And then his back was against the wall and Brad was pressed up against him, and damn if that wasn't the hottest thing ever. He barely had his lips parted before Brad's mouth closed over his, hungry, demanding, desperate.

Drew made needy noises as Brad's tongue pressed against his lips, demanding entrance, demanding his surrender, and he was only too happy to give both. He knew what he wanted, and if this was all Brad was offering, he knew it wouldn't be enough, not anymore. Patience was the furthest thing from his mind as he wrapped one leg around Brad.

Brad reached around to grab Drew's ass. He hefted Drew up, easily lifting him, and Drew wrapped both legs around his waist. Drew just loved having a boyfriend bigger and stronger than he, and Brad moaned appreciatively into the kiss.

But Drew broke off the kiss. "Is this where you want this to go?"

Brad nodded slowly. "Totally."

After this long denying himself what he really wanted, Drew wasn't convinced. He knew if he woke up to a shuttered and withdrawn Brad, or worse, if a regretful Brad crept out in the middle of the night, he'd be devastated, and yeah, at that point, it was all about him. But he wanted nothing to poison his fledgling relationship with Brad and knew that regret would kill their romance in the cradle.

When Drew didn't look convinced, Brad said, "I've already come once with you, remember? And I'm about to do it again, and I'd really like to be naked this time. With you."

"You say the sweetest things," Drew breathed before latching onto Brad's mouth again.

Brad smiled into the kiss and carried Drew to his bedroom. Brad dropped Drew back onto the bed and then fell over onto him.

Drew could tell Brad was being careful not to flatten him, but damn, his double handful of big lug was pushing him into the mattress, and life was oh so good right then. He shuddered as pleasure rippled through him.

Since it had worked so well in the kitchen, Drew ran his hands back up under Brad's shirt. He traced the planes and angles of the muscles along Brad's back, the lats and traps that were so wonderfully developed from rowing.

Brad bit his way down Drew's neck to suck right above the collarbone. "Damn," Drew breathed. "Everyone's gonna know what I did tonight."

"Damn right," Brad said. "I didn't mark you well enough last time. I'm a caveman, remember?"

"My caveman," Drew whispered.

"That's right, your caveman...oooh, damn, you've got about a million years to quit that," Brad moaned as Drew brought his hands around to Brad's front to work his nipples.

"You like that?" He thumbed them gently, feeling them pebble at his touch. He traced the areolas with his fingertips, slowly spiraling back to the center.

"Uh-huh... No one's ever done that," Brad whimpered. "Just you."

Drew smirked, thinking of another surprise that lay in store for Brad, one further south. "I know all kinds of tricks to make you feel good."

"I'll just bet you do." Brad gasped as Drew pinched them hard. "Drewwww...."

Brad sat up suddenly, his eyes almost black with desire. He paused, like he was thinking about something. Then he reached down, tugged his shirt off, and tossed it on the floor beside the bed.

Drew could only stare. He'd seen Brad's shirtless chest before, that day at the water park. Then, he had to be careful not to be caught looking. Now looking was entirely appropriate, and damn, did he look.

"Like what you see?" Brad said.

Drew nodded slowly. Did he ever. Brad's shoulders appeared like they went on for miles. Strong deltoids gave way to large biceps that he knew were not merely ornamental.

Brad followed Drew's gaze. "Bit of a farmer's tan."

"Do you hear me complaining?"

And Drew kept on looking. The hair on Brad's chest—hairy enough to enjoy but not Sasquatch hairy—started abruptly at the top of his rounded pecs, not like some bearish guys he'd been with where the hair went up and over the shoulders and down the back. Drew liked hairy chests, not missing links.

Drew hardly knew where to look next, so he settled for running his hands over Brad's chest. The hair continued down the contours of his abs, but not around his hard obliques. Drew splayed his hands out and ran his thumbs down the treasure trail. He shivered. He was going to see the end of the trail.

"You're amazing," Drew whispered.

Brad blushed. "How come no one's ever noticed but you?"

"They're blind and stupid, and their oversight is my gain. But you know what else?"

Brad shook his head.

"I'm not just talking about your body."

With that, Drew scissored and twisted and rolled, pinning Brad beneath him. He smirked as he held Brad's arms over his head.

"How'd you do that?" Brad said.

"My brief high-school wrestling stint," Drew said.

"You wrestled?" Brad's teasing doubt was clear in his tone.

"I told you it was brief. They told me I was too small, and I switched to cross-country. But I can still take the big ones down when I need to." Drew loved pinning big guys like Brad down. Sure, they both knew Brad could break free, but making him want to stay put, that was the fun of it.

"You don't look that small to me," Brad blurted.

"I got tired of being small, so I started lifting." Drew smirked as he ground against the hard cock he felt straining beneath him in Brad's shorts. "You've been looking, have you?"

Brad blushed harder.

"It's okay, you know. In fact, I like knowing that you're looking, that you admire all my hard work with the iron." Drew had never been one for being built just for the sake of it, but knowing Brad was looking? That'd get him hard every time he thought about it.

"Hey...how come I'm the only one with my shirt off?" Brad said.

Drew looked down at him. "Can I trust you to behave?"

"As much as you ever can."

"Yeah, that's what I'm afraid of. Why don't you unbutton my shirt? That'll keep your hands somewhere I can see them." Maybe Brad's first time with a man would be less frightening, would cause fewer regrets later, if it was something he did with Drew instead of Drew doing to him.

"Can I?"

Drew liked the mixture of hesitation with his man's usual bravado, but right then, he needed to feel Brad's hands. He nodded.

Almost shyly, Brad reached to undo the first button up near Drew's neck. The look of intense concentration made Drew smile. His man could be so serious.

One button, then two, then three. Brad's touch through the fabric teased him, making him tense up with longing, with anticipation.

Then Brad slipped his large hands inside for a moment, and Drew gasped.

"Are my hands cold?"

"No! But slow is killing me," Drew muttered.

"Yeah?" Brad smiled wickedly. "I think I like you desperate."

"I'm there," Drew breathed.

Chuckling, Brad undid Drew's shirt the rest of the way. "This what you want?"

"It's a start," Drew said as Brad began a hesitant exploration.

"You're not as hairy as I am, but I think you're more muscular."

"Yeah?" Drew shivered as Brad touched his nipples.

"You like that too?"

Drew nodded. "Pretty much anything I do to you I'll like in return."

"That's...yeah, that makes sense." Drew could hear a hitch in Brad's voice.

"Who knows what makes a man hot like another man?" Drew said, stroking Brad's chest.

"Yeah, I'm getting that picture." Brad flicked Drew's nipples this time, a little clumsily, but Drew wasn't complaining. "I like making you feel good, like you make me feel."

Drew rewarded him by leaning down and kissing him. It was time to move things along. He didn't want Brad coming in his pants again. He wanted Brad coming in him.

He leaned forward and kissed Brad, just enjoying the gentle caress of lips on lips for a moment. But he had other goals that night, other destinations in mind for his lips and tongue. He nipped Brad's lip before biting his way down Brad's jaw. The stubble might've jarred Brad out of the moment once, but it was just one more reminder that Drew was making love to a man, another piece of wood thrown on the bonfire they built between them.

He sucked on Brad's neck for a few moments, but not enough to raise a mark. They were past that tonight. He had to scoot down off Brad's groin, but the way Brad rocked his pelvis up into him, it was time.

"If you liked my hands, you're gonna love this," Drew murmured. He kissed first one nipple and then the other, slowly lapping at one while sliding his palm over the other. He glanced up at Brad and saw the whites of his eyes through half-closed lids. Yeah, he was a tit pig, all right.

"Damn, baby," Brad panted. "You—"

Then he nipped at one, just enough teeth to zap Brad's cock.

"Drew!" Brad barked. "Oh my God."

Drew continued his ministrations, teasing and even tormenting Brad, whose cries and groans further amped his own need, even though he could tell Brad wasn't quite sure what to do with his hands.

"It's okay to touch me," he said, gently taking one of Brad's hands and placing it over his own cock, almost painfully hard behind shorts and underwear. "In fact, I'd like it."

"Sorry, I just—"

"Don't be sorry." Drew came up from Brad's chest long enough kiss him. "Here, just a minute."

Drew climbed off the bed and made quick work of his remaining clothes. Brad watched him with huge eyes, and Drew knew this was the first time he'd ever seen a naked man, at least naked for the only reason that counted right then. This wasn't a gym locker room, this was a bedroom, and they were there for one purpose.

Then Drew went for the button and drawstring holding Brad's cargo shorts onto his hips, and Brad's eyes grew wider still. Drew looked down, and Brad's gray boxer-briefs were spotted where he leaked pre-cum.

"Hmmmm, I do like that," Drew said, lowering himself down to the bed. He mouthed Brad's length through the cotton, avoiding the leaking head. He wanted to keep Brad revved to a fever pitch, not provoke a repeat of the last time they'd been this hot and heavy.

He smiled as Brad reached down to paw inexpertly at his own equipment. *Gotta love those long arms.*

Then Brad hesitated.

"What's wrong?" Drew asked, trying not to sound too cranky. He could tell something was wrong, but he was really ready for Brad to touch him. Hell, he was ready for Brad to maul him.

Drew sat up. He'd half expected something like this. Brad said one thing, but feelings were feelings and not always so easy to change. He'd be disappointed if they stopped, more than, but he'd be crushed if this became an issue between them. Blue balls hadn't killed anyone yet. "Talk to me, Brad. I can tell something's bothering you."

"I don't know," Brad muttered. "I mean, I want to, it's just..."

Drew sighed. He told himself this was the last time, the absolute last time, he was going to read between the lines. At some point, he had to take Brad at face value, respecting his words as much as he tried to respect his feelings. "Is it the gay sex thing?"

"Yeah, you know me pretty well, I guess," Brad said, smiling shyly. "It's just...I get in trouble when I start thinking. I want to. It's sex with you. But...it's also sex with a guy. Gay sex. That's a lot to wrap my mind around. I don't know about doing everything gay guys do."

Drew rolled his eyes. He couldn't help it. They still had so far to go. "You know, I've never had 'straight' sex. To me, it's just sex, something two people who lo—who want to make each other feel good do. I don't get taking stuff off the table just because it might be 'gay.'"

"I mean, I'm not sure about getting fucked," Brad whispered. "About sucking your cock. You know, the stuff women do."

Drew set that aside. This was not the time or the place for it. "Well, lucky for us," he said, "I'm all over that." He palmed Brad's cock again, pleased to see he hadn't lost much of his erection. "Think you're still up for this, big guy?"

Brad exhaled shakily. "Yeah, I think so."

"You only think so?" Drew pulled down Brad's underwear to free his cock. "Maybe I can do something to make you sure."

"Yeah?" Brad definitely sounded interested.

"Yeah," Drew said before he flicked his tongue against the head of Brad's dick. He ran his tongue up and down the underside to tease.

"That feels good," Brad admitted.

Then Drew took as much in his mouth as he could. He grinned as he reduced Brad to babbling incoherency.

Drew kept at it until Brad's hips started to rock; then he pulled off.

"Damn, Drew," Brad breathed.

"That's yours, whenever you want it," Drew said, slowly stroking him, "or just about. But now"—he looked Brad right in the eyes—"I want you to fuck me."

Brad gulped. "Okay."

Drew thought it might've been easier for Brad if he were lying on his belly. He could fuck Drew and tell himself whatever he needed to, to make it easier. Same deal with Drew on his hands and knees. But that wasn't how it was going to be. While Drew sympathized with what Brad was going through, he refused to be anything other than what he was, a gay man. He'd fought too hard for that identity to compromise or retreat even an inch back into the closet.

Drew also knew himself well. He knew how selfish he could be, and the sight of a hot, hairy, muscled man flexing and thrusting over him rocked him like nothing else. He wanted to see Brad's face when he came. He wanted Brad to see his.

Drew pulled condoms and lube out of the nightstand drawer. "Here's how this works," he said, rolling onto his back. His voice was soft, but his words relentless. He pulled his knees up. "Lots of lube. One finger, and there's a surprise up there."

"A what?" Brad said, giving him a skeptical look.

Drew made a hook with his index finger. "Once you're up to the second knuckle, feel around. You'll find it. Anyway, after one comes two, then three, then this"—he put Brad's cock, still steely hard despite its owner's nerves, over his passage—"goes here."

"Right," Brad breathed, a little shaky. "I can do this."

"*We* can do this, Brad. Both of us. Together."

Brad gave him a look of such relief and gratitude it almost made Drew speak up, made him tell Brad it was okay, they didn't have to do this. But the reality was he very much wanted to, and judging by Brad's cock, he did too.

When Brad fumbled with the condom, Drew sat up. He stilled Brad's hand, and with an amused twist to his lips, he said, "Here, I'll show you something else."

He took the bottle of lube and dripped a few drops onto Brad's rod.

"Damn, that's cold. Are you trying to kill the wood?"

Drew tore open the foil packet and pulled out the rubber. "Sorry about that. A little lube makes it feel better, at least until we've been together long enough to ride bareback."

Brad rolled the condom down over his cock as Drew leaned back and pulled his legs back up.

"Lots of lube," Brad said, squirting some into his hand.

Drew nodded. "Lots. You can't really use too much."

"Gotcha." Brad slicked his finger up and, with a deep breath, put it against Drew's hole.

Drew shivered, smiling, as the electric tingle rolled over him. He loved this, loved that it was Brad.

With a look of utmost concentration, Brad pushed his finger inside, and Drew consciously relaxed. Brad looked so serious and cute that he wanted to sit up and kiss him, but—

"Oh yeah," Drew whispered, shuddering as the first intense wave of pleasure rolled across his body.

"Yeah? I found it?" Brad said, probing with more confidence. He circled Drew's gland with his finger, rubbing around it gently.

Drew nodded, swallowing. "You found it. You've got one too. That's the secret of gay sex. When you do it right, it feels beyond incredible."

"Am I doing it right?" Brad asked, adding a second finger.

"So far, so good."

"I'm big," Brad pointed out.

"I know, and I can't wait to feel it fuck me."

"You know, I'm getting a little impatient for that myself," Brad admitted. He pulled his fingers out and squirted more lube on them before returning them plus a third to Drew's passage.

"You feel so good," Drew said, "and you're about to feel great. Are you ready?"

Brad nodded, withdrawing his fingers. More lube went on his latex-sheathed cock, and then he was up close to Drew.

Drew felt the blunt tip poking at his hole. "Go slow," he cautioned, willing himself to relax. "It's been a while, and like you said, you're big, Mr. Modesty."

"You're cute," Brad said.

"And you're—oh yeah, God, that feels damn good," Drew groaned as Brad slid over—and over and over—his prostate, filling him. The penetration combined with the sight of Brad, big and muscular and just right, looming over him with lust in his eyes, had him close.

"You're so tight. This is...wow," Brad breathed. "I'm not going to last long, not like this."

Brad pulled back experimentally and then pushed back in, filling Drew again, making his body hum. Then again, a little further out, a little faster back in. Then again, deeper and deeper as he gained confidence.

"S'okay, I won't either, now fuck me. You're in. I won't break."

Bracing his hands on either side of Drew's body, Brad leaned over and started thrusting in and out, all the way up to pubes and back out until the head alone remained in Drew's ass.

"Harder," Drew gasped. The fullness was incredible, the slide over his prostate mind-blowing. He felt the heat and light of his climax rising around him as his body sang with pleasure.

Then Brad slammed home, ramming him. "Yeah!" Drew cried as Brad pumped into him hard and fast.

"Gonna fuckin' fill you up," Brad grunted, red and sweaty over him.

Reaching awkwardly around Brad's arm, Drew tried to stroke himself. Brad saw and then shifted his weight to one hand and gingerly took Drew in the other.

"Brad," Drew panted. "Feels great. You're amazing."

Brad's rhythm faltered as he tried to stroke and fuck Drew at the same time, but he got the tempo back together and made Drew fly.

"Getting close," Drew panted.

Brad's breath came harder and harder, matching Drew's own. "Almost there..."

Then, suddenly, Drew was there, filled with light and life and Brad as spots danced before his eyes. His body rocked as he pumped blast after clenching blast of cum onto his chest.

"Drew!" Brad cried, and just like that, he was done, his rhythm slowing as he rode his own cresting orgasm. "Drew," he repeated, softly this time as he caught his breath.

Drew ran his hands gently over Brad's back. Now was the moment of truth. As the lust cleared, would Brad pull out and pull away from him, filled with regret and loathing for them both? Or would he—

Brad leaned forward, into Drew's arms. "Drew," Brad murmured, nuzzling his neck, kissing him softly. "That was...amazing."

Drew held onto Brad, as in the wake of their lovemaking he felt too vulnerable to be alone. To his relief and delight, Brad worked his arms under him and held him tighter, ignoring the cooling, sticky mess between them. "Stay with me tonight?"

"I was hoping you'd ask," Brad said from where he rested his head on Drew's shoulder.

"You never have to wait for an invitation," Drew whispered.

Later, after they'd cleaned up, they cuddled up together, Brad the big spoon and Drew the small one. Drew felt safe and protected and very well fucked.

But one thing tickled at the back of his mind. His boyfriend could barely say the word "gay," and then there were those weird notions of who was the "man" and who was the "woman." Yeah, he'd been pretty damned hot for Brad's cock, but that was some messed-up thinking, and it'd have to be addressed one of these days.

Chapter Twenty

Brad walked through the house, just enjoying the quiet and order. His crew had finished the last of the mopping up the day before, and now it was his turn. With a clipboard, a cleaning cloth, and blue painter's tape to mark any problems, Brad examined first the updated rooms and then the rooms they hadn't touched. Drew prided himself on delivering a quality product, and Brad subscribed to that wholeheartedly. Any problems he identified and fixed before the homeowners found them made Renochuck look better.

No curtains blew in the gentle breeze wafting in the opened windows. Emily would only start her installation once Drew and Brad made sure the house was good to go, and in any event, curtains would only have trapped the dust kicked up by construction, and Brad preferred his crews use industrial vacuums to filter the dust instead of curtains. Too bad they couldn't have waited until the summer heat broke before starting. It was a gorgeous day, not at all like the sweltering oven that had baked the water right out of him when he'd started.

He didn't even mind working on a stepladder up near the ceiling as he checked the crown molding for scratches and visible nail heads. He looked down around the room and out into the hallway beyond. Such a change from just a few months ago. Everywhere he looked, he felt pride in the work he'd helped complete. He'd found it difficult to appreciate the changes on a day-to-day basis. Each day he worked and worked, and while he or the crew completed each individual project, the job as a complete whole had eluded him until now. It satisfied him in a way that rotting in the sales office never would. Philip might be happy driving a desk for Sundstrom Homes, but this just confirmed to Brad that he needed to work with his hands. He needed to create if not beauty, then at least solid workmanship.

He finished checking the crown molding in one room and moved onto the next "room" on his checklist, the hallway, one that connected the public areas with the bedrooms. He glanced into the room on his left. It was one of the rooms untouched by the renovation. That was where he and Drew had made out on his first day on the job. The room in which Brad had confronted seriously for the first time both that he was physically attracted to Drew and that he had feelings for him, despite the fact he was...a man.

Then, Drew's five-o'clock shadow had skeeved him out. Now, Brad enjoyed an emotional and sexual relationship with Drew. That first time had sent him into a bit of a tailspin—he'd had cum on him. Another man's cum on him. It should've sent him screaming for the hills.

But that was the weirdest thing. Usually he was all about dropping his load and leaving. He'd never been much of a cuddler and rarely felt the need to hang around after the deed was done. But that night? There was nowhere else he wanted to be more that evening than with Drew, and even putting up with Randall's shit the next day hadn't taken the shine off it. All it did was make him more determined than ever to get the hell out of his dad's house.

Brad smiled, thinking about that first amazing night as he continued to check the molding for problems. The first night hasn't been an issue, really. By the time they'd made it back to Drew's bedroom, Brad had been so horned up nothing could've derailed him. The beers hadn't hurt either.

But the second time...that had been the weird one, but in for a penny, in for a dollar. Brad let his body take the lead, and that made both of them very happy indeed. After that? Well, it hadn't taken him very long to get used to a regular outlet other than his hand.

Besides, he was with Drew. However improbably that had come about, Brad had fallen for another man, one who had showed him a world full of masculine beauty. That made working out at the gym a whole lot more interesting, even if all he did was look. One guy was all he could wrap his mind around at a time, and he didn't think he'd ever grow tired of Drew.

It showed him just how full of possibility the universe was if he just opened his eyes. Speaking of, Drew was incredibly understanding. This was Brad's first serious relationship, but he had enough experience to appreciate Drew's patience and the fact that he didn't roll his eyes at Brad's struggles to come to terms with things. He still struggled when he thought of himself as gay or even bi. That was just going to take time.

Brad repositioned the ladder, but halfway back up, his cell phone rang. "Brad Sundstrom."

"It's Emily."

"Hey, Emily! How's it going?"

"Have you heard from Drew lately? As in the last ten minutes or so?"

Brad laughed at her direct manner. Usually Emily observed the social niceties, but when she was in a hurry, they flew right out of the window. "No, why?"

"Because I just got the weirdest call from the city preservation office."

Brad shook his head. Those words made no sense. "The what?"

Emily made an exasperated noise. "You heard me. I...I think we got the bid, Brad."

"No way!"

"Way!" Emily said, her voice exaggerated.

"All right, I get it. Not in college anymore."

"Thank you. Where's Drew?"

"No idea, but he should be here any moment to do the walkthrough. One of the two of us will call you back ASAP."

"So, you admit it?" she said archly.

Two could play at that game, and he had the rep for being as dumb as a block of wood. "Admit what?"

"I don't have time for this," she growled and hung up.

Brad tried to resume the quality-control check, but his mind kept jumping around. The bid. He pulled his phone back out and hit Drew's number on autodial. "Come on, answer, you've got that stupid douchetooth—Drew!"

"Hey," Drew said tersely.

"Listen, I just got a call from Emily—"

"I don't have time to talk," Drew interrupted. "I'm on the way to the preservation office. If I hurry, I can make it before they close. Can you call Emily and then get to my house and do something about dinner? Something tells me this is going to be a long night."

"What about the walkthrough?" Brad objected.

"Are we on schedule?"

"Slightly ahead of. I think someone pads his schedule slightly when he draws up a bid."

"Possibly." The sounds of traffic came through the Bluetooth speaker in Drew's car. "We can afford to shove the house off a day. Call Emily—"

"Got it. See you when you get there," Brad said, ending the call.

He scurried through the house, closing windows and doors. Suddenly he was very busy.

Four days later, on a rare Sunday morning at home, Brad wandered out to the kitchen early. He usually spent weekend nights with Drew, but most of his dirty laundry was at home, and he needed to make it clean laundry. He planned to get it all done and then spend the afternoon with his boyfriend. Keeping rowers' hours as he did, it would be easy to run a few loads through the washer and dryer and then get out of there.

Despite the fact little had changed physically about the Sundstrom house since his mother's death years before—Randall allowed nothing to change—Brad no longer thought of the house as his home. He had almost enough saved for his own apartment, but even if he were willing to put up with dorm-like accommodations, he didn't see himself affording the kind of place Drew would set foot in, let alone spend the night. That mattered to him.

To his surprise, Randall and Philip were already awake. Randall sipped at a mug of coffee while Philip stared morosely at a bowl of soggy cereal—Lucky Charms, Brad noted as he glanced over Philip's shoulder.

"Well, to what do we owe this honor?" Randall said. "Did whatever tramp you spent the night with get sick of your snoring?"

Brad inhaled to retort, but Philip caught his eye, shaking his head fractionally.

Knocked off balance by that, all Brad said was, "Gosh, Randall, I missed the warm and nurturing environment of home."

Randall nodded. "Just so. We'll have brunch. See to it, Philip."

Randall strolled out of the kitchen, leaving the brothers to stare at each other.

"I'll start calling around," Philip sighed.

"Don't bother," Brad said. "I'll see what I can scare up at the store. Just be prepared to help me when I get back."

"What's it going to take to get out of here?" Philip muttered, and he headed into the kitchen.

"I'm working on it," Brad said on his way to his bedroom for shoes, keys, and his wallet, "believe me."

Philip grabbed his arm. "Wait."

"Yeah?" Brad said with annoyance.

Philip looked like he wanted to say something, but they weren't the kind of brothers who talked. Closeness and sharing didn't come easily. "Good," he said at last. "I'm glad one of us can."

Brad looked at Philip for a moment, unsure what to say. "I better get to the store. I'll be back as quick as I can."

An hour and a half later, the Sundstrom boys had a complete morning meal ready. It wasn't fancy, but they weren't chefs. Eggs, bacon, pancakes, and fruit salad assembled from pre-sliced fruit from the deli, plus juice and coffee. *If this isn't good enough for Randall, he can go find someplace else to eat,* Brad thought.

There was a knock at the back door, and Alex Beltran walked in. "Hey, boss," Beltran said. He was Randall's oldest employee, the first person he'd ever hired. Brad wasn't sure what to make of him. He'd always been unfailingly polite, but no one who'd worked for Randall Sundstrom that closely for that long had clean hands, and Brad had always thought of Beltran as his dad's sinister henchman. "The city finally assigned the contract for renovation of the Bayard House."

Brad sat still, waiting to see his dad's response. He remembered well Randall's dismissive comments earlier in the summer and so had made little mention of his own work on it.

Randall made a rude noise. "Such a waste of time. Why they don't just light a match to it and start over with something built totally to the city's needs I'll never know." He grabbed the paper from Beltran and read. Then he looked up at Brad, totally expressionless. "St. Charles Renovations," Randall said at last. "Isn't St. Charles the name of that fag you work for, Bradley?"

Brad felt all eyes on him, Philip's and Randall's and Beltran's. His hands clenched. He stood up, overturning his chair. "Drew's not—!"

"Don't raise your voice at me," Randall boomed.

"Drew is not a fag," Brad said, righting his chair. He threw his napkin down and stalked off. He knew Drew was showing homes, but he also knew that with his key, he could hide out there any time.

"They should light a match to that wreck," Randall said, folding the paper and handing it back to Beltran, "and to the fag they gave the contract to."

Early October in the Sacramento Valley. *It doesn't get any better than this,* Drew thought with satisfaction as he ambled along the sidewalk toward to the CalPac field, home of the Titans, the losingest team in the division. But that was okay. That wasn't why anyone went to the games. They went for the same reason Drew and Brad went. To see and be seen. To enjoy the cool—but not cold—fall air now that the leaves had finally started to turn. To root for the home team, even if they didn't stand a chance in hell of winning. You didn't cheer for them because they'd win. You cheered for them because they were yours. Or Brad's. Drew, along with Nick, had graduated from UC San Diego. Tritons, Titans, they sounded the same, or would after a few beers.

Drew trailed along in Brad's wake. That was one advantage to dating a big guy. Crowds were a lot easier to manage with a big moose to clear the way. A mutinous part of his mind whispered that was just about the only benefit, but he squashed the thought as quickly as it had surfaced. Brad had a lot to deal with. Too bad personal growth meant more than a hard-on....

Still not much progress on that front. Drew tried to be patient, but when it came down to it, he failed to understand Brad's hang-ups. All he could do was accept them as long as Brad worked to change them. Drew told himself that a lot these days.

"It's a beautiful night to get out, isn't it?" Drew said once they'd found their seats.

"Yeah, I guess," Brad said. He scanned the crowd, eyes darting here and there. "I just can't shake the feeling it's our last bit of free time for a long time to come."

They'd completed the last of the preconstruction that afternoon. Brad had spent the first week after they received word of their successful bid helping Emily with the detailed plans for the design and build, from the obvious things like furniture and flooring and wall coverings all the way down to the little things like the molds for the glue-and-sawdust egg-and-dart detail for the ceiling moldings in the ballroom, the things people would only notice if they were wrong.

It was the first time Drew had really seen Emily in action, and it gave him a whole new appreciation for the designer's art. But there'd been little time for him to appreciate her work since he'd been swamped with his own. He had crawled over just about every square inch of the mansion while he addressed the requested changes.

Despite those requested changes, not much was being destroyed wholesale, but plenty was being changed. With the list of approved changes in hand, Drew's subs had been called in for a final walkthrough. Plumbing, gas, and sewer upgrades were all fairly straightforward, improvements in what had been installed originally, really, new pipes for old and bringing the various plumbing systems up to code, things of that nature.

He'd spent the bulk of his time with the structural engineers. Drew had expected to have to dig into the walls to bring the mansion into compliance with seismic codes, which hadn't existed back in the day, and the engineers marked out exactly what needed to be done to keep the mansion from collapsing like the proverbial house of cards during a temblor.

But Drew's electric subcontractor had been over the wiring plans, and she'd sprung some nasty surprises for him. None of the wiring could be salvaged, not even the circuits added later in the mansion's history. Since she couldn't guarantee it would carry the loads demanded by modern technology, she recommended yanking it all out and putting new copper wiring in. Drew had agreed. He didn't have much choice, after all, since he knew nothing about electricity except that it could kill him. That was why he hired subs.

Between the seismic upgrades and the electrical work, the original horsehair plaster and lath didn't stand a chance. Just how much would need to be replaced was one of the big unknowns in the project. The masons had some idea how much could be saved, but the final tally depended on the damage from, among other things, the structural engineers and electricians.

If these turned out to be the only cost overruns, then this renovation would go down in the annals of construction. It was par for the course, which struck Drew as a bizarre figure of speech. He'd always hated golf.

"You've got a point, but we can't let the Bayard House swallow all our time. Professionally, sure. We've all got a lot riding on it, but personally?" Drew said. "Definitely not. It'll make us crazy."

"It's already doing that," Brad muttered.

Drew looked at him. "Is everything all right?"

"It's fine," Brad snapped. At the look of hurt on Drew's face, he softened. "Sorry." He took a deep breath. "No, it's not."

Drew waited while Brad gathered his thoughts. Around them in the half-filled stands, the crowd erupted with distracted cheers as the teams took the field. They weren't the only ones using the game as a backdrop for their evening rather than the main event.

"All your friends keep threatening me," Brad said at last.

"They what?" Drew laughed. Then he saw how defeated Brad looked. "What do you mean, threatening you?"

Brad looked around like he wanted to be anywhere but there and talking about anything else. "They keep telling me they'll maim or hunt me down if I hurt you."

Huh. Isn't that interesting, Drew thought, wondering what his friends saw that he didn't. He chose his words carefully. "Well, the reality is I'm dating a guy who's just coming out." He held up a hand to forestall the protest he knew was coming. "Who's bi or just into me or whatever. But that's why they're worried."

"But I'm not even being given a chance. They just assume I'm going to screw you over. I'd never do that."

Not on purpose, Drew found himself thinking. He put a hand on Brad's arm and felt him jump. "They're just worried, that's all. For what it's worth, I'm sorry. I don't think you're going to hurt me, and I'm the only one who counts, right?"

Brad smiled at him. "You're the one I'm dating, yeah." He exhaled noisily. "Sorry to be a downer on our night out. I guess I'm worried about the big job coming up. There's a lot riding on it professionally for us both."

"And personally? I mean, you'll be my boss for a while, and I'm technically your boss," Drew pointed out.

"I hadn't thought of that, so thank you very much," Brad said, a flash of his usual sense of humor shining through.

"Hi, guys," Nick Bedford said, climbing the grandstand steps to where they sat.

"Fancy meeting you here," Morgan added. "Can we join you?"

"Sure," Drew said. "That okay, Brad?"

"Oh sure, like I can be honest now?" Brad said. "Of course, guys. Have a seat."

"You know, in polite circles, people would actually get up and move down so we didn't have to trip over those barges you call feet."

Brad made a show of looking around. "Don't see any of those here, so it sucks to be you, doesn't it?"

"Still keepin' it classy, Brad. Don't ever change," Morgan said.

"Shouldn't you respect your elders or something?" Brad sniped.

Morgan shook his head. "There's a five-year minimum. So, Drew, sure. You? You'd better not linger in front of my car when you cross the street."

"I miss you too. Oh wait... I just saw you this morning. You know, that makes it real hard for the heart to grow fonder," Brad said.

"How can I miss you if you won't go away?" Morgan shot back.

"Who's crashing whose date?" Brad said.

Nick and Drew just smiled as their boyfriends sparred, their jibes and digs lost in the general roar of the crowd.

"So, who's winning?" Nick asked.

"Whoever's playing CalPac," Brad said.

"Your faith in your alma mater's touching," Drew said, laughing.

Brad shrugged. "You know I'm right."

That was interesting. Nick and Morgan showed up, and Brad seemed to relax. Two guys together looked like a date, but add two more guys, and it was just four guys out to watch the CalPac Titans get stomped. Never mind that two of the guys made up one of the most notorious couples on campus.

"Don't you guys worry that you'll be spotted or found out or something?" Brad asked.

Morgan shook his head. "Not really."

But Nick, the more practical of the two, shrugged. "We've already been found out, but yes, it's a concern, given that the school's policy toward us seems to be deliberate blindness. If we call attention to ourselves, that could change."

"But it's a small school, so it's not like we could hide, even if we wanted to." The look Morgan gave Nick spoke volumes.

Drew felt like he and Brad had come into the middle of something, but Brad's question now made much more sense. He was afraid he'd be spotted. With Drew. The realization left a bitter taste in his mouth.

The conversation turned to crew. Drew supposed it was inevitable.

Chapter Twenty-One

It was passive-aggressive, even a little childish, but Drew wanted to see how long it took Brad to figure out that something about their evening upset him. It took the entire football game, a quick bite to eat, and part of the drive back to his place.

"Hey, you're awfully quiet over there," Brad said.

"Yes, I am," Drew said, his tone of voice brittle.

Brad frowned in the darkness. "Uh-oh. I don't like the sound of that."

Drew sighed. He hated "discussions," but he'd sparked this one, so he couldn't very well run from it. "Were you aware how much you relaxed when they joined us?"

"Are you upset Nick and Morgan joined us? *You* told them to sit down."

Drew shook his head. "I didn't say I was upset. I just observed how much you calmed down once they did. Why is that?"

Brad squirmed. "I don't know... I didn't think I did." Drew looked at him levelly but didn't say anything. Brad's shoulders slumped. "I just know a lot of people there."

"We didn't run into anyone you know other than Nick and Morgan," Drew pointed out.

"No, I guess we didn't. Maybe my old friends aren't that into football." It sounded like a question.

"Are you ashamed of me?" Drew said softly, afraid of the answer but needing it all the same.

"Oh hell, Drew. Is that what this is about?" Brad demanded. He looked at Drew, but Drew refused to meet his eyes, looking straight ahead at the road.

"Are you?"

"Of course not," Brad snapped. "No, Drew, of course not," he repeated more softly.

"Then what is it? Because that's sure what it feels like, and I've got to tell you, it sucks."

"What do you want me from, Drew? It's October. In August, I thought I was straight. Now..."

"Now what? What happened?"

"I met you, and now I don't know."

This was why his friends had warned him, why Nick had warned him. He cared for Brad a lot. Lately, he wondered if he were starting to love him, but this hurt. Before he met Brad, he'd always thought that if a boyfriend "did him wrong," he'd react with righteous fury, kicking said bad boyfriend to the curb in a fit of indignation and self-respect. But now, faced with the very real possibility that his closeted boyfriend was embarrassed to be seen publicly with him, all he wanted to do was cry.

"You're quiet. Talk to me?" Brad said.

"It's funny," Drew said in a way that meant it was anything but. "I fought tooth and claw to come out in high school. My family was horrified. I got the shit kicked out of me just about every day for most of my sophomore year by big jerks like you, and now—"

"I'm not a big jerk," Brad said quietly. "I'm just—"

"No, not intentionally, but I'm hurt anyway. It's just kind of ironic, you know? Drew St. Charles, teenaged ambassador to baffled heterosexual high-schoolers, eleven years later is dating a closet case and getting his heart bro—trampled."

Brad remained silent for the rest of the drive to Drew's house.

"Are you coming in?" Drew said from the driveway when he realized Brad hadn't gotten out of the car.

"I wasn't sure you wanted me to," Brad said.

Drew wanted many things, starting with a boyfriend who would, if not hold his hand in public, at least be seen with him. But he also wanted Brad. He wasn't used to compromising. He didn't like it.

"I want you to come in."

Brad sat in the car, just looking out at him, a worried look on his face.

"Please?" Drew held out his hand.

Brad got out of the car and came around to where Drew stood. He reached out to take Drew's hand. "Can...can I hold you?"

"Yes," Drew said, and in a rush, his big lug of a boyfriend enfolded him in his arms right there in the driveway. No, it wasn't public like the football stadium, but at least it was outside. He sagged against Brad, resting his head on his shoulder.

Brad kissed the top of his head. "I can't say I'll be rushing to march in any parades or that what I'm dealing with right now with is easy or anything, but I'm not ashamed to be seen with you. I'm not."

Drew nodded. "Let's go inside. I'm actually getting kind of cold."

Brad led him to the door and then waited while he opened it. Brad closed the door behind him.

Drew opened his mouth to speak, but before he could, Brad grabbed him and held him, kissing him. "I'm sorry," Brad whispered in between kisses. "I never want to make you feel bad."

"I know," Drew said, and he did. But that didn't mean it hadn't happened.

Or that he didn't feel something else right then.

"You still cold?" Brad said, his voice suggestive.

"Warming up nicely," Drew breathed before he kissed Brad.

Drew felt Brad grin as he kissed him. "Because I think I can warm you up some more."

"That's because you're so hot." Drew pulled Brad's shirt up and ran his hands under it. He'd never get enough of Brad's chest, ever. He made a face. "I can't believe I actually said that."

"It was pretty bad," Brad laughed. "Even if it's true." He deepened the kiss, holding Drew's face in his large hands, fanning his thumbs along Drew's cheeks.

"Come on, what're we waiting for?" Drew took off for his bedroom, with Brad half a step behind.

Drew almost made it to his bedroom.

With a grunt, Brad launched himself at Drew. He caught him around the waist and dragged him down to the bed. With a "Ha!" he rolled Drew over and straddled him.

Drew stared up at him with wide, hungry eyes.

Brad grinned at him. "Like that, do you?"

Drew nodded slowly.

"Then I know you'll love this." Brad grabbed one of Drew's arms and yanked it up and over his head. Holding it with one hand, Brad pulled Drew's other arm up and held him.

Just like that, Drew's bones turned to jelly and his cock went rock hard. He closed his eyes and tilted his head, inviting a kiss.

"Someone likes it rough," Brad breathed. He leaned over to kiss Drew, greedy and demanding and plundering. The time for gentleness was past. It was time to show the man who was boss. Brad was inexperienced when it came to sex with men, but he'd been paying attention. He knew what Drew liked. What he wanted. What he needed.

If the first time they made love was all about Brad, this felt to Drew like it was all about him, like Brad was taking everything he'd learned since that night and putting it into practice on and for him.

Brad awkwardly pulled Drew's shirt up to expose him to Brad's lips and tongue and teeth. "Remember the first day of the reno this summer? Making out in that bedroom?" he said.

"Uh-huh," Drew squeaked, distracted by Brad's inexpert but effective lapping at one nipple.

"Remember how I was freaked out by your beard?"

"Yeah." Drew struggled to focus through the rising pleasure.

"There was something else that day." Brad kissed his way lazily across Drew's chest to the other pec as one hand strayed south, palming Drew's erection through his jeans before slipping inside the waistband.

"Braaad," Drew moaned. Had Brad always been this much of a talker? It was making him crazy.

"Wanna know what?"

Drew opened his eyes. "What?"

Brad looked up into his eyes. "I wanted to know what your cock would feel like in my mouth. What it—you—would taste like."

"Jeez," Drew gasped, suddenly unable to breathe.

Brad smirked up at him as he popped the first button on Drew's jeans. "Think it'd be okay to find out?"

"Uh-huh."

Pop.

"Because I don't want to do anything to make you angry," Brad said. He bit playfully at one nip and then soothed the sting with his tongue.

Drew knew what Brad was doing, had apparently taught him the rhythm, in fact. But doing it and feeling it were totally different. That, plus Brad's explorations in his underwear, drove him crazy anyway. "You're...not. You're...this...hot," he said, struggling to focus.

Pop.

"Are you sure? I'm new at this. I'm probably not very good."

Nip. Lick. Kiss. The other nipple lit up under Brad's mouth.

Drew clawed at the duvet. Damn, but the man was a quick study. "You're...fucking awesome."

"Maybe later. But if I'm not doing this right, I could stop."

Brad kissed the middle of Drew's chest. Starting at the top of Drew's abs, he slowly worked his tongue into the ridge between the muscles, the shallow indention that formed the midline of the washboard.

Pop.

"Don't you dare...ohmygod, Brad! Don't stop!"

Brad's tongue ignited a trail on Drew's skin while his hand did the devil's work in his pants, and it was so right and so wrong and he floated in a white-hot burning heaven.

"Well, would you look at that," Brad said in wonder. "Your pants are"—*pop!*—"completely undone. How d'you suppose that happened? And—my goodness, your underwear's kind of messy. Something's leaking in there."

"You're killing me, Brad. Please?"

Brad toyed with the elastic waistband of Drew's boxer-briefs. "Please what? Tell me what you want."

Drew raised his head. "I want you to stop this torture and put my goddamn dick in your mouth already."

Brad flashed him his shit-eating grin. With the tiny part of his brain still capable of rational thought, Drew suddenly understood why Brad had irritated Nick. "Why, Drew, all you had to do was ask."

In one swift motion that belied his large size, Brad was up and over Drew, grasping his pants and underwear. "Lift up."

In their hurry, they caught Drew's erect penis in the folds of his underwear. "Ow! Wait!"

"Something wrong?" Brad said blandly.

"You break it, you bought it," Drew hissed, pulling himself free before Brad yanked his clothes the rest of the way down and off.

"I'll kiss it and make it better." Brad pushed Drew back down to the bed and sat awkwardly next to him. He lapped experimentally at the head of Drew's penis, engorged and leaking pre-cum. Despite knowing it was coming, Drew jackknifed up off the mattress. Or maybe the anticipation stretched his nerves to the breaking point.

"Damn, Brad," he breathed.

Wet heat closed over his cock, so different from fucking. Lighter pressure, yes, but the tongue. Brad's tongue roved up and down his shaft, licking, tasting, playing.

Drew's breath came in shallow gasps, and he lost himself in a sea of pleasure. Brad's technique was far from perfect. There was too much teeth and not enough stroking, but Drew wouldn't have traded it for the world. It was his boyfriend trying, making him feel good, and that made it the best blowjob ever.

Then Drew groaned and pulled his cock out of Brad's mouth. "If I come, you won't get up my ass."

"We can't have that, can we?" Brad breathed, kissing his way up Drew's chest to his lips. But then he kissed his way back down. "Or maybe we can."

"What?" Drew struggled to sit up.

"Uh-uh," Brad said. He smiled and went back to his prize.

"Seriously," Drew panted, "if you keep doing that, I'm going to come."

Brad pulled off him with a wet *pop*. "Maybe that's the plan."

"Wait..." Drew started, but Brad surged up and pinned him again, and didn't that just melt his brain right down to the stem.

"You want it, and I want to give it to you," Brad growled, fumbling with his own fly. He pulled his belt off his pants and wrapped it around Drew's wrists before cinching it snug but not tight. Then he looped the free end around one of the slats in Drew's headboard and tied it roughly. "Now shut it down."

Drew groaned. He still struggled, just a little. It only made it hotter, but he knew he was done fighting. So did Brad.

Brad went back to work, but Drew knew it wouldn't take much longer.

Drew started bucking his hips. Any moment now... "Soon."

Brad redoubled his efforts, humming softly to himself.

"If you don't...mouthful...stop." Drew looked down at Brad bent over him, head moving up and down as he sought to wring the pleasure from Drew's body. And that was all it took. He was there, pumping into Brad's mouth, and powerless to pull away.

And then before he knew it, before he could ask, Brad untied his hands. Drew pulled Brad up. "That was..."

Brad kissed him, and he tasted himself on Brad's lips. "I know."

"But I didn't do anything to make you feel good." He felt a little empty, thinking he'd been alone at his climax.

"Yeah, you did." Brad kissed Drew. "That was so hot for me. Seeing you spread out and helpless like that? I could do that to you for hours. Wanna know why?"

He nodded slowly. Hearing Brad say that made him burn all over again.

"Because at the end of it, I know you're mine, and sooner or later I'll get to tap that fine, fine ass again."

Drew could only nod again, blushing. He was Brad's too. Unsure of just when it had happened, he knew in that instant he belonged to Brad, and that was that.

It scared him a little. He'd always thought that when he gave his heart to someone, he'd be aware of it, that it would be a conscious decision, that he'd have had some control over it, but where Brad was concerned, he was learning quickly he wasn't in the driver's seat.

"Besides," Brad continued, "I came right after you did."

Drew licked his lips, wondering if Brad somehow knew exactly what he was doing or if he were rushing headlong into this too. "You're sure taking to this like a natural."

"Have you looked in a mirror? You would, too, if you had you teaching you." Brad leaned toward Drew. "You... I don't know. You make me crazy, sometimes."

But Drew did know. As passion dimmed and lust cooled, he wondered if that would be enough.

Chapter Twenty-Two

October flew by in a blur of crumbling plaster and sawdust, there and gone as the renovation of the Bayard House kicked into high gear. Like both men knew it would, the renovation consumed their lives.

Brad's days consisted of early mornings on the river helping Nick coach the CalPac rowers, followed by his part-time work for his father at Suburban Graveyard, and more often than not, he spent that fielding calls from his crews at the renovation, since most people who ventured out there seldom bought. Finally, he dashed to the job site, inhaling lunch as he drove and working until the crews quit for the day. Sometimes—the nights he didn't have classes—he stayed late working by himself until the private security Drew had hired told him to go home since he was in the way.

He yawned, swilling down some more energy drink. It wouldn't help, and after five late nights in a row, first studying for exams and then taking them, on top of everything else, he was fried. Still, the mansion wouldn't renovate itself.

Drew'd tried to tell him to take it easy, to pace himself, that they'd built plenty of time into the bid. Brad failed to understand the logic. They had both staked their futures on this high-visibility project, and Brad in particular felt like this was his make-or-break moment.

He wasn't even out of college a year and had majored in physical education. If he had it to do over....

He swore and put the energy drink down. He was too young for regrets. Wasn't he? Maybe Drew, at twenty-nine and with a successful real estate career, could afford to go home when he was tired, but Brad knew it was slacking, not that he'd said so. He wasn't a complete idiot. Still, Drew was stressing hard, so shouldn't he work just as long and hard?

He rested his head on the desk they'd set up in the rented trailer inside the fence at the job site. Just a few minutes of rest.

Initially, he'd worried about working with Drew. They already spent many evenings together, and with Drew's leave from selling houses...well, that promised a lot of togetherness, but the past month had flown by, the days spent in satisfying work and the nights spent making each other feel good. They usually handled their disagreements calmly, and both of them worked to keep the disagreements minor, usually a matter of what Drew envisioned clashing with the realities of engineering and a building almost as old as the state of California itself. At such times, Brad usually found himself serving as the interpreter of the structurally possible to his boyfriend.

It was weird. When they fucked...made love, he guessed, because it had turned into far more than getting his rocks off. Making love. He still struggled claiming the "gay" label, but he definitely had feelings for Drew far beyond what he'd felt for anyone else, and he sure as hell loved plowing him. If that wasn't gay, he didn't know what was. But still, the word.

He felt funny thinking that, but he also felt like they'd passed some threshold or reached some new level. Like they'd established who was boss and who liked what and that was that. Drew liked to be dominated, and Brad liked to dominate him. Drew clearly got off on submission, at least submission to Brad. But he himself just as clearly got off on that submission.

Brad hadn't known that about himself. He wondered if Drew did. From the first time they made out, Drew had responded on a deep, instinctive level to Brad's larger physical size and brash, even forceful personality. Brad could be tender with Drew, but they both knew what Drew liked, and as Brad was learning, his own pleasure lay in giving it to him.

In fact, that time after the football game when he'd gone down on Drew, he'd been firmly in control. He'd held Drew down and given him what he craved. Brad had been the one with the dick in his mouth and the cum down his throat, but he'd definitely been on top, like he had all the other times. But that got him to thinking.

He'd always thought the one who went down was "the girl." That was all his sexual experience had taught him, but when he thought about it, he'd eaten women out before, and he was still all man. He didn't think Drew would've been so into him if he weren't. So maybe oral was oral. Maybe sex was just sex, and what you stuck it in or who stuck what in you didn't really matter.

But then he thought about submitting to Drew, taking Drew inside him. It wasn't like he'd seen a lot of guys' dicks to compare Drew to, but the thought of riding that cock kind of scared him. It meant a lot more than sex. It meant a fundamental change in who Brad thought he was, and he wasn't ready for that.

Still, he'd never been happier, and not even running around like a crazy man between his two jobs, school, and coaching changed that. Not even the daily tedium of

Suburban Graveyard brought him down, not when he had this, and not with Drew in his life. When he thought about it, he might be young and stressed about making it, but he had what he wanted—he was being taken seriously and treated with respect.

He jolted up. Damn, he was about to fall asleep. He glanced down at the blueprints and decided to get going on what he saw. The last thing he wanted was a noise complaint from the neighbors, but a reciprocating saw used deep inside the mansion should be fine. He'd cut the hole for that interior door he'd seen literally right under his nose and then call it a night before security ran him off.

It wouldn't take long, but a few minutes saved here, a few saved there, added up fast, and time was money, right?

"Hey, boss, you need to see this."

Drew looked up from the blueprints for the third-floor private residence. Now that the crews had removed those parts of the rotting floors, walls, and ceiling posing the greatest hazard and temporarily reinforced the rest, the structural engineers were ready to begin the delicate operation of buttressing all load-bearing members, both to hold the building up and keep it standing in the event of an earthquake.

"Bring those with you," Octavio continued.

"I'll be right back," Drew said to the lead engineer. "What's going on?"

"I'm hoping you can tell me. There's a hole for a door where there wasn't one yesterday. Where there shouldn't be today."

"Where?" Drew groaned. He so didn't need this. Too tired and busy for his usual stress releases, he could only push himself to the edge for so long before falling over it. The acid shooting into his stomach right then told him that much.

"Second-floor ballroom," Octavio said.

"Crap," Drew said, following Octavio out of the trailer and up the once-grand main staircase and into the ballroom that would again sparkle in a new gilded age once Emily finished with it.

For now, lath gaped from where the masons had scraped away what couldn't be salvaged. Drew was surprised at just how much of the original walls they'd been able to preserve, both in the ballroom and the rest of the mansion. That meant after addressing load issues to take the stress off original structural materials, repairing and filling cracks, rekeying delaminating plaster, and finally after replacing damaged lath, the entire thing could receive a fresh coat of plaster with marble dust to create a hard, smooth coat that would then be polished with a metal trowel.

Octavio led him to the back of the ballroom, but Drew saw the damage as soon as they walked through the open double doors. The gaping hole where none should be stuck out like a Planned Parenthood clinic in Sun City. "Jesus God," he muttered, dumbfounded by the sight.

"Basically, yes," Octavio replied.

They peered into the wall, although there wasn't much to see. A door-sized hole had been neatly cut through into what was supposed to be a library next door, and the dust had even been cleaned up. A few loose pieces of lath wiggled when Drew poked at them. The cleanness of the cuts surprised Drew, for all this constituted mutilation.

"So, what do we do?" Octavio said.

Drew ground his teeth. What he really wanted to do was hurl his hard hat across the room and then jump up and down on his protective eyewear until it made a nice, satisfying crunching noise. "Why don't you check the dumpsters to see if we can salvage any of the pieces? I'm going to check the workflow log to see who gets a new asshole today and then go grovel to the carpenters and masons to see if they can fix it."

"Don't forget telling the city's historical preservation department. And you wonder why I refuse to be a foreman," Octavio said as they left the ballroom.

"No, I really don't," Drew said.

As he hurried downstairs, Drew knew exactly why Octavio refused any more responsibility than Drew had already forced upon him. But really, what kind of fool clattered around with a saw and no clue where to use it? It had to have been one of his people, if only because vandals weren't so tidy. It was a carefully cut doorway, the result of planning and absolutely stupid blueprint reading.

Fortunately, Drew had a solution. He'd come up with the idea of a workflow log to track the progress of each crew and to know who had done what in his absence. It was looking more and more like he'd be going back to real estate soon, since, as predicted, the city had proved slow to pay, and he had yet to hear back on two pending grants, including a large one from the state redevelopment agency. Given the state's perpetually blinkered finances and with spending freezes looking likely, Drew knew he'd need to raise the cash to keep going temporarily. And now the thought of leaving the renovation in someone else's hands made him long to vomit.

One good thing, he thought, was that door hadn't been there when he left yesterday, so the work wouldn't be too far back. Then he realized something, and it felt like a kick in the gut.

Brad.

Brad had worked late the previous night.

He'd told Brad to go home and sleep, to rest, that he was tired, too tired to keep pushing himself to the limit.

Brad hadn't listened and, like the jackass he could be, charged on ahead, probably fueled by coffee or energy drinks. Drew spun around in his desk chair to check the green recycling bin by the door, and yep, it was full of Rockstar and Red Bull.

He was old enough to realize that you could only go on that kind of amplification for so long. Brad hadn't figured it out yet, but he was about to, just as soon as he arrived at work.

Drew sat at his desk and opened the log to see Brad's handwriting detailing what he'd worked on the day before, including that damned doorway.

A note fluttered out of the log, obviously meant for him.

> *Hey babe,*
>
> *Just a quick note to let you know I got a jump on the next phase and cut the door for the new bathroom in the library wall.*
>
> *This schedule sux. We never see each other. : (*
>
> *xoxo Brad*

"Yeah, buddy, good luck with that." Drew bit each word off and spat it out. He was tired and beyond stressed, and the note should've charmed him. It might even charm him later, if he restrained himself from wadding it up and chucking it in the recycling bin. "Trust me, Brad, right now, you don't want to see me. And will someone please spare me from men too stupid to know their own limitations?"

What he really wanted to do was hit the pathway along the river to pound his stress and anxiety and furor out. Instead, what he would do was mutter rude and unflattering things about his boyfriend under his breath while he wrote a report to the city about the damage to the historic house and then start the cost projections for the repairs. He knew they'd bite into his already tight budget, and they were starting to be strapped for cash as it was.

He remembered thinking this summer that he liked a challenge where both Brad and the mansion were concerned, but there in the trailer-cum-office, he reflected that he'd been full of shit. If a closeted boyfriend who blundered through walls in an historic building that was already devouring his budget constituted a "challenge," the universe lacked all sense of proportion.

A half-hour later, Octavio came in. "Good call on the dumpster. I got some of my guys to help, and we found three big pieces. We pulled them out *very* carefully, so it can probably be repaired."

"Okay, can you oversee this personally?" Drew asked. "Brad's crew—"

Drew shook his head. "Brad's the one who did this. I want someone on it I know won't fuck it up again."

Octavio's eyes widened. He knew the score between Drew and Brad. "You got it, boss." He put particular emphasis on the last word as if to remind him just where the buck stopped. "But in my opinion? This is going to need a restoration specialist. I mean, I can ask the carpenters and masons, but we need this to be perfect so you can assure the city that they'll need radar to find the fix."

Drew regarded Octavio for a moment. "Okay, this conversation never happened, but this will pretty much push the budget into the red."

"But the funding—" Octavio started.

"Between the city and the pending grants, it's tight. I'll have to go over the budget with Emily and see how much I can loan the project, but the reality is I'll probably have to go sell some houses."

Octavio nodded slowly. "Wow. Good to know. So, you want me to—"

"Keep an eye on Brad. He'll be nominally in control in my absence."

Octavio nodded again. "Good luck with that."

"No kidding."

Octavio checked his watch. "I need to get back to work."

"Right. You know how to reach me," Drew said.

As Octavio turned to open the trailer door, it opened, and Brad walked in, along with Drew's renewed anger at the whole situation.

With a last look over his shoulder, Octavio left to get back to work and get out of the line of fire.

"That's odd. What's his deal?" Brad said. "Anyway, did you see the note I left? I hope it helped."

"Helped, you say," Drew said flatly.

"Yeah, what's the problem?" Brad looked at him strangely. "What's yours?"

"The problem, and it's *our* problem, not just mine, is that you cut a door where it didn't belong."

"What?" Brad said stupidly.

"You stayed late when you were dead tired and, I'm guessing, misread the blueprints somehow. You were a room off, Brad. You destroyed a wall that was in pretty good shape," Drew grated out. "Now we have to try to patch it back together and then pray the masons can repair the plaster. You should've gone home and gotten some sleep."

"Shit," Brad breathed. He half turned away.

Drew unclenched his jaw. "Yes, that's one word for it. I might also choose colossally stupid or maybe completely fucked, but sure, we can go with shit. Like shit for brains! How could you do that?"

"At least I was in here doing something!" Brad snapped.

"When you had no business being here!" Drew fired back. "I tried to tell you it was time to go, that you were too tired, but you wouldn't listen to me. You had to be a hero. Now on top of fixing it, I get to explain to the city how this happened."

Brad just glared at him belligerently, but Drew's anger still burned incandescently. "Even you have your limits, Superman. You're not a college jock anymore, Brad! You can't push yourself to the edge and expect to sleep it off by skipping class."

"What the hell is that supposed to mean?"

"It means you've got responsibilities and obligations, and you can't just do what you want. You should've talked to me before striking out on your own on something as major as cutting holes in a wall!"

"So, you're saying you're the boss, and I need to check everything with you? So much for partners! I knew working for you was a mistake."

"Oh, I think not," Drew said. "You were and are desperate to get out from under your father's thumb, and you totally should be, but my job offer was a life-preserver thrown to you, and you know it."

Brad shot him a venom-filled look. "Working for you was mistake, and dating you was an even bigger one."

"You want to mix the professional and personal? Fine, but before you crank up the waaaambulance, keep in mind that you're not the only one who's made sacrifices to this relationship. I've got a boyfriend who still can't say the word 'gay' and who has 'issues' being seen in public in any way that might look like a date."

"Hey, I'm working through a lot right now, I've given up a lot—"

Drew rolled his eyes. He'd heard this so much he could've yelled both sides of the argument. "Yeah, I know. You keep telling me. How about you show me?"

"What the hell have you given up?"

"You mean besides fucking my boyfriend?" At Brad's wide eyes, Drew said, "What, you thought I was nothing but a bottom? Newsflash, I like to fuck guys, not just get fucked by them, and on top of that—ha!—I like to go out."

"You've got a boyfriend—" Brad glowered at Drew's snort. "You've got me, why d'you need to go out?"

"I like to dance. Ask Nick sometime about our adventures at Aspects. It's what gay people do...oh wait, that's right." Drew slapped his forehead. "I forgot. You're not *gay*. You just like to stick your dick up my ass." He shook his head, amazed at what came pouring out of his mouth. For once, it wasn't glitter and rainbows. He'd thought he was fine waiting while Brad made up his mind, but his own needs and wants wouldn't stay buried, not when he ate stress for breakfast and crapped it out before lunch. "I work hard, and dancing's one way I blow off steam. We just passed one of my favorite holidays. Halloween. Did you know there's a charity costume ball I go to every year? It's called the Goblin Ball."

Brad grudgingly shook his head.

"My boss at the real estate agency buys a table every year. Dancing, costumes, a fundraiser for the local HIV/AIDS foundation. Halloween's like Christmas for gay people. And what'd we do on Halloween? Tell me, Brad. What'd we do?"

"Stayed home and handed out candy," Brad muttered.

"That's right. I used to go out. Now we stay in, but not because we're homebodies. No, we stay in because you can't deal with being gay."

"I didn't know any of that. I didn't know you felt that way." Brad looked deflated.

Drew exhaled noisily. "I didn't either, but I've realized I'm really losing patience with having to put your coming out first. I've got needs and wants, too, and I'm figuring out that I can't just box them up, even though I thought I could."

"You...uh, want to fuck me?" Brad asked.

Drew's cheeks colored. "Yeah, I'd love to nail your ass to the wall. Or the bed. The thought of you stretched under me and moaning incoherently while I ram your ass hard never fails to get me off during my own private sexy time."

"You know I'm not there yet." Brad studied the floor.

"I know, but maybe I need to know you're working on it," Drew said.

Brad looked up. "So where do we go from here?"

Drew thought about it. "First, we separate the personal and the professional. We've got two different issues, and the one that matters now is the hole that was cut where it shouldn't be."

Brad nodded. "It sounds like we'd better talk later. For now, can you show me on the blueprints? Because you have to know, I wouldn't do something like that if I weren't absolutely sure."

"I know, but Brad? You've got to slow down. I don't know what the answer is, but this schedule...it's just too much."

He pulled out the thick sheaf of blueprints and flipped to the detailed plans for that part of the second floor. He showed Brad exactly where he'd gone wrong.

"Damn." Brad shook his head. "You're right. I was kind of hoping somehow you wouldn't be, but that's a rookie mistake. I've been around these things long enough I should know how to read them." He rubbed his face. "So how do I fix this?"

"I really don't know," Drew admitted. "I've got some ideas, but it all depends on what our subs say. We may have to call in a restoration specialist."

"That won't be cheap," Brad sighed.

Drew nodded. "I'm probably going to resume selling houses and badger the city to start paying its bills. It'll take a while to get the money flowing again, but it's better than nothing."

"I know it's not much, but I'm sorry." Brad held his arms open. After a moment's hesitation, Drew allowed himself to be held.

"It's funny, but even when I'm mad at you, I can't get enough of you," Drew said, his voice muffled by Brad's chest.

"Lucky for me I'm so lovable," Brad said.

Drew didn't say anything for a moment. "Yeah, you are."

Brad kissed the top of Drew's head. "I know I'm not perfect, but I'm trying."

"Yes, very." Drew elbowed him affectionately.

Chapter Twenty-Three

Later that evening, when everyone else had left the job site for the evening, Brad and Drew walked through the mansion before heading back to Drew's place. Their new evening routine consisted of a workplace safety inspection, checking to ensure that electrical cords for the work and security lights were properly taped along the edges of traffic areas or otherwise away and anything valuable that could attract thieves had been returned to the locked cargo containers.

They couldn't do much about vandals but keep the place discreetly illuminated at night and hire private security. Fortunately, the Bayard House sat on a parcel of land occupied on all sides but the front, and thanks to gentrification, the surrounding properties were both occupied and well cared for. In fact, that the mansion was the neighborhood eyesore was one of the city's reasons for restoring it.

Despite the mild November night, not uncommon in early fall in northern California, the air in the mansion never really warmed up. Then again, the air inside wouldn't become too inhospitable until deep into winter, and both men wore their light jackets loosely.

"I really am sorry," Brad said, "about the fuck-up with the doorway and the things I said."

"I am too," Drew replied, even though he suspected on some level they'd both meant every word.

They didn't say anything for a few moments as they went single file up a narrow staircase at the back of the second floor. When the mansion had been built, the staircase had led to the servants' quarters under the eaves, but Drew planned to the turn the old servants' rooms into a private retreat for the mayor and—currently—his family by knocking down a few walls to open it up a bit, and any resident staff would live in quarters at the back of the property.

The air in the attic was warm, even close, under the influence of the halogen work lamps, and that was another reason to check the mansion before leaving for the evening. They would leave only the bare minimum of lights on not only to spare the neighbors, but also to reduce the risk of fire.

Already the structural engineers had been at work up here, and they saw stacks of lightweight galvanized metal studs to be inserted carefully into the walls before new carrying beams were placed over the existing ones and new doorways and top plates over all of it, essentially creating a modern framed wall inside the old one. Then they'd be anchored from below, and above, the roof would be reinforced and skylights added in select rooms, then insulated and closed in with new lath and plaster for continuity of appearance. The complex, intricate work fascinated them both. Just so long as they avoided the holes in the floor.

Brad looked around. "I can already see this coming together."

"This was your idea, did you know that?" Drew said.

"Uh...no, I don't think so," Brad said.

"That night at the coffee shop after the ballgame? You mentioned the idea of a private space for the family."

Drew smiled and then shrugged. "I hadn't planned anything beyond a suite, not really any different than the public rooms, just closed to the public."

"Oh." Brad smiled. "I didn't think I'd said anything good that night, just kind of running my mouth."

"Oh, I listened all right. I was struck by your energy and enthusiasm, and even then, knew I wanted a part of it. Remember how uncertain you were about what you could contribute to this?"

"And I was right. I screwed up," Brad huffed.

"Yeah, you did. My dad used to say anyone can fuck up, but it takes a real man to make it right. And I know you'll make it right. I'm not sure yet how we'll explain this, but you admitted you made a mistake. You'd be surprised how many people can't."

"Well, if there's one thing I'm good at, it's screwing things up and people over," Brad muttered.

"That's your dad talking."

Brad hunched his shoulders defensively. "I ratted out Nick to the athletic department and almost broke Nick and Morgan up," he said softly. "I'll never forgive myself for that."

"They survived, and they're the stronger for it. Besides, you made it right," Drew said.

"Jeez, I hope that never comes out."

Drew shook his head. "They won't find it out from me."

"But Nick's your best friend," Brad objected.

Drew shrugged. "And you're my boyfriend."

"Some boyfriend," Brad muttered. "I keep you from doing the things you want to do. I still wish you'd told me how much you wanted to go to that Goblin Ball."

"I should've given you the chance to say no instead of making assumptions," Drew admitted. "But I wish you wouldn't be so hard on yourself. I'm not trying to get all rah-rah, and some of this you've pointed out to me, but look how far you've come since this summer. Beer-soaked college pussy hound to a guy who's got a boyfriend."

Brad smiled despite himself. "You're throwing my own words back at me. No fair."

"How's that unfair when you were right?" Drew smiled softly. "I'm sorry for what I said earlier."

"Me too." Brad hesitated. "This is probably really wrong since we're at work, but...can I kiss you?"

Drew nodded and parted his lips, ready for Brad. The kiss stayed tame, a touch of lips to lips, for almost five whole seconds before he realized there were other parts of Brad's anatomy he wanted to explore.

Drew tasted Brad's lips, running his tongue across them. He found traces of breath mints, and underneath that, the apple Brad had eaten earlier. The slide of smooth, slightly moist flesh over flesh made him shiver with need, that one simple act promising intense pleasure to come.

He licked his own tingling lips and then flicked his tongue against Brad's lips, which opened for him.

He reached down to check if Brad felt it, too, pretty sure what he'd find. Sure enough, Brad's not inconsiderable cock was rising to the occasion.

"Jeez, babe, what're you doing?" Brad rasped.

"You know what I'm doing." Drew shifted to straddle one of Brad's legs, grinding against the muscular, jeans-clad thigh. The zing rushed from his groin up his spine. He shivered.

Brad moved his leg a bit, bumping into Drew's crotch. "You sexually harassing me?"

"No, it's makeup sex," Drew breathed as he kissed Brad.

"Never really had it," Brad whispered. He pulled back a little and rested his forehead on Drew's.

"Really? Never?" Drew gasped, shocked despite the moment.

Brad shrugged. "When I screwed up, the woman I was with usually just dumped me."

"Oh, Brad," Drew said, suddenly feeling so strongly for this man who played the blundering oaf but who secretly held a certain shyness, a wounded something about him that made Drew long to take him in his arms and hold and caress and love on him.

So, he did, kissing Brad again, slowly at first. Then Brad opened for him, with increasing heat and passion, and Drew took the lead. He wanted to reassure Brad, wanted to make him feel good and let him know it would all be all right.

He worked his hands under Brad's construction "uniform" shirt of a long-sleeved T-shirt under a short-sleeved one. First the top layer, the short-sleeved tee. He smoothed his hands up along Brad's chest, knowing the friction and texture of the knit fabric rubbing over his nips would heat Brad up fast.

Brad exhaled loudly, and Drew smiled into the kiss. *Yep.*

Then Brad, sometimes naïve where this was concerned but never slow on the uptake, pulled at Drew's shirt. Drew withdrew just enough to make it easier. Brad's touch on his bare skin sent an electric something through him that made his scalp ripple and sent a shiver through him.

"Are you cold?" Brad said, breaking the kiss. "We should stop. Security could find us."

"Don't you dare," Drew hissed. He put his hands on Brad's skin. "That just makes it hotter. Besides, they're used to you working late, right?"

"Yeah, but not like this," Brad said, looking around nervously.

Drew flicked Brad's nips again, but his real interest was further south. He knew the chances of being caught were low, and he really wanted to do this, and—

Drew's horned-up little monkey brain flashed on an idea, a way to break Brad of his notion that some things were for dudes and some things were for bitches.

There was no fumbling involved, because Drew knew exactly what he wanted and where to find it. Brad's belt and button and zipper were in his way, and he dealt with them in short order. He plunged his hand into Brad's underwear and took what he wanted, direct but careful with the goods.

"I didn't know you were this aggressive," Brad moaned as Drew rolled his cock back and forth. Drew loved the feeling of a cock filling beneath his hand.

"Yeah?"

"I think I like it," Brad admitted.

"Yeah?" Drew repeated. "Then you'll love this."

Drew spun him around and, without warning, yanked his pants and underwear down below his ass cheeks. He smacked one firm cheek lightly, making more noise than sting. "Over there. The sawbuck."

"Damn, babe," Brad gasped.

Smack!

"The sawbuck. Bend over."

Brad shuffled the few feet to the sawbuck. "Fuck."

"No, everything but," Drew said, knowing it wouldn't even be that much. He was pushing Brad's limits a little, not trying to spook him.

Brad's eyes widened as he looked back over his shoulder. He gulped. "I'm..." He coughed. "I'm clean. You're the only guy I've ever been with."

That Brad, reluctant to bottom as he was, thought his first time was going to be without supplies and in a building under construction but was willing to do it anyway made Drew fall for him all over again. That kind of trust...damn.

"I'm clean, too, and not until we're both tested and we've discussed it when we're not a couple of horndogs," Drew rasped. He ran his hands down Brad's flanks and then cupped his ass in his hands. "Because the sight of this bare ass? That leaking cock of yours? Short-circuits my brain."

Brad's look flickered from raw lust to something softer. "You're so good to me."

"You make me want to be good to you," Drew said. Then he pushed on Brad's back. "Bend over, damn it."

Brad complied, pants around his ankles and elbows on the sawbuck.

"Before I go on...are you sure?"

Brad exhaled a shaky breath. "Yeah, and it's not like I'm really...like we're really doing it that way. There's no lube or condoms or anything."

"Just spit."

"Spit?"

"Yeah, nature's lube. Don't pretend you've never jacked off with nothing but spit," Drew said. Then he stared. "Are you blushing?"

"A little, maybe, but you've got me going pretty good too."

Drew knelt behind that lovely, sculpted backside. Brad's ass was full and round like a bubble butt, but the muscles were more defined from his time in the gym.

He bit one cheek and Brad yelped. Drew grinned and then laved the bite with his tongue to soothe the sting. He couldn't help himself. He bit Brad again, the other cheek this time, even as he reached around Brad to grab his cock and slide his hand lightly up and down the shaft to turn the bite's gentle sting to pleasure.

"Damn, Drew...what you do to me..." Brad panted.

"Is nothing compared to what I'm going to," Drew rumbled. He leaned forward and rested his cheek against one ass cheek, still stroking.

He moved his other hand up between Brad's spread legs to play with his sac for a moment, feeling the balls pulled in tight. His lover might be afraid of the word *gay* and what they were doing right then, but it turned him on too.

"You like this?"

"Yeah," Brad breathed. "You know just what to do to me."

Brad moaned as Drew pushed gently into the sensitive skin, putting pressure on the prostate from the outside. Brad shook his head to clear the stars behind his eyes. "Damn."

Smirking, Drew changed his attack on Brad's senses. He moved his thumb up to Brad's hole and used his index finger to rub the taint.

He circled Brad's hole, close enough to the sensitive nerve endings to set them off, but far enough to tease. He wanted his man begging for it.

"Aw, jeez," Brad huffed.

Then Drew ran his finger over the hole, just once, and Brad jumped. "This," Drew murmured, inhaling Brad's musk, "is the barest hint of what you're missing."

"Gimme more," Brad grunted.

Drew licked his finger until it was good and wet and then used it to circle the hole a little harder, a little faster. He pressed on the opening, not enough to poke in, just enough to get Brad's attention.

"Oh! Do that again."

Drew spit on Brad's ass and then teased his hole again, sometimes circling, sometimes flicking at the hole with just his fingernail, sometimes rubbing it with stronger, harder pressure.

When Brad started fucking his hand, Drew knew it was time. He stood, reluctantly pulling his hands away.

Brad whined. "Wha—?"

Drew aimed his cock into the cleft between Brad's cheeks, rubbing it up toward Brad's back. He felt his heat rising and knew he'd be splattering that strong lower back with his cum very soon.

"That what you want?" Drew said.

Brad ground back against Drew, who let a streamer of spit fall, slicking the path. He pushed his cock up again and then aimed the head against Brad's hole before letting it slip down between Brad's legs.

Drew thrust slowly, poking into Brad's balls before pulling his cock up to thrust it between Brad's cheeks again. He rubbed it slowly up and down, using one hand to toy with his own nipples, first one, then the other, flicking and pinching them until they were hard little pebbles on his chest. It might not be fucking, but it felt damned good.

Then he leaned forward, holding one hand in front of Brad's face. "Spit."

After Brad complied, Drew reached down and started jacking Brad in time to his own thrusting between Brad's legs. He loved knowing for that moment, at least, Brad was a slave to the things Drew made him feel. It was even hotter than his skin against Brad's large back.

Drew straightened. The sight of that back was just too much to ignore. He spat down onto his cock again.

"Touch yourself," Drew said hoarsely. "I want to enjoy the sight of my hard cock between your cheeks, you know why?"

"Uh-uh," Brad panted. He pushed himself back into Drew's dick, his hips rocking.

"Because someday I'll get to see it disappear between them as I slick it up and slide it into your hot, wet hole."

"Oh, God," Brad groaned, pumping his hand harder. "Drew!"

The sight of Brad's back rippling as his orgasm tore through him sent Drew over the edge, and with a final ecstatic thrust between Brad's cheeks, Drew came in three hard, almost painful spurts.

He stared at his own cum with blind eyes: three blasts, each one lower down Brad's back, the lowest dripping slowly down between Brad's cheeks as it cooled.

He rested against Brad's back. This hadn't been fucking, but it was close. He loved that Brad was willing to do this for him despite his own discomfort. Judging by the size of the cum splatter on the floor, Brad had thought it was hot too.

He loved... Drew staggered back a little, dizzy, but not from his climax.

He loved Brad.

Wow. So, this was what it was. He smiled. Suddenly he got why Nick wore that dopey smile whenever he thought Morgan wasn't watching him.

But Drew had learned a lesson from Nick's experience. He wasn't about to say "I love you" to someone who couldn't say it back, but damn, it was so unfair. He felt it so strongly right then. He wanted to crow with its newness and intensity.

"So, I guess I'm your bitch now," Brad said. His voice shook a little.

Drew rose off Brad's back, wincing at the cold stickiness between them. He smacked Brad's ass again, this time hard.

Brad yelped. "What'd you do that for?"

"Is that how you see me when you fuck me?" Drew demanded, his voice full of machismo and challenge.

Brad, looking like he suddenly wanted to be anywhere but there, mumbled, "Not really."

"Not really? Well, get this through your thick skull. I am *all* man," Drew snapped as Brad turned around. Drew made a show of tucking himself back into his underwear. "And one day—when you're ready—I'll show you what it's liked to be a *man* fucked by another man. Because you're not my bitch, and I'm not yours, you big, dumb, lovable lug. We're two guys who care about each other getting off together."

"Just so long as you think I'm lovable," Brad mumbled as he cleaned himself up.

Drew could only shake his head. Even when he wanted to throttle Brad, he also wanted to hug him and hold him and kiss it away.

Chapter Twenty-Four

Brad knew he needed to talk to someone about all the stuff he was feeling, but he had no idea who. Sure, he had friends, many of them still at CalPac. But the thought of telling Rico and the rest of his old cronies that his *boyfriend* wanted him to take it up the ass and that he kind of wanted to but also kind of didn't, and could he please help Brad sort out his feelings seemed like a nonstarter.

Brad sighed as he hefted a motor for one of the safety launches up onto one shoulder to carry it up to the boathouse. It weighed a lot, but lifting heavy things felt familiar, and he needed that too.

He enjoyed coaching for that reason, even if he preferred rowing. As much of a headache as it could be, and as tired as he was most of the time now, it reminded him of younger, more carefree days. It was a source of stability when everything else about his life had changed.

He dropped the motor into place in the rack next to the others and looked at his hands. They had grease all over them, which meant his parka did too. That was another thing that sucked about life after college—he now had dry-cleaning bills.

Sighing to himself about just how unfair it was that he had to grow up, he trudged off to the locker room. Still, he could admit it had its compensations too. Two of his three jobs gave him satisfaction and sometimes even something to be proud of.

And Drew. Sure, Drew was at the center of all Brad's puzzles lately, and Drew's now-evident unhappiness with the pace of Brad's own coming to terms with their relationship bothered Brad. But there was real affection there, too, and pleasure, both physical and emotional. Brad wasn't prepared to use the l-word, not yet, but he admitted to himself he felt far stronger about Drew than anyone else, ever.

Brad heard voices in the locker room and a word he never thought he'd hear at CalPac.

"No way is Coach Bedford a fag."

He froze outside the door. The word echoed in his ears like a gunshot.

Fag.

"Dude, he totally is. There was a huge scandal last year 'cuz he and Morgan Estrada started going out."

"Whoa. What happened?"

"No one knows. Everything just disappeared. There's all kinds of rumors and shit, but no one's talking."

"Huh. Morgan's Coach's buttboy. I always thought he looked a little queer. If I ever see him checkin' me out, I'll beat the crap out of him."

"No shit."

Like that would ever happen, Brad thought, suddenly sick to his stomach. *Nick and Morgan are totally into each other.*

Brad thought he recognized one of the voices as belonging to a rower who'd moved up to the varsity this year. The other one sounded young, probably junior varsity, maybe even a freshman.

"That's so gay" as an insult was one thing, but "fag" just wasn't something people said at liberal CalPac. The LGBT students looked after themselves very well on campus. The big controversy on campus recently was over a special dorm floor for LGBT students. The "controversy" was that no one in the student body seemed to care.

But CalPac was also known as a safe school for rich idiots. Brad always figured that was how he'd gotten in, at any rate, since that was what Randall had told him. So, who knew what kind of people lurked in plain sight, keeping their opinions to themselves?

Dying inside, Brad gritted his teeth and kicked the door open. "Guys," he said gruffly.

The rowers, and not just the two he'd heard talking, jumped at the sudden intrusion, but that was too bad. Not only did he need to wash his hands and get to Suburban Graveyard, this kind of crap had to stop.

"We were just—"

"Yeah, I heard," Brad said. "Sound carries in the boathouse. You might remember that. The coaches' office isn't that far."

One of the rowers stared at him, and when he spoke Brad recognized him as the one who'd called Nick a fag. Joey something or other. "Is it true?"

"That is absolutely none of your business, or mine, or anyone's," Brad said.

"But doesn't it bother you? What if you were showering and he was looking at you?" Joey demanded.

Brad shrugged, faking a nonchalance he didn't feel. "Let him. If he likes what he sees, then that means my time on the weights is working, doesn't it?"

"What if he makes a move on you?" the rower said, crossing his arms over his chest to ward off imagined prying eyes.

"You mean what if the big bad gay man jumps poor little me? Has that ever happened anywhere? Really?" Brad said sarcastically.

One of the other rowers watching the exchange just shook his head. "Jeez, you're an idiot, Joey. Who'd want to jump your flat ass, anyway?"

The rest of the guys in the locker room laughed, and Brad ignored them, intent on washing his hands and getting out of there as quickly as possible, and not simply because he now had twenty minutes to make a thirty-five minute drive to Suburban Graveyard.

He changed clothes just like he always did, one leg at a time and no thought to who or what was around him. Wasn't that what he was supposed to do in a locker room? But now he felt like eyes were on him, testing him.

Maybe they saw what a coward he'd been. Maybe they saw the sweat beading his forehead, even still, as his heart raced with suppressed anger and fear and revulsion at his own cowardice.

Maybe they saw him kicking himself for not speaking up. He was their coach. He was supposedly some big, strong macho stud, so why was he hiding?

He realized as he drove to work that just by being who they were, Nick and Morgan and Drew were a lot stronger than he was. They were out and open and had to put up with that crap. He'd defended them but not owned it himself. Maybe he could've changed some minds by saying, "You know what, guys? That really offends me. I'm gay, too, and I've never looked at you even once."

But he'd thrown that opportunity away, and even if he found another one, Brad couldn't honestly say he'd do it differently.

He spent the morning at work knowing he needed to talk to someone and knowing there was really only one person he could talk to, if he and Morgan would only leave off busting each other's balls long enough to have a real conversation.

It didn't occur to him until after he'd e-mailed Morgan that, technically, discussing his personal life was inappropriate. He was now Morgan's coach, just like Nick. He sighed. When the hell had life gotten so complicated?

Almost driving off the road one evening on his way to Drew's house also drove the point home that he needed to step back from the crazy. His eyes had drooped shut, just for a second, he was sure, and his car drifted. The thump of the tires against the lane reflectors, as much as the blaring horn of an oncoming car, jarred him awake.

He jerked the wheel hard to the right and returned to his lane. His hands shook on the wheel as he made his careful way to Drew's place.

Drew was right. Something had to give.

What Brad hadn't expected was Drew's reaction.

"You fool! You could've been killed!" Drew bellowed. He ran his hands over Brad's face and down Brad's arms like he was checking him for damage.

"Hey, I'm okay. I didn't crash," Brad said. He held out his arms, and Drew rushed in and crushed his face to Brad's chest.

"But you could've," Drew mumbled.

Brad nodded. "I know, and you're right."

"Of course, I am. What am I right about?" Drew lifted his head.

That was his Drew. He had to laugh. His Drew. That felt good. It felt right. "About me cutting back?" he said as if he were speaking to a small and dim child.

"Oh. Yes," Drew said. Brad thought he looked kind of worried.

"Dude, there's only one choice."

"Did you just call me 'dude'?"

"Yeah, try not to let it get to you."

"You were a lot cuter before you developed this clever wit," Drew groused, pouting.

Brad kissed him on the lips. "Admit it. You lo—like me."

"Yeah, maybe." Drew broke into a stupid grin and shrugged. Then his smile fell. "So, what's this choice?"

"There's not much of one. I'll quit Suburban Symphony. I hate that place."

Drew exhaled loudly. "I was afraid you'd quit the Bayard renovation. It's a gamble, and I can't afford to pay you as much as your dad can. And there was that fight..."

"Awww, babe. You need to know something. I'm happier now than I ever remember being, except maybe on the water sometimes. Yeah, I've got a job with my dad's company, but you know what kind of strings are attached to it too." Brad pulled Drew in for a kiss. "I'd rather take my chances with you than have a sure thing with my dad."

"I'm glad to know I can measure up to everything but crew," Drew said dryly.

Brad held up a warning hand. "Hey, don't flack on crew. If it wasn't for crew, we wouldn't have met."

"True, that." Drew snuggled in closer. "You know, if I go back to real estate, that frees up my salary."

"Oh, babe. Don't do that for me. I know how much you love this. I'll make do. Really."

Drew looked at him steadily and then sighed. "It's not just that. The city's not paying us quickly enough. I could take out more short-term business loans, but when it comes down to it, I'd rather sell houses and loan the project money than owe the bank more than we already do. I'm a lot nicer about collection and charge lower interest."

"It's that bad?" Brad said.

"It's getting there," Drew admitted. "The first payments are only just coming in, and we've been spending money hand over fist for months, and most of the bills for Emily's work won't come in until much later. Commissions for sales aren't a cure-all, but they're better than nothing."

Brad frowned. "But then you'd be working to pay my salary, wouldn't you?"

"Not really. I'd be selling real estate to make the budget stretch until things settle out."

Brad smelled bullshit but decided not to push the issue. He recognized a gift when he saw one, and it reminded him just why it was he cared for this man. "Are you sure?"

"I'm sure. So, when're you going to give notice?"

Brad laughed, but it was devoid of humor. "It's not that simple. I have to tell Randall in person to make sure he gets the message, and since I live with him, that'll make it extra exciting."

"I really don't understand why he's so insistent that two grown men not only work for him but live at home. Most parents can't wait to get rid of their kids."

"So I'm told," Brad said with a sigh, "but Randall's been weird since Mom died. He clamped down after the funeral. I'd have thought it would've eased up over the years, but if anything, he's just gotten worse."

Drew cocked his head. "So how come you're not completely beaten down?"

Brad shrugged. "Because I fight him."

"You? You're one of the most easy-going guys I know."

"Maybe, but where Randall's concerned, it's different. I'm dead weight. If I just sat there on the floor, there's no way you'd be able to move me. I do the same thing to him, only it's mental," Brad explained.

Nodding slowly, Drew said, "You don't engage. When he fights you, you don't respond."

"Sometimes. Sometimes I go along because it's easier. Sometimes I yell back. I pick my battles."

"So why don't you just move out?"

"I really can't afford to yet. Even if I'd stayed working at Suburban Graveyard—and developed an alcohol problem, by the way—it'd be debatable whether I'd be able to afford an apartment that wasn't a complete dump, let alone the kind of place I'd bring you to."

"I'm not that much of a princess," Drew said with a slight smile. When Brad gave him a look, he insisted, "I'm not!"

"Drew, if I put a pea under your mattress you'd toss and turn all night," Brad laughed. "I don't mind. It's what makes you, you."

It made him want to take care of and protect Drew, too, but he didn't say that yet. Couldn't say that yet.

Drew looked like he was weighing something. "You could...you could move in here. If you wanted to."

Brad's heart melted. He held onto Drew for a moment. "You have no idea what that means to me, but I'm just not sure I'm ready. I mean, I didn't know I liked dick this summer, and now I'm in a serious relationship."

"Oh, thank God," Drew breathed. "I'm not sure I'm ready to shack up either."

"Then why'd you ask?" Brad demanded. He knew he'd never understand this man.

"Because you need it," Drew said simply.

That was why Brad tried both to understand Drew and to deal with being gay, but he also tried not to hear the word *fag* echoing in his ears.

Brad took his sweet time telling Randall he'd be quitting Suburban Graveyard. He wasn't necessarily afraid of his father, although that certainly contributed to the week he spent building up to it, but he'd also spent a lot of time—since his mother died—refusing to engage Randall, and he found that habit hard to change.

But life gave him incentive in the week after almost falling asleep at the wheel. There were no more near misses in traffic, but now that he'd noticed it, Brad realized just how tired he was most of the time. By the time he got to Drew's house, one or both of them would be too tired for more than cuddling. That didn't bother him as much as he knew it should.

For one thing, getting it up when he was bone-tired sucked. Locker room bravado aside, Brad knew he was no sex machine, even if Drew usually revved his engine. But truth be told, he was glad for a break from the sex. Hearing one of his rowers call Nick a fag still shocked him. Hearing a hateful word and knowing it applied to him was a new experience, and he didn't like it.

Big bad Brad was afraid of a tiny little word. It wasn't just hearing it, he acknowledged as he sat in the cold and the dark in his car, screwing up his courage. It was hearing it paired with the makeup sex with Drew and what it meant. Because that sex? Drew not quite fucking him over a sawbuck was just about the hottest thing ever, and that scared him.

He was gay. That the hottest sex of his life involved another man made that hard to deny, but it didn't make it easier to take. All the construction worker talk, all the straight male bravado, that didn't vanish just because Drew had gotten in his pants. His body might crave Drew's touch, but his mind still protested. He cared for Drew, might even be coming to love him, but didn't he get a say in something that promised such radical changes in his life?

He groaned and rested his head on the steering wheel, which was kind of sticky from all those meals he'd eaten while driving. He was kicking and fighting, but he hadn't been lying when he told Drew how happy he was. Who knew that Brad, widely regarded as not the deepest of thinkers, was tying himself into knots over all this?

And speaking of fighting... Brad knew what he had to do. He sighed and got out of his car. It was late enough that Randall should be home and parked in front of the idiot box.

Sure enough, as soon as Brad walked in the front door, he heard the television. He walked in and stood in front of the screen.

Randall cleared his throat. "Do you want something, Bradley?"

"Yeah. I..." He took a deep breath. "I need to quit Suburban Symphony. I've got too much on my plate right now, and the sales office just isn't working."

Randall stared at him until he started squirming. Brad hated that. His dad always stared at him during one of their confrontations, stared until Brad backed down in front of the silverback.

"Out of the question. Quit something else. Quit that pointless renovation of that dilapidated waste of money that man talked you into," Randall ordered.

"Why's it pointless?" Brad demanded.

"I just told you, weren't you listening, Bradley? It's a waste of money. There's no way that old firetrap can be made safe, let alone suited to modern needs. I told you not to get involved with it, but you didn't listen. You never listen. And now you're overcommitted. The answer's no."

Brad stared at his old man. Was he losing his hearing or just his mind? "I didn't ask you."

"That's all right, Bradley. I'm telling you. You're not quitting. Now, you're blocking the screen."

Brad shook his head. He knew his dad was arrogant, but this was something else. "Yeah, I am."

"It sounds like you're abandoning this family, Bradley. We work for the family company. I do. Philip does. You do. That's the way it is."

"No, I did work for Sundstrom Homes. Now I work for St. Charles Renovations and the CalPac crew."

Randall glanced away. "You are abandoning this family. Next thing I know, you'll be telling me you're moving out."

"As long as you mentioned it, yeah, once I save enough, I'll be getting my own place," Brad said.

"Absolutely not," Randall gasped, the first emotion Brad remembered him showing in a long time.

"Randall...Dad. It's time. I'm twenty-two. Why the hell Philip's stuck around this long, I'll never know. Once I've got enough saved for first and last month's rent, I'm getting my own apartment."

"This family stays together." Randall stood up. "It has since your mother died."

Brad backed up a step. "Just because I'm finding my own job and want to live in my own place doesn't mean I'm not a part of the family."

But even as he said it, Brad knew it was a lie. He hadn't been part of the family for years, not where it counted, not in his own mind. Not since Randall tied him and Philip to him with ever-tighter ropes in the wake of Helena's death.

"No!" Randall screamed. "I said no, goddamn it. I promised your mother when she died that I would keep this family together. That's exactly what I've done and exactly what I'll continue to do, and the wishes of a foolish child are quite beside the point..."

Brad backed up another step, not sure what to make of Randall's temper. It was the first time he'd seen his dad lose his cool in years.

"So no, Bradley, you will not quit Sundstrom Homes, and you will not move out of this house, do you hear me?"

But this time, instead of ignoring his old man or taking the path of least resistance, he said, "No."

"What?" Randall screamed.

"No," Brad repeated, remembering that he was no longer the gangly kid he'd been when his mother had died. When Randall had intimidated him into compliance when he was young, sometimes he'd retreated into the weight room; sometimes he'd knuckled under to keep the peace. As he got older, he retreated emotionally. "No."

In two quick strides, Randall stood in front of him, his cold blue eyes looking up into Brad's brown ones. "I told you, you will not quit," he bellowed, grabbing Brad's jacket.

"And I told you, I am quitting," Brad said just as loudly.

Then Philip appeared in the doorway. "What's the yelling about?"

"This doesn't concern you, Philip," Randall said calmly.

"Get him off me, Philip," Brad said, never taking his eyes off his father.

"Go to your room, Philip," Randall snapped.

To Brad's disgust, Philip turned and left, sent back to his room like a disobedient child. Then and there, Brad knew he had to get out somehow, money or no.

He brought his arms up and knocked Randall's hands away, but then Randall grabbed him again, and before Brad could stop him, his dad slammed him up against the wall next to the television.

Then again. His head knocked back into the wall, and stars lit up his vision.

Again and again, each slam more bone-rattling than the last.

"It'll only be temporary! Stop!"

Randall stopped but still held onto Brad's jacket.

Brad fought to clear his head. "Yeah, jeez. That hurt." He knocked his dad's hands away again and then ducked away before Randall could grab him again. "I hate you more than you'll ever know, you fucking son of a bitch."

Chapter Twenty-Five

After Brad stormed out, Randall turned off the television, switched off the lights, and went upstairs to the special room across from the master bedroom. It had been Helena's sitting room, her quiet place away from the noisy and boisterous world of a houseful of men, done up in mauve and lavender.

Almost everything was as she had left it when she'd gotten into the car—his car—for the last time, when he'd driven her to her death, T-boned by a drunk driver. He'd walked away from the crumpled ruin of his car; she'd died on the scene.

He never allowed the housecleaners in there and had fired more than one for violating the room's sanctity before he finally gave in and installed a lock on the door.

The only change he had made was the portrait taken a few months before the accident, and even that had not moved since he'd placed it on her vanity table after the funeral. It was his wife's image, frozen in time, the hairdo now out of date, the clothes unstylish, so at odds with the image she'd cultivated in life. Soft black silk draped the silver frame, pooling around it on the table's marble surface. It lent her a severe air, but one he thought suited her.

Randall sat on the tiny bench in front of the vanity. "Bradley's being willful again. Not that he's ever stopped. You were the only who he'd listen to, and you're gone," he said. "Philip's a good boy. He works for me now, as you know. He makes good money. He's dating a nice girl. But he doesn't move out. But Bradley? He fights me every step of the way. He just quit the family firm. It won't be long before he moves out. I can feel it."

Randall lovingly caressed the portrait through the black crepe. "I promised you when you died I'd hold our family together come hell or high water. Water," he mused, "or maybe fire, but whatever tries to split our family apart will be dealt with. Whatever, or whoever."

After the fight with Randall, Brad spent a sleepless night at Drew's followed by an early morning down at the boathouse. He surprised Bob Miller by showing up in the morning, but the contractor didn't mind. It gave Bob a chance to update him on the status of the job and him a chance to break it to Bob gently that he'd be there full-time.

"You quit Sundstrom Homes? Just like that?" Bob asked.

"Yep, just like that," Brad said.

Bob gave him a tight smile. "Are you going to tell me why?"

"Because my dad's an asshole," Brad snorted.

Bob shook his head disapprovingly. "Young man, your father is not an asshole. He's a *fucking* asshole and has been as long as I've known him." He grinned. "I'm glad you finally chewed through your leg to free yourself from his trap."

Brad didn't tell him that his dad had literally beat the concession of his separation from Sundstrom Homes being only temporary out of him. "You know about that?"

Bob put a hand on his shoulder. "Brad, you'll find that the home trades in this area are a very small community, and there's not a whole lot that won't get out eventually. It's something to keep in mind."

"Good advice." Brad nodded slowly. "I wonder if Drew realizes that sometimes."

Bob considered the matter for a few moments. "He'll have a tough row to hoe by being out in this business. Things are changing, but I'm not altogether sure if he appreciates how slowly."

"I doubt it." Brad didn't think Drew had any clue whatsoever about just how homophobic construction workers could be. He knew, and it was one of the reasons he struggled with being out. "Now, if you'll excuse me, I'm going to take advantage of being a man of leisure who only works two jobs to go have lunch with a friend."

Bob laughed and waved him off. It'd been more than a week since he'd e-mailed Morgan, but it was the first time his erstwhile rival could meet during his busy final year of college.

Brad met Morgan between classes, figuring since Morgan was doing him the favor of listening, he could at least not make the man drive to meet him.

Perhaps for the first time, Brad noticed that Morgan looked amazing. Morgan was tall, almost as tall as he was, which was why they'd been paired in the boats, but where Brad resembled a linebacker, Morgan possessed the classic rower's build, defined without being overbuilt, long of limb and lean of muscle. Add to that his dark curly hair and fair skin, and the man looked like a cover model. Brad could see what must've drawn Nick.

But Morgan possessed more than those physical attributes. There was a confidence about him, a natural poise, an ease in any surrounding that proclaimed louder than words that Morgan, sooner or later, got what he wanted. For his part, Brad just assumed he himself was the alpha. No wonder they'd been rivals. Brad had no idea how he'd missed it before.

"Hey, buddy, thanks for meeting me," Brad greeted him outside one of the campus eateries.

"You're welcome. You said you needed to talk about things," Morgan said, "and given how edgy you are and evasive you were in the e-mail, I'm guessing it has to do with being gay?"

"Let's order," Brad said shortly, moving past him into the self-service coffee shop. With a raised eyebrow, Morgan followed in his wake.

After they ordered and found a seat, Morgan said, "So what's going on?"

"I don't want to be gay," Brad blurted. He didn't know Morgan well enough to engage in small talk beyond the crew, and he was too nervous for much of that.

Morgan looked at him levelly. "Interesting. I'd say that you already are and don't have a lot of choice in the matter. I certainly hope you don't think I've got information on reparative therapy."

"There's a cure?" Brad said, not expecting a positive answer. If a real cure existed, he'd have heard about it.

"No, it's a misapplication of psychology that leaves troubled people even more deeply scarred. It's nothing but manipulative bullshit," Morgan spat. "Okay, I have to ask...how come?"

"It's hard," Brad began and then realized what he said. But even as Brad turned redder than a sunburned tomato, Morgan didn't snicker. He had to give the man points for that. "I'm just figuring out that I'm...that I like guys, you know. *That* way."

"Go on."

"It's a lot to deal with at once. I thought it might help to speak to someone who's obviously gay. Wait, I mean someone who's gay and accepts it and...everything," he ended lamely. Why was it he could think this so clearly in his car, but when faced with someone he'd asked for help, he tripped over his own tongue?

"You've gone from just figuring out you might be attracted to guys to being in a serious relationship with a man whose level of comfort with his own sexuality doesn't leave you a lot of room to negotiate or let you get used to this at your own pace?" Morgan summarized.

"Something like that. I mean, I can barely say I'm gay to myself, let alone out loud"—Brad's eyes darted around nervously—"and he wants to go out and hold hands."

Morgan nodded slowly. "I can see how that'd be rough."

"Why can't he just let me do this on my own schedule? When I'm ready? When I'm comfortable, damn it. Why am I suddenly his latest project?" Brad demanded.

"I'll tell you something about Drew St. Charles," Morgan sighed.

Brad frowned as Morgan told him about Drew's high school experiences. "Yeah, he's told me all of that."

"Okay, what he didn't tell you is what it means. He had to struggle to be himself, and that taught him to fight for what he wants. It also gave him the utter conviction that you can only be happy—truly happy—if you're out, and the faster the better."

"Hmm. I guess. Why aren't you as pushy? How long have you been out?" Brad asked.

"I don't really remember not being out." Morgan shrugged. "I noticed boys when my friends noticed girls.

My family noticed me noticing, and it wasn't a big deal. I didn't have to fight to be who I am. Drew did. That makes him impatient with people who aren't on his timeline, and since yes, he likes projects, he's made you one."

"Sometimes I wish he'd just back off," Brad muttered.

"Understandable. Do you wish you weren't together?"

Brad thought about it. "No," he said, after a moment's hesitation. "No. I really like being around him. He's a great guy, and honestly, other than this, I'm pretty happy. I just want to do this at my own pace."

"Tell him that. See how he responds." Morgan grinned. "Remember Nick's Five Cs?"

"Jeez, how could I forget?" Brad groaned.

They looked at each other and laughed. "'Coach, coxswain, crew, communication, and commitment!'"

"It's the communication that's the important one in this case," Morgan said. "So, what's your pace? How out are you?"

Brad shrugged uncomfortably. "Not very, I guess. He hasn't met my friends or anything."

"Your friends are a bunch of frat rats. You need grown-up friends," Morgan pronounced. "What about actual sex? Have you gotten that far?"

Brad felt his face heat right up, and that answered the question.

"Look at you, Mr. Bashful. I'm not sure who this new Brad is, but I like him."

"That's the problem, it's a new Brad, and I need time to get used to him. And yeah, we've had sex."

"So, who's the top?"

Brad choked on his soda. "What'd you mean, who's the top?" he demanded. "Isn't that obvious? I'm no one's bitch."

Morgan leaned back, smirking. "Let's just say Drew's not the total bottom you might think, and—" he looked at Brad intently "—I don't think you're quite the total top you appear."

"What the hell, Morgan? I ask you for help and you—"

"Easy, Brad. Calm down. It's not an insult. If it weren't for the bottoms, the tops wouldn't have anyone to fuck, would they?"

"What?" Brad shook his head, trying to make sense of that. "Maybe that's the problem. I didn't think I was anyone's bitch, but..." He gulped. "I was. Once. Kind of."

"And?"

"I liked it."

"There's nothing wrong with that either," Morgan said gently. "It's called being versatile, or, as I prefer to think of it, a good lay."

Brad hunched his shoulders miserably. "I don't want to be gay. I don't want to be the girl in the relationship."

Morgan stared, mouth agape. "Brad, somehow you've managed to acquire an idea of masculinity—to say nothing of homosexuality—that's long out of date. Sexual position and gender role within a relationship aren't even remotely the same thing."

"They're not?" Brad looked puzzled.

Morgan shook his head. "Uh...no. You've got to separate them. You maybe more than most people need to. They're not the same," he repeated. "The old dude/bitch dichotomy is nothing but homophobia—the inability to conceive of sex as anything other than something between a man and a woman. If someone's doing the fucking, he's a man, because that's what men do. So, the one getting fucked must obviously be the woman, because a woman is by definition the one who gets dicked."

"Dichotomy. That's a big word," Brad said, laughing to cover up his nervousness.

Morgan shot him a look that told him he'd seen right through it. "Try to stay with me, big guy. Those definitions don't apply to us. We're not heterosexuals, we're gay. We're not women and men, we're men. And don't go by appearances. I've known some pretty effeminate-looking guys who were hardcore tops, and some big macho brutes"—Morgan stared him right in the eye—"who couldn't get enough cock up their asses."

"Aww, jeez, thanks for the visual," Brad said. Part of him thought the idea was hot, but talking about this? This made him cringe in shame.

Morgan rolled his eyes. "Any of this getting through to you? I know how much you play stupid, but we both know you're not."

"Has *everyone* figured me out?" Brad demanded. Really, discussing his sex life with his former rival was embarrassing enough without the guy looking through him like he was glass.

"Relax, Brad, your secret's safe with me," Morgan promised. "I don't even think Stuart knows about your serious side. You might give him a chance, by the way. You bust his chops a lot, but he's a great guy and good friend, and he and Jonathan haven't figured out yet that not only are they going to start banging each other, but they're probably going to live happily ever after too."

"Yeah? I thought it was just me, but Nick mentioned something about them too."

"Nick and I talk about it a lot." Morgan smiled. "But I'd like someone else to talk about them with, and maybe be there for them when it's time too."

"That sounds nice."

Brad walked out of lunch feeling buoyed, but still unsure. It was just so hard moving past the idiotic—he saw Morgan's point, rationally at least—notions of male and female he'd picked up from his dad and working construction all those years. Some of those guys had probably been gay, but Brad sure hadn't known it. Hell, he hadn't known it about himself.

Yeah, he was gay, but damn it, why did he have to be? It'd be so much easier if he weren't. But with that realization came the knowledge that if he weren't gay, he wouldn't have Drew, maybe not even as a friend, and Drew... Drew had crept under his radar and into his life before he'd even realized what was going on. Now, he couldn't willingly part with Drew any more than he'd willingly surrender a testicle.

He kicked at a weed in the sidewalk. But damn, couldn't they just go back to the way it had been, him fucking Drew and both getting off without making a federal case out of everything?

Drew loved November in the Sacramento area. The weather was cool enough to justify his favorite suits and sweaters without being off-puttingly frigid, and he spent the weeks before his birthday getting back up to speed with his real estate business. It meant, more often than not, spending the early evenings going over the day's work on the Bayard House with Brad by light of the work lamps, but there was no help for it, just like there was no help for the softening winter home market.

He'd been lucky. His broker had thrown him a few last-minute desperate clients. Even though the commissions might've been lower than he was used to, he was grateful they existed at all, and after his basic living expenses, they all went to the renovation of the mayor's mansion. He'd leave the tax implications to his accountant.

He wished the finances on the project were what he'd projected them to be, but all things considered, the renovation was a success insofar as it was on schedule and close to budget. The city was paying more of Renochuck's invoices, which helped, but really, why seek out small firms and then not pay them on time? He'd never take another public job again.

So professionally, for a man about to turn twenty-nine, life was good, indeed. Personally, however, Drew wanted some changes in his next year of life. This back and forth with Brad over how or even whether to be open...he found it tiresome at best. He knew Brad had some worries about the crew, given Nick's ongoing travails with the oversight committee, but other than that one moment at the dedication of the boat, Drew hadn't been down to the boathouse.

But really, after that brief moment in the Bayard House, Brad seemed to have scampered right back into the closet. Drew didn't know what might've caused it. Was it the sex? They seemed to have backed off that lately. It was one more thing for him to worry about.

Drew doubted anything had happened on the job site. He'd fired more than one person over the years for homophobic cracks. It might be a part of the construction industry, but that didn't mean he'd put up with it when he was paying the bills.

Brad's seriously dysfunctional relationship with his father? God alone knew how Brad had endured that man all those years, but anyone who forced his children to keep living at home after college? As the psychiatrist said to the patient in plastic-wrap underwear, "Clearly I can see you're nuts."

Drew really had no idea what the cause was, but both he and Brad knew these were just proxies for deeper issues. At its root, Brad's problem was with being gay, or at least accepting that he was gay. Drew himself had fought too long and too hard to be exactly who he was to be dragged back into the closet, and that was what the closet did. It imprisoned not just the one in it, but anyone with whom he was intimate. Brad's secret shame was a disease that Drew perforce contracted too.

Since he also had no intention of doing without Brad, the solution—to his way of thinking—was simple. Brad would come out. Everyone should. Drew didn't believe in outing, although homophobic politicians caught with their hands down other men's pants were fair game. But he was certainly willing to force the issue as the price of being together.

Nick and Morgan had invited him to go dancing on his birthday the Monday before Thanksgiving, and he wanted to dance with his boyfriend. Despite his patience this summer and fall, he was going to push the issue.

Chapter Twenty-Six

"You asked what I wanted for my birthday, and what I want is for you to come dancing with me at Aspects," Drew said.

They sat on the sofa in his family room after dinner, their make-out sofa, although lately Brad had been too tired for that. Drew tried to be understanding, since after all, the top had the more physically demanding role, but trying also meant failing. He wanted to dance, yes, but not the closet hokeypokey.

They'd been going around and around on this subject, first via e-mail and now in person, all day. Earlier in the day he'd tried being gentle, but now Brad's reluctance just angered him.

"Jeez, not with the dancing thing," Brad groaned. "You know I—"

"Jeez, not with the self-loathing gay thing," Drew snapped. "And yeah, I know a whole lot."

"Can we...can I take you to a nice restaurant? A Shot of Class? It's supposed to be the best place in town. I...I just don't want to do something so...I don't know...gay?"

Drew sighed. There were so many things he should've brought up sooner—like self-acceptance and accepting him and being out before dating him—but hadn't. He'd been so enthralled by Brad and thrilled that Brad seemed just as interested that he let things go and swept a whole lot more under the rug. Now it was time to deal with it all, apparently.

"I like to dance. As I told you before, I have never pushed you to do anything 'gay'—and sidebar, I hate that you stigmatize something like that—but damnation, can we not just go out as a couple this once?"

"I promise that later we'll go out, but you have to give me more time," Brad pleaded, face anguished. "I'll take you out at New Year's. We'll go dancing on New Year's Eve."

But Drew sat there, his arms folded across his chest, just as unhappy. "You know what? I've given you plenty of time. I'm going out, with or without you. I'm going to spend the evening with Nick and Morgan doing what I like to do, even if I'm not doing it with the one I most want to do it with. I'm tired of you dragging me back into the closet. I suggest you spend the evening deciding what you really want, because this...this creeping around in the shadows with a boyfriend who can't give and take equally, in bed or anywhere else, and who's terrified someone he knows will see him out with me has to stop. I deserve better than that, and frankly, you deserve more out of life than that too."

"What...what're you saying?"

"I'm saying that I want, need, and will goddamn have a boyfriend who's a full partner in life, and not just someone who can barely say the word 'gay' but is perfectly willing to stick his dick up my ass!"

"I'm not that bad," Brad mumbled, looking at the table. He looked miserable, but by that point, Drew had no other idea how to reach him.

"You're a goose down parka and a pair of mittens away from Narnia," Drew said tiredly.

"What's Narnia?"

Drew just stared. "*The Lion, the Witch, and the Wardrobe*? Ring any bells?"

"I never saw the movie."

"It's a book, Brad."

Brad was silent for a while. "I guess I should go...home or something."

"I'd say so, yes. I'm going out."

"Can...can I see you tomorrow?"

"That's up to you," Drew said flatly.

"Are we taking a break?"

Drew knew at any other time his heart would break hearing Brad say that, but that night... "That's entirely your decision, but I can't keep doing this... I can't go on being treated like a dirty secret, so you should probably take some time to decide what you want out of our relationship."

Drew mustered what dignity he had left and walked out of the family room, heading to the garage and his car. He was the one who always said he liked a challenge. Too bad this one beat him.

"Goodbye," he heard Brad say softly when he paused at the door.

"Don't be here when I get home, Brad."

As good as it would've felt, Drew didn't even slam the door behind him. He might've been angry and hurt but stomping and slamming out of his own house would have only been pathetic.

"Where's Brad?" Morgan asked, peering around Drew.

"There is no Brad tonight," Drew said levelly. He wouldn't cry, he wouldn't cry...

"Drew?" Nick said, coming up from behind Morgan and drying his hands on a towel. "What's wrong?"

Morgan pulled him inside and into a hug without waiting for more. "Come here. Nick, will you go put the kettle on? We'll need tea for this."

"I want booze," Drew said, lifting his head from Morgan's chest, "not granny water."

"That'll come later," Morgan said, steering him toward the sofa. It was far more battered and disreputable looking than the suede one Drew'd just abandoned, but at that moment, it looked like the sanctuary he needed.

Nick returned in a few minutes with an electric teakettle and three mugs, tea bags already in them. "It won't hurt to have some water in your stomach before you start drinking."

"I don't actually feel like drinking all that much," Drew admitted.

"Who are you, and what've you done with the real Drew?" Nick said.

"Nick," Morgan warned.

Nick shot Morgan a frustrated look.

"It's okay, Morgan. I know he's just trying to cheer me up, even if he's bad at it," Drew said.

Morgan laughed as Nick sputtered.

"So, do you want to tell us what's up?" Morgan said.

Drew's shoulders slumped. "I told Brad what I wanted to do for my birthday was go dancing. As a couple. He refused."

"I'm sorry," Nick said.

"Thanks. He knows what this means to me. I mean, we talked about it after Halloween. Did you know I sat out the Goblin Ball this year?"

"Wow," Nick muttered. At Morgan's questioning look, he said, "It's a big charity event he goes to every year. I figured he'd go even if he were on his death bed."

"Pretty much, but not this year. I didn't even bring it up because I knew it'd be a nonstarter," Drew, making a face. "I even apologized later to Brad for not giving him a chance to say no to it, for just assuming. I mean, he was pretty uncomfortable at that CalPac football game last month, so why even bring up the ball, right?"

"So, what changed this time?" Morgan asked.

Drew made a face. "I'm just sick of the hiding. Come out, already. He knows he's gay, he's just stuck back there with the old coats and the shirts no one wears anymore."

"That's rough," Nick said.

Drew loved both of them in that moment for not saying "it takes time" or anything like that. For recognizing that he just needed to talk. "And yes, I know you tried to warn me about this possibility, but that doesn't mean it doesn't hurt. So, no need for an 'I told you so,' okay?"

"Do you really think I'd do that to you? Now?" Nick said softly.

"Do you really want an answer?" Drew said, trying to summon some shadow of his usual humor.

"He wouldn't do it *now*," Morgan said, "he'd wait until later, when you've recovered."

Drew laughed a little, and when Nick threw a pillow at Morgan, he said, "You know he's right."

Nick smiled, warm and loving and sickeningly sweet. "Yeah, he is."

Drew watched and tried to stop jealousy from swamping him as his closest friend and his boyfriend exchanged some silent communication. Then Nick nodded.

"You know, that's kind of annoying."

"Hush, you. It's time to get this party started," Nick said, standing up. He held out his hand to Drew.

"First, you're not P!nk, and second, it's not Saturday night," Drew groused.

"We prefer the Shirley Bassey version, thank you," Morgan said.

"You would. Sorry to be such a downer," Drew said. This wasn't how he wanted to spend his birthday evening.

"So, what happens now?" Nick asked.

"We go dancing," Drew replied.

"I meant with Brad," Nick said.

Drew stood up. "That's up to him. I'm done with closet cases. If he wants to be with me—and I hope he does—then he needs to join me in the outside world."

Drew ignored the meaningful look Morgan shot Nick. Couples and their glances. Would he and Brad ever get to that? Or were they done? That hurt to think about, so he knew his answer, but like he'd told Brad earlier, it was all up to him.

Drew didn't start gritting his teeth and faking a smile for Nick and Morgan's benefit until after they arrived at Aspects. They took him to a cute little Salvadoran restaurant, apparently where they'd gone on their first date, equally apparently trying to kill him with cuteness overload. He loved them, he truly did, but sometimes it hurt how into each other they were. It wasn't like they exchanged little secret smiles or fed each other off their forks, because after his rupture with Brad, he would have maimed one or both of them if they had. It was just obvious that they were together. He liked that, since he'd played a role in it, but that night, when he wanted to be there with a boyfriend of his very own, it hurt.

By the time they arrived at Aspects, he actively dreaded the rest of the night. For a Monday night, the bar sported a big crowd, but to Drew it was just obstacles to navigate around. It felt like pinball, and he was the ball. *Zing!* Change course. *Zap!* Change course again. *Bing!* How much longer until he could leave politely?

Most nights he enjoyed the press. He never knew just whom he might bump into, like the next Mr. Right Now. But right then he only wanted the man he'd thought had been Mr. Right to be there to clear a path for him and then hold him tight while they danced.

They got drinks at the bar and then danced together, the three of them, but when the first slow song came on, Drew bowed out. He hated being the third wheel enough as it was.

But he saw Morgan speaking urgently in Nick's ear over the sound of the music. Then he shoved Nick toward Drew. Right then, he knew why Nick loved Morgan so much.

"You've got a good man there," Drew said as he tucked himself under Nick's arms.

"Yes, I do," Nick said.

"Thank him for me, will you?" Drew said as they danced to some slow, sad song.

"Even though he said the sad unicorn needs a hug?" Nick smiled.

Drew shook his head. "You've got a brat there, you know that, right?"

"Yes, I do," Nick repeated, laughing.

They were silent for a moment, just swaying to the music. Then Nick said, "Just make sure he's worth it, okay?"

Drew knew they weren't talking about Morgan anymore. He nodded because right then, it was that or cry.

They finished out the dance, and then they joined Morgan on the sidelines.

"You know what, guys? It's just not happening tonight. I'm sorry. I gotta get out of here."

"We'll go with you," Nick said.

"You don't need to leave just because I'm a downer," Drew said, rolling his eyes. "I'll catch a cab back to your place. You two stay here and have fun. Who knows"—he flashed a hint of his old grin—"maybe you'll flush some more of your rowers out of the bushes."

Morgan laughed as Nick gave Drew a playful shove toward the door.

They'd tried, they'd really tried, but for all the thoughtful gestures like the sticky little drink with a birthday candle stuck precariously in a lime wedge that Nick brought him from the bar, carefully sheltering it with his hand, it was just a bust.

Feeling lower than he had all night, Drew retrieved his coat from the coatroom and headed out into the dark. He breathed deep, pulling the cold air into his lungs. He let it out, willing his sadness to go with it, not that it worked. He was still slinking away from a bar on his birthday, his closest friends inside and his so-called boyfriend nowhere to be seen.

"Hey, buddy, how 'bout a fiver for a sandwich?" a man called from where he crouched on the sidewalk.

Drew ignored him. The indigent population of Sacramento skyrocketed in the winter due to local migration and being bussed in from colder climes. The mild climate meant they wouldn't freeze to death. Drew approved of not freezing to death in theory, but the panhandling annoyed him.

"No, I'm sorry, not tonight," he said, scouting around for a taxi. He should've had the bouncer call him one, but he couldn't take another moment of the mix of happiness and desperation back at the bar. He pulled out his phone and started flipping through the contacts to find a taxi service. Even the tipsy taxi. He could fake being drunk if he had to.

"C'mon buddy, you know you got it."

But just because Drew didn't want the street people dying of exposure didn't mean he intended to treat them all to a meal either. He glanced at the panhandler but saw only scruff and dirt. "I said no. Leave me alone."

"Then how about thirty for a knuckle sandwich?" said a second man, stepping out from between a parked car where he and a third man had been talking.

"What? That has to be the dumbest—" Drew started to say, but then he saw the fist coming for his jaw as someone grabbed the phone out of his hand.

Drew ducked. Then tried to dodge away, but ran hard into one of the other men, who clamped down on his arms while the panhandler held his chin.

"Shoulda given me the fiver," he said before his fist cracked Drew's jaw, slamming his head back hard and painfully.

Then a fist hit his gut, and he was doubled over, and the blows kept coming, and he went down.

There was searing pain and blackness and—

Chapter Twenty-Seven

"Poor Drew," Morgan said as they went to collect their coats. Without the birthday boy, they couldn't muster much enthusiasm for the crowd and the noise when they could be at home dancing on a different plane altogether.

"I tried to warn him," Nick said.

"I know you did, but that's not going to make—"

"Hey! There's someone being bashed out there! Call the cops!" someone screamed into the bar's main door.

Nick and Morgan looked at each other. "You don't think—"

"Come on!" Nick yelled, racing for the door with Morgan right behind him.

Sirens wailed from far away.

They saw a knot of people kneeling around a fallen man, and in the distance, people running.

Morgan took off at a dead sprint.

"Morgan!" Nick screamed, but his long-legged boyfriend ignored him.

Cursing, Nick shouldered his way into the knot of people around Drew. "Drew!"

"You know him?" a woman said. A large badge on her jacket proclaimed her a member of the Lavender Avengers.

"He's my best friend," Nick said, nauseated at the damage and the blood. It was everywhere, running freely down Drew's face and onto his clothes, even onto the sidewalk.

Then flashing red lights bathed them. The ambulance arrived as Morgan loped back toward the bar, breathing heavily.

"Move aside! Paramedics! Let us through!"

Nick looked at Morgan expectantly, but Morgan just shook his head slowly. "They...got away," he said, catching his breath.

A woman in a paramedic's uniform came up to them. "Hey, they said you know this guy?"

Nick nodded slowly. "His name's Drew St. Charles. He's...he's my best friend except for this man here," he said, taking Morgan's hand.

"We're taking him to the UC Davis Med Center. It'd be great if you could meet us there. Any information you have will be a real help."

Morgan put his arm around Nick. "We'll see you there."

"And finally, we have the 'situation' with the men's varsity," Pete Rancilman said. The way he said "situation" made it sound like he smelled dog shit on his shoe.

Brad rolled his eyes. Rancilman just wouldn't let this go. Brad had been trying with minimal success to derail this all autumn, but now he was angry. This meeting on top of the fight with Drew last night was one provocation too many.

This "situation" involved his friend and former coach and, he realized with a start, him. The CalPac crew now boasted two gay coaches, not one. "Just what 'situation' do you mean, Pete?"

Pete looked at him like he was stupid, but Brad was used to that. Lots of people thought he was stupid. "We have a coach preying on his rowers. He's a detriment to the crew and a liability. This has to be dealt with."

"The athletic department investigated it and dropped it," said Prissy Morrain, another member of the committee. "Furthermore, we've heard nothing from anything like the NCAA or USRowing."

Brad had liked her from the start, and not just because she was as skeptical as he about Rancilman's motives. "The only situation I see down at the boathouse when I'm coaching is that the crew is about three times the size it was when I rowed last spring."

"Yes, Brad, we know. You rowed for Nick Bedford last spring. You assistant coach for him now. You saw him in action, swooping in on an innocent undergraduate—"

"Have you *met* Morgan Estrada, this poor pitiful rower you think Nick poached?" Brad said, laughing helplessly. It took him a moment to control himself. "That's the last way I'd describe him. That's hilarious. Did you talk to him about this?" The way everyone looked at him told Brad that they'd never even considered talking to Nick's alleged victim. "He went after Nick, not the other way around. The guy gets what he wants eventually, no two ways about it."

"But is that really the kind of influence we want in a position of authority?" Pete pressed.

"So, what're you proposing, Pete?" asked Steve Mulder, another member of the committee who'd graduated from CalPac long before Brad had been born. "I can't say I'm not concerned by a coach dating one of his rowers, gay or not."

"I think we need to seriously consider getting rid of him," Pete said. He sat back in his chair, smiling in satisfaction.

"For what?" Brad demanded. It was time to shut this down for keeps.

"What d'you mean, for what?" Pete demanded.

This guy's homophobia was off the charts, even Brad could tell that. "Exactly what I said. So far as anything *official* is concerned, Nick Bedford's in the clear. There literally is not a case here that you can support, and you can't fire people at CalPac for being gay, unless you want the school breathing down your neck, that is."

At Rancilman's shocked look, Brad shook his head. "So, in addition to not checking with the crews about Coach Bedford, I'm guessing you haven't looked at the policy and procedures manual for a while? Honestly, if this is how I'd done my homework, I'd never have graduated. I had to go into all of this before the school would even let me be a part-time assistant coach. If you try to fire Nick without an official reason, that school may well drop the crew."

"That damned school sure puts the *liberal* in liberal arts," Pete snapped.

"Liberality has nothing to do with it. It's basic personnel management," Prissy declared, sparing a wink for Brad. "To say nothing of fairness."

"Given all that, we've spent enough time on this," Steve declared. "I move we drop this until such time as either the school finds that Coach Bedford did anything wrong, or we hear from one of the regulatory bodies. We've got other, more important things to deal with, like the urgent need for a bigger boathouse. That's going to cost a fortune and..."

Brad pretended to listen, but his mind was on other things.

This did affect him. Between the word in the locker room and Rancilman's witch hunt, Brad knew he couldn't hide forever. He might not be marching in any parades, but he was gay, and it was time he admitted that without shame, even if only to himself. It didn't make him queasy like it had, and that helped.

Besides, hiding meant no Drew, apparently, and that... He just couldn't go there right then. He pulled his attention back to the meeting, even though he longed to be anywhere but there, anywhere Drew was.

Brad drove home, taking the longest, least direct route he could devise. Slow pokes? Not a problem. He was thinking. He did his best thinking behind the wheel. Some men were toilet men. They only thought on the can. He thought while he drove.

Something had snuck up on him in that meeting. He realized he would have to be out if people were going to go after his friends just because they were gay. That was the job of the big lugs of the world—to be out there in front to protect their friends.

He coached because he missed crew, not because it was his career. If the committee fired him, it was no big deal. If Rancilman wouldn't let this issue die after tonight, Brad would tell him point blank he was gay just to see the reaction.

He might not be entirely comfortable with his sexuality, but homophobia was definitely a problem he faced. He recognized that now.

Brad figured out something else there in the dark. He'd let Drew down, and not just with the dancing thing. Morgan had been right. What he did and liked in bed didn't change who he was.

And what he'd done in bed—or over a sawbuck—he'd kind of liked. It felt weird at first having another man's dick between his legs, but he'd sure come and come hard. All those intense physical experiences with Drew, to say nothing of the emotional ones, had been telling him one thing: "Get over it."

But he hadn't heard from Drew all day, and it was killing him. Drew'd been pretty pissed when he'd left Brad to lock up his house, but he'd also said the next step was Brad's. So, at a stoplight, he hit Drew's mobile number, since he had his douchetooth headset in, his car being too old for a built-in connection. He hated it, but it was easier than a ticket for driving and talking, and he knew that sooner or later the cops would crack down on the scofflaws.

"Hey, babe, it's me. It's Tuesday night," he said when it went to voice mail. "I'm...I'm really sorry. You were right. About a lot of things. I miss you. I just got out of one of those jack-off alumni oversight meetings, and that asshole's still after Nick. I could use your advice..." He stopped lamely when he realized he was babbling. "Anyway, I miss you. Wait, I already said that. I hope you'll call me."

Brad felt about as low as he could after disconnecting the call. Drew must really be mad.

When Wednesday passed without a call back, Brad grew more worried and even depressed. When he checked with security at the job site, they told him no one had seen Drew. Bob Miller did tell him, however, that someone from Drew's real estate office had come by looking for him.

Scared, he bit the bullet and drove to Drew's house, but it was as dark as when he'd left it, newspapers littering the driveway. He left the papers stacked neatly by the front door behind a planter so it wouldn't be quite so obvious that no one was apparently home.

It was late the night before Thanksgiving, but Brad didn't have a whole lot to be thankful for. Tomorrow promised to be an ordeal, a sullen meal and pretending to be a happy family, since Randall only demanded the appearance of a functional family.

Brad left a message for Nick before he left Drew's house. Maybe they'd all gone to Morgan's parents' for the holiday?

But first thing Friday morning, when other people were hitting the sales, if he hadn't heard from Nick, he was hunting him down. It was time for answers.

Nick and Morgan trudged back to the ICU the day after Thanksgiving. Nick hadn't been feeling very thankful, but as Mrs. Estrada had pointed out, Drew was alive and slowly improving. That should be reason enough.

"Don't push this 'brother from another mother' thing too far," the ICU nurse, Jerry Fortier, had cautioned them that first night. Fortunately, Jerry was an ex of Drew's and knew and liked Nick. He'd spoken in the hushed tones that seemed part of the standard protocol in the ICU. "You're in here because I know you and because you're the first person on the ICE list in Drew's wallet. Just be glad he had that much, because his cell phone was apparently broken during the assault. Legally, until or unless we can track down any advanced directives naming you, that's worth less than a bucket of warm spit. Him," he'd said, indicating Morgan with a wink, "I don't know from Adam."

But then Drew's parents had arrived the next morning and told the hospital staff in no uncertain terms that Nick and his boyfriend were to be admitted to their son's presence, if only, as the dramatic Claire St. Charles had said, "Because that's what Drew would want, and woe betide the man who makes his best friend sit in the waiting room."

"Trust me, it's not worth the racket," Drew's father, Edward, had told the attending physician.

"What's his condition this morning?" Morgan asked. He leaned over the desk and set a large latte down next to Jerry.

"Thanks, sweetie. Unchanged from last night," Jerry told them, looking up from the terminal where he was synching vital information from a tablet computer to a patient's file in the hospital's main computer. "He's stable, but until he wakes up, we won't know how bad the head trauma is. The swelling in his brain's almost gone, and that's always a good sign. You're clear to go in."

"Thanks, Jerry. Drew's parents should be here soon," Nick said.

Jerry's eyes went back to his work. "One at a time, though. Morgan can stay out here and flirt with me."

"Go on in, Nick. I think I'll be safe enough. Nurse Ratched talks a good line, but we both know that's all it is," Morgan said.

"That might be funny if I hadn't heard it, oh I don't know, a billion times already in my young career," Jerry said dryly.

Morgan smiled. "You just bring it out in all of us."

"I'll bring it out, all right. A great big paddle to whoop your lily ass. Now get in there, Nick. I've got work to do if this child you snatched from the cradle will let me get to it," Jerry harrumphed good-naturedly.

Morgan laughed softly as he sat down to wait. It was good to hear him laugh, Nick thought. They hadn't had much to laugh about in the last few days. Morgan had been even more upset than he at seeing Drew's crumpled body on the cold pavement outside Aspects. He sometimes forgot about the years separating them. It wasn't that he wasn't shaken, but those seven years between them tempered him a little.

He pushed aside the curtain from Drew's bay and stepped inside. The barely audible hiss of the oxygen flow and the louder beep of the monitors faded to a background buzz as Nick focused entirely on the form on the bed.

Nick still cringed seeing Drew like that. In its own way, it was every bit as shocking as the immediate aftermath of the assault. He pulled a chair closer to the bed and sat down and held Drew's uninjured hand, despite the restraints meant to keep him from worrying at the breathing tube. He was careful not to disturb the IV and set the monitors to screaming.

"Wake up, you drama queen. You've scared us all more than enough," Nick whispered, more to himself than anything. He couldn't tell sleeping from the coma Drew'd been in after surgery in the wee hours of that first terrible day after the beating.

Then Nick stared at Drew. He must've imagined it. But no, he saw movement. Drew opened his eyes.

"Unh," Drew whispered. He tried to move his hand, but the restraints did their work well.

Nick stood so fast the chair flew back and clattered to the floor. "Jerry!" He grabbed his best friend in his arms, tears streaming down his cheeks. "Thank God!"

"Out of the way!" Jerry commanded, shoving Nick aside.

Nick didn't mind. He joined Morgan outside the bay, hovering as people came running, a doctor and another nurse from elsewhere in the ICU. Then he thought of something.

"We need to call Drew's parents," Nick said.

"And Brad," Morgan said. Standing not ten feet from a sign forbidding the use of cell phones, Morgan pulled his smart phone out and dialed. "Mrs. St. Charles? It's Morgan. He's awake." He held the phone away from his ear, and Nick could hear her hysterical sobbing quite clearly. When it cut off, a male voice spoke. He held the phone closer. "Yes, Mr. St. Charles, we'll see you soon."

Nick pointed to the sign. "You're such a rebel."

"If I let other people's rules get in my way, we wouldn't be together," Morgan said.

"Ouch." Nick pulled Morgan into a hug. "I love you so much. Thanks for being here."

"Where else would I be?" Morgan replied.

"Not everyone would be so understanding of my devotion to another man," Nick said quietly.

Morgan shrugged nonchalantly. "I'm not everyone."

"No, you're most certainly not."

Chapter Twenty-Eight

By the time the doctors finished prodding him, Drew had nodded back off again.

"It's about what I'd predict," Jerry explained to them, Morgan and Nick and the St. Charleses in a small conference room away from the droning *beep-beep* of monitors and life-support equipment. "He's been through a lot and lost a fair amount of blood."

"Tell me, Mr. Fortier, is it standard procedure for nurses to give these kind of briefings?" Claire St. Charles said coolly.

"No, but none of the doctors want to do it," Jerry said, smiling slightly. "It seems you've already developed quite a reputation. Now then, starting at the top, his concussion is getting better based on the fact he's awake and lucid. His jaw is wired to deal with the crack in his mandible. The blow, or one of them, also took out several teeth. Given Drew's relatively young age, the periodontist will probably opt for replacements that screw directly into the jawbone itself, but that's not anything we handle here and will have to wait until his jaw heals completely. He'll continue to be fed through a gastric tube. The biggest problem right now is the hemothorax affecting the left lung."

"A cracked jawbone I get, but what's a hemothorax?" Edward St. Charles asked.

"Internal bleeding into the space around the lungs, in this case, the left lung. The more blood and other fluids that collect in the space, the less room there is for the lung to inflate properly. Eventually, if there's enough fluid, the lung collapses."

"My baby," Claire whispered.

"We've got a drain, a chest tube, inserted between the fifth and sixth ribs. Given his cracked ribs, that can't feel too good," Jerry said, "but then those cracked ribs alone aren't going to feel very good. In fact, they're going to make breathing very painful. He's not going to want to breathe very deeply, even once he's off the ventilator. With only shallow breathing, phlegm—that's snot for you, Mrs. St. Charles—collects in the lungs and causes pneumonia. So, until he heals, Drew's going to have some very fine painkillers so he can breathe normally."

"What about the hand?" Edward asked.

Jerry shrugged. "The hand surgeon's set it and done her best. He'll have to have rehab it if it's his dominant hand. I don't remember."

"Remember?" Claire said archly.

"Why yes." Jerry grinned, his teeth startlingly white against his dark, dark skin. "Didn't you know? Drew and I dated for about six months a few years back."

Nick turned away to hide his smile, while Morgan bit his lip to keep from laughing. Claire St. Charles could be a dramatic, even melodramatic, woman, but Jerry did a fine job of refusing to let her cast herself in the role of the Tragic Victim's Mother.

"Where were we? Oh yes, he'll have to learn to use his other hand for various...bodily functions, but I'd imagine Drew'll rise to the occasion. So. Rehab, and for the fractured patella and damaged knee joint too. He'll be on crutches for a while, then maybe a walker or a cane. It just depends."

"How long?" Edward asked quietly.

"About six weeks on the jaw. Roughly the same on the hand, maybe a little longer on the knee since it's load-bearing." Jerry consulted the tablet with Drew's medical records. "What else? Oh yes. The item of biggest concern right now is the blood in his urine. It—"

"Blood?" Clare gasped. "In his urine?"

Jerry nodded. "Have you noticed the rosy color coming down through the catheter and into the collection cup?"

"Yes, but I'd assumed it was blood or lymph or something draining, maybe from that collapsed lung you mentioned," Claire said, one hand clutching her necklace.

"That tube is further up," Jerry said. "It's indicative of internal bleeding, and if it doesn't stop, it'll mean more surgery."

Edward sighed. "More surgery. Poor Drew. What about that—"

"What about that horrid tube in his mouth?" Clare demanded. "I want it out so he can talk to me."

"That 'horrid tube,' Mrs. St. Charles, is right now the only thing keeping him breathing, and yes, it prevents him from talking because it goes down the back of his throat, in between his vocal cords and into the top of his lungs," Jerry acknowledged.

Nick squirmed uncomfortably at the thought of something going so deep. "So how long before he can ream us out for all this?"

"It won't be fast. He'll have to be weaned off the artificial breathing, and even once he is, the tube will be left in until we're sure he won't need it again," Jerry said. "It's better than having to put it in again. It's pretty common for the tube to stay a couple of weeks after he leaves the ICU." Jerry held up a hand. "Before you ask, I don't know. That's up to the doctors. A week or two here, a few weeks more in the trauma nursing unit, then a rehab facility until he can take care of himself."

Jerry looked at each of them. "Drew's going to need everything we can give him."

"We can't stay away from work that long, but we'll try to fly up here again," Edward said.

Claire looked at them. "That means it's up to you boys."

Nick and Morgan nodded. "We won't let him down," Nick promised.

"Hi, Drew. It's me. I don't know what's going on, or where you are, but I hope you're okay. I...I guess you're really mad at me and don't want me around anymore. I'm sorry. I never meant to hurt you."

He disconnected that call and made another one.

"Nick? It's Brad. What the hell's going on? Drew's disappeared, and this is the third message I've left you."

Brad ended the call. Usually he just slept the day after Turkey Day, but this year he could only worry helplessly. First Drew had disappeared, and then Nick and presumably Morgan, since those two had more or less been grafted together.

All the people he wanted in his life weren't taking his calls, and the ones he didn't want and frankly hated stuck to him like ticks. Randall, for sure. Philip could go either way. His brother's retreat during his confrontation with their dad filled him with contempt, but then, so much did about life in the Sundstrom home.

Brad got up to go rummage through the fridge for leftovers. Randall might be an asshole, but he set a good table. Not that Brad was hungry, but it was something to do, and then he might feel guilty enough to go work off his nerves at the gym.

His cell phone's bleating interrupted his mental ramblings on the way to the kitchen. Nick's number flashed on the display.

"Nick! Where've you been?" Brad said, quickly returning to his room and locking the door to his cell behind him.

"Hey, Brad. Sorry. It's been...rough," Nick said, his voice cracking. He coughed. "Shit. I totally spaced on calling you. I'm so sorry, I—"

"Dude, what the hell's going on?"

Nick was silent for a moment. "Drew was attacked Monday night on his way out of Aspects."

Brad fell back onto his bed. "What? How...who...God."

"We don't know who yet. Morgan and some of the witnesses chased them, but they got away. The police are treating it as the hate crime it so obviously is."

"Where were you and Morgan?" Brad demanded.

"We were still inside. Drew wasn't in the best mood," Nick said. Nick didn't say anything else, but he didn't have to. Even a block of wood like Brad knew what those unspoken words meant.

Brad swallowed. Drew. His Drew. "So, what happened?"

"Drew left early to take a cab back to my place to get his car. Morgan and I left shortly after. But in that interval, three men attacked Drew outside the bar and severely beat him. It looked pretty bad, but I'm not sure his life was ever in that much danger."

"Jeez," Brad breathed. Nick's description of the injuries made him sick to his stomach as his imagination scrawled blood and wreckage on his mental image of Drew.

"Sorry I didn't call you sooner. We've been spending a lot of time at the Med Center, and I keep forgetting things like my cell phone charger. I think the only reason I've been home to shower and change clothes is Morgan's insistence," Nick said tiredly. "Drew's in the ICU for a while longer. At least with school out this week for Thanksgiving we haven't had coaching to worry about."

"Do you think it'd be okay to visit him?" Brad asked quietly. At least he knew why Drew hadn't returned his phone calls, but after that, he doubted Drew would even want to see him.

"I'm not sure that's a good idea right now, honestly," Nick sighed.

"Right." Brad squashed his hurt. He should've known better than to ask. "Thanks for letting me know."

"I have to go, Brad. I'll talk to you later."

Brad didn't bother to say goodbye as Nick ended the call. He didn't see the point.

Guilt washed over him like a tsunami. He should've been there. If he'd been there, he'd have been able to protect Drew. If he'd been there, Drew would never have wanted to leave his own birthday celebration.

He might as well have kicked Drew himself. People could say what they wanted, but he knew the truth. This was his fault. He should've been there.

Brad stared at the ceiling, ignoring the ache in his chest and the knot in his stomach and the tears escaping the corners of his eyes. He couldn't shake the image of Drew lying battered and broken and bloody on the ground.

Drew must've been furious with him to have left his own house just to get away from him. Intellectually, Brad knew Drew was pretty unhappy, but it must've been a lot worse than he'd ever dreamed. And now? Now Brad knew that Drew hated him. How could he not?

His first real relationship was down in flames, and he had no one to talk to but Drew's best friend and that guy's boyfriend. They were the only gay guys he knew.

He'd failed. He was a failure.

He spent the rest of the day there, staring at the ceiling, mired in despair, listening to the refrain of failure echo in his head.

Nick hated him too. He'd heard it in his voice. Why wouldn't he? Brad had let Nick's best friend down, had left his best friend to be savagely beaten. Brad would hate him too.

He knew it was best for all of them that he not return to coaching in January. If he were honest with himself, what he liked most about helping Nick was being on the water and around a boathouse, not the coaching per se. He'd finish out the semester, but once the crew was off the water for the holidays, he was done. Rather than resign officially, he'd send Nick an e-mail and then just slouch off into the murk of a foggy valley day.

Then it hit him. Work. He worked for Drew. This was why people didn't work where they slept. He'd have to crawl back to his old man and beg for his job back. He'd told Randall it was only temporary, but he knew Randall. There might well be begging involved.

Brad rubbed his eyes. He needed a beer. Better to do this buzzing. That he hadn't eaten since breakfast would help. He got up and opened a can of liquid courage and sucked it down. It was a little past its best-by date, but that wasn't an issue. Then another.

Thus fortified, he headed out to humiliate himself. He heard voices as he approached the family room where his dad held court with the television.

He heard Alex Beltran, and he sounded angry. "You did *what*?"

"I did what I thought was necessary," Randall said calmly.

"Sir, you shouldn't go around me like that to contact my men directly. If this gets out..."

Randall sounded unconcerned, but then, he always did. "It won't get out."

"One of them already told me about the 'special job' he did for the big boss. How do you know they're not in a bar bragging about it right now?" Beltran demanded.

"You worry worse than an old woman," Randall said placidly.

"Somebody has to," Beltran muttered as he stomped out of the room, almost knocking Brad over.

Beltran gave him a long look that probably meant something, but Brad couldn't figure it out. The beers didn't help.

Brad knocked on the wall. "Can I talk to you for a moment, Randall?"

"The world seems intent on interrupting me this afternoon. What is it, Bradley?" Randall said.

He hadn't thought to prepare any kind of justification. "I need my old job back," he mumbled.

"Yes, I suppose you do. I'd imagine that ridiculous renovation's on hold, now that one of the principals is in the hospital for the foreseeable future. Yes, Bradley, you may have your job at Suburban Symphony back starting tomorrow."

Relief washed over him. "Thanks, Dad."

"And Bradley?"

"Yeah?"

"If it weren't for the family business, you'd be working as a personal trainer in a third-rate gym in the suburbs."

Brad shuffled back to his room. Randall was right. He was a failure. But how had Randall known about the assault?

"Hey, former roomie," Morgan said, bending down to hug Stuart, who was seated at a table in the now-deserted student commons at school. "How's it going? Sorry I haven't been around much."

"No worries. I know you and Nick have been spending all your free time with Drew," Stuart said. CalPac was on break for the winter holidays, but he still had books open, studying ahead of time to compensate for the demands crew would place on his life this spring.

"Not having to listen to me whine also freed up your time for Jonathan." Morgan set a bag containing a sandwich, apple, and bottle of water down in front of his friend.

"He's gone home for the holidays, and what's this?"

"Lunch. I knew you'd be studying and thought you could use some," Morgan replied, digging into his own sandwich. He'd stopped on the way to meet Stuart, figuring that Stuart had skipped lunch and knowing funds had something to do with it.

"So, how is he?" Stuart asked, poking around in the bag.

"Better. I mean, compared to a month ago...there's no comparison. He's awake when he's supposed to be and sleeps when he can. You know, with all the prodding and checking of vital signs. I honestly think it's the breathing tube that pisses him off the most. Well, that or the feeding tube."

"He's still on that?" Stuart gasped. "That's not good, not good at all."

"They weaned him off the breathing tube already, but I guess they leave the tube in, just in case he backslides."

Stuart shook his head. "I don't know him like you do, but even I can tell the man needs to express himself."

"He does that plenty well, believe me." Morgan made a face. "His parents must be doing well for themselves, because on their last day here, his mom gave him an iPad."

"You're kidding," Stuart said flatly. He took a bite of his sandwich.

Morgan shook his head. He himself was never at a loss for spending money, but he knew it was an issue for Stuart, and he never flashed cash in front of his friend and now former roommate. He also never let on that he knew Stuart was strapped for cash. "Nope. I guess watching him scribble notes on a steno pad with his nonwriting hand was too much. She said, 'Think of it as a gift to all of you. He'll be unbearable if he has to communicate that way one moment longer.' Mrs. St. Claire's kind of a bitch, in my opinion."

"So, Drew comes by it honestly?" Stuart said. "Okay, sorry that was bad."

Morgan laughed but soon fell silent, considering. "What I'm about to tell you is for your ears only. No one else's. Not Jonathan's. No one's."

"All right. You've succeeded in making me curious."

"Nick's getting out of coaching."

Stuart stared at him. "I couldn't have heard that right. The crew's never done this well."

"No, but he's quitting all the same. The investigation by the school and trouble with the oversight committee, to say nothing of the possibility of investigation by USRowing hanging over his head like the sword of Damocles...it's worn him out. You know physical therapy's always been his plan B?"

Stuart nodded.

"Well, it's now his goal. Seeing what Drew's going through and knowing what's to come...that's given my Nick a lot to think about."

"He thinks too much," Stuart said.

"I know, but that's who he is. We'll both finish up this June, and then..." Morgan shrugged.

"Looks like that spreadsheet of yours will come in handy, after all." Stuart referred to the file he'd seen on Morgan's computer that correlated credentialing programs for him with schools that offered courses in PT for Nick.

"Guess so," Morgan said.

They ate in silence for a few minutes.

"Does Drew know? That Nick's quitting coaching because of him?" Stuart asked.

"No, that's the last thing he needs. He's pretty depressed right now."

Stuart paused in taking a drink. "Wouldn't you be?"

"Yes. He's got reason enough just with the hate crime and then that huge renovation project being put on hold by the city council. I mean, it's great that they're so understanding, even if the politics of a gay bashing forced them to do it, but there's the Brad situation too."

"I thought they were going at it hot and heavy."

Morgan nodded. "They had been, right up until the night of the assault. They had a huge fight, Drew walked out, and Brad went home. Other than calling Nick the day after Thanksgiving, no one's heard from him since."

"Maybe he feels guilty," Stuart said. "Who knew he had it in him?"

"Brad's deeper than you think and coming to terms with being gay's been hard for him. I guess with his family in construction, it's pretty homophobic. That's got to be hard to put behind you," Morgan said. "But this vanishing shit? While Nick doesn't have the time to deal with it right now, I'm not particularly happy."

"I can see that. So, let's talk about something else, now I've finished shrinking your head. Again."

"I...you...I'm not that bad," Morgan yelped.

"I told you once that most of my time's spent dealing with the drama you freakishly tall men dish out," Stuart reminded him. "I wasn't lying, and it hasn't changed."

"So, let's talk about you. Tell me how it's going with Jonathan."

"It's complicated," Stuart said.

When several moments ticked by without follow-up, Morgan said, "That's it?"

"Yes, It's complicated. What do you want me to say?"

"And you wonder why we never talk about you. So, changing topics again, since this one died on the vine, are you still coming home with me? Mom's expecting you."

"Absolutely. I wouldn't miss it for the world," Stuart replied with a big smile.

That warmed Morgan. "I may not stay as long as usual. Nick's staying here, only coming up for Christmas Day, and I want to be here for him."

"That's really sweet. You can come get me before school starts up again."

Chapter Twenty-Nine

Drew couldn't show the holidays, to say nothing of the trauma nursing unit, his backside soon enough. His life would be so much better if people would just stop wishing him a happy new year. It was a week ago. It wasn't happy. At least he'd been declared strong enough to move to a rehab facility.

Still, without Nick and Morgan, he knew it would've been so much worse. Their faithful attendance at his bedside was perhaps the biggest reason he was healing as fast as he was. His parents hadn't been able to stay too long, although he knew they called Nick every day, and that iPad had been a godsend. Even without his voice, thanks to that damned breathing tube, he'd been able to pay his bills electronically. He'd never trusted AutoPay before, but it seemed marginally preferable than having his utilities cut off and his credit rating trashed.

His parents' gift, which they refused to consider an early Christmas present, had also allowed him to start catching up on his e-mails. But those took energy, and he lacked that commodity. More often than not, checking his e-mail consisted of deleting spam and sweeping the inbox for any sign of Brad, although by the time Christmas rolled around, he knew that was a wasted effort.

Nick had spent part of Christmas with him, even bringing him a Christmas tree in the form of a little potted evergreen with a few lights and tacky little ornaments. Drew loved it, the only holiday cheer he'd had. Or allowed.

The nurses had removed the breathing tube before the move to the rehab facility, but it still hurt to talk, and with his jaw still wired closed, he didn't try. Based on the latest X-rays, he only needed to endure it—and that wretched gastric feeding tube—another week or three. The therapists told him his returning temper was a good sign. He knew he'd be grateful for their attentive care once he was fully recovered, but for now his irritation needed an outlet.

Not that his therapist and chief antagonist put up with much. Deanne gave as good as she got, even typing pointed barbs back to him on his iPad when she really wanted to jerk his chain.

Right then, Deanne was making him walk to re-accustom his shattered knee to bearing weight. The crutches dug into his armpits and made his barely healed hand scream from gripping the handles.

"Good," Deanne said. "Now do it again."

"'Urts," he grunted through his teeth.

Deanne just tapped her foot and pointed to the floor in front of her.

With a grunt of pain, he started his slow way back. Plant the crutches, take a step, steady himself, repeat.

"Good," she said. "Now we're going back to your room."

His eyes bugged. He'd never gone that far on the crutches before, but she picked up her clipboard and his iPad and held the training room door for him.

He grimaced and bent to it.

Brad pulled his head out of the fridge in the back room when the bell over the door to the sales office jangled. "I'll be right out," he called, cramming more water and soda in. "Sorry about that, I was just...oh. It's you two."

"Yes, it's us," Nick said. "I didn't know how to contact to you since you pulled your vanishing act over the winter break, especially since you're back to not answering e-mail."

Morgan stood there with his arms crossed over his chest, glaring rebelliously from one man to the other, and Brad could already tell how this conversation was going to go. Apparently, he wasn't Morgan's favorite person right then.

"So rather than try to keep pinning you down, we decided to drive out here after practice," Nick said.

"We?" Morgan grated, and Brad felt the air chill further.

"Yes, *we*," Nick said firmly, steering Morgan to one of the chairs in front of his desk. "Sit!" he ordered.

To Brad's surprise, Morgan sat. He'd always kind of figured that Morgan called the shots, but maybe he hadn't given Nick enough credit.

Brad moved around them to his desk. "Well, here I am. What do you want to talk about? I'm at work, and I'm kind of busy."

Morgan snorted, but Nick ignored his boyfriend. "We need to talk about Drew."

"How's he doing?" Brad asked, afraid of the answer yet desperate for news.

"Now he wants to know?" Morgan snapped.

"What's your damage, Morgan? You've been an asshole since you walked in here," Brad fired back.

"You just up and abandoned him!"

"He dumped me!" Brad cried.

"That's not what he told us," Morgan said.

"He might as well have. He wanted something I just couldn't give him," Brad said.

"Yeah, like being true to yourself," Morgan said.

Nick put a hand on Morgan's arm. "Morgan."

Morgan had opened his mouth to unload on Brad again, but at Nick's touch, he snapped it shut.

No, Brad definitely hadn't given his former coach enough credit. The sight of the proud, sometimes imperious Morgan Estrada brought to heel with a single gesture brought a smirk to Brad's face.

Morgan glared at him. "Why're you smiling?"

"You. Dude, you are so married," Brad said.

"And we'd really thought you two were headed in that direction," Nick said softly. "Do you want to tell me what happened from your perspective? My boyfriend's pugnacious attitude aside, we really do care about what happens to both of you."

Brad sighed. The thought of rehashing all that hurt...but then again, maybe he owed it to them. Maybe he hadn't burned his bridges as thoroughly as he'd thought. "I guess Drew told you about the fight?" When they both nodded, he continued, detailing his last encounter with Drew, every detail painfully clear in his memory. He shrugged uncomfortably. "So, he told me I had to be out or I couldn't be with him."

"It sounded to me like he was just trying to jar you the rest of the way out of the closet," Morgan said.

"It didn't sound that way to me," Brad snapped. "My family's always been pretty macho, and I was around a lot of homophobia from an early age. As messed up as life with my dad is, it's all I know. I can't just wave a magic wand and be out, loud, and proud."

"No calls, no e-mails, and you haven't even been to see him," Morgan said. "That's what I don't get."

Brad could only stare. "He told me not to," he said, pointing to Nick.

"He... Nick what?" Morgan turned to Nick.

"I what?" Nick said.

"Don't you remember?" Brad said bitterly. "When you finally called me back the day after Thanksgiving, you told me you didn't think it'd be a good idea for me to go see him. So, I didn't."

"Nicholas Bedford," Morgan said ominously.

Nick sat back in his chair, racking his brains. He wiped a hand across his face, the strain showing. "I remember, but Brad, I just meant right then while he was still in such critical condition. I never meant stay away completely."

"How the fuck was I supposed to know that?" Brad yelled. Then, more softly, "How should I have known what you meant?"

He put his head on his desk, sick to his stomach. That whole time his maybe-ex-boyfriend had been in the hospital and Brad hadn't even dropped by. Right then, he hated Nick more than he'd hated anyone before.

"Brad...I'm sorry," Nick said, putting a hand on his shoulder.

Brad knocked it away. "Don't. Just fucking don't. You're not my favorite people right now."

"I think we should go," Morgan said quietly. "But Brad, Drew's in the rehab facility, and they've finally taken the breathing tube out. He can talk, and he's always had Internet access. Here's the number—"

"Get out!" Brad said, still hiding his face.

Brad ignored them as they left. He knew he'd forgive them, forgive Nick, but not just yet. Sure, he and Drew had had a nasty fight, but Brad knew that in ignorance, he'd abandoned Drew when he'd needed him most. Ignorance seemed to be how he did everything. One more thing that made him feel stupid.

He wanted to throw up, sick at the situation, sick with dread, sick at the thought of Drew alone and hating him. He'd run away, but something told him he'd feel just as shitty wherever he ended up. He'd still be Brad Sundstrom, Fuckup and Loser. Randall probably already had cards printed up somewhere.

He picked up the piece of paper with the rehab facility's number on it.

He punched the numbers into his cell phone, but overcome by nerves, he ended the call after the first ring. What made them so sure Drew even still wanted to talk to him? How did they know Drew wouldn't just swear at him for being so stupid and then hang up on him? He wasn't sure he could handle the sting of Drew's rejection again.

More nervous than when he'd placed that first call to Drew last summer, he hit the key to call Drew's mobile line, still the first number on autodial, his home second. It went right to a canned service message, and he disconnected.

He hit the number to autodial Drew's house.

"We're sorry. The number you have dialed is unavailable or has been disconnected. Please check your local listing or try your call again later. If you feel you have reached this recording in error..."

Brad killed the call. The message was clear enough. Drew had changed his phone numbers to cut him off.

That was enough rejection for Brad for one day. He crumpled up the piece of paper on which Morgan had jotted down contact info for Drew at the rehab place.

There was no one in the sales office of Suburban Symphony to see Brad's eyes, bright with unshed tears, as he flipped the sign on the door to "Closed" and sat in the back room, trying to get his act together.

Drew knew he should count his blessings. But lying there in bed to recover from the morning's therapy, it was easier to rehash his curses. The city had placed the Bayard reno on indefinite hold. Emily had come to him in the ICU that first week and dropped the bomb. The mayor's office had publicized that out of concern for the health and well-being of the owner of a small, independent business and under the circumstances, the project would wait until he'd recovered. While he was appreciative, he was also aware of the role politics and PR played.

That was all very well and good, and while one day he might be grateful for even the appearance of consideration, in the short term it made for the very real possibility of financial ruin. No completed job meant not meeting payroll or paying off the short-term loans he'd taken out to bridge the gap while he waited for the city to pay up. It meant bankruptcy for Renochuck, and since he'd loaned the company so much money, it meant bankruptcy for him too. There in rehab hell, he knew it meant losing his dream of moving from real estate into reconstruction, losing his house, and losing his boyfriend. That hurt most of all.

And Brad. He missed Brad. A lot. Even though their last time together had been a wicked fight, he missed his boyfriend. He missed his goofy smiles and the shy ones. He missed the thoughtful little gestures. He missed his big, larger-than-life presence. He missed getting pounded.

Sometimes, in those quiet, dangerous moments when he thought about their last fight, Drew wondered if maybe he hadn't been too harsh, if perhaps he should've been happy with what he and Brad had, because right then, they apparently had nothing. Less than nothing.

But then he got angry at Brad. Not once had the big jackass come to see him. So far as he knew, Brad hadn't even tried. No calls. No e-mails. Nothing. Yes, they'd had a fight, but Brad had abandoned him in his moment of need. That sounded so melodramatic to his inner ear, but it was the truth.

That Brad had run like a frightened bunny at the first sign of real trouble told Drew all he needed to know. It also made him sad. He thought he'd loved Brad, but he hadn't known for sure until Brad was gone.

Drew knew he'd been right to stick to his guns, to insist that Brad stand up and be counted as gay. But being right hurt like hell.

Brad looked up from the television, depressed by sappy Valentine's Day-themed shows on the tube and annoyed by the interruption to his evening routine, but someone was knocking on his cell door. He muted the television. "What?"

"It's me," Philip said. "Can I come in?"

"Yeah," Brad said curtly.

Philip tried the door, but it was locked.

"Just a minute," Brad grumbled. He heaved himself out of his recliner. He stumbled to the door and fumbled with the lock as he leaned against it. Then he lurched back to his chair. Philip could open the door himself.

He grunted as he dropped the last foot back down. It was late, and since he'd been drinking his meals lately, he was drunk. Not blackout drunk, but beyond buzzed. He knew it wasn't a good thing, but he didn't care. What else did he have to do? Twenty-two, and his life was over. That called for another one.

Philip looked at him for a moment. "Are you drunk?"

"Yep."

"Been doing that a lot lately, haven't you?" Philip sat on Brad's bed.

"Fuck off. I can drink if I want to," Brad snapped.

Philip held his hands up. "Easy, Brad. I'm just concerned, that's all."

"I'm fine," Brad muttered belligerently. "I mean, why wouldn't I be here in our shiny, pretty prison?"

Philip acknowledged the point. "It's just...you seemed so happy last year, before the holidays. Now your calories come from a can, and honestly, you look like hell."

"I feel that way, Philip."

Brad stared at the television, brooding. He'd been doing a lot of that since he found out about the accident. He lost Drew because he was too chickenshit. Then Drew was almost killed, and it was his fault because he wasn't there to protect him. And why wasn't he there? Because he was a pussy and couldn't be seen in public with a boyfriend, a boyfriend whom he'd realized too late just how much he cared for. Was on the way to loving.

But then Nick basically told him to stay away. He was surprised at how much that hurt. He was surprised how much Nick and Morgan meant to him, and not just because they were the only gay guys he knew. Morgan had called him a few times, but he knew it was just to ream him out, so he let the calls go to voice mail and then deleted them.

"Do you want to tell me why?" Philip asked gently.

Brad sighed. He didn't, but what did he have to lose? He'd already screwed his life up. "Because I loved someone, and I threw it away."

Philip didn't say anything for a while, and Brad resumed his own hazy thoughts. Just when he was about to turn the volume back on, his brother said, "Was it that guy I saw you with at the dedication of the boat?"

Brad jerked his head around to stare at Philip. So, he had been there. A denial was on the tip of his tongue, but then he thought, *That's what got me into trouble in the first place.* "Yeah."

"Do you want to tell me what happened?" Philip leaned back on Brad's bed.

"You're not surprised?" Brad said.

Philip smiled. "Not really. I saw you kiss him at the boathouse. I've had a little while to get used to the idea."

And when Brad opened his mouth, it all came pouring out. "So, I screwed up."

Philip shrugged. "Maybe. At the very least, it sounds like some epic miscommunication. I think you need to call your old coach, for starters."

"I need to get out of here," Brad muttered, reaching for another beer. He paused and then grabbed a water instead.

"So, what's it like?" Philip asked. "Kissing another man? You looked pretty happy."

"I was," Brad said. He looked at his brother with a hint of his old humor. "The facial hair came as something of a surprise, at first."

Philip laughed. "I can imagine. He must be something special."

Brad smiled sadly. "He sure was."

"Okay, what about...um...the, *you know*." Philip made gestures with his hands.

"The butt sex? Dude, you've got no idea. It's *so* much tighter. If I'd known that, I'd have come out sooner."

Then the door banged open. "Come out? What the hell are you boys talking about?" Randall demanded.

"Get out!" Brad thundered, up and out of his chair in a flash.

"This is my house, and I'll go where I please," Randall said. He spoke softly, but over the years Brad had mastered the art of interpreting his father's lack of tone, and this one meant fury.

Brad grinned. It might not be smart, but what the hell. "Yeah, Randall, I'm gay. A cocksucker. A fudge-packer. A butthole bandit. A—"

Then Randall was on him, knocking Brad back into his chair. Both men were impaired, Randall by his rage, Brad by his beer. But Brad was used to beer, and he brought his knee up hard into his father's groin.

Brad shoved his father off and stood up. This time, Philip jumped between them. "Knock it off, both of you!"

"You disappoint me, Bradley," Randall said, apparently back in control.

"Like that's anything new." Brad rolled his eyes. "You'll rant and you'll rave and then you'll do what you always do: go back to ignoring me, and I'll go back to hating you, except that I never stopped."

Randall shook his head. "Well, I guess I taught you to stand on your own two feet, and this is the thanks I get."

"No," was all Brad said.

"No, what?" Randall demanded.

He knew what Randall wanted. The "sir." But Brad'd be damned if he was going to give it to him. "No, Mom taught me to stand on my own two feet. You taught me to be afraid and to think I'm not worth anything. It's taken me a while, but I think I'm finally remembering Mom's lessons."

"Oh really?" Randall said. He pushed Philip out of the way, who slipped out of the room.

"I'm not going to fight you," Brad said. It figured Philip would bail sooner or later.

"You always were chickenshit," Randall sneered.

Brad's own fury rose to match his father's, and he almost took the bait. The gangly, hurting kid in him wanted nothing more than to pummel the older man. He knew he could. He was bigger and stronger, even if Randall was meaner. His jaw ached from the pain of clenching.

"You're not worth a prison record," Randall sneered.

"This whole situation is just stupid. I'm moving out as soon as I find a place, and as soon as the Bayard House renovation is back on track, I'm done at Suburban Graveyard," Brad said as he forced himself to relax.

"If you quit, you're fired!" Randall shrieked, losing control again.

"For being gay, Randall? Isn't that against company policy? I'm pretty sure it is. You try it, and I'll file a complaint with the state for wrongful termination, and who knows, maybe I'll tell them about a few of the other shitty things you've done over the years too." Brad was bluffing, but the look on his dad's face said he'd hit closer to the truth than he knew. He filed that away for future use.

He spent the next morning at Suburban Graveyard making calls about apartments. He'd been a little worried about first and last months' rent, but Philip had quietly slipped him a check with the words "no-interest loan" written on the memo line, and just when he was about to write him off again. It certainly surprised him how by not caring and risking it all to tell Philip he was gay meant he now had a brother, probably for the first time since their mother had died.

He found a few places in decent parts of town, just studios, and it looked like he'd be using a laundromat until he could afford a place with a washer/dryer hook-up. Still, it was funny how priorities could change, and right then, freedom, dignity, and self-respect looked like pretty nice amenities.

He was about to leave to grab lunch before viewing the first of them when he was struck by a thought. He pulled up the webpage for the Capital City Rowing Club, the local masters rowing outfit. He knew they were there. They were the older guys wobbling back into their dock when the CalPac boys were heading out. He never gave them much thought, since masters rowing started at age twenty-seven, but after all that beer, he needed to get back into regular workouts, and he didn't think he'd be able to pull off the Sundstrom corporate gym membership too much longer.

He fired off a quick e-mail.

I graduated from CalPac in June and rowed for Nick Bedford. I'm looking to get back into crew. If you'll haul my underage ass around for a few years, I'll pull my hardest for you.

Later that afternoon, Brad sat in a coffee house and considered his apartment options. One was near the freeway, which would make getting to Suburban Graveyard easier, but given his plans to bail on that just as soon as things got going with the Bayard House again, that was at best irrelevant and possibly a negative factor. One was close enough to the Bayard House that he could bike there, although from what he'd seen of drivers downtown and in Midtown, that seemed risky. The third...the third was close to Drew's neighborhood. That tugged at his heart. He knew they weren't a couple because of him, but the thought that maybe they could sleep in the same zip code at night comforted him.

He figured there were worse reasons for taking a given apartment. That decided, he checked his e-mail on his smart phone. One from the men's coach at the masters rowing club.

There's a new younger age category, so you can race too. Come check us out!

Just knowing there might be another rowing home for him, on top of a new home-home, buoyed him. He felt more optimistic about life, maybe even better about himself, than he had since...since right before that fight with Drew.

On a whim, he drove by Drew's house. The two of them had made a real mess of their relationship, with a little help from Nick, but Brad was honest enough with himself to admit he felt strongly for Drew.

What he saw when he pulled up in front of Drew's house appalled him. The yard looked like the Middle East after an American military incursion. He circled the block and then parked across the street.

He had an hour or two to get back to the rental office to check out that apartment close by. Not a lot of time, but Drew's yard needed more than he could give it in a single afternoon, anyway.

He checked to make sure he still had his key, jogged up to the house, and rang the bell. If Drew were home, he'd act like he was just returning the key, but based on appearances, no one had been by for a while.

He let himself into the garage by the side door and located the key to the back shed containing the lawn mower. He'd see what he could get done, maybe enough to appease the neighbors, maybe enlist Nick and Morgan. It wasn't like they—or at least Nick—didn't owe him.

Drew stared at the calendar on the corkboard over his desk in his home office. It still displayed November's page. He had left home to go dancing for his birthday and hadn't come home until late February. That was some trip, he thought as he ripped pages. When he found the back cardstock, he realized he didn't have a new calendar for this year.

He sighed. One more thing that he hadn't done while he healed. He knew he had no reason to complain. No breathing tube. That had been utter hell. The next time he deep-throated something in the future, it'd better be flesh.

No feeding tube inserted into his stomach, either, and his jaw worked again, even if it hurt to talk too much or chew anything too tough.

Nothing to show for his ordeal but some aches and pains that would fade in time and scars that would never disappear entirely.

He tried not to look in the mirror much. He couldn't stand to see where his teeth had been, even though he wore a decent temporary bridge and would soon have replacements that screwed directly into his jawbone, now that his jaw had healed. He didn't like seeing the new wrinkles, either, and just as soon as he'd sold a few houses, he'd be investing in some ruinously expensive man cosmetics.

He still needed a cane, but that, too, was temporary. His physical therapist assured him he had made good progress, but some days—most days—it felt like all pain and no gain. In the meantime, he limped along and rested when he had to, grateful every day for his blessedly temporary handicapped parking placard.

Speaking of selling houses, his broker had been so understanding Drew was giving serious thought to nominating the man for sainthood. The broker had allowed him to come creeping back into the business knowing full well that when the renovations of the Bayard House resumed, Drew would give real estate less than his full attention. It helped that when he was at his best, Drew was a damned good agent. He just wasn't at his best and wouldn't be for a while.

At least he could catch up on life now. The first hurdle for a man used to near-constant connection was to retrieve messages left for him. Despite periodic sweeps of his voice mail, his home and work mailboxes were full, and who knew how many calls he'd missed?

Then there was his cell phone. He'd been grafted to it. His attackers had crushed it. He'd kept the account current by paying the bill online, but he hadn't been able to replace the phone until recently. He had no idea if there were even any way to retrieve old messages or if the calls were just lost. If that one message he most wanted had been lost or had ever existed, now he knew a call from Brad would never come again.

Not long before his release from rehab, Nick had come to see him, and he knew something was wrong immediately. The last time he'd seen Nick that upset and nervous had been when he and Morgan had been on the skids. Before that, it'd been when Nick came out to him. When Nick told him what was up, Drew understood. In that moment, and for the first time, Drew hated his best friend.

Despite their fight, Brad had been wild with worry when he hadn't been able to track down not only Nick and Morgan, but Drew as well. And then Nick had told him not to visit. The thought still raised the bile in his throat. Brad had wanted to but thought he was unwelcome, because of their fight. So, he had left Drew one final message, and when Drew finally was able to access his voice mail, it broke his heart to hear. It looked like they were done. At this point, he didn't see a way out of the sorry, tangled mess of miscommunication. Too much time had passed, and feelings were too hurt all around.

It made thoughts of filing for his disability insurance and dealing with creditors seem trivial, but that trivia needed attention. He took a portfolio of documents related to his assault and hospitalization, things like the police report and newspaper stories and discharge papers from the hospital and rehab. It helped smooth things over when he went to pay past-due bills in person.

The city had frozen the Bayard House project not long after his assault, so he had a little time on that, although bills still came due. He just hoped the city would unfreeze the money so he could pay them.

When it came down to it, he could run errands and sell homes with a limp and a cane. But what really limped along was his heart.

He flipped half-heartedly through his thousands of e-mails, mostly business related at first, although his broker had set up an autoreply to let people know. Later messages mostly consisted of good wishes.

He wondered if there were a support group for people who'd been in the hospital for a long time to help them readjust to life on the outside again. Group therapy for victims of violent crime? Check. Individual therapy to cope with that and adjusting to his physical status? Check. Not coping with rattling around his house as he tried to re-establish his old work habits? Not so much.

He gave up and stared out of the window at his backyard. The flower beds looked good, and his raised vegetable beds appeared ready for the spring planting. The lawn was winter-browned but would come back well enough in a month or three as the weather warmed up. At least it was still well tended.

His lawn was well tended. He started out of his chair. What the—

He grabbed his cane and gimped to the window. Whoever'd been taking care of his yard had butchered his roses, but they thrived on abuse and would be back in a year or two. The rest?

Someone had been tending his yard. Someone. Who was he kidding? Nick and Morgan were just the sweetest men sometimes, even if they were motivated by guilt.

He hobbled back to his desk and called their landline. There was no need to disturb them at school. "You guys. Thank you *so much*. The yard looks amazing. We'll get through this. Talk to you soon." He made a few tired-sounding kissing noises and hung up.

Suddenly exhausted, he walked slowly to his room and sat on his bed before carefully swinging his legs up. Between a lack of endurance and the painkillers, Drew fell deeply asleep almost as soon has his head touched the pillow.

He roused with a start hours later. He was groggy, and it was dark in and out, but the phone's insistent buzzing woke him.

He checked caller ID. *Sac City Fire.* He frowned and answered.

"Yes, this is Drew St. Charles."

He listened as disbelief and horror raced each other to the pit of his stomach to see which would make him sick first.

"Yes, I see. Thank you." He hung up. Then the crying started, and he threw the handset across the room.

Chapter Thirty

"Sorry, sir, no one's allowed into the construction zone," the police officer said.

Brad held his driver's license out. "But I'm the job foreman on the renovation. The fire department called me and told me to come down here."

Red lights still flashed, but the sirens were silent, and the acrid smell of smoke permeated the air. Water soaked the ground around the burned wall of the Bayard House, and Brad could just imagine how much water was inside.

The officer guarding the open chain-link fence considered the matter and then flagged down a passing firefighter. "This man says you guys called him?" He sounded dubious at best.

"What's your name?" the firefighter demanded.

"Brad Sundstrom."

She spoke into her radio for a moment. "Come with me, sir," she said, much less tersely. "The captain's expecting you."

Brad flipped his hard hat up onto his head and ducked under the yellow caution tape. He followed the firefighter to one of the engines where several people in turnouts huddled. "Captain Douglas? Brad Sundstrom's here."

A man who looked to be in early middle age glanced up. Brad took one look at the man's chiseled features, accented with soot, and the strong build apparent even beneath the bulky turnouts, and his jaw fell open. Drew's appeal had been both physical and emotional, but this man, the fire captain, triggered raw, animal lust.

Brad shoved that aside. He hadn't been called to the Bayard House to cruise firemen, even if he'd had the first idea how to do it.

"Mr. Sundstrom?" the captain asked, looking at him speculatively.

Shit. Caught looking. "Call me Brad. What happened?"

"I was hoping you could tell me," Captain Douglas said, looking him up and down. "I thought this job had been put on hold."

Brad nodded, suddenly warm. "Yes, after my boss was assaulted and spent a month in the hospital and more time in rehab."

"So, there was no active work going on here, then?" the captain asked, frowning.

"No. I doubt any of the crews were here, either, since the money was held up by the city even before the work stoppage."

"That confirms my first impressions, then. This looks like arson."

"Damn," Brad muttered. "Is there any way I can see the damage?"

Captain Douglas thought about it for a moment, staring into Brad's eyes. Then he nodded. "Yes, I think so. Since you've got a hard hat and the fire's out. I'll show you personally."

Brad followed the captain around to one side of the mansion, mind spinning, wondering what exactly was going on.

"We think they cut the fence on the far side of the lot and then snuck around to this side of the building, where they used a crude incendiary device—"

"And that is?" Brad said.

"Sorry, occupational hazard," Captain Douglas said, smiling sheepishly. "A home-made bomb, probably gasoline or maybe lighter fluid, in a bottle with a gas-soaked rag for a wick. Break a window, light the rag, throw it inside and run around to the other side of the property and out the cut fence when security comes to check it out."

Brad felt sick to his stomach. "Is that what happened?"

Captain Douglas shrugged. "The exact details will depend on the analysis of residues by the lab, but it's probably pretty close and my—" he paused, giving Brad a loaded look. "—physical investigation. Neighbors reported seeing people loitering after hours, and knowing the project's on hold, they called the police. Other people reported the sound of breaking glass just before seeing a flash. I'm told there might be physical descriptions, and I'll follow that up with the police in the morning. Want to look around inside?"

"Yeah, sure, that'd be great. I need to know what we're dealing with here." The captain's attentions unnerved Brad in a way that made him need to adjust himself, but he didn't think it'd be a good idea to reach into his pants right then. He also needed to check out the damage, even if what he wanted to check out was Captain Douglas.

"Watch your step. It's wet in there," the captain warned him. "Here's where we think it started." He pointed to a gaping hole where there had only been a wall the last time Brad was there.

Brad would have to check the plans, but he was pretty sure this had originally been the mansion's parlor, and now he could step in from what would one day be part of the gardens. He was extremely aware of the captain's proximity to him, just as he was aware of the not-quite-casual way Captain Douglas brushed his hand over his turnouts.

"Why would someone do something like that?" Brad asked. "It's just an old house. It's not like we're building on sensitive habitat or sacred ground or something."

The captain shrugged. "Who knows? Vandals don't need a reason. It could even have been gang members trying to make a name for themselves."

"Lovely." Brad shook his head. "So, what happens now? What's the procedure?"

"Given the historic nature of the building and the importance of the project to the city, I'll get on the investigation first thing in the morning. Honestly, it looks fairly cut and dried. Strictly amateur."

"Can I go in?" Brad asked. He needed to move away from this man.

"Sure, like I said, just watch your step." Captain Douglas took hold of Brad's arm to steady him as he climbed awkwardly through the hole. Brad pretended not to notice the gleam in his eye, although his cock sure felt it.

The captain pulled a flashlight out of his turnout coat and shone it around. "As you can see, the damage doesn't extend very far into the room, which tells me that they didn't throw it far and possibly that they didn't throw it with enough force for the bottle to shatter. So, the gas would've leaked out and ignited, but not splattered everything with burning drops." Standing close behind

Brad, almost breathing in his ear, Captain Douglas pointed his flashlight to the ceiling. "But note how bad it is up there. I'd say most of the damage is to the ceiling and the floor above it. I shouldn't take you up there in case the floor's been weakened by the fire, but I might be able to make an exception."

Brad swallowed, his throat gone dry. The smoke, it had to be the lingering smoke. "No, that's okay. Safety first!" he squeaked, thinking about what he and Drew had done upstairs.

And then he remembered that Drew didn't want him anymore, not for who he was, a man only just coming to terms with being gay. Like it or not, he was single, and they say the best way to get over someone is get under someone else. It'd always worked in college...

Taking a breath, Brad backed up against the captain. "Sorry," he said, but he didn't move.

"No worries." The captain skimmed his tongue over Brad's ear. He moved his crotch into Brad's ass and held it there.

Brad knew where this was heading. He had a choice. He could see where this led, see how it was with another guy, a man other than Drew. See if he really was gay. Or he could carry the torch for a man who wouldn't take him as he was.

Not quite believing he was doing it, Brad ground his ass against the man standing behind him, sending him an unmistakable message. He knew what he'd do if Drew ground back into him like that. He'd have him bent over a table in seconds. Or would if they were still together. That cooled him a little.

Then he felt a hand, a stranger's hand, another man's hand, rubbing his own too-hard cock through the jeans he'd thrown on when the call had come in. Thanks to the beer diet he'd been on, the formerly loose jeans hugged his body, and there was nowhere for his arousal to hide. It felt unreal. It felt incredible.

Brad reached back and returned the favor, setting up a long, slow stroke over the thick fabric of the captain's protective clothing. Maybe it was just the thickness of that gear, but good goddamn. The captain felt huge under there.

"Jeez," the captain breathed. "You'd better be prepared to follow up on that. I'm taking a huge risk, but I've been hard since you got here."

"Me too," Brad said, a little nervous but also incredibly hot. "And yeah, I think you'd better...uh, show me the situation upstairs." He coughed. "I...uh, it wouldn't be right bringing crews back in without...uh, assessing the damage in person."

With a look that smoldered in a way that had nothing to do with the fire his brigade had just quenched, Captain Douglas led Brad upstairs and dragged him into the first room that wasn't open to the stairs.

Before Brad knew it, the captain shoved him up against a wall. "You like this?"

"Yeah," Brad breathed, and he did. "So, what's your name, hot fireman?"

"It's Owen." He sucked Brad's lip into his mouth. "I've wanted to do this since you walked in."

"I think I noticed," Brad breathed. He hesitantly reached into Owen's pants and pulled at his shirt. "Is...is this okay?"

"More than." Owen shoved Brad's hand further down over his hard-on. "Yeah, like that."

Brad kissed Owen back, biting his way down Owen's neck as he worked his hands into his pants. It had always revved Drew up, and it worked on Owen, too, judging by his jagged breath.

Then Owen tugged at his own jeans. "Let that out. Fire needs air before it can burn."

"Do you always talk about fires during sex?" Brad asked.

"Only when the guys are as hot as you," Owen replied. Then he looked at Brad, and they both laughed. "Sorry, that was really bad. Let me make it up to you."

"How?" Brad squeezed Owen's prick and played with the fluid leaking from its tip.

"Like this." Owen sucked at Brad's neck briefly before he fell to his knees before Brad's open jeans. He reached into his underwear like it was a box of buried treasure and tenderly pulled Brad out, stroking his cock gently with one hand while he used the other on himself.

"That feels good," Brad breathed, leaning back against the wall.

"That's nothing," Owen said before taking Brad in all the way.

"Oh God," Brad moaned as the soft tissue at the back of Owen's throat muscles fluttered around the head of his cock as Owen took him all the way in.

Owen pulled off, looking smug. "Told you."

"Don't stop," Brad urged, and smiling, Owen bent back to his task.

Brad was on his way to heaven when his mind took a detour. He'd tried to deep-throat Drew but couldn't. They'd both enjoyed the attempt, however. It was them. He still missed Drew.

"Stay with me, Brad," Owen murmured around his cock, looking up at him. Then he started humming, a low throaty rumble that notched everything up a hundred times.

And Brad could only think about what Owen was doing to him. He concentrated on the sensations. It was impossible not to, but it was likewise impossible not to think of his boyfriend...ex-boyfriend.

His hips thrust of their own volition, and he suddenly knew just how close he was. "Almost there, buddy."

Owen backed off, stroking them both hard and fast.

"Oooh!" Brad gasped as he shot in two hard blasts, splattering the front of Owen's chest. Moments later, Owen grunted out his own climax, narrowly missing Brad's shoes.

Brad leaned back, catching his breath. As intense as the blowjob had been, he recovered fast. Then he noticed what he'd done. "I'm sorry."

"I'm not," Owen said with a smirk, rubbing his hand through Brad's load. He held it up and smelled it before wiping his hand on his pants and zipping up his coat. "The memory of this? I'll be jacking off for months to this."

"Yeah," Brad said, barely over a whisper.

"Who is he?" Owen said softly.

"What?" Brad blinked, unprepared to hear soft words on the lips of a stranger who'd just blown him in public.

"The man you thought about."

"He...he's my boyfriend, my first. I guess now he's my first ex," Brad said, sniffling. He told himself the sniffles were because of the smoke. Same with the tears in his eyes. All that smoke.

Owen stood and took Brad in his arms and held him gently. "You want to tell me about it?"

And strangely enough, Brad did want to tell this not-quite-total stranger with his cum on his chest. It felt good to be held, even like this.

"So, there it is." Brad wiped his eyes. "The whole sorry story."

Owen released Brad enough to look in his eyes. "You need to call this man. If he's still jonesing for you the way you so obviously are for him, this will all be a bad memory in the rearview mirror before you know it. But you won't know if you don't reach out."

"I have called him," Brad mumbled. "He didn't call back."

"Then call him again, at least one more time. You owe it to both of you to give this another shot."

"I guess so."

"I know so, and—"

"Hey, Captain!" someone called from downstairs.

"Up here! Be right down," Owen—Captain Douglas again—called. "I'm just showing the project foreman the damage."

"Yeah, all over the inside of your jacket," Brad whispered.

"Bad!" Owen hissed playfully. He pulled Brad in for a quick kiss. "One more thing. If this guy really doesn't want you, trust me, when you're ready, you won't be single for long."

Brad didn't say anything as he followed the fire captain downstairs, instead trying to school his expression out of freshly blown into something more serious, since he'd just been shown the smoke and fire damage to the second floor. Allegedly.

He left quickly after that, something they both seemed to want. Captain Douglas had a job to do, and

Brad had a lot to think about on the drive back to his apartment, so close to Drew's house and yet so far away from the comfort it once held.

Owen was right. Brad owed it to himself and Drew to try again.

But jeez, did he have "bitch boy" written on his forehead? How'd Owen known he was gay? And if he and Drew weren't together, why did it feel like cheating?

Chapter Thirty-One

The entire next week, the first week in March, Brad felt like his skin didn't fit. No matter what he did, how hard he pulled in the boats or pumped in the gym, nothing worked.

With the fire at the Bayard House, Sundstrom Homes and Suburban Graveyard held him fast like the La Brea Tar Pits. He decided to take advantage of the perks and keep going to the gym. One of the few, to his way of thinking. Not that it worked. Nothing set him at ease. Perhaps nothing could.

Where his life had been looking up and he felt like he was regaining his mojo, suddenly it was the suck again. Life, work, Drew, all of it.

The very next day after the fire, he called Drew on his landline, since calling him on his mobile line had yet to accomplish anything besides eating up Brad's own minutes.

Psyching himself up, he promised he would be perfectly calm when what he wanted more than anything was to beg and whine and plead like an Irish setter for Drew to take him back.

"Hi, Drew. It's me. I'm still really sorry I couldn't give you what you wanted. But...can we at least talk about this? I miss you. Please call me."

Drew had to be call screening. No one in business for himself could afford to be this hard to reach. Or maybe

Drew was showing houses. Brad was too afraid to call the real estate office, although at this point, he'd long ago parted company with his pride. He heard the echoes of his father's words. He really was chickenshit.

Feeling worse when he hung up the phone, Brad just stared out of the window. Spring made its presence known in fits and spurts, and that day was a pleasant one, although with his luck, it'd rain for tomorrow's practice.

Brad hated not knowing about the fate of the Bayard House, but until Captain Douglas completed the arson investigation, the entire thing was up in the air. He'd spoken unofficially to the city's preservation office and to the mayor's office, but until the report came back, both agencies were noncommittal, and since he wasn't a principal on the project, they couldn't tell him much that was official.

Captain Douglas. Owen. Brad still couldn't believe he'd done something like that, but it left no question in his mind. He was gay. No doubt about it.

Even though the memory still quickened his pulse, and yeah, he'd jacked off a couple of times thinking about it and thinking about Owen getting off remembering what they'd done, lingering regret permeated the memory. He didn't want built firemen. He wanted Drew, but Drew didn't seem to want him back anymore.

Fuck. What was he going to do? How was he going to get over Drew? Getting under someone else hadn't worked. He'd thought of Drew so much Owen had called him on it.

The *ping!* of his corporate e-mail pulled his mind back to the present. Just what he wanted, an e-mail from his father.

Against his better judgment, Brad opened it and regretted it almost instantly. Randall had written to him to gloat about the fire at the Bayard House.

On the Thursday the week after the fire, during another interminable afternoon in the sales office, Brad's cell phone rang, but he didn't recognize the number.

"Brad Sundstrom."

"Hi, Brad. It's Owen Douglas."

Brad's stomach turned a little somersault. "Hey, Owen. What's going on?"

"Like I told you, I fast-tracked the investigation, and I just wanted to let you know that I'm done. It's safe to resume work," Owen said.

"Now if only the city would let us."

"I've recommended as much in my report. As long as the mansion's empty and incompletely renovated, it'll be a target, either for vandals or for squatters from the homeless population. That might well mean more fires, too, since they light them to stay warm. It wouldn't take much for one to get out of control," Owen told him.

"You said you thought it was arson. Was it?" Brad asked.

"Oh, definitely. I don't have many leads, but that's a job for the police, and I've turned everything related to that over to them. There's not a whole lot to go on, however, so we may never catch the arsonists." Owen paused. "Are you doing all right?"

"Yeah, sure," Brad said a little too fast, "but should you be talking about this on a fire department phone?"

"Good dodge there, but as it happens, this is my personal cell phone. I'm just trying to look out for you,

Brad. You seem like a nice guy, and as corny as it sounds, I only want you to be happy."

Brad didn't say anything right away, because to tell the truth, he felt like dirt.

"Brad? You with me here, big guy?" Owen said.

Brad didn't know if he'd chosen those words on purpose, but it sounded like what he'd said when they were...when they were back at the mansion. "Yeah, I'm here. And yeah, I feel pretty bad about it, like I cheated on him or something, which is ridiculous, since he won't even take my calls."

"Betrayal is a state of mind and not a reflection of whether you're together or not," Owen said patiently. "For what it's worth, that only says good things about you, you know."

"Yay me." *Damn.* Brad hated feeling this way. Sometimes, he just hated feeling.

"Call him, Brad," Owen urged.

"I have," Brad said softly.

Owen said nothing for a moment. "I'm sorry."

It was just business after that. Brad had to hand it to Owen. On learning Brad was apparently single, he had most emphatically not offered his phone number or tried to hook up.

But who cared about a sterling character when feeling like this was what it got him?

Brad sleepwalked through the next day and that whole weekend. He showed up for work and practice, but he just went through the motions. He spent a morose weekend around his apartment, but at least he kept his face out of the beer. He might be miserable, but he knew a budding problem when it bit his ass.

Monday was looking like more of the same when his mobile phone rang. The office phone rarely rang, but suddenly his own phone was chirping like a cricket in the night.

"Brad Sundstrom."

It was a subcontractor who needed answers and money. Brad promised to at least get him answers by the end of the day.

Well, wasn't this a pig fuck? A project on hold, a principal who'd apparently vanished, an ex-boyfriend he still cared for so much it hurt. He leaned back in his office chair and flicked a pencil up into the acoustic ceiling tiles. Oddly amused, he threw a new one up and stuck it next to the other one. He'd never managed it when he'd tried in middle school and high school.

Flick.

The Bayard House was again safe to work in.

Flick.

The subcontractors needed answers.

Flick.

There was no reason not to resume work.

Flick.

No reason, other than having to call Drew again.

Drew was incommunicado.

Flick.

Owen was right. He had to call.

Or maybe not.

There was another principal on the project.

He hadn't had much contact with Emily lately. They'd planned for her to get involved once they had a place for her to put the furniture and hang the wallpaper.

Maybe they didn't need Drew to get started. Maybe, just maybe, he could use this to prove himself to Drew.

Showing more excitement and verve than he had in months, Brad pulled up Emily's phone number and called her.

"This is Emily Schoenwald."

"Hi, Emily, it's Brad. Can I talk to you about the Bayard renovation for moment?"

"Brad," she said flatly. "What a surprise."

"Uh...yeah. Listen, I've got subcontractors calling me needing answers."

"So?"

"So?" Brad repeated. "What'd you mean, so? It's time to get back to work, only I can't reach Drew. I think he's just given up."

"Wouldn't you?" she demanded.

"Look, I know he's been through a lot, but—"

"You have no idea, you silly boy," Emily snapped.

He'd really thought that as a gay man, he wouldn't have to put up with this kind of bullshit from women, since they didn't have what he now wanted. "I don't know what you're talking about, but can we just—"

"No, I don't suppose you do," Emily sighed. "What'd you want, anyway?"

"I told you." Brad clenched his fist. "It's time to get this project back on track."

"Did you not hear about the fire?"

"I was down there while it was still smoldering, and I've been in nearly constant contact with the fire department since then," Brad said with exaggerated patience.

"Then you know how bad it is."

"Better than you do!" Brad snapped. "Look, are you going to help me or practice being a cunt? Because I have to tell you, you're already pretty good at it."

"When?" Emily said, resignation writ plain in her voice.

"At the job site in an hour. Bring your hard hat." With that, Brad hung up.

Brad met Emily at the gate. She peered around him. "It doesn't look that bad from out here," she admitted grudgingly.

Brad nodded. "It's really not nearly as bad as it could've been. I'll show you. I don't feel like cranking the power just for this, but I've got lights." He handed her one of the two large battery-powered lanterns.

He waved at the security service, now paid for by the city, as they walked by. "Just looking at the damage," he called, and the guard nodded and radioed the others.

Brad unlocked the main doors and held them for her with an exaggerated show of gallantry. He needed her on his side.

"So, where's the damage?" she asked. "It's sure a far cry from the last time I was here."

"You won't say that when we come to the parlor. That's where the fire was started," Brad said.

"Yeah, that's what they told me a day or two ago, but how're you getting such detailed information?"

Brad shrugged, hoping she chalked the blushing up to the cold air in the mansion. "Just a good working relationship with the fire captain on the scene, I guess."

Emily slid one parlor door back into its pocket enough for them to slip through, although even in the dim light of their lanterns, they saw the soot clouding the cut glass inset into the wood.

Emily made a mew of distress when she saw the hole burned through the outside wall, now covered with plywood. "Any idea who did this?"

Brad shook his head. "Captain Douglas wasn't sure they'd ever catch the people who did it, but he's turned that part of the investigation over to the police."

"Still, I have to admit, you were right. It could be a lot worse."

He rolled his eyes and then flashed his lantern up to the ceiling. "Look up."

"Oh, shit."

"Yeah, smoke and fire rise. Who knew?"

Emily turned to face him. "Brad, seriously. It could be worse, but it's not good. Between damage and bad renovations in the past and modern codes, saving the Bayard House was a stretch in the first place. Maybe it's time to think about invoking the escape clause. You know, cut our losses and move on."

Brad hated the thought. Despised it, even. "There's a rowing expression: 'The only race pace is suicide pace, and today looks like a good day to die.'"

"That's...hardcore."

"I'm hardcore," he said, and suddenly, he knew it was true. In crew, during that last all-important race, he'd gone so far into the pain cave he never thought he'd see the sun again. They all had. And they won.

In life, like crew, he might've been beaten down, but he would not be beaten. He could do this, for himself...and for Drew. Life had dealt Drew a severe blow and even smacked Brad around. But Drew had an ox for a boyfriend, and that boyfriend wasn't going down, not without a fight, not at all if he could help it.

"Hear me out." Brad's voice was full of possibility. "Obviously, we're going to have to repair the wall, but it's possible we'll need to replace that section of floor too. How is up to the structural people. But this could've been so much worse. Since there's nothing in here, there's not that much to decontaminate, maybe just the plaster on the walls and ceiling where smoke got to it, plus water damage, but hardwood's easy to restore." He swept his arms around him.

Emily considered his words, and he could tell she was coming around. "And with past floods, the water didn't even damage the historical integrity of the building, not really."

"With the city behind this, you as one of the principals can get the money flowing again. We can use this to revise the budget and hire more crews. There's no reason on earth we can't finish this."

Emily nodded slowly. "Okay. You've convinced me. There's just one more thing."

"Yeah?"

"What the hell happened between you and Drew?" she demanded.

Brad groaned. "What's that got to do with anything?"

"I know something bad happened between the two of you. I've never seen him this devastated. He's never isolated himself like this."

"You know, I really don't want to go into the details of my personal life. It's really none of your business."

"Drew's a dear friend, and that makes it my business, Closet Boy," Emily snapped. "I told you once I'd rip your balls off if you hurt him."

"Enough, you pint-sized bitch. I'm fucking sick of Drew's friends butting in and threatening me. The fact is,

I'm a foot taller and over a hundred pounds—" he stopped, looking her up and down. "—make that seventy pounds heavier. If you threaten me one more time, I'll kill you myself and bury you in the garden."

Emily smiled. "I knew I liked you. You'll be strong enough to stand up to Drew."

Brad just shook his head. She was too complicated for him. "We can do this. We can get this back on track. Are you in?"

"Why're you doing this?" she asked, looking him straight in the eye.

"For Drew. This is his dream, and it can still happen. I let him down once. I won't do it again." But he was also doing it for himself, to prove if only to himself that he wasn't a quitter and a failure.

Emily looked at him intently. "Do you love him?"

Brad didn't even have to consider the question. "More than anything."

"Then call Bob Miller. He'll know what to do."

"What about the city?" Brad asked.

"You leave that to me. Drew too. If you want to do this to make it up to him, then it needs to be a surprise. But be prepared, he might not take you back, and he might not like being surprised."

"I have to risk it. Right now, I've got nothing."

Chapter Thirty-Two

Spring had a firm grip on the Sacramento Valley, although unsettled weather was possible even that late into April. But Drew didn't care. There might've been dark clouds on the horizon, but for him, the clouds were mostly gone, the storms of the winter departing, the waters calming.

Only two real problems remained in his life, the unsettled fate of the Bayard House and Brad. Emily had taken over all aspects of the project six weeks ago, and to his surprise, he was happy for her to do so. He'd had too much on his plate as it was with just returning to health and some semblance of life as he'd known it before the assault. The Bayard renovation had been pie in the sky, and he presumed she was in the process of winding it down and would contact him for signatures in due time. Sure, losing a dream hurt, but his therapist worked with him in accepting it.

And Brad. He surprised himself with how much he still ached for the man. Brad had worked his way in deep and getting over the big jackass would apparently take time. He tried to tell himself he'd never really seen anything in Brad, that it had just been lust, but in his quiet moments late at night, he knew the truth.

But that night wasn't a night to whine or bemoan his fate. He wanted to celebrate. While his psychological wounds would only clear over time, his doctors and physical therapists just that morning cleared him to return to full physical activity. He planned to celebrate tomorrow by going for a walk, since he'd have to build back up to running.

Tonight, he'd insisted on treating Nick and Morgan to a good dinner out. He knew that on student budgets, even with parents as affluent as Morgan's, dinners out were a rare treat. He wanted to show his gratitude for all their help during his recovery in some way, as well as make it clear that as much as losing Brad hurt, he was over Nick's role in the miscommunication.

Drew rose to greet them, hugging first Nick and then Morgan. All three men wore suits, and if Drew's hung a little loosely, no one mentioned it.

"Wow, this place is pretty fancy," Nick said, looking around. It was kind of adorable how uncomfortable he looked in a suit and an upmarket restaurant.

"How come you never took me places like this when we were dating?" Morgan said. For his part, he looked born to wear designer suits like the one his parents had bought him at Christmas. Too bad he was destined for the classroom, because he and Nick wouldn't be able to afford them until they both finished grad school.

Nick looked hurt. "You've seen my bank balance. You know I would if I could."

"I meant him," Morgan said with a twinkle in his eye and nod of his head. "You took me to some stupid crepe place on that faux date Nick put you up to. Who knows, maybe if you'd taken me here, things would've worked out differently. Maybe I might've fallen for you, Drew."

Drew and Nick exchanged amused looks. "Highly unlikely," Drew said, shaking his head. He remembered well just how much Morgan had wanted Nick, and their relationship had only increased in intensity.

Still, Drew was pleased that Morgan had gotten over his hurt and forgiven him for his part in that ridiculous charade. "So, tell me about San Diego? How was the Crew Classic?"

"Fantastic! They missed a win in the men's varsity by a mere second," Nick said.

"Yeah, but we got creamed in the men's open," Morgan muttered.

"Which is full of ex-Olympians," Nick said.

"Which is cold comfort when boats walk by you," Morgan said.

Drew shook his head. Things would be better for them once Nick didn't coach Morgan. "But are you glad you went?"

Morgan nodded. "Yeah, but I sure wish Stuart hadn't—"

Interruption came in the form of a reporter for the local birdcage liner and her pet photographer. "Excuse me, Drew St. Charles?"

"Yes?"

"I'm with the *Sacramento Picayune*. Now that the Bayard House is nearly completed, and given the cost overruns inevitable in any building project, plus the problems associated with the fire, how is it you're back on schedule but haven't run afoul of union rules? Is it true you have ties to the mob?"

Drew tried not to let his shock show on his face. "As even you must know, I've been in the hospital and then in intensive rehabilitation. I'm only just getting back up to full speed. I'll have to defer all those questions to my foreman, Brad Sundstrom." He signaled the maître d'. "These reporters were just leaving. Can you point them toward the door?"

"Immediately, sir, and please accept my apologies. They should never have been allowed to disturb you in the first place." She positioned herself between them and the reporters. "If you'd be so good as to follow me?" she asked in a tone that implied if they weren't good, she'd summon the police.

"What the hell was she talking about?" Drew muttered as the maître d' and two stout busboys made sure the journalists departed posthaste.

"I can't imagine," Morgan said blandly, ignoring Nick's pointed look.

"Anyway, guys, thank you. You've done so much for me while I'm recovering. Visiting me in the hospital, and in Nick's case, haunting my PT appointments—"

"Even if he does have another motive," Morgan said.

"I mean, you guys have even been taking care of my yard, and I know you don't have the time to do that," Drew said. "Even with the Bayard fiasco, I'm getting back into the swing of things and can take over again."

Nick and Morgan exchanged a freighted look.

"What's that look mean?" Drew asked.

"We haven't been mowing your lawn," Nick said.

"I wish we could say it was us," Morgan said, "but the reality is, we're just too busy this semester."

"If not you, then…who?" Drew said, baffled. "Because otherwise it's kind of creepy."

Morgan shrugged. "I think you should do what you told that reporter to do and call Brad."

"Did he do it? Or are you two both just so stubborn that neither of you will give an inch?" Drew demanded.

Nick looked at him with pity. He hated that. "I know he hurt you and that you hurt him."

"And we know he's tried to get ahold of you," Morgan said.

"Not for a while," Drew mumbled.

"If you've been keeping him dangling on purpose…" Nick warned.

Drew crossed his arms. He knew it made him look like a petulant child. "But what about what he did to me?"

"What is this, *Queen for a Day*? A contest to see who's the most aggrieved party?" Morgan snapped. "Grow up."

"Ouch," Drew said. "Unfair."

Morgan glowered at him. "I've been listening to the two of you for months. Get your shit together, or I'll take steps."

"And just what does that mean?" Drew demanded. Honestly, where did this boy of Nick's get off?

"You probably don't want to know," Nick said. "I sure don't. Just call him."

"I don't want to talk about this anymore." Drew picked up his menu and hid behind it.

"Of course, you don't, sweetie. Admitting you're wrong is haaard," Morgan whined.

Drew put his menu down. "It's just…it's gone on so long. He hasn't tried calling in a while."

"Leaving aside the fact that you knew he'd called," Nick said, "yes, it is hard, and no, you have to do it. The Drew I know was never one to duck his responsibilities."

"One thing I've learned during my convalescence is that not doing anything is a lot easier," Drew said. Then a sharp, stabbing pain lit up one shin. "Ow! That was my good leg."

Morgan leveled a straight stare at him. "Next time, it'll be your bad one."

"Oh, all right, I'll call him," Drew muttered.

"There, now that wasn't so hard, was it?" Morgan said, patting his hand.

Drew went home and did was he was told. The talk with Brad had to be one of the most strained, awkward conversations he had ever had with anyone in his entire life. Long silences throbbed with the words they didn't or couldn't say to each other. But they finally established that Brad would pick him up at three o'clock the next afternoon.

Drew looked out his front window at 2:55 and saw a strange SUV pull into his driveway. But out jumped Brad. Drew thought he looked different somehow. Maybe a bit trimmer, but more confident somehow. He had to admit, it looked sexy as hell on the big lug. His big lug.

Drew twitched the curtain closed and acted like he wasn't standing right behind the door by counting to twenty before opening it when Brad rang the bell.

"Hi," Brad said quietly. He waved shyly.

"Hi," Drew said back, drinking Brad in with his eyes.

They stood there for a moment, lost in each other's gaze. Brad broke the spell. "Are you ready? Have your hard hat?"

Drew held it up. "Yep, let's go."

Brad waited for him to lock the door and then hurried past him to open his car door for him.

"Thank you." Drew was unsure just what was going on. "New car?"

Brad shook his head. "No, I rented it. I wasn't sure how your leg was, but I figured you wouldn't have to bend too much to get into something like this."

"You rented a car. To take me to the Bayard House. Last night."

Brad scratched the closely cropped hair at the back of his head. He was red from his neck to his scalp. "Uh...yeah."

"Thank you." Drew had to admit, Brad sure seemed to be making an effort. Despite his reservations, it charmed him.

"No sweat," Brad mumbled, looking at the ground.

But Drew knew perfectly well that as late as their call had been, renting a car most likely involved a great deal of effort, at the very least a trip out to the airport, and whether it was last night or this morning, the airport was still out there to hell and gone.

They drove in silence to the Bayard House. It felt to Drew like several times Brad had opened his mouth to speak but never said anything, and he himself stared studiously ahead. He had to admit, however, he found it hard to keep his anger up around Brad. The SUV was such a caring gesture...

And then they pulled up to the Bayard House.

"What the fuck?" Drew burst out before he could stop himself.

Brad rewarded him with one of his sly grins. "What d'you think?"

Drew walked slowly away from the SUV until he stood on the promenade leading to the Bayard House's grand entrance. Carpenters buzzed about the outside front of the mansion, installing the remade gingerbread details on the reborn Victorian mansion. Elsewhere, painters applied careful coats of custom-mixed colors by hand for a period look while trying not to drip on the landscapers.

When Drew turned around, Brad grinned his cocky grin, but underneath it, Drew saw an edge of nerves, as if he weren't quite sure what Drew would make of it all.

"Care to explain this?" Drew said.

"Want to see inside?" Brad countered.

Drew had to admit he did.

Brad stopped him before he could enter the house, holding up clean-room booties. "Here," he said, kneeling. "Let me. I don't want you to tax your knee."

"Brad, I'm fine. I've been cleared for exercise. In fact, that's what I'd be doing if I wasn't here." But he lifted first one foot and then the other like some obedient horse for the farrier.

Brad slipped booties on over his boots and then held the door for him.

The first thing Drew noticed was the smell, beeswax, not urethane or some other synthetic, and the expanse of restored wood floors gleaming dully in the afternoon light.

"Go on in," Brad said quietly. "Go check out your design."

The plasterers had largely completed their work before the flooring contractors had restored the floors, but here and there someone worked at repairing a scrape or ding in the pristine white of the walls.

"Let me show you the parlor." Brad's voice shook in the empty mansion. "That's where the fire was."

Bemused, Drew followed Brad into the house. Brad slid one door back for him and then waited for him to enter. Drew walked in and stopped. "I don't remember there being a set of French doors there."

Brad shook his head. "There wasn't. But that's the wall that burned. The carpenters decided the remaining wall was strong enough to stand up with a certain amount of reinforcement. The preservation specialist suggested the French doors. I hope it's all right."

"They look really good there, like they were meant to be there," Drew admitted. He wanted to find fault, but for some reason, he just couldn't.

Brad crossed the room to the doors in question, beckoning Drew to follow. "If you look out, you actually have a pretty good view of the folly."

Drew looked but then turned around. Brad stared intently at the floor, almost as if he didn't dare look at Drew.

"Brad...how?" Drew asked, shaking his head at the enormity of it all.

Brad shrugged sheepishly. "After I got the call from the fire department...well, it was pretty dispiriting. On top of an already rough time." Brad looked at him and then glanced away again. "I'd made a lot of plans around this job, and then having them go up in smoke... I was pretty down, and when the fire captain told me it was arson? I was even more upset. But then he called me a week later, and the place was cleared for us to get going again. As I sat there in the office at Suburban Graveyard, I realized that with Bob and Emily's help, I could do it. I tried calling."

Drew looked down, realizing he hadn't been the only one to hurt. "I'm sorry."

"Water under the bridge," Brad said.

"Wait... how're you—we, I—paying for this?" Drew demanded.

"The money came through from the city and state. You should've seen Emily. I've never seen a more shameless performance. She dressed to look like a vulnerable little woman, she cried, all of it. They never stood a chance. She even talked them into the revised budget so we could hire double crews and make up for lost time."

"And then some." Drew nodded slowly. Then something dawned on him. "My yard. That was you the whole time, wasn't it?"

Brad looked at the floor, scuffing his foot bashfully in dirt that wasn't there. "Yeah. Well, Nick and Morgan helped when they could." He blushed again. "I started it and kind of bullied them into it, although it really didn't take that much."

"How'd you know when I was out?" Drew asked.

"I... um." Brad hesitated. "Not to sound like a stalker or anything, but I've got an apartment not that far from your house. It wasn't hard just to swing by and check. Also, I finally called your boss at the real estate agency, and he tipped me off via text message when you were showing properties."

"Broker," Drew corrected absently. This was absolutely the last thing he had expected, and it was a lot to take in. "This is amazing, but also overwhelming. Would you mind taking me home?"

"Sure," Brad said softly.

"Did you ever sleep?" Drew asked as they drove back to his house.

"No, you wouldn't let me. Every time I closed my eyes, I saw you." Drew could tell Brad was choking back tears. "I saw you battered and bleeding on the sidewalk. And I wasn't there. So, I worked until I dropped and then got up and did it again. And I'll keep doing it, whatever it takes, until you take me back."

"I never let you go. You just ran," he said as Brad pulled into the driveway.

Brad shook his head. "No, you got hurt, and then I thought you hated me because I was too chickenshit to be out. But I'm here now, and I'm not leaving. This time, I'll protect you."

The more Drew thought about it, the more he realized something. He *still* loved Brad. But he had to know. "Do you love me?"

Brad closed his eyes and then opened them to look fully into his. "More than I can tell you. Yes, Andrew St. Charles, I love you."

Brad leaned over, and Drew met him partway, their lips touching. Brad's kisses still made him tingle.

"Take me inside?" Drew asked.

Brad quirked a shy smile, the kind that made Drew both tender and hard. "Of course."

Drew never remembered entering his house, only moving into the bedroom with Brad, where they apologized with their bodies. Kisses that started out chaste quickly heated to the point of liquefying metal. He fumbled with the buttons of his shirt, but Brad whispered, "Let me."

Brad unbuttoned his shirt with an agonizing, slow sweetness, starting by gently kissing his neck but then sucking and biting a trail south, down across his chest. He caressed the dwindling scar from the gastric pump for a moment before making short work of the belt, button, and zipper on Drew's slacks.

Brad gently pulled Drew's pants down over his leaner, post-recovery hips. He stopped at the knee that had been broken, gently laving the scars with his tongue. Drew found it strangely erotic the way this man, his boyfriend, his lover, made love to the scar. As if hearing his thoughts, Brad looked up. "It's you. It's a part of you, and I love it like I love all of you."

At the question in Drew's eyes, Brad said, "I had a lot of time to think. This is who I am, and who you are. And it's good."

"Yes, it is," Drew whispered, amazed at the changes Brad had worked in himself since November.

Brad held Drew steady while he stepped out of his pants and then stood up. "How come you're still dressed?" Drew asked.

Brad smiled again, but not so shyly this time. "You want me naked?" he asked, eyes never leaving Drew's.

"You have no idea how much I want you naked right now." Then Drew gasped as Brad stepped up to him and cupped him through his boxer-briefs.

"I think I do," Brad smirked.

Drew groaned a little as Brad withdrew his hand and started to undress slowly, staring into his eyes the entire time.

"You're killing me," Drew breathed.

"How? I'm not even touching you." When all Brad's clothes were on the floor, he whispered, "Touch me."

Drew touched him, running his hands across Brad's broad, hairy torso and stopping just short of the end of his treasure trail, a chest and belly he'd missed so much over the previous months. "I thought about you."

"I thought about you too. All the time."

"I thought about this," Drew said, hands settling over Brad's pecs as the nipples hardened beneath his palms.

"Me too," Brad moaned, his head tilting back.

"It's how I knew I was getting better." Brad's neck was too much for him to resist. "If I could get hard, I was healing. I got hard thinking about you."

Brad moaned. His hands sought out Drew's underwear of their own accord. "Now who's wearing too much?"

Drew yanked his underwear down, eager to get back to his prize.

But Brad just turned around, exposing his ass, his epically muscular, lightly furred ass.

"You can't expect me to ignore something like that. I'm not made of stone," Drew said. He was shocked at just how much he needed to push Brad over and fall on top of him.

Brad reached back and felt his cock. "I don't know, that feels rock hard to me."

"I'll show you rock hard," Drew growled, smacking one plump cheek.

Brad gasped. He looked over his shoulder, his eyes on fire. He moved back until Drew's cock rubbed between his cheeks.

"You want to do that again, huh?" Drew said, a little disappointed. He'd thought—hoped—someone would be getting fucked.

Brad shook his head. "No. I want you," he whispered, caressing Drew's now-leaking cock, "this, in me."

"You mean—"

"Yeah, I want you to fuck me, or," he said, squeezing, "are you not man enough?"

This new Brad of his was just asking for it. "I'll show you man." Drew pushed him down. "It's on, Muscle Boy, on like Donkey Kong."

Laughing, Brad fell to the bed. He wiggled his ass at Drew until he smacked it again.

"Are you sure?" Drew said. "I mean...."

Brad turned his head to look up at Drew, eyes full of love and trust. "It's you. It's us. Now shut up and do me."

Drew pulled condoms and lube out of the nightstand. All that skin, and it was all his. He felt like a starving man presented with a buffet, hardly knowing where to look next or what to start with.

He climbed onto the bed and settled himself over Brad, reaching up to interlace their fingers. For a moment, he didn't move, only enjoying the feeling of Brad spread out beneath him. That this man, this huge, powerful man, loved him enough to put him in control when before he'd feared to, rushed to his head. He had to make love to this man, and soon.

Drew rubbed his cock across Brad's cheeks. He let go of Brad's hands and pushed himself up. "I wish you could see how hot you look," he said as he bit the back of Brad's neck.

Gasping, Brad thrust up into him.

Taking it as a sign, Drew moved down so he could appreciate that fine ass properly. He kissed the top of the cleft as he caressed the cheeks.

Then he ran one hand up to tease at Brad's hole, tickling the entrance.

"That feels...good," Brad breathed.

"Yeah? I got something that'll feel so much better," Drew said. He spread Brad's cheeks and kissed his way down from the top of the cleft, inhaling Brad's scent. It wasn't something he did with all his boyfriends, but Brad was his last boyfriend, and he deserved it all.

Drew flicked his tongue against Brad's hole.

"Oh!" Brad gasped.

"Like that?" Drew teased between forays against the puckered opening.

"Jeez, yes, don't ever stop," Brad almost sobbed.

When he'd reduced Brad to a needy, begging creature, Drew sat up. "I think you're ready."

"I hope so," Brad rasped, "because I really want to feel you in me."

Drew smoothed a condom down over his cock. Then he warmed some lube in his hand before carefully opening Brad up. One slick finger became two, then three, and at each addition, Brad rocked up into Drew's touch.

Then Drew grazed Brad's gland, grinning as a shudder racked the man beneath him. "That's what I've been talking about."

"Uh-huh," was all Brad said.

It was time.

Straddling him, Drew used a finger to guide his cock to Brad's hole. With only the gentlest pressure, he pushed inside the virgin ass.

"Oh my God. This feels...you feel...wow," Brad huffed.

"Tell me if it hurts, if it's too much," Drew said tightly, taking it as slowly as he could.

Brad groaned. "So full. So...the slide over my prostate."

Drew slid in, inch by inch, until Brad had taken all his shaft and his pelvis met Brad's cheeks. He lowered himself down so his chest rested against Brad's back. He sighed with pleasure, staying there a moment. He loved that soaring feeling, a feeling like no other, and knew he'd come from it alone if he lay there long enough, buried to the hilt in the tight, wet heat of his lover.

He pushed up and pulled back a little and then slid home again, taking it very slowly, each stroke pulling out a little more before inching in again.

He felt Brad shaking beneath him as the exquisite pleasure verged on torture. "Please," Brad sobbed.

Bracing his arms on either side of Brad's wide shoulders and rippling lats, Drew took up a rhythm that would bring them both to satisfaction.

Beneath him, Brad thrust back against him, seeking his own release.

Drew pulled out momentarily. "Up!" he commanded, spanking Brad's cheeks.

When Brad was up, he thrust in again. "Yeah!" he cried.

Then he reached around and grabbed Brad's cock with his lube-slicked hand. From the feel of it, Brad was making enough of his own, and Drew rubbed the pre-cum around, adding it to the mix, amazed that he could do this for his boyfriend.

"Oh God, babe...almost there," Brad said.

"Me...too!" Drew grunted, Brad's cries driving him higher. One thrust, then another, and he was over the edge. His body burned with the fire of his climax as he pumped out his life into his lover in an eternal instant and took it all back into himself.

"Aaaah!" Brad cried, his own orgasm overtaking him. He pumped into Drew's hand, his spunk spilling over onto the bed, but Drew didn't care. His man laid out beneath him, helpless after coming, was the most beautiful thing he'd ever seen.

Brad rested on his elbows, head on the bed. "I can hold you up a long time," he said after a few minutes, "but I'd rather hold you."

Drew pulled out, holding onto the condom. He tied it off and dropped it on the floor. Then he stepped into the bathroom and brought back a towel and cleaned Brad up.

Brad pulled the comforter back and climbed in. Then he held out his arms. "C'mere, you."

Drew smiled and climbed in, settling into his favorite place on earth—tucked under Brad's arm. "Stay with me?" he said.

"Tonight?"

"Forever."

Epilogue

JULY

"Will this Owen person be there?" Drew asked as he tied his bow tie.

Brad glanced down, sorry he'd done it and even more sorry he'd confessed it to Drew. "I don't know. I guess it's possible. I don't control the guest list for the gala celebrating the completed Bayard House. Will it be a problem if he is?"

"No, I guess not," Drew said softly. "I mean, it won't be a problem." Then he brightened. "You might have been the foreman, but now you're my partner in St. Charles Renovations."

Brad kissed Drew's forehead. "I hate to break it to you, but since I got my contractor's license and bought into it, I *am* St. Charles Renovations. You sell houses."

"Boy, some people come into money and it swells their heads right up." Drew rolled his eyes.

"I didn't 'come into' money. My dad's right-hand man for the last thirty years went to the police and ratted him out, and the cops indicted Randall for the arson at the Bayard House and paying a few of his workers to beat you up. Then my brother pulled the ultimate power move. Or maybe it was a dick move."

"Maybe it was both." Drew tried not to laugh as Brad made an utter hash out of his own bow tie.

"Both, definitely. I mean, forcing the old bastard out of the company he'd founded and then stripping him of everything while he's in the slammer awaiting trial? I'm glad I'm not Philip's enemy."

"Enemy? I should say not. That buyout was incredibly generous, and even after buying into Renochuck, you're still loaded."

"Yeah, I'm a regular trust-fund brat, now." Brad winked.

"You were always a brat. That the lawyer controlling the fund decided Renochuck counted as making something of yourself and gave you control doesn't change that." Drew shook his head. He batted Brad's hands away from the bow tie. "Let me. If you don't, we'll never get out of here."

Brad leered at him wolfishly. "We still might not. I had no idea how hot you'd look in a tux."

He grabbed his boyfriend playfully around the waist and ground his crotch against Drew's. Every day he gave thanks that this man, this wonderful, funny, intelligent, and gorgeous man, loved him.

A knock at the door prevented Brad from seriously wrinkling Drew's tuxedo. He peeked out. "The car's here. Are you ready, partner?"

Drew looked at him, and Brad saw the world in his eyes.

"Ready, partner," Drew said softly.

And they were.

Acknowledgements

My husband, Burch Bryant Jr., continues to support my work and believe in my writing, and I'll always be grateful for that. Our son thinks it's pretty cool that his "Daddy made a book," even if he won't be old enough to read them for years to come.

Various people generously shared their expertise with me, and once again, the rowing mafia came through. I'd like to thank Shep Harper for information about arson investigations and Erik Spiess, RN, for information about traumatic injuries and recovering from them. Any factual errors are entirely mine and in no way reflect on the information they gave me. Likewise, I'm pleased to acknowledge Brian Todd and the Gay and Lesbian Rowing Federation for their enthusiasm for my work and help promoting it to the rowing community.

Thanks, too, to Aimee Hasson and Matt Fuller for their information about what it is a real estate agent does besides "just sell houses." Whatever errors and mischaracterizations there are belong to me alone.

Dahlia Adler Fisch and Burch Bryant Jr. read various drafts of *Tipping the Balance* and helped me catch all kinds of typos, plot holes, and inconsistent characterization. It would be a far poorer book without their efforts.

I'd like to thank my editor at NineStar Press, Elizabeth Coldwell, for her help making this a better book. I'd also like to thank Natasha for her lovely cover, Rae for giving this book a new home, and everyone else at NineStar for their efforts to bring *Tipping the Balance* to press.

About the Author

Christopher Koehler always wanted to write, but it wasn't until his grad school years that he realized writing was how he wanted to spend his life. Long something of a hothouse flower, he's been lucky to be surrounded by people who encouraged that, especially his long-suffering husband of twenty-nine years and counting.

He loves many genres of fiction and nonfiction, but he's especially fond of romances, because it's in them that human emotions and relations, at least most of the ones fit to be discussed publicly, are laid bare.

While writing is his passion and his life, when he's not doing that, he's a househusband, at-home dad, and oarsman with a slightly disturbing interest in manners and the other ways people behave badly.

Christopher is approaching the tenth anniversary of publication and has been fortunate to be recognized for his writing, including by the American Library Association, which named *Poz* a 2016 Recommended Title, and an Honorable Mention for "Transformation," in *Innovation*, Volume 6 of Queer Sci Fi's Flash Fiction Anthology.

E-mail: christoarpher@gmail.com

Facebook: www.fb.me/Christopher.tells.stories

Twitter: @christopherink

Website: www.christopherkoehler.net/blog

Other NineStar books by this author

The CalPac Crew

Rocking the Boat

Coming Soon from C. Koehler

Burning It Down

CalPac Crew, Book Three

Four months into his new job as battalion chief for Sacramento City Fire's second battalion and Owen Douglas still couldn't sit still. Sure, he knew the job from a theoretical standpoint, and every day he learned more from a practical standpoint, but he couldn't ignore the niggling discomfort he felt when he saw those bugles on his collar. Like his new uniform didn't fit quite right, and perhaps from a certain point of view, it didn't. No matter how he squinted or how many times he turned it this way or that, he couldn't see all that much light between his investigation into the arson at the Bayard House at the beginning of the year and his promotion to battalion chief. More to the point, neither could the men and women under his command.

Not to mention every time he opened his mouth, unicorns crapping glitter and rainbows popped out. At least, that was what people seemed to be waiting for. He liked to think he was discreet, that nothing at work proclaimed him Big Gay Owen, no snapshots of boyfriends, no photos of him shaking his ass on a Mardi Gras float, no matter how much fun he'd had in Sydney, just a subtle rainbow on his battered 4Runner, a bar no bigger than the head of a toothbrush. He tried not to play the gay card, but he was the first out battalion chief in the fire department's history, and well he knew it. More to the point, the people under his command knew it. Maybe he was just making too big a deal out of it or felt guilty for being promoted over the heads of more senior firefighters.

His intercom buzzed with his secretary on the other end. "Yes?" Owen said.

"Prissy Morrain to see you."

"Oh! Send her in, please." He dashed to his office door. He didn't expect her until tomorrow.

Owen routinely left his office door open, but he quickly got out from behind his desk to greet his visitor, and not just because she outranked him.

"Chief Morrain! I'm so sorry! I must've made a mistake in my calendar. I wasn't expecting you until tomorrow—"

Prissy Morrain waved a manicured hand. "Retired Chief, and I'm a day early. We both have better things to do than make small talk over hors d'oeuvres over at some white-tablecloth restaurant. Did you bring your lunch today?"

Owen nodded. Since he was a "first" for the department, he'd sought out the advice of another "first," the first woman battalion chief, now retired from active firefighting and promoted off to one side to do something less dangerous involving paperwork. "I'll grab it out of the fridge. There's a nice park a block away. We can eat there."

"That'll do fine."

Prissy Morrain was a handsome woman, Owen thought; really, she could've been one of those older models, the ones with silver hair and flawless skin who pitched vitamins to women of a certain age. Her wrinkles weren't so much age lines scoring her face with years but delicate lines of character radiating out from her eyes and around her mouth to accentuate a ready smile. How she'd managed that with a career spent fighting fires and sexism, he'd never know.

He spent the short walk to the park rehearsing what he wanted to say, but when Prissy asked, "So what's the problem?" Owen could only blurt, "I'm just not clicking with the people under me. This station, sure. My office is here, but the other stations in this battalion not so much, and there's one station that when I walk in everything stops for a few minutes while I walk back to talk to the captain on duty, and that's just creepy."

"Have you talked to human resources?"

"Don't be absurd" slipped out before he could stop it.

Prissy laughed. "Smart man. You don't want this on your record."

And that was why he'd contacted her. "Team-building exercises aren't my thing at this point and are just a waste of time. I'm not in a burning building with these guys. They simply need to function with each other and work in coordinated groups, and they do. But I don't like getting the stink eye either."

"Look, hearts of gold, most of these guys, but it's a conservative profession. The younger ones are yours," Prissy said, arching one eyebrow, "maybe even literally. There's more than one gay man among the recruits, and you're a fine-looking specimen yourself."

Also Available from NineStar Press

Connect with NineStar Press

www.ninestarpress.com

www.facebook.com/ninestarpress

www.facebook.com/groups/NineStarNiche

www.twitter.com/ninestarpress